SUMMER'S END

A NOVEL

KATHRYN B HULL

SUMMER'S END

A NOVEL

KATHRYN B HULL

ARPress
45 Dan Road Suite 15
Canton MA 02021
  Hotline: 1(888) 821-0229
  Fax: 1(508) 545-7580

Ordering Information:
Quantity sales. Special discounts are available on quantity purchases by corporations, associations, and others. For details, contact the publisher at the address above.

Printed in the United States of America.

  ISBN-13:   Softcover   979-8-89676-652-0
              eBook   979-8-89676-653-7

Library of Congress Control Number: 2025924888

DEDICATION

For my family, Laurice, Craig and Eric,
and friends, too numerous to name.

God has not given me the spirit of fear,
But of power, of love, and a sound mind.

- II Timothy 1:7

ACKNOWLEDGMENTS

To Rosemary Chiaverini, Rebecca Estrada Hull, and Chris Griego, superb editors, who spent countless hours reading the manuscript and making appropriate suggestions.

To Deputy Joshua Van Gorp, La Quinta Police Department, for clarifying information regarding police policies, arrest protocol, and line of command.

CHAPTER 1

The last day of summer began like all the others, but it was the end of the day that made it unforgettable for Jeanne.

She strolled along the water's edge, the waves gently kissing her feet, and made her way to the large outcropping of rocks at the end of the sandy strip. With careful footing, she climbed to the crest, breathing in the cool salt air as she took in her favorite view—the endless stretch of sea melding into the horizon.

But when she turned to descend, her breath caught. In the crevice of the rocks below, she spotted what looked like a man's leg. Her pulse quickened. She stared, willing it to move.

"Hello," she called out, her voice cracking. "Are you all right?"

No response.

Heart pounding, she carefully moved down toward the leg. As she got closer, she saw the rest of the body, fully clothed, lying in an awkward position, deathly still.

She looked up and down the beach—no one to call for help. Swallowing panic, she scrambled off the rocks and ran to the nearest house. She banged on the door. She stood trembling until a tall, dark-haired man opened it.

"Please," she gasped, "call the police! There's a man—either he's dead or unconscious—lying in the rocks at the end of the beach!"

Without hesitation, he grabbed the phone. Jeanne stood by the door, trembling as he spoke, giving clear directions to the dispatcher.

He turned to her. "They're on their way. By the way, I'm Jonathan."

"Oh... I... I'm Jeanne." Her eyes welled up unexpectedly. For a moment, she wasn't on the beach. She was back in her kitchen the day her husband left. Their twins had just graduated from high school. He'd said now the kids were on their own, she could be, too.

Jonathan's voice broke through, "You okay?"

"Yes," she said quickly, wiping at a tear. "I was just thinking about... Never mind."

Moments later flashing lights appeared. Police officers and a coroner moved swiftly, methodically examining the scene. Jeanne stood frozen until they lifted the body onto a stretcher. Her knees gave way. Jonathan caught her before she fell.

"Some women just can't take the sight of a dead body," the older officer muttered. "We need to speak with her, and you. Is your house close by?"

"Yes, that one," Jonathan pointed.

"Take her inside. We'll join you shortly."

Jonathan scooped Jeanne up and carried her across the sand. Inside, he laid her on the sofa and fetched a cold, damp cloth, placing it gently on her forehead.

Her eyes fluttered open. She squinted at him. "Where... Why am I here?"

"You fainted," Jonathan said calmly.

Jeanne sat up abruptly. "I have to go—" She wavered as she tried to stand. Jonathan steadied her.

"Sit down," he said. "The police want to ask us a few questions. Just rest until they get here."

She hesitated, swallowing hard. Her voice dropped to a whisper. "That was Roger."

Jonathan frowned. "You knew him?"

"He was my husband."

Silence.

What else was there to say?

A knock on the door broke the silence. Jonathan opened it and two officers entered. The taller one, with a grey mustache, stepped forward.

"I'm Detective O'Neal." Gesturing to the younger officer behind him, he said, "This is Officer Brandt. May we ask you a few questions?"

"Of course," Jeanne said quietly.

"Can you tell us how you happened to find him? Was anyone else around?"

"No, I saw no one, I just wanted one peaceful walk before summer ended," her voice trembling. "It was when I descended from the rocks that I saw his leg." She put her hands over her face and moaned, "Oh, Roger. What happened?"

"What do you mean?" the officer asked.

"He was my husband."

The officers looked at one another questioningly.

"That puts a whole new spin on it," Officer O'Neal observed. "I think we'd better go down to the station and get a full statement from each of you." He directed them to the patrol car.

"Jeanne, do you have an attorney?" Jonathan asked.

"No. Do I need one?"

"You might. I'd be happy to represent you. I'm an attorney with Crown, Best and Carruthers. I'm Jonathan Crown."

"Oh... that's where I'm supposed to start working tomorrow," Jeanne said with surprise. "At least I was." Now she wondered if they would want her. She was fortunate to be hired at her age. She knew she had good skills, that she was intelligent and reasonably attractive. Strange how much importance men put on looks, but if that's what it took to get a job, she presented herself for the interview with perfect makeup and a well-tailored suit in a color to bring out the blue of her eyes. An energetic personality had worked—she was hired on the spot by one of the most prestigious law firms in the city.

As they settled in the policeman's car, Jeanne closed her eyes trying to keep the tears from escaping. She sighed in short, jerky breaths. Jonathan reached for her cold hand, gently clasping their fingers.

"It will be okay," he said.

Jeanne looked into his warm, brown eyes as a slight smile reached the corners of her mouth. "Thank you. I wouldn't know what to do."

"That's all right. We'll figure it out together."

The patrol car stopped at the front entrance of the station. "Here we are," the detective said. "Just follow me."

They entered the building and walked through the lobby, down a long hallway, and into a small grey room.

"Have a seat," Detective O'Neal said as he pointed to two chairs on one side of the table. He took a chair on the opposite side. Officer Brandt remained standing near the door.

"May I get you anything? Water or coffee or...?"

"I'd like some water, please," Jeanne said.

Officer Brandt was asked to bring water for everyone. Then Detective O'Neal began questioning Jeanne.

"I need you to tell me everything—no detail is too small. How long were you married to the deceased?"

"About twenty-five years."

"Do you have children?"

"Yes, I have two. A boy and a girl—twins."

"Do they live with you?"

"Currently, they are away at school—at the university," she answered. "Oh, I should call them!" she said reaching for her phone.

Detective O'Neal said, "Please wait until everything is clarified, then you can call them."

"Of course," Jeanne agreed.

His tone changed. "I know this is difficult. When did you last see your husband?"

"When he left in June, nearly three months ago. We've been separated."

Officer Brandt returned and handed Jeanne the water. She took a sip, her hands still shaking.

"Do you have any idea why he would be on the beach where he was found?"

"No. Our home is only a short distance up the beach, but he hasn't been there. At least not that I know," she said with a slight frown.

"Do you know where he's been living since he left?"

"No. I never asked him. However, our children might know. He probably stayed in touch with them."

"Could you give me their contact information?"

"Sure, but may I talk to them first?" Jeanne asked with concern.

"Yes, of course. You need to let them know what happened."

The detective handed her a paper, on which she wrote the necessary information for her children, Mark and Mandy.

"Do you have friends here that he might have been visiting?" he continued.

"Not really..."

"Where have you been the last twenty-four hours?"

"I drove out to the beach house alone Friday afternoon and I haven't left. I needed some quiet time. I haven't seen anyone—not until this afternoon."

"And you, Mr. Crown?" O'Neal turned to Jonathan.

"I've been here since Saturday morning. I needed time to relax and to concentrate on a court case. I had not left my desk until Ms. Blomgren knocked on my door."

The detective made a few notes. "We'll need to confirm both your statements, of course. I think that will be all for now. Oh... here are the things found on your husband—his wallet, clothes, and miscellaneous items."

"Thank you," Jeanne said as she hesitated. She finally took the bag that held them.

"Officer Brandt will take you home." Then he added, "We'll be in touch with you when the autopsy is completed. It appears to be an accident. He may have slipped on the rocks, hitting his head as he fell, but we must be sure."

"I understand," Jeanne said. She turned to leave, and looking up at Jonathan, said, "It looks like instead of my working for you, you may be working for me."

"I'd like that," he said as he escorted her to the officer's car.

CHAPTER 2

They rode in silence—thinking about Roger and what could have happened. Her thoughts returned to reality. How was she going to tell the children? What arrangements need to be made? There were myriad questions racing through her mind.

"Jonathan? Since our divorce isn't final, am I responsible for...?"

"Let's discuss this later."

The police car stopped in front of Jonathan's house, at his request. He thanked the officer and took Jeanne's hand as she stepped out of the car.

"Let's go to my house first and have a cup of coffee... or tea?"

"Thanks. That would be nice." After a pause she said, "Perhaps I should go on home. I need to call the children." She hesitated for a moment and then said, "All right, maybe just one cup."

Jeanne wandered around the room looking at the furnishings and the artwork. "You have a lovely home. Have you lived here long?"

"I've owned the house for several years, but use it only on occasional weekends. Before I lost my wife we spent more time here. It's not the same now."

"I can understand that. What was her name?"

"Elizabeth. She was the younger sister of one of the secretaries in our office, Phyllis, who currently is working for me. She has blamed me for her sister's death, though I don't know why."

"Perhaps she was jealous... you married her sister and not her." Jeanne stood in front of a painting of an ocean scene. "Is this a painting of this beach?"

"Yes, it was done by an artist who lives here. I think he captured the ocean at sunset perfectly."

"I agree. It is beautiful. So peaceful... like I usually find it."

Jeanne sat on the stool at the counter drinking her coffee and looked across at Jonathan in the kitchen. He was quite handsome with the build of an athlete—broad shoulders, a muscular torso with lean long legs. "I really am glad you were here today. I don't know what I would have done if I had been alone."

"I'm glad I could help. And I will continue to help you." After a quiet moment, Jonathan continued, "Jeanne, about starting your job.... When you're ready it will be waiting for you."

"I really appreciate that. I couldn't concentrate on starting a new job right now."

"Don't give it another thought."

Jeanne finished her coffee and slowly stood up. "Thanks so much for your kindness. Now... I must go call my children."

"I'll walk with you."

"You don't need to."

"But I'd like to," he said as he led her out the door and onto the sand. Jeanne's home was only a couple of houses down from his.

As they went up to her house, Jonathan handed her his business card. Jeanne said, "I'll call you when I hear from the police." She went in and slowly closed the door. She leaned against it letting out a big sigh with a silent prayer. Jonathan walked toward his house, but turned back, looking through the glass to see Jeanne standing there—wondering.

CHAPTER 3

After a restless night, Jeanne awakened early with the events of the previous day on her mind. Questions presented themselves. Why was Roger here—on the beach? What if I hadn't seen him lying in the rocks? How long would he have lain there? I must not think about it. She recalled walking along the water's edge leaving footprints in the sand. The tide was coming in and soon and the footprints would disappear, *just like my former life*, she thought. She had stood at the crest of the rocks looking out at the great expanse of sparkling blue water. "Free. Free to be me," she had said into the cool ocean breeze which tossed her blonde hair across her face as she stretched her slender arms toward the sky.

When she talked with her children last night they had been devastated, asking numerous questions for which she had no answers. She tossed off the blankets and headed for the shower. After a quick shampoo, she felt clean and refreshed. She put on her silk robe and headed for the kitchen. She wasn't hungry, but freshly made coffee was what she needed to clear her tired brain. The ringing of the phone interrupted her thoughts. The caller ID indicated it was Detective O'Neal.

"Good morning, Detective," she said trying to be alert.

"Good morning to you, too. Did you talk with your children?"

"Yes, shortly after I got home last night I called them. They were concerned."

"Will they be coming home?"

"Not right away. I thought there was no urgency. Since the school year has just started, I thought it best for them not to come home until it was necessary."

"You're right. We may have a few more questions for you. Will you be available later today?"

"Yes. Just let me know when," Jeanne said.

"How about two o'clock?"

"That will be fine. I will be going to my apartment in the city later this morning. Should I have Mr. Crown, my attorney, with me?"

"I don't think that's necessary, but if you would feel more comfortable you may."

Jeanne slowly released the phone and looked at the business card Jonathan had given her. *Should I call him? Should I go to the police station alone? I've always been independent, and am capable of handling things myself. What if Roger's death was not an accident?* The thought struck Jeanne as a possibility. *If so, is that why they want to talk to me again?* A slight panic set in, her heart rate increased and her breathing became more intense. Her hand trembled as she reached for the phone to call Jonathan. She entered the numbers hoping he would be available.

"Crown, Best and Carruthers attorneys at law," a cheerful voice answered. "How may I help you?"

"This is Jeanne Blomgren. I'd like to speak with Mr. Jonathan Crown, please."

"Please hold for a moment." The line went quiet.

In a few seconds a different voice said, "This is Phyllis, Secretary to Jonathan Crown. How may I help you?"

"I need to talk to Mr. Crown. It will only take a minute. Just tell him it is Jeanne." Tears were forming behind her eyes. *Get control of yourself,* she said silently, and with a slight tremble in her voice she said, "Perhaps you could just ask him to call me. I need to talk to him before noon."

"All right. Give me your number and I'll give him the message."

"He has it," she said abruptly and disconnected.

Even though she was filling in for his secretary who was on an extended leave, Phyllis was familiar with everyone in his life. She wrote the information on a message slip and took it into his office. As she placed it on his desk, she frowned and said, "So who is this Jeanne that I've not heard about?"

"Jeanne? Oh, did she call?"

"Yes. She wanted to talk to you."

"Why didn't you put her through?"

"I try to screen your calls, as you asked."

"Thanks. That will be all," Jonathan said as he reached for the phone.

Phyllis left the room, leaving his door slightly ajar. She stood just to the side where she could hear him.

"Jeanne, are you all right?" he asked as soon as she answered. "What's happening?"

He was quiet as Jeanne told him she was to go to the police station after lunch. She asked him if he should be with her.

"Absolutely," he said. Then he spoke so softly Phyllis could not hear what he said. Jeanne told him how to find her apartment. He checked his calendar and called to Phyllis.

"Phyllis, please come in."

She quickly entered the office, pad and pen in hand. "Yes, sir. What can I do for you?"

"Cancel my afternoon appointments. I will be out of the office for a few hours. There is a new client I have to meet with. It's urgent."

"I'll need to have information on her," Phyllis said with an air of efficiency.

"It doesn't matter now. I'll give everything to you later. That's it for now," and he ushered her out of his office and closed the door.

Phyllis was annoyed Jonathan had never been like this before. *What's going on?* she wondered. She always knew his schedule, where he went, to whom he talked. He was being secretive with this new client. *Why?* Phyllis thought about how she could find out. *No one talks to my boss without my knowledge,* she said to herself.

Shortly before noon, Jonathan walked out of the office without a word, briefcase in hand and entered the elevator. Phyllis's emerald green eyes followed him while tapping her pen on the desk.

CHAPTER 4

Just as Jeanne finished applying her lipstick, Jonathan arrived to take her to lunch before their appointment at the police station. "I'm sorry to bother you," she said apologetically, "but I wasn't sure what I should do."

"You did the right thing," Jonathan replied. When they exited the building, Jonathan's red Mustang was waiting. As they buckled up, Jonathan said, "Until the cause of Roger's death is verified, do not speak to anyone without my being present. Knowing how the police often think, you may be considered a suspect, or at least a person of interest."

"Oh, I hadn't thought of that. But I'm innocent. You believe that, don't you?"

"Yes, but we may have to prove it."

Jonathan had chosen the Rusty Robin Restaurant, which lent itself to conversation. Over a quick lunch they discussed Jonathan's role as her attorney, possible questions the police might pose and how Jeanne should answer them. Then they headed to the police station.

"You have a very logical way of thinking. I like that," Jonathan said.

"I'll take that as a compliment," Jeanne responded.

"It's meant as one. Here we are. Now check with me before you answer any questions."

"Yes, sir," she said with a minimal salute. Jonathan smiled.

They approached the window and Jonathan told the officer that Jeanne Blomgren was here to see Detective O'Neal.

"Oh, yes. He's expecting you. I'll let him know you are here." She spoke briefly into a phone and in a few seconds Detective O'Neal appeared.

"Thanks for coming in," he said as he opened the door to admit them. She felt a little uncomfortable walking down the cold, sterile hall to the last room on the left, a corner office with windows. "It will be a couple of days before we get the autopsy report on your husband. However, we have some questions for you."

"All right. How can I help?" Jeanne asked.

"We need to work out a time line for the day when you found his body. Could you tell us about your day? What time did you get up?"

"It was around nine o'clock."

"And then what did you do?

"I made coffee and fixed a light breakfast. Do you want to know what I had to eat?"

"No, that won't be necessary," the detective said with a smile. "Did you go out that morning?"

"No, I stayed in. I was to start a new job on Monday, so I needed to close up the beach house and pack for going to my apartment in town."

"So how did you happen to be out on the beach in the afternoon?"

"Since it was to be my last day at the beach I just wanted to relax and enjoy the sun for a little while. I took a book with me and sat outside to read. Before going in I decided to take a short walk."

"Why to that end of the beach?"

"No special reason. I often climbed up on the outcropping of rocks just to look at the ocean. It was one of my favorite places."

"Did your husband know that?"

"Know what?"

"That it was one of your favorite places?"

"I don't know. I never told him." Jeanne began to wonder about this line of questioning. "What difference does it make?" she asked.

"We're just trying to get all the information to create a time line of the day's activities. Did you see anyone else on the beach that day?"

"No. I was engrossed in my book and didn't look up until I finished it. Then, as I told you, I walked along the shore, climbed up on the rocks, and when I turned to descend, I saw the body. I looked around, but saw no one in the area. That's when I ran to the closest house, which was Mr. Crown's."

"Thank you. One more question. Do you know if Roger left a will? If so, who is his beneficiary?"

"That's two questions," she said smiling, then continued, "I would think he had a will, but no, I do not know the details of it. You'd have to ask his attorney."

"That can wait until later."

Detective O'Neal turned to Jonathan. "Now, Mr. Crown, were you home all day?"

"Yes, I was working at home. It was only when Jeanne knocked at my door that I left my desk."

"Did you notice anyone on the beach during the day? Do you know if any of the neighbors were at home?"

"No, I don't know. I never saw anyone nor did I look for anyone."

"And, Ms. Blomgren, were you aware of any of your neighbors being at home?"

"I didn't see anyone that day. We mostly keep to ourselves."

"So why did you go to Mr. Crown's house that afternoon?"

"As I said, I ran to the closest house to call for help, and it happened to be his."

"Had you ever talked to him before?"

"No. I had never even seen him. I didn't know who lived there."

"It's not a very friendly neighborhood, is it?" Detective O'Neal asked with a grin. "Well, that will be all for today. You've been very helpful. We'll be in touch when we get the results of the autopsy; then we'll tell you when we can release the body. I'm sure you need make arrangements."

"Yes, we do." Jeanne stood to leave.

"That went well," Jonathan said as they approached his car. "He may try to contact some of your neighbors just to verify your information. I just hope he will be discreet."

Jonathan dropped Jeanne at her apartment. He did not go back to his office, but instead drove to his beach house. He wanted to find out if there were people at home who could possibly help in Jeanne's defense, if needed. At his house, he quickly changed to casual attire, donned his sunglasses and walked out onto the sand. He headed down toward the outcropping of rocks and climbed up to look out over the ocean. He understood why Jeanne liked this place—it was quiet and isolated. He scanned the row of beach houses with windows facing the ocean.

If he went to the door of a house, what would be his reason? Last Sunday afternoon was when Jeanne climbed up on the rocks. *Did she have her book with her? She didn't say. Perhaps she did and dropped it. I can ask if anyone found it. That would work.* So with that scenario in mind he walked to the house next to his.

He punched the door bell and heard a slight ringing inside. He waited a few seconds and when no one answered, he went on to the next house with the same result. He thought most of the occupants were weekenders and this was the middle of the week. However, he did try one more house. After the second ring, someone appeared.

"Can I help you?" a lovely young woman asked.

"Yes. Hello. I live near you, but I'm not sure we have met. I'm Jonathan Crown."

"I'm Margaret." She was wearing a colorful sun dress, her dark hair was tied back in a ponytail and she was barefoot.

"May I ask you a question?"

"Sure. What is it"

"Were you here last Sunday afternoon?"

She hesitantly answered, "Yes, I arrived here early in the afternoon. Why?"

"I'm wondering if by any chance you may have walked out on the beach over by those rocks," he said pointing to the outcropping. "Did you happen to find a book that my friend may have dropped?"

"I did walk out to the water's edge, but not by the rocks. I didn't notice a book."

"Thanks. I was also wondering if you saw anyone else in the area that afternoon."

Margaret frowned. "I do remember someone going by that last house up toward the street just as I arrived."

"Could you recognize them?"

"No. I didn't look that carefully. We really don't know our neighbors very well. I do think, however, that it was a woman. She was wearing a wide-brimmed hat."

"Thank you. That's very helpful. I'll keep an eye out for someone with that description to see if she found the book."

Jonathan went back to his own house. Now he'd wait to see if Detective O'Neal would ask the same questions.

CHAPTER 5

At the office, Phyllis did not ignore the fact that Jonathan left without telling her where he was going or who he planned to see. In the break room over lunch, Phyllis told Judy, the secretary to another partner, about Jonathan's new secret client, a woman who had drawn him out of his office in the middle of the day. "I think he has a secret love. Shortly after he had a call from a woman, he just left the office."

"I'm sure he has a good reason."

"I will find out, I promise you," she said with resolution, then immediately changed the subject. "Did I tell you about the wonderful man I'm dating?"

"No. Who is it?"

"His name is Roger."

"When did you meet him?" Judy asked.

"About a month ago. I was having a glass of wine at my favorite bar one evening and he was there—alone, too. We started talking and had an instant connection. He said he was in the process of getting a divorce. We have been seeing each other often ever since we met."

"I'm pleased for you," Judy said. "It's not easy meeting decent people."

"Well... he's not another Jonathan," she said with a smile. Judy was the only person she told about Roger.

Jonathan came in early the next morning, called Phyllis into his office and gave her the information she needed about Jeanne. He didn't mention that she would be an employee in the near future, nor did he tell her the details of the case.

A few days passed before Jonathan heard from Jeanne again. This time, when she called, Phyllis knew Jeanne was a client, so patched her straight through when she asked to speak to Jonathan.

"What's new?" he asked.

"The autopsy is complete and Detective O'Neal wants to see me. Can you join me?"

Jonathan heard an intake of breath, and it wasn't Jeanne.

"Of course. When?"

"Tomorrow morning. First thing."

"I'll be there. Shall I pick you up?"

"That would be nice. Thank you."

Jonathan waited a few seconds before disconnecting the line. He sensed that Phyllis had been listening in on his conversation. He walked out of his office and approached his secretary's desk. "Phyllis, did you listen in on my last phone conversation?"

She hesitated, biting her lower lip as she thought about her answer. "Well... not really. I may have heard just a little... at the beginning."

"I don't like you listening to my conversations. If there is anything you should know, I will tell you. Is that clear?"

"Yes, sir," she said looking down at her hands folded on her desk.

"Now, about my schedule tomorrow... do I have any early appointments?"

She looked at his calendar. "No, none until eleven."

"Thank you. I'll be out in the morning, but will be back by eleven."

Phyllis was curious about his new client. Jonathan seemed to be rather secretive about her, which made Phyllis all the more interested. *How is this one different?* She was determined to find out.

Jeanne's apartment in town overlooking the park was very comfortable for one person, and for the twins when they came to visit. A plus was that it was within walking distance to the law office, assuming she still had a job. She had furnished it with Danish contemporary style furniture, with splashes of colors in pillows and accent pieces. It suited her perfectly. The best part was that it was all hers.

Even though it was just for another meeting with Detective O'Neal, she was eagerly looking forward to seeing Jonathan. She opened the door as soon as she heard his soft knock. "Good morning," she greeted him with a smile. "I'm ready."

"Then let's be on our way," Jonathan replied.

It was only as they silently descended in the elevator that Jeanne said, "I'm afraid, Jonathan."

"I understand, but at this point you need not be concerned. The police are just being thorough. It takes them a while to get all the information to build a case, if there is one."

They exited the front doors. "Thank you, Alexander. We'll be back in an hour or so," Jeanne told him.

"I'm glad you have Alexander at the door to your apartment building. Apparently you had mentioned I was coming."

"Yes, I thought I'd better, since he didn't know you."

During the short ride to the police station, Jonathan reminded Jeanne to not answer any questions without checking with him. He did expect this visit would be informative, but one could never know what conclusions Detective O'Neal would make, or may have already made.

When they arrived, the officer at the front desk recognized them and immediately called Detective O'Neal. "He's expecting you, so go right in," she said as she opened the door to the long hallway.

The detective greeted them at his office door. "Come in, come in," he said as he motioned them to the chairs facing his desk. "Well, we got the results of the autopsy of your late husband," he said addressing Jeanne. "He appears to have died from blunt force head trauma. He also had a severely broken leg. Perhaps he slipped on the rocks and twisted his leg as he fell in the rocks below. There were no other signs of injuries or unusual markings."

"So it was an accident?" Jeanne asked.

"Yes, we believe so. Do you have any idea why he would be there alone?"

"No. I hadn't seen or heard from him since he left in June."

"We did find something interesting in his pocket—someone's business card from your office, Mr. Crown.

"Who was that?"

He handed the card to Jonathan. "It was yours."

Jonathan's face registered surprise. "How can that be? I've never met the man."

Jeanne spoke up. "Could it have been from your secretary. She may have had your card."

"If you think it was from your secretary, I would like to speak with her," the detective said. "Could you have her come in?"

"Certainly. It is strange... how would she have known Roger?" He frowned. "I guess we will find out."

"Now, Ms. Blomgren, we can release your husband's body whenever you want. Just tell us where you want it sent."

"I'll call you later today with the information."

"Thank you." He stood up indicating they were finished. "My sympathy to you and your children," he said with sincerity.

They drove back to Jeanne's apartment with more questions now than before.

"Would you like to come in?" she asked.

"Yes, for a few minutes."

Jeanne let them in, and Jonathan paced about the room. "I am puzzled as to how my card got into Roger's pocket. If Phyllis was the one who knew him, why give him my card? How did she know him?"

"I think you are going to have to talk to Phyllis."

"Yes, of course." Jonathan was lost in thought, trying to make sense of everything. "This somehow involves you and me in Roger's death. I must get answers." He stood by the door and stated, "I need to get back to the office. I'll talk to Phyllis this afternoon before I take her down to meet Detective O'Neal. I'll let you know what happens. You have things to take care of so call if you need me," and then he was gone.

CHAPTER 6

B y noon, Jonathan was eager to talk to Phyllis. He walked out of his office and asked, "Phyllis, how would you like me to take you to lunch today?"

"Yes, that would be wonderful," she said with excitement.

"Can you get away now?"

"Whenever you say."

"Then let's go. Bring your calendar with you. I need to check some dates with you."

They walked to the little French restaurant at the corner of the block.

Phyllis asked, "What did I do to deserve being taken to lunch?"

"I just needed to talk with you and I thought you'd be more comfortable out of the office. I have some questions for you," he said in a serious tone.

"Sure. Anything I can do to help."

As soon as they entered the restaurant, they were seated. Jonathan took a deep breath and began with the first question. "Do you know a person named Roger?"

Phyllis sat up straight, blinked her eyes in surprise and said, "Yes. I met him about a month ago at a bar. Why do you ask?"

"He was found dead at the beach last weekend."

"You said he was dead? How? When?"

He ignored her questions. "He had my business card on him. Did you give it to him?"

"He told me he was going through a divorce and might need an attorney. I suggested he contact you."

"When did you last see him?"

"I'm not sure. A few days ago, maybe last week."

"Why don't you check your calendar?"

She picked it up and turned to the current pages. "Well, last weekend he wanted me to meet him at our bar. Then he suggested we drive out to the beach. He wanted to show me his house. It was a Sunday morning."

"Do you remember what time you got there?"

"Why do you want to know?'

"Just answer the question. What time did you arrive at the beach?"

"I'm not exactly sure. It was probably late morning."

"Did you see his house?"

"No... Yes. He pointed it out to me, but that was it. We walked down by the surf and then he said we should go back, so we did."

"Did he mention his wife's name?"

"No."

"That's it?"

"Yes," she answered while biting on her lower lip. "That's all we did."

When they had finished their lunch and were ready to leave, Jonathan said, "By the way, Detective O'Neal at the police station wants you to come in to talk to him. He has some questions for you. You may be the last person to have seen Roger alive."

A look of panic appeared on her face and Phyllis said, "How could that be? He was fine when we left the beach."

"Just answer his questions honestly and you'll be okay."

"Will you go with me?" she asked hopefully.

"Certainly. And I think we need to do it soon."

They walked back to the office in silence. Phyllis rushed to the restroom and splashed cold water on her face and repaired her makeup. At her desk, she checked appointments for her and Jonathan and decided they could leave the office by four o'clock. That would give her time to collect her thoughts and prepare answers to his questions. Phyllis had a hard time keeping her mind on her work. She was anxious about the questions the detective might ask. Jonathan exited his office and said, "Come on. Let's get this over with."

Phyllis grabbed her purse and followed him to the elevator. "I'm a little nervous. I've never been in a police station before," Phyllis said.

Jonathan didn't respond.

When they arrived at the station, Phyllis asked, "Did the police tell you why they wanted to see me?"

"Only that they found my card in Roger's pocket, and since you are my secretary and I didn't put it there, they wanted to see what you might know. Just routine questions, I'm sure."

After a few minutes, they were ushered to Detective O'Neal's office. "Please, come in and have a seat. Good to see you, Mr. Crown," he said with a nod. "It's nice to meet you, Phyllis," and he shook her hand. "Thanks for coming in. I have a few questions for you."

Phyllis clasped her hands together in her lap to keep them from shaking.

"I understand you are Mr. Crown's secretary. Correct?"

"Yes, I am."

"What is your full name?"

"Phyllis Louise McNeil."

"How long have you been working for Mr. Crown?"

"For less than a year. I'm assigned to him temporarily, but I've been with the firm for a little more than two years."

"I see. For whom did you work before you went to Mr. Crown?"

"I was a secretary to Mr. Best, one of the other partners."

"How did you know Roger Anders, the deceased?"

"Oh, I didn't know his last name," she said with surprise. "I met him in a local bar one evening. We had a couple of drinks and seemed to hit it off. We dated a couple of times."

"When did you first meet him?"

"About a month or more ago. I told all of this to Mr. Crown."

"I understand, but you need to tell me. Where did you go on your dates?"

Phyllis told him of having lunch a couple of times and about going to the beach one weekend, just as she had told Jonathan. She also mentioned his impending divorce.

Detective O'Neal leaned his chin on his folded hands as he studied Phyllis while considering all she had told him. Finally, he thoughtfully said, "I appreciate you telling me about you and Roger. I still have concerns about the circumstances of his death, but we will get it all sorted out in time. You've been very helpful." He escorted them to the door. "I would like you to be available in case I have more questions. Should I call you at Mr. Crown's office?"

"Yes, that would be best," she answered and looked at Jonathan for assurance. As they walked back to the car, Phyllis said, "Well, that wasn't so bad. I don't know why I was so nervous."

"Any new experience can be a little unnerving. You did fine." Even though she told the same story to the detective as she had told him, it seemed a little rehearsed. He felt there was something she wasn't telling him.

As they walked to the car, Jonathan said, "By the way, I never did ask you why you left Mr. Best and wanted to work for me?"

She blushed a little. "I liked you better. You are the senior partner, and it would be a step up. Plus, you did give me a raise."

CHAPTER 7

Jonathan was quiet on the drive back. He thought about the many times when Phyllis found a reason to talk to him or come to his office. She observed his comings and goings, accidentally met him at the elevator at the end of the day, had him walk her to her car... He just hadn't been paying attention to the signs. He had never encouraged her, but he did notice how happy she was when he'd asked her to lunch. He would not do that again.

He dropped Phyllis at her car. He didn't want to return to the office, and he didn't feel like going home, so he pointed his car in the direction of Jeanne's apartment.

Phyllis opened her car door, got in and sat without turning on the ignition. She took a deep breath, feeling relieved that the interview with the detective was over. *If I hold to my story, all will be well,* she told herself. She caught a glimpse of herself in the mirror and immediately relaxed the frown she saw there. She didn't want to get wrinkles prematurely. It was enough just to have the sprinkling of freckles across her nose.

Alexander, the door man, recognized Jonathan immediately and ushered him into the apartment building. Jonathan pushed the button for Jeanne's floor and leaned back against the elevator wall. The thought of seeing Jeanne made his heart skip a beat. He had to be careful—she was his client. Once the elevator doors opened there she was standing before him dressed casually wearing sneakers and a small hat.

"Oh, I didn't expect to see you. I was just going for a walk," she said with a warm smile. "Why don't you join me?"

"That would be nice. I rarely take time for a walk."

As they exited the building, Jonathan removed his suit jacket, handed it to Alexander and asked, "Would you put this in my car, please?"

"Of course, sir."

While they walked, Jonathan told her about the conversations with Phyllis and Detective O'Neal. "She didn't know Roger's last name, so they must not have known each other very long. By the way, when I found out it was Anders, I wondered about your name being Blomgren."

"That's easy. When Roger left, I decided to take back my maiden name. I was becoming my own person with a new life."

"I can understand that."

They walked in silence, enjoying the fresh September air. At the edge of the park, they stopped to rest on a stone bench. The sun was low in the sky making long shadows across the lawn. A small bird was chirping on the branch above them.

"This is my favorite time of the day," Jeanne commented.

"I'm glad you suggested this. It was just what I needed." He sighed. "Now I think we should walk back. I have work to do at home."

"Are you sure? I thought maybe I could make a simple supper for us at the apartment."

"Simple is very tempting. However, I don't like to impose on a client," he answered with a grin.

While Jeanne put a healthy salad together and sliced a French baguette, Jonathan opened a chilled bottle of Pinot Grigio, a California white wine. "You have very good taste in wine."

"We have Roger to thank for that. He did like good wines, and kept an adequate supply on hand. I do enjoy a glass of wine with dinner, which I have nearly every night."

"A civilized woman. I agree with your custom," he said with a smile.

During supper, their conversation covered many different topics, none of which included Roger, the police, or work. It was a time to get to know one another on a more personal basis. When the wine bottle released its last drop, Jonathan looked at his watch and rose from his chair.

"One last question... will you be ready to start work next week? We could use you soon."

"My children are coming home this weekend for Roger's service on Sunday, and then they have to return immediately for school. So, yes, I could come in Monday."

"That would be great, if you don't think it rushes you."

"No. I can be ready to begin my new career the next morning," she said with a smile.

"Would you like me to attend the service Sunday?"

"Oh, yes, of course. And I'd like you to meet my children. Please, do come."

"I'll be there." And he was gone.

CHAPTER 8

The twins were arriving Saturday—that's tomorrow, she realized with surprise. Roger's attorney had the reading of the will scheduled for that afternoon. The service Sunday afternoon was being handled by their pastor in the chapel of the Presbyterian church. She didn't think many people would attend, but some of those who had been their friends before the proposed divorce might come, and of course, his office colleagues.

She was ready for the final goodbye to Roger. She was curious, however, to know if the police had found the person or persons responsible for his death. They had the details in the coroner's report and so there was no reason to delay Roger's cremation. Detective O'Neal would let her know if, or when they came to a conclusion. They knew the cause of death, just not how it occurred, or maybe by whom. It could be just a simple accident if he had climbed up on the rocks and then slipped and fell, or...

Just before the day ended, Jeanne called Jonathan's office. Phyllis intercepted the call, telling her that he was in a meeting. "May I take a message?"

Jeanne hesitated. "Just tell him that Roger's service is at two o'clock Sunday afternoon."

Phyllis hesitated and then asked, "Does he know where it is?"

"Yes, I did tell him that."

"I'll give him the message," and she disconnected the call.

As soon as Jonathan returned to his office, Phyllis gave it to him.

"Thanks. I needed that."

"She said you knew where the service was?" she said with a question in her voice.

"Yes, at the Presbyterian chapel. I know where it is."

Phyllis was glad to know since she would be going, also. After all, she did know Roger. She wanted to see who his wife was. She had thought of her as her competition even though Roger was divorcing her. Phyllis returned to her desk feeling satisfied. She would play the role of the sympathetic friend.

At the end of the day, as everyone was leaving, Judy stopped by Phyllis's desk and asked what she was going to do on her days off.

"Why do you ask?" Phyllis asked.

"I just wondered if you were going to see your special friend."

"Who do you mean?"

"Roger. The one you told me about."

Phyllis stopped short and a look of panic swept across her face. She immediately changed it to a half smile. "No, not this weekend. He said he would be out of town."

"I'm sorry. Would you like to join me for a glass of wine before going home?"

"No, thanks. I have things to do." Phyllis did not want to go to the local bar again, the one where she had met Roger.

"Okay. See you Monday," Judy said as she turned to leave.

Phyllis sat at her desk thinking about the recent events. If only she had not met Roger, but he was charming, thoughtful, and quite good looking. She had begun to think he might be the one. But in only one month she knew that would not be the case. *How easily one can be fooled by a smooth-talking gentleman. Now I no longer have to deal with him,* she thought with relief. She gathered up her personal things and left the office.

Jeanne went to the airport to meet the plane Saturday morning.

"Hi, Mom," Mark said giving her a hug. "I can't believe Dad's gone. How are you doing?"

"Thanks, son. I'm okay. I have a wonderful attorney who has been helping me. You will meet him tomorrow at the service."

They walked to the car with Jeanne asking questions about school and the children asking about their father's death. Mark said, "I was surprised when Detective O'Neal called and asked a few questions about Dad."

"What kind of questions?" Jeanne asked.

"Things like did I know who his attorney was, did I know if he had a will, did I have an address of where he had been living, and then how did you and he get along, things like that. He seemed concerned about you."

"He seems to be doing a very thorough job in investigating your father's death." As an afterthought Jeanne said, "I guess the police have not completely ruled it a simple accident."

"Oh? Why is that?" Mandy asked.

"I don't know, but the detective said it's just a feeling he has." Jeanne understood what he meant. She, too, often had a feeling about Roger in the last several weeks of their marriage. "It's a kind of intuition, something you can't put your finger on, but you know there's something that's not quite right."

At the apartment, Jeanne opened the door and Mandy exclaimed, "Oh, Mom. This is lovely. When you first bought it, I was not sure, but now ..." and she gave her mother a hug.

"Yeah, it's okay," Mark said with approval. "Where shall I put my stuff?"

"You may have the room down the hall, second door on the right. And Mandy, you can have the one directly across from him. When you get settled, we'll have a light lunch. We have an appointment at three o'clock with your father's attorney for the reading of his will."

While the twins unpacked, Jeanne put a chicken salad together. She had fresh rolls and a chocolate cheesecake for dessert. She knew how much Mandy liked chocolate—in any form.

"Mom, I really like your new apartment. It suits you. And the view from here is great. I'm glad you changed from our old house," Mark said with more enthusiasm than Jeanne had ever observed.

"Thank you. I was concerned that you would miss coming home to the old one, but I felt I needed to make this change after... you know."

"Don't be concerned about us. We'll be away for at least four years, and who knows what we will do, or where we will go after we graduate?"

"True," Mandy said as she entered the room. "I doubt if we will ever live full time at home again. However, I do hope you keep the beach house. We love to go there for the summer."

"Yes, I will keep the beach house. It is so peaceful compared to living here in town. I probably will enjoy it often on weekends."

They were quiet as they ate their salads. Jeanne looked at her two children observing how they had grown into beautiful young people. Each had characteristics of both her and Roger. They were typical Swedish blondes with blue eyes, tall and slender. She had to admit that Roger had given a lot to them over the years. He was good with them, but different with her. They had a good relationship for years, but they had gradually grown apart. When he told her he was leaving, she almost felt a sense of relief. Not that she didn't love him, but the relationship had dissolved until they no longer had a connection. She didn't feel sad or angry, just empty. The twins were the one good thing from their marriage.

Over dessert, Mandy asked, "Did you get chocolate cheesecake because you know it's my favorite, or because you want to entice me to stay longer?"

"Maybe a little bit of both," Jeanne answered with a warm smile. "Indulge me in a little wishful thinking."

"I promise I... we will come home for holidays. Isn't that right, bro?"

"Absolutely," Mark responded as he put the last piece of cheesecake in his mouth.

"I will expect you both then. We can spend Thanksgiving weekend at the beach house. Now, we need to leave soon. We can walk to the attorney's office."

She enjoyed her role as a mother, but she must remember her children were becoming independent adults. She recalled reading once that the values you taught your children by the age of twelve would remain with them. They were now five years past that. She hoped they had done it right and their teachings were instilled in them, guiding them in their life choices.

CHAPTER 9

As the family left the apartment, Mark asked, "Mom, did you sign the divorce papers?"

"No. I planned to do it when summer was over. And then... everything changed. Why do you ask?"

"I just wondered."

They walked in silence.

"Well, here we are," Jeanne said as they stopped in front of the tall office building of a law firm. Upon entering they were greeted by the receptionist. "We have an appointment with Mr. Welford."

"It's Ms. Welford. What is your name, please?"

"Jeanne Blomgren, or Jeanne Anders." She didn't know which was the proper name to use at this point. She thought of herself as Blomgren, but legally she was still Roger's wife.

The receptionist lifted a phone and said, "There is a Ms. Blomgren-Anders here to see Ms. Welford. Thank you." As she disconnected, she said, "Ms. Welford's secretary said to come right up. The elevator will open to her office on the seventh floor."

Mark said, "Wouldn't you know Dad would hire a woman attorney? She's probably beautiful, too." He punched the seventh floor button and they waited without another word.

A young man greeted them when the door opened and said, "This way to Ms. Welford's office," indicating with his hand.

Ms. Welford stood to shake hands with each of them. "Thanks for coming. I'm glad we could schedule this meeting while the twins were in town. Your father spoke very highly of you. He was proud of you both." The twins just smiled. "Please sit down," she offered as she pointed to the three chairs opposite her desk.

Mark whispered to Mandy, "Just as I thought, she is beautiful."

Mandy grinned as she punched him with her elbow.

"Now, I know you have limited time here. I understand the memorial service for Mr. Anders is tomorrow. Would it be acceptable for me to attend? I've known him for a long time, and even though I had not met any of you, I feel as though I know you."

"Of course, you may. It's not a closed service," Jeanne responded.

"Yes, I would like to. Now, let's get to it." She picked up a large folder. "I've asked my secretary, Gerald, to sit in and take notes in case there are questions."

"Just for the record, please state your names," Gerald said.

"Mark Anders."

"Mandy Anders, or should I say Melinda Anders?"

"Jeanne Blomgren-Anders."

"I was told that Roger had no siblings or other children. Is that correct?" Ms. Welford asked.

"Yes, that's correct. As far as I know we are his only living relatives," Jeanne said.

"This was written and filed with us nearly one year ago. He did not update it after he filed for the divorce. We had encouraged him to consider doing it, but it seems he wanted to let it stand as it was at the time. So... here it is."

She began reading all the whereas and herein legalese statements, finally getting to the distribution of assets section, which was the area of most interest to the twins. "Two-thirds of my financial assets will be divided equally between each of my children, the twins Mark and Melinda Anders, to be used exclusively for their education, with any remaining funds after they receive their degrees, to be used or invested at their discretion. The remaining third of my financial estate goes to my wife, Jeanne Blomgren-Anders. In addition, the beach house goes to Jeanne, the mortgage of which has been paid. Any of my personal belongings may be distributed, donated or destroyed as determined by my wife, Jeanne. Love to you all. Roger Anders."

There was complete silence for a few seconds, when Mark finally asked, "How much money is in his estate? What are we talking about?"

"Gerald, would you please give a copy of Roger's financial statement to each of them? From that you will be able to determine the amount you will receive. It is a substantial amount, so I suggest you work with a financial advisor so that Roger's wishes will be carried out and that you will handle the amount you receive responsibly. There are some papers for you to sign, after which you will each be given a check in the amount indicated on the forms. Any questions?"

"Do we need to pay you for your services?" Jeanne asked.

"No. Roger took care of that prior to his passing. You owe us nothing."

"This is truly amazing," Mark said as he looked at the financial statement. "I had no idea Dad did so well financially. He always made us think we had to be very careful with our expenditures."

"I'm not sure I know how to handle this much money," Mandy said. "I definitely will get a financial advisor. I'm just relieved my education costs are covered. I would never be able to afford it without Dad's help. It's interesting, he never told us that he could take care of it."

"I guess he wanted you to be careful and responsible with money," Jeanne said. "You always had what you needed, maybe not always what you wanted."

Ms. Welford handed each of them the form which indicated the amount they would receive from Roger's estate. It also was releasing her and their firm of any ongoing responsibility regarding his estate. "Please read it carefully before you sign. You've heard it said, 'always read the fine print,' well, I'm asking you to do just that."

Mandy finished reading the paperwork first, and signed where it was indicated. She sat quietly waiting for the others. Mark was next. He looked over the papers carefully with a puzzled expression.

"Do you have a question, Mark?" Ms. Welford asked.

"Oh... no, I guess not. I was just wondering, how did he have so much money and we didn't know about it?"

"That's something you should have asked him. All I can tell you is that he made some very good investments over the years and saved his money."

Jeanne finished reading all the printed words and gratefully signed where indicated. She let out a long sigh, releasing all the tension from her body. "I'm glad this is finished and we can move into our new life. Even though Roger didn't want to remain married to me, he did take good care of me."

"Yes, I would agree that he did," Ms. Welford said.

"Since I never signed the divorce papers, I guess that now I can destroy them."

"Because of Roger's untimely death, it is good that you had not signed them. His will might have been changed otherwise," Ms. Welford explained. "As it is, you were still his wife at the time of his death. Now his settlement seems very fair to all of you."

All three of them stood up, thanked Ms. Welford as they accepted their checks, and turned to leave the room with big smiles on their faces. As soon as they were in the elevator, they embraced in a group hug. Mark was the first one to say it. "It was good of Dad to provide so well for us."

"I'm overwhelmed," Mandy said. "I've never seen such a big number following a dollar sign. I think I will have to learn about investments."

"That would be a wise thing to do," Jeanne said.

"I think I need time tonight to think about it. What is it they say when you have to make a big decision—sleep on it?"

"Right. Good point," Mark agreed.

They arrived at the apartment feeling elated at the outcome of the will. Now they had to deal with the memorial service tomorrow. Jeanne put some music on, Mark went to his room and she and Mandy kicked their shoes off, sat down on opposite ends of the sofa and put their feet up. This is how they often sat when they had an issue to discuss—and they had a big one this time.

Mandy was quiet for a while, and then said, "You were going to tell me how you met Jonathan. Now is a good time."

Jeanne took a deep breath and let it out slowly as she began to recall that fateful day at the beach. "It was the last day of my time at the beach house for the summer. I was starting a new job the next day. I walked to the rock pile, one of my favorite places, for my last visit. That's where I saw your father's body which had fallen in the rocks." She paused and her body shivered. "I went to a house to get help, and there was Jonathan." She continued telling her the story of their fortuitous meeting. "I don't know what I would have done if he hadn't come to my rescue."

They sat in silence for a time. Tomorrow would be their final goodbye to Roger.

CHAPTER 10

After a good night's sleep, Jeanne was ready to face the day. She decided to attend the early morning church service. She left a note for the twins telling them when she'd be back, and to make their own breakfast.

Sunday morning traffic was light. She tuned the car radio to the classical music station. A Bach Prelude was playing. *Most appropriate for going to church*, she thought. By the time she arrived at church, she felt at peace. She was confident that her life, as well as the twins' were going to be okay. Just as she started up the steps to enter the church, a hand touched her shoulder. Startled, she looked around and was surprised to see Jonathan.

"Good morning, Jeanne. What a surprise. I didn't expect to see you out so early."

"I'm surprised to see you, too. I woke up early with my mind spinning. I thought perhaps church might calm it."

"Do you mind if I join you?"

"Of course not. I'd love it."

They selected a seat in the sanctuary just as the organ began the prelude, a Bach Chorale. Jeanne whispered, "This is my favorite music in church. If I hear Bach on the organ, I know I have been to church."

As they sang the opening hymn, *Joyful, Joyful We Adore Thee*, Jeanne was aware of what a beautiful baritone voice Jonathan had. She matched his with her soprano voice. Just the act of singing filled her with peace, and to do it with Jonathan beside her filled her with joy.

At the conclusion of the service, they remained seated listening to the grand organ postlude. When the last note died away, they slowly stood and walked out into the sunshine.

Jeanne turned to Jonathan and asked, "Would you like to come to the apartment for a quick lunch? Then you could go with us to the memorial service."

He hesitated, smiled at her, and then said, "I'd love to, if you're sure the twins won't mind?"

"Not at all. I would like you to meet them. I'll go on ahead and you can come at your leisure."

On the way home, Jeanne was wondering how the twins would respond to Jonathan being her friend in addition to being her attorney. She left her car with Maurice and took the elevator to the apartment. Jeanne kicked off her shoes and sat down next to Mark. "We have a guest coming for lunch."

"Who?" he asked.

"Mr. Crown, Jonathan, my attorney. I met him at church and invited him to come for lunch. He's planning to go to your father's memorial service so I thought he could go with us. Is that okay with you?"

"Makes no difference to me."

"Good. I think I'll go see what Mandy is up to. Did you both have breakfast?" she asked as she walked out of the room.

"I did. I don't know about her."

"Mandy," she called as she softly knocked on her door. "May I come in?"

"Yes, of course," she answered.

Mandy was still in her PJs leaning against pillows on her bed holding an open book. "I'm reading a novel to keep my mind busy. I don't like thinking about Dad and what might have happened to him. Will we ever know for sure?"

"I understand, dear," she said as she sat down on the edge of the bed. "I, too, keep wondering and asking unanswerable questions. I'm just glad we have my attorney to help us. He's investigating the incident along with the detective. I'm sure they will figure it out.

"Meanwhile, I wanted to tell you that Jonathan, Mr. Crown, is coming here for lunch. I met him in church this morning, and since he was planning on attending the memorial service I thought he might as well go with us. And besides, I'd like you to get to know him," she said as she left the room.

The doorbell chimed, announcing Jonathan's arrival. Jeanne scurried to the door and opened it to a smiling Jonathan holding a wine bottle in one hand and a nonalcoholic beverage in the other. "One for us and one for the twins," he explained as he entered the door.

"How thoughtful of you. I'm sure they will be delighted," Jeanne said as she took them from him. The twins entered and stood side by side.

"Well, here are the famous twins," Jonathan said, looking at them with a big smile.

"Yes. I'd like you to meet Mandy and Mark. This is Mr. Crown, my attorney," she said.

"I'm so pleased to meet you. Your mother is very proud of you. She talks about you often."

"I hope it's all good," Mandy said.

"As long as she doesn't tell you everything, I think we're safe," Mark said with a grin.

"I won't divulge any secrets she may have shared," he responded.

While they continued chatting, getting acquainted, Jeanne excused herself to get lunch on the table. She had prepared a cheese and mushroom soufflé, a sample of fruit slices, and fresh croissants. The oven bell chimed announcing the soufflé was ready. As she lifted it from the oven, she called, "Okay, everyone. To the table. This must be served immediately."

The lunch was quite pleasant with easy conversation between the twins and Jonathan. Jeanne loved listening to them. They could have continued talking into the afternoon, but it was time to go to the memorial service.

In the elevator no one said a word. They were sobered as each thought about what was next. Roger was dead, her husband and their father was dead, and life would be different. And there still were questions to be answered.

"Have each of you thought about what you will say at the service?" Jeanne asked.

"As long as we don't have to give a long speech, I'm okay," Mark said.

"I agree. I'll just share some of my best memories of Dad," Mandy added.

"That would be perfect. Just say what's in your heart," Jeanne said.

CHAPTER 11

The large double doors were standing open and people already were gathering at the chapel. Jeanne parked, walked around the car and took the hand of each twin. Together they entered the chapel with Jonathan following.

The flowers gracing the front platform were bouquets of yellow and blue with sprays of white orchids. A large photograph of Roger was placed in the center. As they walked to their seats, they focused on the picture. He looked happy in the professional photograph taken a few months ago. The quiet organ music filled the chapel's space with peace. The sun glinted through the small stained glass windows, each one depicting an event in the life of Jesus. They sat quietly with their own thoughts waiting for the service to begin.

At the appointed time, the minister entered, greeted the audience and spoke briefly about life and the passing on to the next. Then he asked if anyone would like to say anything. Each of the twins took their turn speaking briefly about their memories of their father. Jeanne also said her goodbye to her husband of nearly twenty-five years, thanking him for their time together and for giving her their wonderful twins.

At the conclusion of the service, every one stood and sang his favorite hymn, *How Great Thou Art*. The minister announced a reception was in the fellowship hall next door where everyone could greet the family. They were escorted out and the guests followed.

One by one people came first to Jeanne, offering words of condolence and remembrance, then on the Mandy and Mark. Occasionally, someone said something that triggered the beginning of tears. They were relieved when the last person passed by them, but then one more came to Jeanne.

"I didn't know Roger well. I met him only a couple of months ago, but he was a wonderful person. I am Phyllis, secretary to Jonathan."

"How nice to meet you. Jonathan has been a great help to us," Jeanne responded.

Jonathan came over and said, "I see you have met my secretary, Phyllis." He hesitated a moment before saying, "By the way, Phyllis, Jeanne will be starting work with us tomorrow."

Phyllis opened her mouth, but nothing came out. Her eyes opened in surprise. "That's wonderful. I will look forward to getting to know you. If I can ever be of help, just ask."

"Thank you. I'm sure I will be asking often at first."

Then Phyllis pulled Jonathan aside. "Why didn't you tell me about her?"

"We just decided on her start day. She interviewed with us a few weeks ago." He gently pulled away and went back to Jeanne.

Phyllis said, "I'm glad to have you come on board. We can use the help. Jonathan is on overload most of the time." She smiled up at him and patted his arm.

Jeanne observed her subtle claim on Jonathan and was curious about her act of intimacy. Perhaps they had a relationship at some level. She'd have to be careful around her.

Mark brought a glass of punch to his mother.

"Thank you, Mark. I really needed that." She turned from Phyllis and walked across the room to sit down. Her feet were tired and she didn't want to talk to any other guests. Her thoughts went to Roger and tears began to form behind her eyes. They were not so much for the loss of Roger, but more for the loss of her marriage.

Mandy joined her, took her hand and said, "Mom, we're going to be okay. I will miss Dad, but I have good memories of him and our family together."

"How sweet of you to say that. I will miss you when you're away at school. You must promise to come home as often as you can." She looked for Jonathan to see if he, too, was ready to leave. He seemed to be cornered near the refreshment table by Phyllis. Jeanne quickly stood up and said, "Let's go. Would you ask Jonathan to come along? Unless he wants to stay longer."

Mark went to Jonathan. "Mom wants to leave now. Will you be coming?"

"Yes, yes. Sorry to keep you waiting." He turned to Phyllis, handed her his glass and left her without saying goodbye. She just stood there looking after him.

Jonathan put his hand on Jeanne's back to subtly direct her from the room. "Sorry if I kept you waiting."

"No problem. Undoubtedly your secretary had things to say to you."

They remained quiet on the ride back to the apartment. Jeanne parked in the garage and they took the elevator up to their floor. Upon entering the apartment, the twins went straight to their rooms.

"Would you like to come in for a glass of wine?" Jeanne asked Jonathan.

"Thank you, but I think not. You are tired, and besides you need to get ready for starting your new job in the morning. I want you to be well rested," he said with a teasing smile. "I'll see you at nine o'clock tomorrow. Sleep well." And he was gone.

Jeanne was tired, emotionally as well as physically. She turned on the classical music station and curled up in the corner of the sofa. While she listened to a Beethoven symphony, she reflected on the memorial service and the many good comments made by friends. Roger really was a good person. *It was just… Perhaps she could have worked harder at their relationship, but then, so could have Roger. He was gone a lot during the last few months and when he was home, he seemed preoccupied. Now there is no use wondering about what might have been.* She had to think about the next stage of her life.

The phone rang intruding in her thoughts. "Yes, Maurice. What is it?"

"Someone is here with flowers for you. Shall I send him up?"

"Who is it?"

"He says he is from the church."

"All right. Send him up." She wondered why they would be bringing flowers to her now. Following the gentle knock on the door, she opened it to see only two large arrangements of flowers. "Is there someone behind this wall of color?"

"Yes. I'm the custodian from the church," he said as he peeked around the bouquet. "I hated to leave these beautiful arrangements to wilt and die in the chapel, and thought you might enjoy them for a few days."

"How thoughtful of you. Yes, come in, please. You can put them right here on the table."

"Mrs. Anders, I am sorry for your loss. Mr. Anders was a good friend. We will miss him."

"Thank you for your kind words, and thanks for bringing the flowers here. We will enjoy them, I'm sure." And with that she ushered him out the door and slowly closed it.

The twins packed their bags. It was time to leave for the airport. Mark was relegated to the back seat—Mandy had already commandeered the front seat. Conversation was nonexistent. Jeanne said she would miss them and looked forward to Thanksgiving when they'd come home for a few days. There was little traffic until they neared the entrance to the airport.

"I'll just drop you here in front. It's too hard to find a place to park. Is that okay?"

"Sure, Mom. We can give you a hug and be on our way," Mark said. He grabbed the bags from the trunk and handed Mandy hers.

Jeanne exited the car just long enough to give each of them a hug, saying, *"Jag alskar dig"* to them in Swedish. "I love you both and I'm so proud of you." They said they loved her, too, and then disappeared into the cavern of the airport, turning briefly to wave goodbye... they were gone. Jeanne went home alone, reflecting on the events of the weekend.

CHAPTER 12

Jeanne greeted Monday morning with trepidation. It had been years since she worked professionally. Because she had not asked about parking, walking two blocks to the office helped her relax.

The receptionist greeted her when she entered the glass doors. "Good morning. How may I help you?"

"I'm Jeanne Blomgren. I'm starting to work here today. I think I'm supposed to meet Jonathan Crown. Can you tell me where I should go?"

"Just a minute. Let me check." She punched in a number and spoke into her headpiece. "Phyllis, there is a Ms. Blomgren here to see Mr. Crown. Shall I send her up?"

"Thank you. She said to go right up. She will meet you at the elevator on the ninth floor. That is the Executive floor," she said giving Jeanne a warm smile.

True to her word, Phyllis greeted Jeanne as she stepped out of the elevator. "Welcome to Crown, Best and Carruthers, Attorneys at Law. I'm glad to see you again." She pointed with her hand to indicate Jeanne should follow her. "This way to Mr. Crown's office. As you know, I'm his personal secretary. It's only temporary, but I'm hoping he will keep me. I like working for him. He's a great boss."

"Here we are." Phyllis lightly knocked on the door with the distinctive letters in gold **Jonathan B. Crown, J.D., Esq.**, and opened it. "Ms. Blomgren is here to see you."

"Great," he said as he stood up and came around the desk to greet her. "Come in, Jeanne. Thank you, Phyllis. I'll call you when I need you." Phyllis closed the door. To Jeanne he asked, "How are you this morning?"

"I'm a little nervous. I haven't worked in an office for some time, as you know."

"Yes. As you are aware, Phyllis is assigned to me as my secretary only temporarily. Right now, I'd like to have you as my assistant. I need help with paperwork—mostly research, routine stuff that you can learn very quickly. You may do research for the other partners as well. Does that sound okay to you?"

"Well... I think so. As long as you're patient while I'm learning," she said hesitantly.

"I think I can manage that. You'll need to go to Personnel and fill out what will seem like a ream of forms in order to get you on the payroll. I'll have Phyllis take you there. She will help you get oriented to the various offices and employees' areas, and introduce you to other staff members. Any questions?"

"Not yet, but I'm sure there will be many."

"Phyllis, will you come in please?" he called into the intercom.

She entered immediately. "Yes, sir?"

"Will you take Ms. Blomgren, Jeanne, to the personnel office? She needs to fill out the required forms for employment. Then, please show her around so she knows where the staff room is, as well as the ladies' room, the copy center, and any place else necessary so she won't get lost. Also, introduce her to some of the other staff. She will be my assistant. That's it for now."

"Yes, Mr. Crown. Will do," she said with a surprised expression. "Come with me, Jeanne, and we'll take the tour." Jeanne followed Phyllis for her orientation. "I didn't know Mr. Crown was looking for an assistant. He usually tells me everything. We work very closely together. You must be special."

"I don't know about that. I was surprised to get hired so quickly. I was interviewed by a gentleman in the personnel office. I guess he knew what the firm needed, and I was it."

They stopped in front of a desk, and Phyllis said, "Judy, this is Jeanne. Judy is secretary to one of the partners, Mr. Carruthers. Jeanne will be an assistant to Mr. Crown. Surprise."

"Welcome, Jeanne. Let me know if ever I can be of help."

"Thank you. Will do." And they walked on.

They took the elevator down to the personnel office. "We need to have our new employee, Jeanne Blomgren, fill out the employment forms," Phyllis said to the receptionist. "Also, I think she needs to meet the head of the department. Is he available?" After a few minutes, they were ushered into his office. "I want you to meet our newest employee, Ms. Jeanne Blomgren. She will be working with Mr Crown."

"Thank you, Phyllis. It's good to see you again, Ms. Blomgren. I heard you were coming in today. Mr. Crown seems very pleased to have you on his staff. Please sit down," and he pointed the chair opposite his desk. "Phyllis, I'll call you when we are finished and you can escort Ms. Blomgren back to her office."

"Yes, sir," she said as she turned and left.

"Now, tell me more about yourself. From your name I would guess you are Swedish, or perhaps Norwegian."

"Yes, I'm Swedish. That is my heritage."

"Do you have family... children?"

"Yes, I have twins. A boy and a girl."

"Do they live with you?"

"Not presently. They are away at the university."

"And what university is that?"

"Stanford in Palo Alto."

"A very good choice. I recall from our interview a few weeks ago that you have not worked for several years. How do you feel now about getting back in the business world?"

"A little nervous, but eager to be busy. As you know, my husband passed away recently and being on my own, I felt I needed to do something worthwhile with my time."

"I'm aware that you have kept up your skills through your volunteer work, so this transition will be easy for you. We're delighted to have you join us. Do you have any questions?"

"Just the usual like what holidays do we observe? When is payday? And, of course, what is my salary? We never discussed it because I was just happy to get hired."

"You will be given an employee's handbook which has all the answers to your questions. I will have to talk with Mr. Crown about your salary. I'm sure he will let you know what we decide. Now, to the paperwork. Here are all the forms you need to fill out. Because our firm works with all types of cases—private individuals, family, business, government, a few criminal and pro bono—we require a lot of information about our employees. You will have no secrets," he said with a smile. "You may sit at the table just outside my office. My secretary will let Phyllis know when you are finished so she can come get you. Just take your time."

"Thank you." Jeanne picked up the stack of papers and settled at the table where she began to study the material in front of her. So many questions addressing things she had not thought about in a long time.

The secretary interrupted her concentration asking, "What department will you be working in?"

"Mr. Crown told me I'm starting as his assistant."

"Oh! A good place to start." She turned back to the work on her cluttered desk.

Jeanne continued filling in the blanks with answers to a variety of questions. She had no idea how long she had been writing when she decided she was finished. "I think I've done all I can. Shall I leave this with you?"

"Yes, that's fine. I'll call Phyllis and tell her to come for you. You might get lost if you went on your own."

"I'm sure I would."

They were soon back on the ninth floor and outside Jonathan's office. Phyllis knocked on his door and walked in. "Jeanne is back. Where shall I tell her to go? Have you selected her desk?"

"Have her come in. Then we'll discuss it."

Jeanne entered his office and sat down with a sigh. "You were right. It was a ream of papers filled with questions. I haven't written that much in years. I think I have writer's cramp."

"The hard part is over. Things get easier now. I understand we never did discuss your salary. After talking with the head of the personnel office, we have agreed on a figure. I hope you will be willing to accept our offer." He named a figure for her monthly salary to start.

Jeanne gasped. "Are you sure I'm worth that much?"

"Absolutely, and I know you will prove it, too."

"Now we must find a desk and adequate space for you to work. Come with me." They walked out of his office, turned left, and opened the next door. "This will be your office."

Jeanne was impressed. It was comfortably large, with a lovely wood desk and matching upholstered chair, a small file cabinet, a computer and printer, and best of all, a window looking out toward the park. "Why do I get such a lovely office? I don't deserve it."

"You are my assistant, and you deserve it."

"I love it. Thank you." She looked around and asked, "May I bring my own artwork?"

"Of course. It is your office. Make it comfortable for you."

Phyllis poked her head in the door and said, "It's almost lunch time. If you don't have plans I thought I'd take you to our cafeteria. It has good and reasonably priced food, and besides you'd get to meet some of the other people in our firm. Sometimes we go out to the deli down the street, but the cafeteria is just as good."

"That would be perfect. I hadn't given a thought to lunch."

Jonathan asked Jeanne to stop at his office when she returned from lunch and they'd lay out her work schedule.

Upon entering the cafeteria on the third floor, it looked just like a nice restaurant. Tables were scattered around the room, fresh flowers were in the center of each one, the lighting was subdued and soft music was playing through the speaker system giving a quiet relaxed atmosphere. The delectable aromas were enticing.

With an exclamation of surprise Jeanne said, "My, this is not what I expected when you said we were going to the cafeteria. It's lovely."

"The firm likes to keep its employees happy. This helps. Come on, let's see what's on the menu today."

Jeanne was surprised and impressed with all the wonderful dishes available. One could have a complete meal here, which she might do sometimes so she wouldn't need to cook dinner at home.

After settling at a table, Phyllis said, "It's interesting that you and Jonathan have something in common."

"Really? What's that?"

"Your late husband died in an accident and Jonathan's wife died in an accident. Doesn't that seem like a coincidence?"

"Not particularly. They died a few years apart and on different continents. I was told Jonathan's wife died when they were on vacation in Europe."

"That's true. I just found it interesting. You know, the death of Jonathan's wife has remained a mystery, and now they are not sure how Roger died. Again, a coincidence?"

"What are you insinuating?"

"Oh, nothing. I just found the similarities interesting."

They continued eating in silence. When Phyllis had finished her lunch, she said, "You know, Jeanne, you can talk to me anytime about anything. I want to be your friend, and in a place as big as this one, you need a friend."

"Thanks. I'll keep that in mind."

She was relieved to get back into her own office. She went to see Jonathan and found his door wide open. "Hi. Are you ready to put me to work?"

"Yes. Do come in and close the door."

Jeanne entered, closed the door and sat across from Jonathan. She held her hands in her lap waiting for an assignment. For a moment they just looked at each other, finally Jonathan said, "As I told you, we do work for many different types of clients. Often I'm working with several at once, like now. That's why I need your help. Knowing how you think I'd like you to do some research for me. Have you seen our library?"

"No. Phyllis said it was on the floor below, so I think I can find it."

"Good. Here are the files for two of my clients with questions to which you need to find answers. No rush, but I'd like to have answers by the end of the week, if possible."

"I will give it my best." She left the office, files in hand, and made her way to the elevator, but stopped. She decided to use the stairs and walked down to the next floor. She entered a room the size of the entire floor. Jonathan had told her the section to work in, and so she asked the attendant to point her in the right direction. She was on her own for the rest of the afternoon.

CHAPTER 13

When the phone on Phyllis's desk rang, she picked it up with a cheery response, "Mr. Crown's office. How may I help you?"

"This is Detective O'Neal."

Phyllis's heart skipped a beat as she gave a gasp.

The detective continued, "I'd like to speak with Jeanne Blomgren. Is she available?"

"Not at the moment. She is in the library, but I can have her call you back in a few minutes. Just give me your number."

Phyllis jotted it down, took a deep breath and was relieved the call was not for her. She took the note down to the library and delivered the message. "I told the detective you'd call him back soon."

Jeanne asked the attendant for a phone she could use and was directed to a small room nearby. She closed the door and dialed the number.

"Hello, Detective. This is Jeanne. You called?"

"Yes. I have a question for you. What kind of car did your late husband own?"

"It was a silver Mercedes-Benz. Why?"

"It's curious that he was found dead at the beach, but his car was not there. Do you have any idea why, or where it might be?"

"No..o..o..." she said thoughtfully. "That is strange. Do you think it may have been stolen?"

"At this point, anything is possible. We'll continue checking into it. Thanks for getting back to me so quickly."

Jeanne left the room with another question about Roger's death. *Why wouldn't his car have been there? Phyllis said they had driven out to the beach Sunday morning. Perhaps they drove Phyllis's car. Then his car should be in his garage.* She called the detective back and suggested he check the garage at Roger's place to see if the Mercedes was there. Then she realized, she would have to clear out Roger's personal things from his apartment. Meanwhile, she had to concentrate on the work at hand. Jonathan would be waiting for the information for which she was searching. At the end of the day, she had made great progress with one of the files.

When she returned to her office, she saw that Phyllis had left for the day. Jonathan's door was open. She stuck her head in and asked, "Do you have a minute?"

"Sure, come on in. How did it go down there today?"

"Okay. I'm almost finished with one of the files." She paused, then continued. "I wanted to tell you Detective O'Neal called this afternoon and asked about Roger's car. It wasn't left at the beach. I suggested he check the garage at Roger's apartment. That reminded me that I need to clear out his personal things from there. I'll do that this weekend. I don't have his address, but I can get it from Detective O'Neal."

"Good idea. Would you like some help?"

"Maybe. Are you free?"

"I can be. What time would you like me to come by?"

"Not early. Say around ten? It shouldn't take long."

"It's a date. Now it is concerning that no car was at the beach. Do you have any ideas?"

"Phyllis did say he invited her to go with him to see his beach house. Perhaps they drove in her car. But then why would she leave Roger there?"

"Good question. I think it invites more investigation. Phyllis may have more questions to answer."

The apartment greeted her with the scent of flowers. Memories came flooding back. Memories of when the family was together, of her and Roger in their good days, of the twins before leaving for the university, and of the past summer at the beach house. The end of summer was when all of their lives changed.

I really enjoyed my first day at the office, she thought as she turned on the music channel. She changed into casual clothes and checked the refrigerator. After a quick reheating of leftovers, she sat down with the unfinished morning paper.

The phone rang. It was Mandy. "Hi, sweetheart. Is everything okay?"

"Yes. I just wanted to check in and see how your first day of work went."

"The first part of the day was spent filling out forms and getting a tour of the building. Phyllis took me to lunch in their cafeteria. You wouldn't believe it. It's like a restaurant, and good food. I think Phyllis will be a good friend."

"That's great. You need a friend."

She was awakened in the morning with a Mozart Sonata and stretched. The phone rang. It was Detective O'Neal.

"Good morning. Sorry to call so early but I wanted to catch you before you went to the office."

"That's okay, but I haven't had my first cup of coffee so I may not be too alert."

"I checked your late husband's garage. His car was not there. I checked with the police barn that houses tow-aways that have not been claimed. It's not there either. Of course, a stolen report would not have been made since he wouldn't have... couldn't have. Do you have any idea where it might be?"

"Did you check with Phyllis? Since she may have been the last person to see him alive, perhaps he said something to her about his car. Did they go to the beach in his car or hers?"

"No, I haven't talked to her yet, but I will. Thanks, and have a good day."

Jeanne was puzzled by the detective's report. But that was not her problem. On the other hand, Roger's car was now hers. However, she was sure she didn't want to be driving it.

Phyllis greeted her cheerfully when she arrived at her office to start her second day. "Will I see you for lunch?"

"Maybe. Call me when you're ready," Jeanne said as she walked to the stairs.

She immersed herself in research. By noon, she had finished as much as she could for one file. She decided to take it up to Jonathan. As she approached his door, Phyllis asked, "Is it time for lunch already?"

"Almost. I just finished with this file and thought I'd bring it up to Jonathan. Is he free?"

"I think so. There's no one in his office. Just knock."

After a soft tapping on the door, he called, "Come in."

Jeanne entered. "Good morning, Jonathan. I finished this file so I thought I'd bring it in so you could check and see if I need to do more, or something different."

"I'm sure it will be fine. Just leave it here," he said as he pointed to his in basket. He seemed busy so Jeanne turned to leave. She stopped and said, "Detective O'Neal called to say they can't find Roger's car."

"Well, I'm sure it will turn up somewhere. He'll keep us posted." And he turned back to the work on his desk.

Jeanne slipped out and closed the door. "He seems to be very busy today," she told Phyllis. "I'll be in my office until you're ready for lunch."

"It will be just a few minutes."

Jeanne enjoyed the solitude of her office. She planned to bring in a plant or two, and shop for some decent artwork for the walls.

Phyllis stuck her head in the door ready to go to lunch. As before, they took the elevator down to the cafeteria floor. Today the special was Szechuan chicken with rice, Jeanne's favorite. She asked the server if there was MSG in the dish. There was not so she ordered that with a small green salad.

"Why did you ask about MSG?" Phyllis asked.

"I have an allergy to it. Several years ago MSG was used a lot, particularly in oriental food. I nearly died one time after an oriental meal. I could never again enjoy a Chinese or Japanese meal. Not even Thai. Now the restaurants rarely, if ever, use MSG, but I always ask."

"That must have been terrible. Do you have other allergies?"

"None that are that serious. I have a little reaction to red wine, so I just stick with white. My favorite are California white wines, like Pinot Grigio, Chardonnay or Sauvignon Blanc. I like the taste of red wines but even a sip makes my throat feel numb."

"That must keep you from going wine tasting."

"I guess it would be pointless," she said with a soft laugh.

They remained quiet, Phyllis digesting the information she had just learned, and Jeanne feeling good about her new friend.

The end of the day came quickly. As Jeanne was leaving, she passed by Jonathan's door and he called out to her. "Jeanne, I just wanted to let you know I will be out of the office for a day or two, in court. I hope it will not extend into more than couple of days, but we never know. In any case, as we agreed, I will help you Saturday. But we'll talk before then."

"Okay. Thanks."

"So... what are you doing Saturday that you need Jonathan's help?" Phyllis asked.

Jeanne was surprised that Phyllis was listening to her conversation with Jonathan. "He's going to help me clear out Roger's apartment."

"I could have helped you. All you have to do is ask."

"I didn't ask Jonathan. He offered."

"I see. If anything changes, or he can't make it, I'd be glad to help. Here is my home phone number," she said as she handed a small note to Jeanne. "Call if you need me."

"Thank you. I appreciate it." She took the note and left.

The rest of the week proceeded uneventfully, except on Friday, Phyllis received a call from Detective O'Neal. She was asked about Roger's car.

"No, I don't know anything about his car."

"Did you drive to the beach in your car or his?"

She quickly said, "We took my car, because I have a convertible and we thought it would be perfect for such a beautiful day."

The detective agreed that it would make sense to take her car. "Did Roger say anything about his car. Was it being serviced, was it in his garage, parked on the street? Anything?"

"No, nothing. We didn't talk about his car. We had more important things to talk about."

"Yes, I'm sure you did. Well, if anything comes to mind, give me a call."

"Will do," and she disconnected the line. She sat for a few minutes wondering what she should do.

CHAPTER 14

Jeanne woke up early Saturday ready for a day of physical work. She had collected a few boxes to put Roger's things in, even though she had no idea how much there would be. Just as she finished breakfast, Jonathan called. "You're up early," she said as she answered the phone with an energetic voice. "Are you ready to put in a day of labor?"

"Good morning, and yes, I'm dressed in my work clothes—jeans and a tee shirt. When shall I come, or shall I meet you there... wherever *there* is?"

"Since parking probably is limited at his apartment, you'd better come here, and we'll take my car. There's more room in it than in yours."

"Good plan. I'll see you in about a half hour."

As soon as the call was disconnected, Jeanne called the manager of Roger's apartment to tell him she would be removing his things. That was when the manager said, "You know, it is a furnished apartment, so it's only his personal items you will take."

"Oh, I didn't realize that. I'll be there around ten this morning."

"I'll be waiting."

She dressed in her jeans, a printed tee shirt, and sneakers. She tied her hair back in a ponytail and applied very little makeup. As soon as she added lipstick, the bell rang. "You do look like you're ready to work," she observed as she opened the door and glanced at Jonathan's attire. "But so am I," and she swung her arm indicating her jeans. "I just found out that Roger was living in a furnished apartment, so we won't have much to remove. It will make for a much shorter day."

"That sounds good. Then we might have time to do something else."

"What do you have in mind?"

"I haven't decided yet. It may depend on how tired we are when we are finished."

"Okay, then. Let's go to work."

They drove out into a lovely fall day. A cool breeze stirred the leaves falling from the trees. White clouds floated in the azure sky creating moving shadows. It was a short ride to Roger's apartment. Fortunately, there was a parking space not far from the front entrance. Jeanne easily slide her car into it.

"I'll check with the manager to get a key and let him know we are ready to remove Roger's belongings."

Jeanne rang the bell on Unit No. 1. In a moment, the door opened to a middle-aged man dressed in a leisure suit which looked almost as old as he. "Yes, what can I do for you?"

"I'm Jeanne Blomgren-Anders. I called you about taking the personal things from Roger Anders' apartment. This is my attorney, Jonathan Crown."

"Oh, yes. Let me get a key and I'll take you up. It's just on the second floor." He was back in a few seconds and led the way to the elevator. "We could walk up, but I don't do well with stairs, which are right over there."

Once in the elevator, Jeanne took a deep breath and slowly let it out. She was apprehensive about going into Roger's apartment. Even though they had been married for more than twenty-five years, recently they had been on their own.

The manager led the way down the hall to No. 203. "Here we are," he said and slipped the key into the lock. The door swung open and he handed the key to Jeanne. "Just let me know when you are finished, and you can return the key."

"I know you said the apartment came furnished. Does that include dishes, kitchen ware, linens and...?"

"It does not include linens. Those are his, as are the house plants and personal hygienic items. If you want me to walk through with you, I can."

"I'd appreciate it. Since I'm not sure what he may have brought with him, I want to be sure we take anything that was his, but nothing of yours."

Jeanne held her breath as she stepped into the small room that had been Roger's. The air was stale since it had been closed for some time.

"I think Mr. Anders had a cleaning service that came in every couple of weeks, but after I found out he had died, I told them not to come. It's a bit stuffy in here. You can open the windows or just turn on the air conditioner."

"Yes. We need to get some fresh air in here," Jonathan said as he opened a window.

They walked through the small apartment pointing out what stayed and what was Roger's. Not much was his.

"If you have any questions, you know where to find me. Feel free to take your time."

"Thank you. We'll be fine," Jeanne said. She closed the door with a big sigh. "Where shall we begin?"

"Let's start in the kitchen," Jonathan decided.

There were not many items to set out, just some towels and a few spices. A look in the refrigerator found it nearly empty. The few things that were there and in the freezer had been there several weeks or longer. They were thrown into the garbage can, all except a couple of cokes.

"We can enjoy these later,' Jeanne said. "This won't fill even one box. This task may be easier than I thought." She turned on the dishwasher which held several dishes, pots and utensils. "At least we can leave clean dishes for the next tenant. Let's do the living room next, then finish with the bedroom and bathroom."

Jonathan noticed a door in the hall and opened it. It held linens—sheets, towels, a blanket and a pillow. He took them out to put in a box. As he separated the towels, a stack of money fell out. There were several hundred dollar bills, some fifties and a few twenties. "Jeanne, come look at this!"

Her mouth fell open as she saw the money fluttering down to the floor. "Where did that come from? How much is there?" she asked with astonishment.

"I don't know, but it was placed in this stack of towels. Why would he hide it here?" He quickly counted it. "There's at least a couple thousand dollars or more. Here's a little bit to add to your piggy bank."

"I think I'll save it until the twins come home and share it with them." She tucked it into her purse. "I wonder if we'll find any other surprises. We'd better look through everything carefully."

The next room to tackle was the bedroom. They stripped the bed, looking under the mattress and putting everything into one large box to go to the laundry. Jeanne opened the closet door to see it only half filled with his clothes. A couple of pairs of shoes sat on the floor. There was nothing on the top shelf except one small box. She lifted it down, only to discover it was empty. *Why would he save this box?* she wondered. It was a lovely box from a very exclusive jewelry store in the city. *I wonder what it contained?* She took the box, picked up the picture of the twins that was sitting on the chest and commented that Roger really did love his children.

"It seems he down-sized quite a bit after leaving home," Jeanne observed. "He must have been living a very Spartan life since he left. This meager selection is a surprise." She placed everything in boxes to go to the cleaners before giving it away. She emptied all the drawers, of which there was very little. However, at the bottom of one drawer she lifted a file folder with several sheets of paper in it. It was a copy of their divorce papers, unsigned. The second file under it contained letters. She looked at the first one and saw that it was from a person named Phyllis.

"Jonathan, you have to see this!" She handed the file to Jonathan and watched his face as he read some of the letters. "What do you think of these? Are they from your secretary?"

"They certainly seem to be. They sound as if she was having, or least was wanting to have an affair with Roger." He continued reading them and then exclaimed, "She talks about me! She says she was in love with me. She may have been using Roger hoping to make me jealous. I had no idea."

"She sounds like a mentally unbalanced person."

"Yes, she does. And her last letter is dated the day before Roger died. I wonder if there is a connection?"

"I think we should give these letters to Detective O'Neal, don't you?"

"Absolutely! Don't say anything to anyone about finding them." He gave the file folder back to Jeanne.

Everything was put in the elevator and Jeanne closed the apartment door, closing the chapter in her life that had included Roger. She returned the door key to the manager and gave him her name and phone number.

On the way back to Jeanne's apartment, they stopped at the cleaners and dropped off his clothes and left the boxes of linens at the laundry. The rest Jeanne left in her garage to take care of later. It had taken them only a little more than a couple of hours, so they still had the rest of the day to do something. Jeanne didn't want Jonathan to leave so she invited him to come in for lunch. She made ham and Swiss cheese sandwiches on rye, with a brownie for dessert. She put out a selection of teas and poured hot water into two cups. Jonathan selected green tea.

"I understand this is supposed to be very healthy," he said as he placed it in his cup.

While sipping their tea, Jonathan had a suggestion. "Let's drive out to the beach this afternoon. We're dressed in casual clothes so we're ready to go."

"A great idea. We can check on our houses. I haven't been back since Roger's accident. You've been very busy and I know I've been under a bit of stress, with the new job and dealing with Roger's affairs. So... let's go."

"Let's take my car. Alexander kept it out front for me." After a brief pause he continued with a big smile, "I think he likes me."

"And why wouldn't Alexander like you? You are a very likeable person."

"Why, thank you. But wait until you get to know me better."

They were quiet as Jonathan drove out into the city streets. He turned on the classical music station. "I'm glad we both like the same type of music. That way we won't argue about what station to turn on."

"Yes, we are compatible in that area."

"I hope we find that is not the only area in which we are compatible," Jonathan said with a glance at Jeanne, who just smiled.

"Do you go to your house at the beach often?" Jeanne asked.

"No, I don't go there much since Elizabeth died."

"I'm glad you were there the weekend of Roger's accident, otherwise I may never have met you."

"I believe God has a plan for each of us. I'd like to believe that in His plan, we were to meet. It just happened that day at the beach. If it was not that day, it may have been when you started to work in our law firm."

"What if I had decided not to start working after all that happened?"

"I think you would have because you had made a commitment and because you wanted to keep busy. Then you would have been assigned to me." He smiled and looked at her as he said, "It's just that we met a little sooner."

"Maybe you're right. Whenever we would have, I'm glad we did. Yes... it's all in God's plan," Jeanne said thoughtfully.

When they arrived at the beach, Jonathan parked in his driveway. They entered his house and Jeanne was surprised at how spacious it was. Obviously, it had been designed and furnished with Jonathan's wife in mind. It definitely was not a bachelor's pad.

"Would you like to see the rest of the house?" he asked noticing her interest in his space.

"Yes, if you don't mind."

Jonathan gave her the tour downstairs. Jeanne was impressed with the artwork in each room.

"Did you or your wife select the paintings and sculptures you have?"

"Elizabeth was the artistic one, but she always asked for my opinion."

"I'm particularly fond of sculptures, and you have some lovely pieces."

"We secured some of them on our trips to Europe. In fact, the one on my desk is the one we purchased on our last trip there. It was Elizabeth's gift to me on our anniversary."

"It's a beautiful bronze, very sensual. It calls for one to touch it. I can understand why you keep it on your desk."

Jonathan looked at it with sadness in his eyes, undoubtedly thinking of his late wife. He took in a deep breath and asked, "Would you like to see the rest of the house?"

"Of course, but only if you want me to see it."

They went up the curved stairway to a space overlooking the living area. From there hallways led them to three bedrooms, each with its own bath. The master bedroom was very inviting with soft blue dominating the space. There was a huge walk-in closet and an elegant bath with a shower and a round tub large enough for two. The whole house was very luxurious for a beach house.

Jeanne's favorite place was the balcony off the master bedroom. "Did Elizabeth spend time on the balcony? It seems like a great place to relax and enjoy the ocean view."

"Yes, sometimes she was there. Most of the time she was on the lower floor, just to be near me, she said. And I liked having her nearby."

Jeanne could tell that Jonathan had a very special relationship with his wife. She wished hers had been that close with Roger. It was in the beginning of their marriage, but it didn't last. The change was so gradual that she wasn't aware of when or why they drifted apart.

As they descended the stairway, Jonathan put his arm around her shoulders and said, "Thanks for letting me share this part of my life with you. You're the only person who has seen this part of my house."

"Thank you. I feel honored that you let me see it with you. It is a lovely space and I can see why you like to spend time here."

"Now, I think we should check out your house. Just to be sure everything is okay."

"Good idea. It has been a few weeks since I was there."

They walked out and turned to go to Jeanne's house when she glanced toward the outcropping of rocks at the end of the sandy strip. Someone was standing up at the top of it.

"Oh, I hope that person knows how dangerous that can be," she said with concern. A picture of Roger lying in the rocks flashed through her mind. "I don't think I will ever want to go up there again."

"That's understandable. Perhaps we should go warn that person, or at least find out who it is and if he belongs here."

They walked across the sand, watching the person who seemed to be looking for something among the rocks. As the figure turned they could tell it was a woman. She was holding a wide-brimmed straw hat.

"Hello, there. Is everything okay?" Jonathan called.

The woman looked up, startled at seeing someone. She nearly lost her balance on the rocks. The wind blew her hair from across her face.

"Phyllis! What are you doing here?" Jonathan asked in surprise.

"I was looking for something I may have dropped the day Roger brought me here."

"The police went over this area very thoroughly. If there was something here, I'm sure they would have found it."

"Can we help you?" Jeanne asked after recovering from her shock of seeing Phyllis.

"No. I think it's lost forever. I need to get going," she said as she carefully climbed down from the rock pile. "I didn't expect to see you here. Quite a coincidence."

"Both Jeanne and I have houses here, so we came out to check on them."

"Oh, I didn't realize that," Phyllis said, feigning ignorance.

"Neither one of us had been back since her husband's death, so we thought we'd take advantage of a beautiful day at the beach and check our property," Jonathan explained, not that he needed to. However, Phyllis's explanation for being there was questionable.

Phyllis walked up past the beach house to the street, leaving Jonathan and Jeanne looking after her with questions.

"I wonder what that was all about," Jeanne said. "And I wonder what she was looking for? If it was something she dropped the day they were here, why look for it now and not a few weeks ago?"

"It is strange that she'd be here the same day we drove out. Coincidence? The fact that she said she was looking for something she may have dropped makes me think that she knows more about Roger's death than she has said. What do you think?"

"I think you may be right. Perhaps we should tell Detective O'Neal about this."

"Meanwhile, let's finish our task and go check on your house."

"To be fair, perhaps I should show you through my home. Would you like a tour?"

"Absolutely, only to be fair," he said, grinning at her.

Jeanne walked him through the rooms, watering the wilting plants along the way. "Now, let's go upstairs, and you can see my favorite room."

They climbed the split-level staircase and walked straight into a room of all glass from floor to ceiling and wall to wall. It was almost like being outdoors. Some of the glass walls slid open to let the cool ocean breeze in, and one could walk out onto the balcony that stretched the entire length of the house.

"I can see why this is your favorite room. It has a spectacular view of the ocean and the entire beach area. It is a unique design. It must be the only one with a view like this. I thought I had a great view, but this outdoes mine."

After spending several minutes enjoying the view where a sailboat was skimming through the blue-green waves, Jeanne led him through the bedrooms and baths. There were original oil paintings and a special color scheme making each room unique. The aqua-colored master bedroom was welcoming and comfortable with teal-colored overstuffed chairs facing the windows. She enjoyed her home and was glad she could share it with Jonathan. No one had been there since Roger left.

"Everything seems to be in order, so perhaps we should head back to the city," Jonathan said reluctantly.

"What would you think if we stayed here a bit longer? We could run down to the market, get something for a barbecue and a salad and have dinner here. Could we?"

Without giving it much thought, he agreed. "I think that is a great idea. Let's do it."

They drove to the market, picked out a couple of steaks, items for a salad, a small baguette, and a couple of bottles of good wine.

"The day I was dreading with its unpleasant tasks is turning out to be very enjoyable," Jeanne said as they drove back to the beach house with their purchases.

"Since I have an almost new barbecue at my house, shall we go there?" Jonathan asked.

"Since you are going to do the cooking, I think that's a good idea. While you tend to the steaks, I will prepare the salad."

It didn't take long for dinner to be ready. Jeanne found crystal wine glasses, and Jonathan poured red wine for himself and white wine for her.

After finishing their meal, they took their refilled wine glasses with them out to the enclosed patio and sat to watch the ocean waves. As the sun disappeared in the darkening water and an array of colors filled the sky, they knew it was time to leave.

CHAPTER 15

Monday morning, Jonathan had to be in court, and so Jeanne had time to reflect on the weekend with him. She didn't want their personal relationship infringing on their time at the office. Their personal and professional lives must be kept separate.

As soon as she walked into the office, Phyllis approached her with an exceptionally friendly attitude. "Sooo... did you and Jonathan have a good time at the beach this weekend?" she asked with a sly smile. "I was surprised to see you there—together."

"We did not spend the weekend at the beach. Jonathan helped me clear out Roger's apartment and when we finished we decided to check on our houses at the beach. We hadn't been there for a few weeks."

"I must say that Jonathan is being a bit more attentive to you than he usually is to a client, or even an employee."

"I'm sure he is just being helpful as I get back into the working world after having lost a husband. I appreciate a sympathetic attorney and an understanding boss."

"Yes, he is that. He has been very good to me, too."

"Well... I must get back to my solitude of research. Later..." And she left Phyllis looking after her with a jealous glare.

Phyllis had a hard time concentrating on her work. She had to figure out a way to make Jonathan forget about Jeanne, or at least not trust her. In time she would find a way. Meanwhile, it was best to pretend to be her friend.

Jeanne began to feel a little bit smothered by Phyllis's attention. She finally told her that sometimes she would like to have lunch with other staff members or just be alone. Then Phyllis invited Judy to join them for lunch. It was a step in the right direction, but Jeanne would have enjoyed time alone with Judy.

"Jeanne and Jonathan went to the beach last weekend," she told Judy with a hint of mystery in her voice.

"Really?" she responded.

"We didn't just go to the beach. We both have houses there and so we went to check on them. He had helped me in the morning to clear out my late husband's apartment. He is my attorney, as you probably know."

"Yes, Phyllis told me, and that he is particularly attentive to you, more than with most employees."

"Perhaps because of how we met and also that I'm a new employee, it may seem that way. We have a completely professional relationship," she said while looking at Phyllis. "So tell me more about yourself, Judy. Are you married?"

"No."

"How long have you been working in this firm?"

"I started before Phyllis was hired, so I guess I'm the most senior secretary on staff, not that it gives me any privileges," she said smiling.

"You seem to enjoy working here. You must have a good boss."

"Yes, all of the attorneys here are wonderful."

"Now it's time to get back to work. I enjoyed having lunch with you, Judy. Perhaps we can do it again."

"Absolutely." She didn't say anything to Phyllis. They went their separate ways.

Phyllis decided that since Jonathan was going to be out for the rest of the day, it would give her time to check his office. There was no one to observe her. Besides, as his secretary she had a right to be in his office. However, he had told she should be there only when he was in.

She entered his office with trepidation and closed the door most of the way. She first looked at the pile of papers on his desk. In it was a letter from one of their largest clients. She quickly read it and realized it was something that no one else should see. She put it back in the pile where she had first seen it hoping Jonathan would never know she had read it.

Next, she went to the files in his desk drawer. There was one with her name on it. She pulled it out and saw that it contained his evaluation on her. She couldn't help but read it. It was a favorable report, but the last line made her catch her breath. It read *I must be careful of any information given her. I cannot fully trust her.* The file was returned to its place in the drawer. Other files contained papers on their active clients, all of whom she was aware. She pulled the one on the large client whose letter was on Jonathan's desk. *Perhaps I can use this to persuade Jonathan that Jeanne is the one he cannot trust.* She took the file, looked out the door, saw no one near and went to her desk. She hid it in a drawer, way in the back so no one could see it. Of course, when Jonathan noticed it missing and asked about it, she would know nothing. She was sure her plan would put her in good stead with Jonathan when she found the file, and discredit Jeanne. Now all she had to do was wait.

Phyllis met Judy in the staff room having a cup of coffee and joined her with a coke. "So, Judy, what do you think of Jeanne?"

"She seems very nice."

"I'm still puzzled by Jonathan's behavior around her. He's known her for less than a month, and he is with her a lot. More than he is with any other employee."

"Phyllis, don't stress over it. He can do what he wants. Maybe he likes her company. And they do have something in common.

"What's that?"

"They both lost a spouse recently and they're probably a little lonely. That would draw them together. You need to let it go."

"I guess you're right," she said with a sigh. She continued sipping her coke in silence while pondering her next step.

When Jeanne left the library and went to her office, she noticed Phyllis was not at her desk. She looked in Jonathan's door to see if he might be there.

Just as she turned back, Phyllis came up behind her and said, "What are you doing in his office? No one is to go in when he is not there."

"Oh, I didn't go in. Since you weren't here, I just looked to see if he was there, and when I didn't see him, I turned around."

"Why should I believe you? With no one here to see you, you could have been in there for a while, looking at who knows what. You two seem quite friendly so maybe you feel free to go into his office anytime. Is that it?"

"I did not go into his office. I would not go in without his permission."

"Well, that's what you tell me now."

Jeanne had never seen Phyllis so angry. Either Phyllis was being over-protective or she was feeling guilty about something.

Phyllis cleared off her desk and prepared to leave for the day. "Are you leaving now?" she asked Jeanne.

"In a few minutes. I just want to put my work away and read the e-mails I may have received while hidden away in the library. I'll see you tomorrow."

Jeanne went to her office and sat at her desk. She stared at the bare wall for a few minutes thinking about Phyllis's unusual behavior. It was as if Phyllis accused her of doing something unethical. Obviously, something was bothering her. She seemed to exude a sense of guilt.

"Hey, there," Jonathan said startling Jeanne out of her chair. "What are you so deep in thought about?"

"I was just pondering an unusual behavior Phyllis exhibited a few minutes ago."

"Why? What did she do?"

"She seemed very angry that I had looked in your office to see if you were there. I didn't go in; I just stood at the doorway. She yelled at me asking what was I doing, that I was never to go in your office."

"That is out of character for her. I've never seen her get angry." Jonathan was quiet for a few seconds and then said, "Perhaps she is jealous of you. Remember the letters we found? She did see us at the beach and possibly jumped to some conclusion."

"You may be right. I've tried to be a friend to her."

"Don't worry about it. It may be a one-time thing. Maybe tomorrow she will be sweet and friendly again. Would you like me to speak to her about it?"

She responded quickly, "No, no. I don't want her to think I tattled on her. That would make it worse."

"You're right. Now... are you ready to leave?"

"Yes. I was just going to put these files away and check my e-mails. Give me five minutes and I'll walk out with you."

They walked together to the elevator without saying a word. Everyone else had gone. "I think I'll be finished with our court case sometime tomorrow," Jonathan said. "If so, we should give the letters we found to Detective O'Neal. Do you want to go with me?"

"Of course. I'm curious as to what he will say."

"She was my secretary..."

"And he was my husband."

"So we both are in this together," Jonathan concluded.

"It would seem so."

CHAPTER 16

Jeanne was asked by Mr. Carruthers to do some research, and so she spent several hours in the legal library. It was beginning to feel like her permanent office. However, she did escape every day to go to lunch with Judy, Phyllis or just to have a little quiet time alone.

One day she had lunch with Phyllis and was asked, "How long were you and Roger married?"

"A little over twenty-five years."

"You seem like an easy-going person, so I was wondering why Roger wanted a divorce.

"Phyllis, that is a very personal matter. I'd rather not talk about it."

"I understand. I was just curious since I had only recently met Roger. At first, he seemed very personable, fun and attentive."

"What do you mean, at first?"

"Oh, nothing... I dated him only a few times so I didn't get to know him very well. However, he became a little controlling wanting to know where I was going and with whom, like he was checking up on me. Was he like that with you?"

"As I said, I don't want to talk about it."

"Okay. Sorry I asked."

Jeanne was surprised at the personal nature of her questions. When she returned to her office, Jonathan's door was open. She knocked lightly. He looked up and motioned for her to come in.

"I finished the work for Mr. Carruthers, and so I wondered what I should do next."

"Since it is Friday, let's not start a new project. In fact, I think I can get away a little early. Let's see if Detective O'Neal is available and can look at those letters we found?"

"Yes, I was wondering when we could get them to him."

Jonathan made the call to the station. "Detective, Jeanne and I have something to show you that I think you will find interesting. Could we come by this afternoon?" After a few seconds, he said, "That will be fine. We'll see you then."

"He said he will be available any time after four o'clock."

"Since we have a little while to wait there is something you can help me with. You can look for a file I seem to have misplaced. It's for one of our major clients. The letter that was to go in it is on my desk, but I can't locate the file."

"I'll do my best."

Jonathan pointed her to the file drawer where it should have been.

Just as she opened the drawer to begin her search, Phyllis appeared at the door. "What are you doing?"

"Jonathan asked me to look for a file he may have misplaced."

"Yes, Phyllis. Jeanne has a little free time. You haven't been able to locate it, so we can use some assistance. It's an important file for an active case."

Phyllis just glared at him. "Are you sure you can trust her? She is new to the firm and a lot of our files are filled with highly crucial and personal information."

"I know. She has been cleared to have access to all of my files, so don't worry about it."

Phyllis grudgingly returned to her tidy desk with an angry glance at Jeanne.

"I don't want to cause Phyllis to be upset at you."

"You're not. I'm the boss, not Phyllis. She needs to remember her position."

"Perhaps she feels threatened by me. I'm not trying to take her job, which I couldn't if I wanted to. I'm not qualified to be a personal secretary."

"I think you're qualified to do just about anything you put your mind to. For now, how about finding that file?"

"Yes sir, boss." Jeanne smiled as she settled into a chair and began looking for the client's lost file. Thinking the file had probably accidentally slipped into another or between some she checked each one carefully. In the process she was getting acquainted with names of their clients.

As four o'clock approached, Jonathan said it was nearly time to leave. "Make note of where you are so you can begin where you left off. I must have that file next week."

"If it's here, I will find it," Jeanne said with confidence.

"I'm sure you will. Let's go," he said as he picked up his briefcase holding Phyllis's letters.

"I'll just grab my stuff and meet you at the elevator."

Jonathan told Phyllis he had an appointment out of the office, and would see her Monday morning.

"I don't have anything in my appointment book for you. Are you meeting a client?"

"Yes, no... not exactly. It is for a client. Never mind. See you Monday."

Phyllis was annoyed by his lack of information. She noticed Jeanne left her office and did not return. She casually walked toward Judy's desk just in time to see both Jeanne and Jonathan enter the elevator. *Just as I thought they are going out together.*

"Judy, did you notice Jeanne and Jonathan leaving together? I wonder if they are dating."

"Of course not. She is an employee. They have a right to be together. Don't start rumors where there are none."

"If you say so, but I'm not so sure they are just that." She returned to her desk where for the rest of the day she pondered the Jonathan-Jeanne relationship.

While Jonathan drove, Jeanne glanced at some of the letters again. She was surprised at how many Phyllis had written in the brief time they had known each other. She appeared a bit desperate, particularly in her last letter. She wondered what Detective O'Neal would think.

As before, they were ushered directly into the detective's office. "Good to see you," he said. "I'm curious about what you have found."

"Letters from my secretary, Phyllis, to Roger." Jonathan handed the file to the detective and waited until he had read some of them.

"Where did you find these?"

"They were in the bottom of a drawer in Roger's apartment. We found them when we were clearing out his things. I find it strange that he even kept them."

"As I recall, Phyllis had known him for a little more than a month. She must have been immediately infatuated with him, and maybe a little desperate," the detective observed.

"That's our impression, too. The last one written the day before he died seems a little different. Read it and tell us what you think."

The detective took his time, rereading parts of it. With a frown creasing his forehead he finally looked up at Jonathan and Jeanne. "I don't know what to make of this. I'd like to have our staff psychologist look at these. Would you mind?"

"Not at all. I think she sounds unstable. She's worked for me for nearly a year and I haven't seen this side of her. I have noticed that she seems jealous of Jeanne."

"After Dr. Meredith, the psychologist, reads them he may want to talk with Phyllis. I'll let you know. There may be more to Phyllis's relationship with Roger than is apparent." The detective stood up and said, "I'll be in touch as soon as I get a report back from Dr. Meredith. Thanks for bringing these to my attention."

"You're welcome. We'll be eager to hear from you." Jonathan led Jeanne out to his red Mustang. Jonathan took his place behind the steering wheel but didn't start the engine. He put both arms on the wheel, leaned over and stared out of the windshield. They sat in silence for a few seconds. Finally, Jonathan turned and looked at Jeanne.

"I can hardly believe that my secretary had such an intense affair with Roger. She never mentioned it to me, or anyone else in the office that I know of."

"She did mention him to Judy. I don't know when. Maybe before I started working here. You'd have to ask her what she knew."

"I'll wait before talking to her. Meanwhile, we can do nothing until we hear from Detective O'Neal and the psychologist."

Silence ensued as Jonathan started the engine and slowly pulled out of the parking lot. In a few minutes, he asked, "Would you like to stop someplace for a glass of wine?"

"I'd love to. We need to talk."

He made a couple of turns and pulled up in front of an exclusive club. "Have you ever been here?"

"No. What is it?"

"I hold a membership in this club but rarely have time to enjoy it. I thought it would be a nice quiet place where we will have privacy."

As Jonathan turned the engine off, a parking attendant appeared and asked to see Jonathan's membership card. He produced it and was immediately warmly greeted "It's been a while since we have seen you, Mr. Crown. Welcome."

"I've been unusually busy, but I'm glad to know I've been missed," he said as he exited the car. They entered The Club through large intricately carved double wood doors. There was no name to indicate what it was, only that it was private. Jeanne knew it was a very exclusive club and was thrilled to be able to enter it. The receptionist greeted them and ushered them into the club's private quarters.

They were escorted to a table in the corner of the room and sat in smooth leather chairs.

Jeanne was properly impressed with the elegance of the facility. It spoke of old world wealth and charm. "Obviously Roger didn't run in the same circles as you. He would have been out of place here," Jeanne observed.

The hostess approached their table greeting Jonathan. "It's been some time, Mr. Crown. I'm glad to see you back, and with such a lovely guest," smiling at Jeanne.

"Thank you, Debra. This is my assistant, Ms. Blomgren."

"I'm glad you could join Mr. Crown. He doesn't get here often enough. Now, what would you like?"

"We'd like a glass of wine. The burgundy we keep on hand, and Jeanne would like a glass of the California Central Coast's Pinot Grigio."

"Yes, sir. Right away," and she disappeared.

"You keep your own wine in the wine cellar here?"

"Yes, that way I know it always will be available."

The glasses were placed in front of them, the hostess filled them and immediately left. They were the only ones in the room so they could talk freely.

"What did you want to talk about? Anything in particular?" Jonathan asked.

Jeanne hesitated before saying. "I'm concerned about Phyllis. Not just about her letters, but about our relationship in the office—hers and mine. Sometimes she is very friendly, trying to be my friend, and other times she seems angry with me."

"I've noticed that, too. I do think she is a little jealous of you working for me. She was the only one for quite a while."

"She seems very protective of you. I've told her we have a professional relationship; you are my attorney and my boss. That's it."

"That's true, but I think of you as my friend, also."

Jeanne looked at him. "Yes, I think of you as my friend, too. I think we have been careful about keeping that aspect of our relationship out of the office."

"And I expect to keep it that way," Jonathan agreed.

"Judy tells me that Phyllis is the office's gossip queen. I think she has tried to raise questions about us. For instance, she saw us leaving the office together at the end of the day and jumped to an erroneous conclusion. And then there was that day when she saw us at the beach. I don't want our friendship to interfere with your position at the firm. So, I guess what I'm suggesting, is that we be careful about being together at the office."

"I understand. But since you work for me, we have to be together sometimes. We just won't leave at the same time. Does that sound okay?"

"That should work. I don't want to cause any problems for you or Phyllis."

"I appreciate that."

"Now that this is cleared up, let's not talk about Phyllis. Tell me, what do you hear from the twins?"

"They are doing well, beginning to make friends and seem to be keeping their grades up."

"What are they majoring in or is it too soon for them to decide?"

"Mark wants to study architecture or possibly web design. Probably both. Mandy is interested in health sciences. She doesn't want to be a nurse or a doctor, but would like to work in research discovering new cures. Both have high ambitions, but I'm sure they will succeed in achieving their dreams. They are very bright and have the necessary determination."

"You must be very proud of them."

"Yes, I am. They were both valedictorian for their high school graduation. The school gave it to them as if the twins were one person."

"Did they receive scholarships for their university programs?"

"Yes, they each were granted very generous scholarships in their respective fields of study. At the time, we didn't know their father had money set aside for them. I feel now that we should give at least some of it back for students more in need. Of course, if they each follow their current course of study we know there will be more than four years at the university. Mark will need at least three additional years before he will be a bonafide architect. I don't know how much will be required in the research science field for Mandy. It could be ongoing. But we will not ask for a renewal of the scholarship after this first year."

"That's very generous of you," Jonathan said as he drained the last of his wine.

"I've talked long enough. Now it's your turn."

The hostess appeared with wine to refill their glasses. "Will you be staying for dinner?"

He looked at Jeanne. "If you don't have plans, would you like to have dinner here?"

"I have made no plans, so yes, it would be nice to stay for dinner."

The hostess returned with menus. Jeanne was impressed with what it offered. She ordered the baby spinach salad with bacon crumbles, the pecan encrusted veal cutlets, and herb seasoned rice with grilled vegetables. Jonathan ordered the same salad and vegetables, but chose the prime rib with garlic mashed potatoes.

After placing their orders, Jeanne said, "This is wonderful. I never expected to have such a wonderful evening. It's almost like going on a date."

"Let's make it a date. I haven't been on one in a long time."

"Neither have I."

"Let's hope this isn't our last," Jonathan said looking deep into Jeanne's eyes.

"I would like that," she responded with a shy smile.

Their meals were served and they ate in silence for a while, then Jeanne said, "As I said, it's now your turn to talk. Tell me about Elizabeth. How long were you married? What was she like?"

After taking a little time to think about what he wanted to tell her, he said, "We were married for more than twenty-five years. She was a beautiful person, inside and out. We had a lot of fun together. She enjoyed traveling so we went to Europe nearly every summer. She was artistic and carried a sketchbook with her. Her sketches became the basis of some of her paintings. She spoke several languages. She was fluent in French and Italian, had a smattering of German, enough to get by as a tourist. She was an excellent cook. She could prepare a gourmet meal as easily as I could grill a steak." He stopped talking long enough to take a bite of his roast beef.

"She sounds like a wonderful person. Very interesting and a great companion. You were fortunate to have her in your life as long as you did."

"Yes, I was. I still miss her every day." He remained pensive while continuing to eat his dinner. "I have never told anyone that much about her. What is it about you that encourages me to share so much personal information?"

"Thank you. I feel honored that you trust me enough to share it. I hope you always are comfortable with me... and I with you." Jeanne laid her fork down and looked up at Jonathan. "Thank you for bringing me here. This was a wonderful dinner. And I like the privacy we had."

"We'll have to do it again. It will become our place," he said with a warm smile as he reached across the table and placed his hand over hers. Her heart skipped a beat and she could feel a rush of heat to her face. She was glad when the hostess appeared.

"Would you like dessert?" she asked.

They looked at each other, and Jeanne asked, "What do you have that's chocolate?"

"We have a home-made brownie with vanilla ice cream topped with hot fudge."

"It sounds perfect. I'll have that," she said with enthusiasm.

"How about you, Mr. Crown?"

"I'll have a cup of coffee and a bite of hers," he said grinning at her.

"I'd like coffee, too," Jeanne added.

Jeanne glanced at her watch and was surprised to find that they had been there for over two hours. Conversation and good food made the time slip by quickly. She experienced a sense of freedom that she had not had in a long time. She smiled to herself.

"What are you thinking about?"

"Oh, nothing special."

"Whatever it was, it made you smile."

"I was just thinking about how good it felt to be so free, to not have to answer to anyone. I've really enjoyed this evening."

"I'm glad if I have contributed to making you smile. I, too, have enjoyed it."

The decadent dessert appeared with two spoons. Coffee was poured for each of them.

"Would you like cream or sugar?" the hostess asked.

"No, thank you," they said at the same time.

"That's something else we have in common," Jeanne said. "Did you know there are two Swedish clans? One that drinks their coffee black, and the other who uses cream and sugar. Each one thinks the other is wrong. As you can guess, I am a purist; I drink it black. And besides, I like coffee so why cover the flavor with cream or sugar?"

"I agree. There is nothing better than a good, unadulterated cup of coffee."

They took their first bite of the rich chocolate dessert and immediately went into a state of ecstasy. Nothing needed to be said.

After the dessert trappings had been removed and a second cup of coffee consumed, they reluctantly left the club. The short drive to her apartment was in silence. They had shared at lot and there was nothing more they needed to say. Jonathan dropped her at her front entrance.

CHAPTER 17

Jeanne rose full of energy. She made coffee and took a cup to sit where she could look out over the park. The trees scattered among the evergreens were just beginning to change colors. The phone rang interrupting her quiet time. It was Jonathan. She said a cherry, "Good morning."

"Good morning. I just wanted to tell you I really enjoyed yesterday with you."

"I did, too."

"I was wondering if you wanted any help with the boxes you left in the garage?"

"Oh, I'd forgotten them. No, I'll take care of them later today."

"Okay, but call me if you need help... or just to talk." The call was disconnected before she could respond.

Jeanne reclined in the chair, smiling as she sipped her coffee. She was startled to hear the bell announcing someone at her door. She looked out the peep hole to see the apartment's building manager standing there with a frown on his face.

"Good morning," she said cheerfully as she opened the door.

"And good morning to you, too."

"What can I do for you this lovely day?"

"I was wondering about the boxes in the garage. I believe they are yours."

"Yes. I left them last night since it was late when I got home. I was just on my way down to retrieve them."

"Good. We don't like anything left sitting out in the garage."

"Of course. You wouldn't happen to have a trolley I could use, would you? It would keep me from making several trips."

"Yes, I do have one. It's in the garage. I'll go with you and get it."

"Thank you. I'd appreciate it." She paused. "I just cleaned out my late husband's apartment. This seems to be all that's left of his life," she said as the elevator door opened and she pointed to the boxes stacked by her car.

"I'm sorry to hear that. Here, let me do that," he said as he began to stack the boxes on the trolley.

With surprise Jeanne responded, "I could do that, but I really appreciate your help."

"Glad to be of service. Anytime you need assistance, just let me know. Here we are," he said as he wheeled the trolley into the elevator. "Wait. Why don't I help you get them unloaded, too. I'm not busy at the moment." She let him take the boxes and set them just inside her door.

"Thank you so much. I'm sorry I left them in the garage last night."

"No problem. Now they are all yours." He closed the door behind him.

She was not eager to unpack them. First, she was going to sit down and finish reading the morning paper. She opened the unread section of the paper. As she turned to the first page, she was shocked to see a picture of Roger and the headline "BODY FOUND AT BEACH." *Who would have written this article?* It was a few weeks ago that she had seen Roger's body lying in the rocks. *Why was it not in the paper then?*

The article was brief giving very little information on his life or the cause of his death. It did state that he had owned a house on the beach where he was found. Her name as his widow and the twins were mentioned as being his survivors, his only known relatives. She had just finished reading the article when the phone rang.

"Hello?" she answered without checking to see who it was.

"Good morning. I just saw the article in the paper and wondered if you had seen it yet," Jonathan stated.

"Yes, I was just reading it."

"I was surprised to see it appear now. Why not right after he was found at the beach?"

"That was my question, too. Perhaps the police released the story now hoping that someone reading it might come forward with additional information. What do you think?"

"I think you should call Detective O'Neal and see if they did indeed place the story. If so, I'm surprised he didn't tell you."

"Good idea. I'll check with him right now."

She hesitated not wanting to seem critical of the detective. If he was the one who gave the information to the newspaper he undoubtedly had his reasons, which she would like to know. She dialed Detective O'Neal.

"Good morning. This is Jeanne Blomgren. Is Detective O'Neal available?"

"No, he's not in today. Can someone else help you?"

"If you hear from him, could you please have him call me?"

"I will give him the message, but I doubt if he'll check in before Monday morning."

"Thank you." She hung up the phone disappointed she would have to wait another day to get answers. She called Jonathan to report that she would learn nothing until Monday. Just as her hand released the phone, it rang, startling her.

"Jeanne, this is Detective O'Neal. You probably saw the article in the paper this morning. I'm sorry I neglected to advise you of its publication. I didn't know it was coming out today."

"I was wondering about that, and left you a message. What's going on?"

"As you know, I'm not completely satisfied with the details on the death of Mr. Anders. I think somebody knows something we don't. Since there hasn't been any new information, I thought perhaps someone seeing an article with some of the information might stir up feelings of guilt and maybe they would slip up with a casual comment. It's worth a try."

"I agree. The article gave very little information other than it looked like an accident. That would make the guilty party feel relaxed."

"That's what I'm counting on," the detective said. "I want you to be aware as you have conversations with anyone when, or if they talk about the article. A simple word or two could be significant."

Jeanne was quiet for a few seconds as she registered his meaning. Her thoughts drifted to Phyllis. "Yes... yes. I understand," she assured the detective. She remembered the comment one neighbor at the beach made to Jonathan about seeing a woman with a wide-brimmed hat leaving the beach the same day as Roger was found dead. And then the day she and Jonathan were there seeing Phyllis with a wide-brimmed hat looking for something near the rocks. *Could that have been the same person?*

As Jeanne unpacked the boxes she realized how little there was to show that Roger had existed. She wondered if her life would be the same at the end. *We put so much emphasis on what we do today with little thought to the legacy we leave.* She vowed to do more with her life.

CHAPTER 18

Monday morning, Jeanne turned on her computer and saw an e-mail she couldn't identify. She hesitated opening it. The subject line said *new information*. She decided to wait and check with Phyllis or Jonathan to see if they recognized it.

"Good morning," Phyllis said cheerfully as she popped her head in Jeanne's office door.

"Good morning, Phyllis. There's a message on my computer from someone I don't recognize and I hesitate to open it. Could you see if you recognize it?"

"Sure. Let's take a look." After a few seconds she said, "No, it's not one I know."

"I think I'll just leave it unopened for a while. If I don't respond, they may try again."

"Good idea. See you later," and she was gone.

It was time to continue searching for the missing file in Jonathan's office. As Jeanne passed Phyllis's desk, she asked her if they could have lunch today.

"Of course," she said enthusiastically. "I'll meet you in the cafeteria."

"No. I was thinking perhaps we could go out to the deli you mentioned. I haven't been there yet."

"Okay. Come by here when you're ready."

Jonathan appeared and Jeanne said, "Well, good morning. Now that you are here, I should continue looking for the missing file. Is this a good time?"

"Sure. Come on in."

Jeanne glanced at Phyllis as she entered Jonathan's office, and noticed her deep frown. Obviously, she was not happy about her being in Jonathan's office. Jeanne opened the file drawer and searched carefully, starting where she had left off. Finally she said, "I have finished searching through all these files and have not found the missing one. Are there any other places it could be?"

"Check with Phyllis. I think she has a file someplace for old, closed cases."

"Thanks." She went to Phyllis and asked her, "Where are the closed-case files?"

"Why do you want to know?"

"Jonathan suggested I look in them in case the missing file was put there by mistake."

"I'm sure it would not be there. I am the only one who does the filing."

"I need to check, just in case."

"Whatever, but it's a waste of time. Here are the closed cases, in these two drawers. Just be sure you don't mess them up."

"I'll be very careful," Jeanne said as she pulled open the first drawer. She searched carefully and found nothing out of place. When it was approaching lunch time, Jeanne closed the file drawers and turned to leave. "Whenever you are ready to go to lunch let me know," she told Phyllis as she passed by her desk.

"I'm ready now, so let's go."

As they walked to the deli, Phyllis asked, "How do you feel about your job, now that you have a few weeks behind you?"

"So far I like working here. Everyone is friendly, the cafeteria has great food, and I have a beautiful office."

"Yes, you do have a nice office. Better than... Here we are." Phyllis pushed open the frosted glass door to the deli. They were seated at a small table. "Their sandwiches are to die for. You can have your choice of bread with the filling stacked so high you can hardly get your mouth around it."

"Great! Since I'm hungry I think I'll have one."

After they placed their orders, Phyllis asked, "Why did you want to have lunch with me today? For the past few days it seems like you have been avoiding me."

"Not really. I've just been busy, and a little preoccupied. But there is something I'd like to ask you."

She looked surprised and said, "Sure, what is it?"

"Are you and Jonathan an item?"

"What! No. No, of course not. Why do you ask?"

"I just wondered because you seem to have a rather personal demeanor with him, more than just being his secretary."

"Well, I do like him... a lot... but we've never dated. He's never encouraged a relationship."

"I think office romances never work. One needs to maintain a professional relationship in the office."

Their sandwiches were served and conversation ceased. After enjoying several bites, Jeanne continued, "I was curious about the time we saw you at the beach. What were you looking for? You said you lost something. Did you ever find it?"

"Yes. It was just a small, jeweled comb for my hair that was a special gift from a friend and I hated to lose it. I thought I was wearing it the day we drove out to the beach. I found it later on the floor of my car."

Jeanne gave a knowing smile and said, "Was this friend a boyfriend?"

"Why do you ask that?"

"So... are you going to tell me who he is?"

Phyllis opened her mouth to say something, then closed it again. After finishing another bite of her sandwich, she said, "I'd rather not discuss my personal life with you... or anyone in the office. Sorry, but I don't feel comfortable with sharing personal information."

"No problem. I understand. Sorry I asked. Well, I'm glad you found it. Was it a gift from Roger?"

"Why do you ask that?"

"You were wearing it the day you went with him, and so I thought it might have been a gift from him. Has he given you other gifts?" Jeanne asked as if she was interested.

"No. Why would you think he'd give me gifts?"

"No reason." She remembered the empty jeweler's box on the top shelf in Roger's closet. "I'm aware that you hadn't known him very long, but he is, or was a romantic person."

"Yes, he was that. He was always a gentleman, very attentive. Sometimes, too much so. But I did enjoy the attention—for a while."

Continuing the conversation, Jeanne asked, "What changed?"

"I was beginning to feel smothered. I think I have been independent for too long. Don't get me wrong, we did enjoy each other's company, but he became too attentive. Was he like that with you?"

"I can't say that he was. In fact, he had grown distant in the last few months of our marriage. He seemed to be preoccupied most of the time. Then when he left, I never heard a word from him."

They both signaled the server for boxes to take the remainder of their sandwiches with them. After asking for a refill for her coffee, Jeanne continued," Phyllis, you mentioned that you had driven out to the beach with Roger in your convertible. Was that the only time you had gone there?"

"Yes. I didn't know he had a place at the beach until that day when he took me to see it. He had not told me anything about you, except that he had filed for a divorce, but at the time, I didn't know from whom. Since he wanted me to see the beach house, I assumed it belonged to him."

Jeanne had hoped Phyllis would talk more about Roger, and based on the content of her letters to him, one would think she'd want to. *She was eager to share her thoughts with Judy about Jonathan and me; why not about me and Roger? Maybe I should talk to Judy.*

A voice called to them, "Hello, ladies. I see you know the best place for lunch." It was Detective O'Neal and Officer Brandt.

"Well, hello," Jeanne responded. "Yes, it is a great place if you're hungry. It was too much for us, as you can see by our takeout boxes," which she held up as they continued walking.

"Good day, ladies. Until next time," Detective O'Neal said with a wave of one hand, the other holding half a sandwich.

While walking back to the office, Phyllis said, "I don't know why, but whenever I see a policeman, my blood pressure rises and my heart beats faster. Those two are very pleasant, not at all threatening, so why do I get nervous?"

"Maybe you are feeling guilty about something? Maybe an experience in your childhood? Do you have an outstanding parking ticket?" Jeanne asked in a joking manner.

"Not that I know of."

"Don't worry about it. As long as you're not guilty of anything, you're okay. I think of them as my friends, or even my guardian angels."

"That's a good way to think about them. I'll try that." However, she knew that she would always be uneasy around them.

"Did you ever tell Roger that you were feeling smothered?"

"Not in so many words. I did tell him I needed some alone time."

"Now you have all the freedom you want," Jeanne said.

"Yes, and it feels good."

They returned to their respective desks and Phyllis asked Jonathan, "Have you or Jeanne found the missing file?"

"Not yet." He went to Jeanne's office and knocked on her door as he entered.

"Oh, please come in," she said, "and close the door. I have another e-mail that I don't recognize. It has a different address from the last one, but this one says *something you should know*. Here, take a look."

"I don't recognize the address. Is it different from the other one?"

"Yes, it is. What do I need to know?"

"I don't have a clue," Jonathan said. "I wonder how many more messages you might get."

"Shall I just wait and see?"

"What else can you do? Maybe you should forward them to Detective O'Neal and see what he thinks."

"Good idea. I'll do that immediately. Do you have his e-mail address?"

"I think it's on his card. I'll go get it," and he dashed out of her office.

As he rapidly walked past Phyllis's desk, she called after him, "May I be of help?"

"Not right now," and he went right back to Jeanne's office and closed the door.

"Here it is. There was another reason I came to your office. I wanted to ask if you learned anything worthwhile over lunch with Phyllis. Did she say anything that might indicate what kind of relationship she had with Roger?"

"Yes, she did share a little. Apparently, Roger was smothering her with attention, and she wanted more freedom, which she told him. And that thing she was looking for the day we saw her at the beach was a jeweled hair comb that was a gift from a friend, and it was special to her. She later found it on the floor of her car, so she says. What do you make of that?"

"It's very interesting. Do you believe her?"

"Not completely. When I asked if Roger was *the friend,* she didn't say yes, but I had the impression he was."

"I think you should write down everything you and she said at lunch while it's still fresh in your mind and give it to Detective O'Neal. Her comments may prove helpful eventually."

Jeanne sent the e-mail messages to Detective O'Neal explaining how they had just appeared on her computer, but that she had not read them. She spent the next few minutes typing her notes on her conversation with Phyllis, and then forwarded them to the detective with a copy to Jonathan's personal e-mail. She received an answer back from the detective almost immediately.

Jeanne, thank you for forwarding the messages to me. I, too, am puzzled by what they mean and there was no explanation in the body of the message. I will have our staff find out who sent them. They have a way of searching, but I don't know how they do it. As to your report on your talk with Phyllis, thank you. I do think she is not telling us everything. Just continue to keep your ears open. I'll let you know when we know more. You do the same. - O'Neal

Jeanne was surprised that Detective O'Neal didn't learn anything from the forwarded e-mails. At least he would pursue finding who sent them. Meanwhile, she still had not found the missing file. It had completely disappeared. She had looked everywhere. She was beginning to think she was incompetent. The only place she hadn't looked was in Phyllis's desk.

"Phyllis, would you mind if I looked in your desk to see if somehow the missing file may have slipped into it? I know you have a lot of paperwork, so it's possible."

"Oh... No. I'm sure it's not here."

"It's nearly time to leave, so perhaps we could do it together tomorrow."

"Okay, first thing tomorrow morning would be fine. Just let me grab my stuff. I'll meet you at the elevator." As soon as Jeanne left, Phyllis quickly took the file from her desk drawer and placed it in the back of one of the file drawers Jeanne had already searched. Then she joined her at the elevator.

Jeanne said, "I was wondering if you'd like to go shopping with me this weekend. Since I haven't been in a professional job for a few years, my wardrobe is limited. You can help me select appropriate business attire. Would you like that?"

"Of course. I always enjoy spending other people's money," Phyllis said with a smile. "Besides, I could use a couple of new outfits, too."

CHAPTER 19

Jonathan was concerned about the messages Jeanne was receiving. He wondered if they related to Roger's death. The e-mail messages started after the notice of his accident appeared in the paper. The person who sent them said there was additional information. He could only wonder if someone knew something but didn't want to be identified.

The detective was still waiting for a response from the psychologist about the letters Phyllis had written to Roger. *Was there a connection?* Jonathan would call him tomorrow. He felt there was more going on than was obvious. *What role did Phyllis play in it? Was there anyone else involved? If so, who... and why?* Now with all these questions running through his mind, he couldn't get to sleep. When he finally drifted off, disturbing dreams entered his subconscious.

Early the next morning, Jeanne received a phone call from Detective O'Neal. "Sorry to call so early. I hope I didn't awaken you."

"No. I was awake, but since I haven't had my first cup of coffee I may not be coherent. So what's up?"

"I had a thought about Phyllis. After you told me about seeing her at the beach a few weeks after Mr. Anders' death, and then you showed me her letters, and her response to our questions about his car... I think we need to pursue questioning her further. What do you think?"

"Well," Jeanne said thoughtfully, "that is not for me to say, but I, too, have a feeling about her not being totally forthright in her answers and the information she shared."

"We can't make accusations just on feelings. We need to dig further. If you have any suggestions, please feel free to tell me."

"There is one secretary in our office that Phyllis seems to be friendly with. It's possible she may have told her about Roger being her friend. I can ask Judy about it. What do you think?"

"If you can talk to her, it wouldn't hurt. Any bit of information could help us."

She pondered the questions relating to Phyllis and how she could approach Judy to glean a little more information about Phyllis's relationship with Roger. She sat down with the morning paper. As a result of the article last week, there was a small report that the police had received several calls about the body found at the beach. They followed up on all the leads, but so far none proved credible. This information could provide the opening Jeanne needed for a conversation with Judy about Phyllis.

The brief walk to the office always gave her time to get her thoughts together. Just as she reached the end of the block, someone called her name. She turned but saw no one she recognized and so continued walking. She heard her name being called again, this time closer. She stopped and waited to see if someone approached her. A young man who looked a bit familiar, but whom she didn't know, came up beside her.

"I hope I didn't frighten you."

"You did just a little. Who are you?"

"I'm Danny. I deliver mail to your office."

"I'm sorry I didn't recognize you. What can I do for you?" Jeanne asked as they continued walking to their building.

"It's probably none of my business, but I read about your husband being found at the beach a few weeks ago, and then the brief note in this morning's paper about no credible phone calls to the police. It got me to thinking." He paused.

"Yes, thinking about what?"

"Well, you know... when I deliver mail to the various offices, I often overhear parts of conversations. Now, don't get me wrong. I never stop to listen, but sometimes I hear a few of their words."

"What have you heard that you want to tell me about?"

"I heard Phyllis talking on the phone about finding a place to park her car. Now why would she need another place? She has a garage at home, and of course, her space here when she is at the office. I just wondered if she was getting another car. I hesitated to ask because I didn't want her to think I listened to her conversations."

"I understand. Thank you for telling me. I will check it out but not mention you."

Jeanne now had more information to digest. "Good morning, Phyllis," she said as she passed by her desk. "Could you have Jonathan see me as soon as he comes in?"

"Certainly. Anything I should know?"

"Not really. I just have a couple of questions for him."

While waiting to hear from Jonathan, she perused the files on her desk deciding which one to tackle first.

"Where are you off to?" he asked with a grin as he entered her door.

"Oh, you know. Back to the dungeon."

"It's not that bad is it?"

"Not really. It's just that I feel a little isolated."

"So... what did you want to see me about?"

"Come in and close the door."

Jonathan did as she asked. "What is it?"

"I had a very interesting conversation on my way to work this morning with Danny, who delivers our office mail. He approached me and introduced himself. I was embarrassed that I didn't recognize him. He told me that after seeing the newspaper articles, he recalled a conversation he had overheard of Phyllis on the phone asking about a place to keep her car." She continued to tell him all that Danny had said.

"I think this information is important," Jonathan said. "Have you told anyone about this?"

"No, I wanted to tell you first, but I do think Detective O'Neal should know."

CHAPTER 20

Jonathan called Detective O'Neal, leaned back in his ergonomically correct chair and waited for him to answer.

"Good morning, Jonathan. How are you this beautiful day?"

"Very well, thank you. I gained some interesting information I think you might like to have. I learned of it just this morning."

"What is it?"

"One of our employees overheard a bit of conversation that has us intrigued." Jonathan told him of the conversation Danny had heard Phyllis having with someone. "Do you think it might be worth pursuing?"

"Definitely. Could you have Phyllis come in... or should I ask her?"

"It might be best if you ask her. I don't want her to think we listen to her conversations. You needn't indicate how you learned of it. However, would you want to talk with Danny to hear his comments first hand? I'm sure he would be willing to come in."

"You're right. I should talk with him first." He was quiet for a few seconds and then asked, "Could you bring him in around ten o'clock?"

"Let me check and I'll get back to you." He hung up and called, "Phyllis, could you tell me if I have any appointments this morning?"

She checked her schedule and said, "You have nothing on my calendar until this afternoon. Did you want me to arrange something for you?"

"No. I will be out of the office a little before ten for an hour or so. I have an appointment downtown."

She was curious, but she had learned that Jonathan would tell her what she needed to know later. She wondered if it involved Jeanne again. She'd keep an eye out for her.

"By the way, Phyllis, when is the mail usually delivered to the office?"

"Not until nine o'clock or after," she said. "Did you want me to watch for something?"

"No. Nothing for now."

He walked out of his office toward the elevator, stopped at Judy's desk, and asked her what floor the mail room was on. Learning it was in the basement, he took the elevator down to a place he had not been before. The door opened to a cavernous space with several shelves and cubby holes aligned throughout. It was a busy place with young people sorting and distributing pieces of mail into their proper bins. Since he didn't know which one was Danny, he asked the supervisor, who offered to have Danny come meet him.

"Is there a problem?" the supervisor asked.

"Oh, no. I just need to get some information from him."

"Danny!" he called over the speaker system. "Come to the front, please."

In a few seconds a young man appeared with a look of concern on his face. "Yes, sir. What did you want?"

"This gentleman needs to ask you something."

"Yes, Mr. Crown, what is it?" he asked feeling intimidated by the most important partner.

"Can we speak in private?"

"Certainly, sir. Right over here." He led him to the small room.

As soon as Jonathan closed the door, he said, "Now, don't be concerned. You're not in trouble or anything. I just need to ask you about some information you shared with Jeanne Blomgren this morning. It's about the conversation you overheard by Phyllis, my secretary. It may be very important. Would you be willing to go to the police station with me this morning to tell the detective what you heard?"

"Yes, if you think I can be of help."

"Fine. Meet me by the front doors at nine forty-five this morning. I'll arrange with your supervisor for you to be away for an hour or so. You should not mention this to anyone."

"Yes, sir. You can count on me."

"Good. I'll see you in a little while," and he left the room, stopping by to tell the supervisor that Danny would be out with him for a little while this morning. He assured him that he was not in any trouble, but was helping him on a case. He returned to his office and placed a call to Detective O'Neal. He told him he and Danny would be there at ten o'clock.

He left his office telling Phyllis he would be back in a couple of hours, and walked with long strides to the elevator. Phyllis surreptitiously checked to see if Jeanne joined him. She didn't.

When he met Danny they drove directly to the police station. "Detective O'Neal is expecting you so go right in," the officer said while unlocking the door.

Danny felt a little anxious since this was the first time he had been in a police station. When they arrived at the last door on the left, Jonathan knocked.

"Come in, Jonathan." The Detective greeted them with a smile and a handshake. "Good to see you. So this must be Danny. I'm glad you could come in. I'm eager to hear what you have to say."

Danny felt more relaxed with the friendly attitude of the detective. "As I told Mr. Crown, I just want to be helpful if I can."

"I'm sure anything you can tell us will help in our investigation. Jonathan told me you overheard a conversation by Phyllis that puzzled you. Tell me everything you can remember."

"As you may know, I deliver mail to the various offices in the firm's building. Occasionally, I overhear comments as I pass the desks, but I never stop to listen."

"That's a good rule. So why was this day's conversation different?"

"I know Phyllis drives a convertible. I asked her about it once and she commented that it's always parked in her garage so she doesn't have to put the top up at night. So when I overheard her asking about renting a garage for her car, I thought it curious since she already has a garage, as well as the space at the office. I didn't listen to more of her conversation, but she did say that the location would not be a problem."

"That's very interesting," the detective said with a slight frown. "Perhaps she was having someone visit her and there was not parking space at her residence." He pondered the information as he stroked his graying mustache.

Jonathan commented, "That's a possibility, but she has not mentioned anything to me about having a visitor. Normally she would."

"Danny, do you remember what day it was that you heard Phyllis talking?"

"I'm not sure, but I think it was sometime a couple of weeks ago. I do remember it was on a Friday because she mentioned that she would see the garage the next morning, which she would not be able to do if it was a workday. Unless she had asked for the morning off. Mr. Crown would know that."

"She did not ask for any time off in the last couple of weeks, nor was she out of the office at any time that I recall," Jonathan said.

"Well, it seems that it might be wise for me to have another chat with Miss Phyllis. Thanks for coming in, Danny. We appreciate the information." He stood up indicating the conversation was over.

As they walked out of the police station, Danny said, "That wasn't so bad. I just hope it helps with the case he's working on."

"I'm sure it will. One never knows when some small bit of information will make a big difference."

CHAPTER 21

The next day was uneventful for Jeanne. However, Phyllis was not so fortunate. Detective O'Neal called asking her to come to the station to answer a few more questions.

"Jonathan, Detective O'Neal wants me to come see him as soon as it's convenient. Can you go with me?"

"Yes, of course. You know my schedule so you tell me when."

"Could we do it around eleven?"

"That's fine."

She told the detective when she would be there. She wondered what else he needed to know since she had already told him everything. When it was time to go she stuck her head in Jonathan's office. "It's time..."

When Phyllis entered his car, she questioned, "Do you have any idea what the detective wants to ask me?"

"No. He doesn't share his work with me. It's probably just more details he is trying to clear up."

The short drive to the station was completed in silence. The officer at the front desk greeted them saying, "It will be just minute. Detective O'Neal is on the phone. Please have a seat until he is free."

"It's the waiting I don't like," Phyllis confided in Jonathan. "It gives me time to wonder..."

"Just always tell the truth and answer every question to the best of your ability."

When they went to the detective's office, Jonathan led the way. He knocked on the door. "Come on in," the detective responded. "Thank you, Phyllis, for coming in again. There's just something I need to clear up. I received some new information and so I have a few questions."

"I'll help in any way I can," she responded without hesitation. "What do you need?"

"I remember you said you and Mr. Anders had driven out to the beach the day of his death in your convertible. Is that correct?"

"Yes, sir."

"So we can assume he left his car in his garage. However, could he have left it parked at your place when he joined you in your car?"

Phyllis shifted in her seat, looked at her folded hands, and slowly said, "That's possible."

"Do you know what kind of car he drove?"

"We had only a couple of dates and we met downtown at a local bar, so I'm not sure what make of car he owned."

"I see." He waited for several seconds before asking, "Why were you looking for garage space to rent?"

She made a short gasp, looked surprised, and asked, "Why would you ask that? No one knows..." She stopped, not wanting to say more.

"You have a garage where you live and probably keep your convertible in it. Is that true?"

"Yes, that is the only garage I have."

"I have a witness who heard you asking about renting a garage for your car, that you would see the space the next day. Did you rent another garage?"

"I'd rather not answer that," she said glancing at Jonathan. "But, no, I do not need or have another garage."

"Is that your final answer?"

"Yes, sir."

"Thank you. That will be all for the time being. I will contact you again if I have more questions."

Phyllis rose unsteadily and exited with Jonathan. Nothing was said as they got in Jonathan's car. Finally, he asked, "Phyllis, were you telling the truth to Detective O'Neal? You can be honest with me. What you tell me remains confidential."

Phyllis waited a few seconds before answering. "I was talking on the phone one day about renting a garage, but it wasn't for me. I have a friend who needed a place for her car, and I was just helping her find one. That's all."

"Why didn't you just say so?"

"I don't know. His question caught me by surprise. I shouldn't have been doing that at the office. I'm sorry."

Jonathan quickly picked up on the fact that no one had mentioned she was overheard at the office, so why did she mention it? *Perhaps she is not telling the truth.*

Judy called Phyllis to see if she wanted to have lunch at the Deli. "It's been a while since we were there. How about it?"

"I'd love to." She was glad to go out since the morning visit to the police was unsettling.

As soon as they left the building, Judy asked, "So what's new?"

"Why would you ask?"

"I saw you leave with Mr. Crown this morning, so I was curious."

"Oh, it was just a business appointment and he needed a secretary with him." Then Phyllis asked, "Are you dating anyone interesting?"

"Well... there is this one guy who seems promising. He's an assistant manager, or something, in the local bank. We've only dated a few times. So how about you? Anyone new in your life?"

"No, not at the moment," Phyllis responded with a tone of sadness.

"What about the one you met in a bar several weeks ago?"

"That didn't last. We ended it a couple of weeks ago."

"Sorry." There was nothing more to say.

By the time Phyllis was ready to leave at the end of the day, everyone else had gone. She sat at her desk for a few minutes reflecting on the conversation she had at the police station. She wondered if Detective O'Neal believed her. Roger's car was at her place. It was a beautiful new silver Mercedes-Benz. What was she thinking, driving it home and parking it in plain view? She knew she'd have to find another place for it. But where? *Think, think* she said to herself as she rubbed her temples.

On the way home, she had an idea. *I could rent a garage or a storage space and park Roger's car there.* As soon as she got home, she looked up garages in her area to rent. There was one not far away. She called; it was no longer available. Next, she checked storage units, only to find that they were not large enough for a Mercedes. It really didn't matter where it was because she was not going to be visiting it very often, if at all.

Finally, one person had an available vacant garage. She drove to the address, which was only a couple of miles from her. It was in a nice area, and the garage was not visible from the street. Perfect. She punched the button by the front door and waited impatiently until the door opened a crack.

"Yes? May I help you?"

"I'm Phyllis. I called about renting your garage."

"Oh, yes. Just come around out back, and I'll show it to you."

Phyllis walked beside the house and waited for someone to come to the back door. When it opened, an elderly man came out leaning on his cane.

"Sorry to keep you waiting. I don't move so quickly these days. I've had to give up driving, and so I sold my car. Now, this space is empty," he said as he opened the garage door.

Phyllis was impressed with how clean it was, almost as if it had not been used. "This is perfect. I may need it for quite a while. Will that be a problem?"

"It's available as long as I still live here, and I have no immediate plans to move. Only if my son tells me I need to go to the old folks home. They call it a senior retirement facility, and I have no intention of doing that."

"I'll take it. I assume I can rent it by the month. How much would that be?"

"I really don't need the money. I would just give it to you, but I'm told I should ask something to make it legal. How about $30 a month?"

"That's very reasonable. I'll do it, and I'd like to pay for the first six months now," she said as she peeled out the bills. "Just one question. Can we keep the garage locked so no one else will have access to it?"

"Certainly. Here is the key to the lock. You can put anything in it you want and it will be safe. I'll just need your phone number in case I get sent away," he said with a grin.

She gave him the information he needed and walked to her car with a great sense of relief. Now she had to find a way to get the Mercedes in it.

CHAPTER 22

Saturday morning, Jeanne was eager to go shopping with Phyllis. She took inventory of her closet and realized how meager the selection was. She arrived at the Boutique at the appointed time and was greeted by a sales clerk.

"How may I help you?" she inquired.

"I'm waiting for a friend, but we want to look at professional attire. I recently started working in a law firm, and find my wardrobe somewhat limited."

"I'll be happy to assist you with that. Just tell me your preferences for..."

Phyllis rushed in and said, "Good morning. I see you beat me."

"Not by much. I told this sales person we want to look at office attire."

The sales clerk showed them to the appropriate area. "When you're ready to try something on, just let me know." She left them to search on their own.

They each chose a couple of suits, then blouses, and finally looked at dresses. Jeanne selected one suitable to wear at the office and one for evening—perfect for dinner with Jonathan. After spending nearly two hours in the Boutique, they paid for their purchases and left.

"That was fun. You make a good shopping partner," Jeanne said. "You have great taste for colors and styles. It's been such a long time since I had shopped for these kinds of clothes, I didn't realize how styles have changed. Or maybe it's I who has changed."

"What do you mean?"

"I have this new life. I'm single and working in a professional field. Before, I was married with a family—being a mother and a housewife." After a few moments of quiet reflection, she said with amazement, "I am different. But I like it."

Phyllis was quiet for a time. "I'm thinking of getting a new car pretty soon. What do you drive," she asked.

"I have a Toyota Camry. I like it. It's comfortable, economical, dependable. Roger, my ex, had a Mercedes, but even though it would be mine now, I wouldn't want to drive it. It's too big and is more costly to keep up. But at this point we don't know where it is."

"That's strange," Phyllis said and quickly continued, "I drive a convertible. Perfect for Southern California's climate."

"Yes, it would be. Why do you want to get a different one?"

"The convertible is getting older and needs a new top soon. It's been a good car, but after a certain age anything can go wrong." She paused, then continued, "However, after this shopping spree, it may be a while."

"Do you still want to go to the Deli? Unless you'd like to try a new place?"

"There is this little, out-of-the way place I've heard about. Are you game?"

"Sure. What kind of food do they serve?" Jeanne asked hesitantly.

"I really don't know since I've not been there, but I heard it was really good. It's just around the corner from here."

"Okay. This is a day of new experiences, so let's do it."

They grasped their parcels and trudged down the block where they saw several people standing in front of a small restaurant.

"Several people are waiting. That's a good sign," Jeanne observed.

"Let me check and see how long it is for seating." Phyllis went in and was told it would be about thirty minutes. "Do you want to wait or go someplace else?"

"Let's wait. I'm eager to try this place. I just read the menu posted by the door, and it sounds interesting."

"Fine. My car is not too far away and since we have thirty minutes, we could walk there and deposit our purchases in the trunk. I'll ask the receptionist to keep us on the reservation list."

They quickly walked the two blocks to her car.

"This really is a beautiful car," Jeanne said. "Why would you want to give up a convertible?"

"I may not. I'll think about it."

Back at the restaurant Phyllis checked to see where they were on the list. "We're up next. Good timing."

"Yes, timing is everything," Jeanne agreed. She pondered the reaction Phyllis had about cars. She sensed something was bothering her, but there was nothing concrete she could identify.

During lunch, Jeanne felt she was getting to know Phyllis a little better. When Jonathan's name came up, she noticed Phyllis's demeanor change. Her voice became softer, more pensive. *Perhaps she really is in love with Jonathan.* She knew Jonathan was not in love with her. Their's was strictly a professional relationship—the boss and his secretary.

"I really have enjoyed working for Jonathan. He is a great boss, and a wonderful person," Phyllis said. "I would like to become his secretary permanently."

"Why can't you?" Jeanne asked.

"The person he had before was promised she could have her job back when she returned from her leave. I'm not sure when that will be, but I have to be prepared for another change."

"I can understand why you'd like to remain as Jonathan's secretary," Jeanne said with sympathy. "I, too, enjoy working for him." They were quiet as they walked back to Phyllis's car. "Thank you, Phyllis, for spending this day shopping with me. I had a good time."

"I enjoyed it, too. We'll have to do it again sometime... after we save up for it," she said with a chuckle.

By the time she got home, Jeanne was tired. It had been a good day; however, she was concerned that she'd not learned anything about Roger's car. She was sure Phyllis knew more than she was saying. It was just a feeling she had.

At home, Phyllis thought about the Mercedes and the questions Jeanne brought up concerning its whereabouts. She knew she had to get it into the rented garage. She couldn't ask anyone to pick her up after she left it there, so she had to find a way to get back home. *Of course, why didn't I think of it before?* She changed into casual attire and left her house. She got in the Mercedes that was still parked on the street, and fortunately, it started with only a little coaxing. *Amazing that no one noticed it when the police posted a missing car report.*

She approached the house and drove to the garage behind it. She unlocked its door, which lifted easily. The Mercedes fit comfortably in the space. She quietly closed the doors, secured the lock on the door, and walked out to the street. She called an Uber driver to pick her up at the corner and waited, relieved to have the car out of sight.

While riding home, she thought about the problem she created by keeping the Mercedes. *What was she thinking? It would be great to own such a beautiful vehicle, but how can I make it legal? It was listed as missing or stolen, and as soon as I tried to register it or renew its license, it would be flagged, and I would be caught.* She decided to make no decisions immediately. Let it sit for a few weeks while she figured out what to do with it. She paid the Uber driver with a generous tip when she arrived home. Now she could relax.

CHAPTER 23

Monday morning, Phyllis was eager to get to the office. Today was the day she would find the file and blame Jeanne for misplacing it. If it went according to her plan, Jonathan would be grateful to her for locating it and at the same time discredit Jeanne for her incompetence.

"Good morning, Phyllis," Jeanne said cheerfully as she walked by her desk. "You're in early."

"Good morning. Yes, I needed to get an early start looking for the file you couldn't find."

"So you haven't found it yet either?"

"No, but if it's here, I know I will find it."

Jeanne went to her office and sorted through the messages on her computer. The one from Detective O'Neal she opened immediately. He needed to talk with her and asked if she would come to the police station sometime today.

Jonathan stuck his head in the door. "Good morning, Jeanne. I trust you had a relaxing weekend."

"Yes, I had a great time shopping with Phyllis. Do you like my new suit?" she said as she did a slow spin to show it to him.

"Absolutely beautiful, and so are you," he said with an approving smile.

"Why, thank you, sir." She hesitated, then said, "I have a request from Detective O'Neal to come see him, so I need to be out of the office sometime today. Will that be a problem?"

"Of course not. Just tell me when. It's important that you see him when requested."

"Thank you. I'll let you know when I get an appointment."

Phyllis had overheard their conversation and decided the best time to *find* the file was when Jeanne was out of the office.

Jeanne called the detective and told him she could be there whenever he said.

"How about eleven o'clock this morning?" he asked.

"I'll be there."

Jeanne went by Jonathan's office and told him when she was going to see Detective O'Neal.

Phyllis stopped her and said, "I heard you say you would be going out at eleven. Do you know when you will return?"

"I'm not sure. Maybe not until after lunch. Why?"

"No reason. I just like to know approximately when you will return in case someone asks for you. Just being a good secretary. By the way, you look great in your new suit."

"Thank you." Jeanne continued on her way to the library.

She arrived at the station promptly at eleven and was greeted warmly. She took a deep breath and said, "I'm here to see Detective O'Neal."

"Of course. Go right in. He's expecting you."

She knocked lightly on his door.

"Come in, Jeanne," the detective called.

She entered. "Good morning, sir."

He looked down at his hands folded on top of his desk. He was quiet for several seconds and finally said, "You probably are wondering why I wanted to talk to you. There's something I learned that I wanted to ask you about, or at least tell you about."

"What is it?" Jeanne asked with curiosity.

"Someone called the station to report some unusual activity in her block. It was regarding a car that had been parked near her house for several days. She hadn't paid any attention until one of her neighbors commented that she wondered why such an expensive car wasn't being used. She watched it for a few days. It was a silver Mercedes and no one was seen entering it nor was it moved. She was about to report it to the traffic division when one morning, a woman got in it, and even though it took a little coaxing, she got it started and drove away. It hasn't been back."

"Did she get a license number?" Jeanne asked.

"She didn't think to get it. She is an older lady who keeps to herself. She says she doesn't like to get involved."

"Did she recognize the woman who drove it away?"

"She says she never saw a face, she just knew it was a woman, but didn't know how old. She moved like a young person, not as old as she, which was seventy-eight."

"Why did she decide to call the police?"

"She just thought it was unusual, and since it was a very expensive car, perhaps it was being stolen. In case it was Roger's car, I wondered if you had heard anything."

"Not a word." She hesitated a bit then said, "However, last weekend during lunch with Phyllis, she mentioned that she was thinking about getting a new car. When I asked why when she had a beautiful convertible, she said it was getting older, needed a new top, and thought it would be a good idea to start shopping for one."

"That is interesting."

"I had a feeling that she was hiding the real reason she asked about a car. Do you think it's possible that it was she who drove the Mercedes away from its long-time parking space?"

"That crossed my mind. But if so, where would she take it? And why wasn't it seen when we put out the notice of it missing? Obviously, the traffic officers didn't do a thorough job since it was parked on the street the whole time." Detective O'Neal was quiet as he strummed his fingers on his desk. "It does make one wonder, doesn't it? Perhaps I should have another talk with her. In the meantime, keep your ears open for any comments she makes and see if you pick up on anything. Thanks for coming in. We'll stay in touch."

Since it was close to lunch time, Jeanne decided to go home before going back to the office. She pondered the detective's report about a Mercedes. *Was it Roger's? If so, why wasn't it seen days ago? And where is it now?*

"Jeanne, Jonathan wants to see you in his office immediately." Phyllis was very curt in her request as she confronted her in the doorway.

Jeanne was surprised by the way Phyllis spoke to her, but she went directly to Jonathan's office. She knocked on his door and waited until she heard him call, "Come in."

"You wanted to see me?" she asked.

"Yes. Please sit down." He looked more stern than she had ever seen him. He just sat quietly looking at her.

"Is there a problem?" Jeanne asked.

"You might say that. You know the file of an important client that you looked for and couldn't find?"

"Yes. Did you find it?"

"Not exactly. Phyllis found it in your desk. Perhaps you can tell me how it got there."

Jeanne's eyes and mouth opened with surprise. "No, sir. I did not put it in my desk. Is that it on your desk?"

"Yes." Jonathan slid it across the desk to Jeanne. She saw the name of the client.

"No, sir. I have never seen that file. It was not in the files when I searched them. It is very clearly marked and I would have seen it had it been there."

"Are you sure? You could have overlooked it."

"No, I was careful. Even if it had been misfiled I would have seen it. Obviously, someone removed it and then discovered it later. Someone wants to blame me for something I didn't do."

"At this point I only have your word against Phyllis's. The main thing is I have the file before my meeting with the client. This is the first time I've had this problem, and this is the first time you have worked in the office files. I just want to be sure this doesn't happen again."

"It won't. I'm sorry," Jeanne said as tears began forming in her eyes. She stood up and turned to leave the room.

"Jeanne, I'm sorry, but I have to be sure you can handle the work here. The files are extremely important to our clients' welfare."

"I understand. Perhaps I should not be handling any of the files, for you or the other partners."

"You may continue doing your work. Just be very careful with all the files." He turned back to the work on his desk, dismissing Jeanne.

As she left his office, Phyllis asked her, "Is everything all right?"

"It is now," she said with tears glistening in her eyes. She had never been reprimanded so firmly. "I'm just glad you found the client's file. Where did you find it?"

"It was in your office," she said with a smile. "I know how things can get misplaced accidently. Since you had been working on many different files, I thought I'd check to be sure it hadn't been mixed in. I hope you don't mind my going into your office."

"I'm just glad you found the file, but I wish you'd asked me earlier. I know it wasn't there. It makes me think someone is trying to discredit me by moving the file. However, I can't prove it. Have you seen anyone go into my office?"

Phyllis hesitated, bit her lower lip as if she was thinking. "Not that I'm aware... but then, I'm not always at my desk."

"No matter. It's all done and over with now." Jeanne slowly walked back to her office pondering how this could have happened. She knew someone had planted the file in her office, but who, how could she find out, and why?

Phyllis was feeling very proud of herself for pulling off the discrediting of Jeanne. Jonathan had no suspicion she had done it. Perhaps this would be the beginning of the end of whatever relationship there was between him and Jeanne. Now she had to think of a way to get rid of her entirely.

CHAPTER 24

Jeanne was conflicted about the appearance of the file. *How could it have been placed in my office? And why? Was someone trying to get me fired? If so, who? Phyllis would have been the one who had access to the file, but why would she want to get me in trouble? I thought she was my friend.* She gathered up her work and headed for the library, glad she would be alone for the rest of the morning.

Judy called to her as she passed her desk, "Jeanne, is everything okay?"

She hesitated, then answered, "Yes, it is now."

"You look upset. Did something happen?"

Jeanne wasn't sure how to answer that. She didn't want to blame Phyllis when she had no proof, but she didn't want anyone to think that she was incompetent and had lost, or misplaced an important file. Finally, she asked, "Can I trust you to keep this quiet?"

"Of course. What is it?"

Jeanne told her about Phyllis finding the file that Jeanne had spent hours looking for. "I know it was not in my office. Someone put it there while I was out this morning, but I don't know who. Phyllis is the one person who has access to the files, and my office. Jonathan was quite upset at me, but I think he believes me... that I had not misplaced it."

"That is upsetting. I'm surprised anyone, even Phyllis, would do that to you."

Jeanne continued to the library where she put it out of her mind and concentrated on her work. She was glad when the disconcerting day ended.

After arriving home, she sat down to a light supper. As soon as she took the last bite, the phone rang. It was Jonathan. Jeanne hesitated before answering, wondering if he was still upset with her. She picked it up and quietly said, "Hello, Jonathan."

After a long pause, he said, "I've called to apologize for the way I talked to you this morning. Phyllis was listening and I wanted to seem serious when I reprimanded you for being careless, which I know you weren't. My gut tells me that she had something to do with the file's disappearance, and then reappearing. Now I just need to find out why."

"Thank you for telling me. You played your role very well, leaving me quite upset."

"I'm so sorry."

"No, you did the right thing. I think Phyllis may be trying to get you to fire me, and I wouldn't blame her. She is very protective of you. I think she wants you to herself and she feels I'm getting in her way."

"That may be. However, she is hurting only herself. She is a very responsible secretary, but I cannot tolerate game-playing in the office. Until we can prove she placed the file in your office, I can't confront her. I just want you to understand that I trust you. Let's just play along with her game for a while."

"I understand. Thanks for telling me. Now I can put my mind at rest."

"Just be careful, now that we know Phyllis can be vindictive."

"I will... and I will continue trying to be her friend. What is it they say? Keep your friends close and your enemies closer... or something like that."

"That's a good idea."

Jeanne was glad Jonathan had called. He wasn't upset with her after all, but she understood why he disciplined her as he did in front of Phyllis.

When she entered the office the next morning, Phyllis greeted her by saying, "You look tired. Didn't you sleep well last night?"

"As a matter of fact, I had a restless night. A lot was on my mind."

"So, what was bothering you?"

"You were. I was pondering why you want to make me look inefficient."

"What do you mean?"

"You know. I'm sure you are the one who hid the client's file, and then later said you found it in my office. No one else could have had access to it. I just want to know why." She continued to look directly at Phyllis, waiting for an answer.

Phyllis looked uneasy as she bit on her lower lip thinking of a reply. She began speaking in incomplete sentences. "Why do you think... You know I wouldn't... I like you and I only want... I don't know what to say..." She looked down at her folded hands and after a brief pause she said, "I don't appreciate you blaming me for something I didn't do. You can't prove that I had anything to do with that file."

"That may be, but there's no one else who knew about the file." She turned and walked away leaving Phyllis looking after her with her dark green eyes ablaze in anger.

She stopped by Judy's desk on her way to the library. "Judy, would you like to have lunch today?"

"Yes, I'd like that. What time?"

"Let's go on the early side of noon."

By eleven thirty, Jeanne was finished with the current research. She walked by Judy's desk and said, "Meet me at the front doors in ten minutes."

She stuck her head in Jonathan's office. "I'm off to lunch," she said. and she hurried out ignoring Phyllis. She was eager to talk with Judy about Phyllis's behavior. She hated office dissension, but she really needed to talk to someone who knew Phyllis. Something was not right.

"I feel like I'm escaping from a... I don't know what, but I'm not comfortable around Phyllis," she said to Judy when she met her.

"I understand. She has not been honest with you. What does she have against you?"

"I have no idea," Jeanne said hesitantly. "But I do know she feels I'm coming between her and Jonathan. She seems very possessive of him."

They were quiet for a few minutes as they jostled the crowd on the sidewalk. Jeanne continued, "Her attitude changed when she learned that my ex was the man she had started dating, and was found dead at the beach where Jonathan and I have houses. Did she ever say anything to you about Roger?"

"Yes, several weeks ago she told me about this wonderful new man she had met at the wine bar whose name was Roger. When I asked her about seeing him one weekend, she said he'd gone out of town so she would not be going out with him. Usually, she likes to brag about her dates, but she never talked about him again after that. I found that a little curious."

When they were seated in the deli, Jeanne asked, "What has she said to you about Jonathan? I'm curious whether they have a relationship outside the office."

"I do believe she would like to be more than just his secretary. She requested the assignment when Marianne, his former secretary went on an extended leave. It's unusual to reassign a secretary to another partner when there was no problem with her current position. She was rather insistent, as I recall. Then she bragged to me that she had been requested by Jonathan to work for him, which was not true. One partner would never ask an employee to leave her boss to work for him. I don't know how she managed to get reassigned, but she is persistent in getting what she wants."

"So when she dated Roger, did she tell Jonathan about him?"

"Of course. She wanted to make Jonathan jealous hoping he would pay more attention to her, but we know that never works."

"Right. I'm interested, also, to know if Phyllis ever talked to you about the day she and Roger went to the beach."

"She did tell me they went there one weekend in her car. She didn't say much about it, other than he pointed out his house to her. He didn't take her there, however. She was disappointed not to see it. That's about all she said."

"One day recently when Jonathan and I went to the beach to check on our houses, we saw Phyllis in the area where Roger was found. As you may know, Jonathan and I have houses just a few doors from each other, but we had never met until the day I found Roger dead in the pile of rocks. Well, when we asked Phyllis what she was doing there she said she had lost a jeweled comb, which had been a present from a good friend, and she was searching the area where they had been. She thought perhaps she had lost it that day."

"That was strange. I'm sure the area was searched carefully by the police."

"Exactly." Jeanne continued, "I also wanted to ask you about Phyllis being overheard searching for a garage? She has one at her place as well as a parking space at work. Why would she want another garage?"

"I've heard nothing about that. It is strange…"

"She told Jonathan she was looking for a garage for her friend. What friend?"

"As far as I know, she doesn't have any friends. She never mentions them," Judy said thoughtfully. "That reminds me, was your ex's car ever located?"

"Not yet. That's another question. Personally, I think Phyllis has the answer to that. Don't tell anybody I said that. I shouldn't have said it."

"I won't, I promise," Judy said with sincerity.

They went out of the deli with the left-over sandwich boxes in their hands. They had walked less than half a block when a police car drove up and stopped abruptly beside them. Detective O'Neal jumped out of the car and called, "Jeanne, I'm glad I caught you. I just left a message for you at your office. I think I may have a lead on your ex's car."

"Really! That's great."

"Yeah. Could you stop by the station later today, and we'll talk about it?"

"Sure. I'll let you know when after I check in with Jonathan.

"Fine. Good day, ladies," and the car sped away.

"Well, that's interesting," Judy said. "I wonder what he's learned."

"Me, too. I guess I'll find out when I see him."

Back at the office, Jeanne stopped at Phyllis's desk and asked if she had any messages.

"No, no one called for you," she said, not looking at Jeanne.

"Oh, thanks. I was expecting a call. I guess I'll hear later." She walked on, wondering why Phyllis would tell her there was no message when the detective said he had left one at the office. Jonathan's door was closed and so she asked Phyllis if he was available.

"No. He's on the phone with a client. I don't know how long he will be."

"No problem. I'll catch him later." On her way to the library, she stopped by Judy's desk and asked, "Didn't Detective O'Neal say he left a message for me at the office?"

"Yes, he did."

"So why would Phyllis say there was none? What game is she trying to play?"

"Maybe Jonathan took the message?"

"That's possible. I'll ask him."

Shortly after she was in the library, she called Jonathan. "I want to ask a favor. I need to be out of the office for a little while this afternoon. Would that be all right with you?"

"Of course, if it's important. Just let me know when."

Jeanne called Detective O'Neal. "What time would you like me to come in?" she asked.

"You could come by any time after four o'clock? I'm eager to talk with you."

"I'll be there." She went back to her work, but an hour later she decided to quit and go back to her office. When she went by Jonathan's office, his door was partly open and she quietly knocked. Phyllis frowned at her as she went in and closed the door. "A couple of things I need to talk to you about. First, Detective O'Neal wants me to come in after four o'clock today. Will that be okay?"

"Of course. Did he say why?"

"Yes. He may have some information regarding Roger's car."

Jonathan frowned as he said, "I wonder what it could be?"

"I have no idea, but I will find out. The other thing I wanted to tell you is that I saw the detective on our way back from lunch. He told me he left a message at the office for me to call him. When I asked Phyllis about it, she said there was no message for me. Why would she do that? Or did you take a message?"

"No, I didn't talk to the detective. Let me ask Phyllis about it." He opened the door and called to Phyllis. "Did you take a message for Jeanne from Detective O'Neal this morning?"

"No, I did not. If I had I would have given it to her," she said abruptly.

"Thank you." He turned to Jeanne and said, "Confirm with Detective O'Neal what time and with whom he left the message. I'm not sure what is going on."

"I'll do that. It is unusual..."

She left Jonathan's office telling Phyllis that she would be leaving early.

"Oh? Do you have a date?"

"Nothing like that. Only some business to take care of." She kept walking.

CHAPTER 25

At the police station, Jeanne immediately went to Detective O'Neal's office. She put her head in the doorway. "Hi, I'm here."

"Oh, good. Come on in."

Jeanne sat down facing him. "I'm eager to hear your news. Do you know where Roger's car is?"

"Not yet, but I may have a lead on it." After a long pause, he continued, "I had a call from an elderly lady reporting suspicious activity on her street." He continued telling Jeanne what she had said about the car that had been parked near her house for several days, and then a young woman driving it away. "When I asked for her address, I was surprised to learn it was near Phyllis's house."

"Do you think it was Phyllis who took the car?"

"I can't be sure, but it sounds as if it could be. Have you learned anything new from her? Has Phyllis mentioned her friend or if she found a garage?"

"Unfortunately, no. Judy did say Phyllis has never mentioned a friend. She doubts if she has any."

"That wouldn't surprise me," he said and then quickly added, "I'm sorry. I should not have said that."

"I understand. I have thought the same thing. I'm finding her to be a difficult friend. She was really upset with me in the office and blamed me for something I didn't do. I got the feeling she was trying to discredit me with Jonathan."

After a thoughtful pause, he said, "If it was Phyllis who drove the car away from the parking space near her neighbor, where would she take it? She'd have to drive it occasionally to keep the battery charged. Of course, she may not know that."

"I doubt that she would think about it, but you never know. Do you think I should ask her about her friend? The one who needed a garage?"

"If you feel comfortable asking her, go ahead. Just keep a record of your conversation."

"Of course." She stood up to leave but turned back. "I might ask Judy join us since Phyllis may have mentioned her friend to her. What do you think?"

"Sure. You might feel more comfortable having a witness to your conversation."

"I'll let you know what happens." She turned to go out, and stopped to ask, "By the way, what time did you leave the message for me this morning?"

"It was around ten or so. I was told you were in the library and would call when you returned."

"With whom did you leave that message?"

"It was Phyllis. Why?"

"She told me there was no message."

She left the police station and did not go back to the office. She needed time to consider this new information. As soon as she got back to her apartment, she wrote down everything she could recall from her conversations with Judy and Phyllis. She felt there was a connection somehow to Roger's car.

The next morning, she opened her computer to check e-mails and saw one that caused her to stop. It was from a familiar address, but she wasn't sure if it was the same as an earlier one. The subject just said *Listen*. She forwarded it to Detective O'Neal.

Jonathan peered into Jeanne's office and said, "Good morning. Did you learn anything new from Detective O'Neal yesterday?"

"Yes. Come in and close the door. It seems that an elderly lady who lives near Phyllis observed a car being driven away by a young lady. It had been there for several days. She couldn't give him much information but thought perhaps someone was stealing it and maybe she should report it."

"Did he think it might have been Roger's car?"

"The lady didn't know the exact make, but her description was close to a Mercedes. I will talk with Phyllis today and ask about a garage."

"Good. Keep me posted."

Upon entering the staff break room, Jeanne saw Judy. She poured herself a cup of coffee and went to her table. In a few seconds, Phyllis came in and joined them. Jeanne was delighted to get them together.

"Phyllis, did you ever find a garage for your friend?"

Phyllis made a quick intake of breath and nearly choked on her coffee. "Yes. No... well, almost. I have a lead on one."

Judy asked, "Is your friend from out of town?"

"Yes, of course."

"How long will she, or is it a he, be here?" Judy continued teasing.

"I don't know. A few days, perhaps. And it's a she."

"When is she arriving?"

"Why are you asking so many questions?" She seemed nervous. I'd rather not talk about this. It's personal." Phyllis stood up to leave saying, "You both are too nosy."

After she was gone, Jeanne said, "She was uneasy about the subject of a garage, and she didn't want to tell us anything about her friend."

"I don't think she has a friend. I think something else is going on."

"I agree. But how can we find out?"

"Maybe casually ask later if her friend has arrived, or if she found a garage."

"Let's stay in touch and see what else we learn."

Once in her apartment, she relaxed with good music and wine which put anything to do with the office out of her mind. The phone's ringing startled her. It was Jonathan.

"Hi. I'm glad it's you," she said with a light tone.

"Hi, and I'm glad to hear your voice, too. Are you busy?"

"No. I'm just reading. However, I'd rather talk to you."

"So... what shall we talk about?"

"You're the one who called. Did you have something on your mind?"

"Not really. It's a quiet evening and I was thinking about you."

"And what were you thinking? All good, I hope."

"Of course. Have you heard from Detective O'Neal about the e-mails? I'm curious about who is sending them."

"I am, too. But, no, I've not heard from him. I'm hoping his on-line sleuths come up with something soon. Another unidentified e-mail came with only *listen* in the subject line. I forwarded it to Detective O'Neal."

"Jeanne, changing the subject, would you like to go to a concert this coming weekend?"

"Maybe. What concert is it?"

"So you are particular?"

"Well... kind of. For instance, I don't enjoy jazz enough to hear more than five minutes of it. And I don't like rock at all, neither progressive nor acid. Some of the oldies but goodies, such as the big bands, are okay, and the popular music of today is boring. It seems to be based on rhythm with no discernable melodies. As you may have concluded, I am a classical junkie."

"Then I think I am in luck. The Philharmonic is performing at the Music Center Saturday—an all-Beethoven concert. Would that appeal to you?"

"Absolutely! I'd love to attend that one."

"Then it's a date. Perhaps we could even have an early dinner at The Club before the concert. Would you like that?"

"That would be lovely." When the call was disconnected, Jeanne sat still for a few minutes thinking how fortunate she was to have met Jonathan. He turned out to be a great boss, a talented attorney, and best of all, a good friend. She was content with her life as it was evolving.

CHAPTER 26

Phyllis wanted to invite Jeanne to her home for dinner, but she debated on whether to invite Jonathan also. After giving it careful thought, she decided to invite Judy. *Perhaps if I were more friendly they would stop asking so many questions.* She chose next Friday as the evening for the dinner. She would prepare Jeanne's favorite meal—Szechuan chicken, for which she had found a simple recipe.

At the office, Phyllis asked Judy if she liked Szechuan food. "Yes, I do. I know it can be rather spicy, but it's one of my favorite oriental dishes."

"That's great. I'm planning to make it for dinner Friday and I'd like you to join me."

Judy was surprised by the invitation and was curious as to the reason she was invited, so she said, "Yes, I'd love to. May I bring something?"

"No, that won't be necessary. However, if you really want to bring something, how about some ice cream for dessert?"

"Sure. That would go well after a spicy dinner."

"I've invited Jeanne to come also. I'm making her favorite dinner."

"Oh. So it's girl's night?"

"Yes, I guess it is."

Phyllis returned to her desk feeling good about her plan. When Jeanne walked by, she stopped her and said, "Judy is coming to my place for dinner Friday evening. I'd love to have you come, too. I'm preparing Szechuan chicken, which I think is one of your favorite dishes."

"Yes, that sounds wonderful. May I bring something?"

"That isn't necessary, but you could bring some wine. I understand you are a connoisseur of good wines."

"And who told you that?" she asked with a smile.

"Jonathan mentioned that you had an excellent wine collection."

"I would be happy to bring the wine for dinner. And thank you." Jeanne was surprised by the invitation, especially after the recent conversations she and Judy had with her.

Jeanne told Jonathan that she and Judy were having dinner at Phyllis's on Friday. She was glad Judy was included and wondered why having dinner alone with Phyllis made her feel uncomfortable. She knew Phyllis was making an effort to be a friend but she had a sense that there may have been more to her invitation than just being friendly.

After changing into slacks and a silk blouse, Jeanne selected two bottles of white wine to take with her. Just as she was ready to leave, the phone rang. She hesitated before answering, but took time to identify the caller. It was not a number she recognized, but it was local. She took a chance and answered it as she wrote the number down.

"Have you been getting my messages?" a male voice asked.

"And what messages might that be?" she asked.

"I told you I had additional information. You didn't respond."

"I don't know who you are. Why didn't you just leave the information in the e-mail?"

"No one else may see it, or know what I want to tell you."

"Tell me now what I need to know."

"Not over the phone. Can you meet me in a public place tomorrow?"

"I'm not sure that is a good idea."

"It's important. I think you really want to know what I have to tell you. So, please meet me at ten o'clock at the coffee shop on the corner of Sixth and Market."

"But I won't know you..." Jeanne started to say, but the line was dead. Now this was a request she didn't know how to handle. She would ask Jonathan if she should have the meeting. Meanwhile, she had a dinner to get to. She picked up the wine and left the apartment. Now she wished she had not answered the phone. While driving to Phyllis's she pondered what information she should know and who the person was that she was to meet. She put it out of her mind determined to have a pleasant evening with her co-workers.

Phyllis greeted Jeanne almost before the bell stopped ringing. "Do come in," she said in a friendly voice. "I'm looking forward to the evening with the two of you. I just hope you'll like the dinner I've prepared. Judy just arrived."

"Thank you for having us. I'm sure it will be just fine," Jeanne responded with a warm smile. "Hi, Judy." She continued, "I hope I'm not late. I had a phone call just as I was leaving. I shouldn't have answered, it but I have a hard time ignoring a ringing phone."

"I know what you mean," Judy said. "If I don't answer I keep wondering if I missed the call of a life-time or one from the handsome man I just met or... It's probably just wishing for something wonderful to happen."

"Yes, you just keep on wishing," Jeanne said. "Someday your prince will come along."

They all laughed and went to the kitchen where Jeanne poured a glass of wine for them.

"Let's just sit for a minute and enjoy this delicious wine," Phyllis suggested. "Jonathan tells me Jeanne has quite a nice collection of fine wines. Isn't that right?"

"Yes, my husband was a knowledgeable wine connoisseur and so we have always had a good supply of wines. I'm not sure I will be able to maintain it. However, I will try to replace them as I use them."

"Good plan," Judy said. "I know nothing about wine other than there are red ones and white ones."

Phyllis added, "But there are pink ones also, such as Rosé." Then she continued, "I will leave you two to discuss various wines, or whatever, while I put the finishing touches on dinner.

Jeanne started to get up saying, "May we help you?"

"No. No, not at all," she said quickly. "I like to work in the kitchen alone."

"Well, tell us if you need any help. Otherwise, we'll stay out of your way," Judy said.

In a few minutes Phyllis called and said, "Perhaps you could put some ice in the glasses and fill them with water."

Judy bounced up and said, "That's something I can do."

"Jeanne, you can toss the salad. The dressing is right there on the counter," Phyllis said as she handed her the salad tongs.

While the salad and water were being taken care of, Phyllis added the rice to a large bowl. She then poured the chicken Szechuan into another serving bowl and placed them on the table.

"It's all ready, so let's eat." She pointed to their respective chairs inviting them to sit.

"May I pour the wine?" Jeanne asked. She turned and said, "Now, let's make a toast to Phyllis for hosting this lovely dinner."

They lifted their glasses and touched them before taking their first sip. "Oh, this is exquisite!" Judy exclaimed.

"Thank you," Jeanne responded. "Now let's dip into this delicious smelling food."

"Help yourself," Phyllis said. "Bon appétit."

Jeanne first served herself the salad and then passed it along to Judy. "I hope you like light dressing. I didn't want to overdo it."

"I'm sure it will be perfect," Judy said. "I never like my salad drowned in dressing."

Phyllis slid the bowl of rice over to Jeanne. "I'm sure you want this first, then add the chicken to it."

Jeanne placed a couple of spoonfuls of rice in the center of her plate. "It smells wonderful," she declared as she inhaled the chicken dish.

After everyone had served themselves, Phyllis picked up her fork and took the first bite of the Szechuan dish. After a few seconds, she declared it delicious. Judy followed suit and agreed. Jeanne hesitated a moment, looking at the aromatic dish thoughtfully. She remembered the first time she had eaten this dish and nearly lost her life.

"What's the matter, Jeanne? I thought this was one of your favorite dishes," Phyllis said.

"Oh, it is. I was just having a flashback, but I'm okay now," Jeanne said. She took a generous bite, and she, too, declared it delicious. "You have captured the flavor perfectly."

"I'm glad you both like it. So... eat up."

In about a minute after Jeanne had eaten a couple more bites, she reached for her water and gulped. She began choking.

"You must have swallowed wrong," Phyllis said without paying any more attention to her. However, Judy noticed Jeanne wasn't just coughing—she wasn't breathing. She jumped up and yelled at Phyllis, "She's not breathing. Help her!"

"Maybe something's caught in her throat. Do you know the Heimlich maneuver?"

"I've never done it. Have you?"

"No, but let's try it," Phyllis said as she stood behind Jeanne.

There was nothing caught in her throat, but she couldn't breathe. Judy dashed to the phone and dialed 911.

"What are you doing?" Phyllis asked.

"Calling for help." She gave the location information to the responder and that the person was not able to breathe. Within seconds, sirens were heard approaching the house.

Meanwhile, Phyllis just stood there watching Jeanne turn blue and finally pass out, falling to the floor. She didn't move to help her at all. Judy stared at Phyllis with disbelief. She didn't seem concerned that Jeanne was in distress. Judy tucked a pillow under Jeanne's head, but she still couldn't intake any air. *How long can one go without air?* Judy wondered.

The paramedics arrived, pounding on the door, which Phyllis made no move to open. Judy dashed to the door and opened it, directing them to where Jeanne lay on the floor. They assessed the situation quickly, and after giving her an injection of something to counteract the allergic reaction, they were able to partially open her air passage. She first took very shallow breaths, but soon was gasping for air. Her color slowly returned to normal.

"She's lucky you called as soon as you did. She was nearing the place of no return," the paramedic said. "Just give her a few minutes, and I think she'll be okay." They began packing up their equipment. One of them spoke to Judy, saying, "You did the right thing. Thinking something caused her to choke would have been my first guess. But never hesitate to call for help."

"I'm just glad Jeanne's okay, thanks to you," she said as she gave him a big smile.

"By the way, I'm Michael, and my partner is Jim. We're glad we were able to help."

At that point, Phyllis stepped in and said, "I'm Phyllis, and these are my friends, Judy and Jeanne. We all work together."

"Just be careful of what you feed them next time," Michael said with a smile as he turned to leave.

Phyllis frowned at him, turned back to the table, and said, "Now maybe we can finish our dinner." She sat down and began eating as if nothing had happened.

Judy was dismayed at Phyllis's lack of concern for Jeanne. "What's with you?" she asked.

"Well, there was nothing we could do, and I had prepared this dinner for you. I don't want it to go to waste."

Judy went to help Jeanne. "Are you okay now? Do you need anything?"

"I need to go home. You go finish the dinner with Phyllis." Then quietly, she said, "I think she tried to kill me."

"What do you mean?"

"I think she put MSG in the Szechuan chicken when she knew I was allergic to it."

Judy stared at her, eyes open in shock. She walked Jeanne to her car and then returned to the dinner with Phyllis. They continued eating without saying a word. Finally, Judy asked, "Phyllis, did you put MSG in the chicken dish?"

"I'm not sure. I may have, but only a little to help with the flavor"

"Did you know Jeanne was allergic to it?"

"Of course not. How would I know that?"

"She said you knew about her allergy, and that you may have done that on purpose."

"What are you saying?" Phyllis asked as she got up from the table and turned her back to Judy. "Perhaps you should leave, too."

"Perhaps I should." And with that Judy left without thanking Phyllis for dinner.

CHAPTER 27

Jeanne called Jonathan as soon as she arrived home. He answered on the first ring. "Jonathan, I just had the most horrifying experience. I think Phyllis tried to kill me."

"What!? Are you okay? Where are you?"

"I'm home. Can you come?"

"Yes, I'll be right there. Stay on the line with me." He put the phone in his pocket and headed out the door on a run. As soon as he was in the car, he punched the phone on. "Are you still there?"

"Yes. Are you on your way?"

"Yes, I'm in the car. I'll be there soon." It seemed that he could not get there fast enough. Thinking about what Jeanne had said filled him with anger at Phyllis and concern for Jeanne. He jerked the car to a stop in front of her apartment building, practically threw the keys at Alexander as he ran into the building, and punched the elevator button hard.

When he knocked on Jeanne's door, it was opened almost immediately. He rushed in and grabbed her in his arms in a grateful hug. "Are you sure you're okay?" he asked as he stepped back to look at her.

"I'm okay, now that you are here," she said in a shaky voice. She led him to the sofa. "Sit down, and I'll tell you all about it." She took a deep breath. "Phyllis invited Judy and me to dinner this evening. She prepared one of my favorite dishes, Szechuan chicken. It tasted perfectly delicious, but within a minute after taking a couple of bites, I couldn't breathe. I remembered my allergy to MSG, and my last thought was that Phyllis put it in the food when she knew I was allergic to it."

"Why would she do that?"

"I think she wants me dead. Anyway, the next thing I remember, I was lying on the floor looking into the very kind eyes of a paramedic. It felt so good to be able to breathe again."

"Where was Phyllis at that point?"

"She was just standing there doing nothing. It was only when the paramedic gave his name to Judy that she stepped in and introduced herself in an almost flirtatious way. As soon as they left, Judy helped me up and Phyllis went back to eating as if nothing had happened."

"How callous of her."

"I didn't say anything to her. I just told Judy I wanted to go home. She walked me to my car and I left. I think she went back inside."

"Perhaps I should take you to the hospital to be checked out. Do you have any idea how long you were without oxygen?"

"No, but long enough to lose consciousness."

"Come on. We are going to emergency to be sure you really are okay."

They went down to Jonathan's car. "Alexander, I'm sorry for being in a rush when I arrived. Jeanne had just had a medical episode and I was eager to see if she was okay. I'm taking her to the hospital to get her checked."

"I'm sorry to hear that," Alexander said as he gave the keys to Jonathan.

As soon as the engine roared to life, he peeled out of the driveway and took the shortest route to the local hospital. Even though Jeanne was not in an emergency state at the moment, Jonathan felt as if she was. He kept asking her questions. "How do you feel now? How long were you unconscious? What did Phyllis do? And Judy, was she okay?" He didn't give her time to answer as they pulled into the emergency entrance to the hospital.

They checked in at the desk, and Jonathan gave the reason he brought Jeanne in. "She had a strong allergic reaction to some food and was unable to breathe for quite a while. We just want to be sure she is okay and has no lasting effects from oxygen deprivation."

"I'll have her see a doctor shortly. Meanwhile, please fill out these forms. Is she capable of doing that herself?"

Jeanne immediately said, "Yes, I can do it," as she reached for the papers. "I'm just fine."

Jonathan wasn't so sure and said, "As soon as the doctor tells me you have no residual effects from your experience, I'll agree with you."

They took seats, and Jeanne began filling out the forms. She had no problem doing it. She hesitated at one question and said, "I know my birthday, but I can't remember the year. Do you remember how old I am?"

Jonathan looked at her and said, "I think you're 43. Is that right?"

"You're sure you didn't just invert the numbers?" she asked with a smile. She was surprised she couldn't recall her birth year.

She had barely finished entering all the requested information when she was called to go see the doctor. Jonathan went with her.

"Good evening. I'm Doctor Larsen. And you are her husband?" he asked Jonathan.

"Oh, no. Not yet," he answered. "I'm just her attorney."

"Well, Jeanne, tell me, what's the problem?"

She told him about her severe reaction to the Szechuan chicken, to which she was sure Phyllis had added MSG. "That is the only thing that could have caused my reaction."

"Had that happened before?"

"Yes. Several years ago, I nearly died before they discovered my allergy to it."

"Had you told your hostess about your allergy?"

"Yes, she knew because I mentioned it when we had an oriental lunch a few days ago and I asked the server if they used MSG in their recipes. I was told they did not, and that is when I explained my request to Phyllis. She could have forgotten, and I neglected to ask her. I thought she knew."

"What was your reaction this time?"

"Within a minute after eating a couple of bites, my throat began to close. I tried to drink some water, but I just choked on it. I couldn't talk enough to tell them what was wrong. And then I guess I just passed out. I don't know how long I was unable to breathe, because the next thing I knew I was on the floor looking into the face of a very handsome paramedic, gasping for air."

"It would have taken several minutes for the paramedics to arrive after they were called. And you don't know how soon they were called, do you?"

"No. I didn't think to ask. I'm sure Judy would know. She's the one who called 911."

"Even without knowing for sure, we know it could have been several minutes before you were treated. Have you had any indications that you were not thinking or acting normally?"

"No... only just now I couldn't remember my birth year when I was filling out that form," she said, pointing to the paper in the doctor's hand.

"Sometimes we don't want to remember," Doctor Larsen said with a smile. "I doubt if that is a serious indication of any mental problem. However, I think it would be wise for us to run some tests. Would it be all right to schedule it for tomorrow morning? I think you are tired, and besides, our technicians are through for the day."

"That would be fine," Jeanne said. "What time shall I come in?"

"Check with the nurse on your way out. She will schedule your time."

"Thank you, Doctor Larsen. Now I can relax tonight."

"Yes. You need to do just that. I think you handled your event very well. Good night, now." And he left the room.

They checked with the nurse and were told to come in early—8:30 on Saturday morning.

They remained quiet on the drive back to Jeanne's. Jonathan had myriad questions, but they could wait. He knew he would have to talk to Phyllis and Judy to get the full story. Could he wait until Monday when they'd be back in the office? He wanted to get more information now. He didn't have Judy's number at home, but he could find it at the office. He went straight there after seeing Jeanne home.

He left his car at the front entrance telling the night security guard he would be only a few minutes. At his desk, he looked for the personnel directory. He couldn't remember Judy's last name. He started at the beginning looking for a Judith. After going through a couple of pages, he came to the name. Judith was a secretary, so this must be the one he wanted. He jotted down the phone number and dialed it.

He glanced at the time and noticed it was nearly ten o'clock just as she answered. "Judith, are you the secretary to Mr. Carruthers?"

"Yes, I am," she answered. "Is there a problem?"

"Yes... no. This is Jonathan Crown. I'm sorry to call so late, but I just came back from taking Jeanne to the emergency to have her checked out. I wanted to ask you a few questions about what happened earlier this evening."

"Is she okay?" Judy asked with concern.

"Yes, we think so. They are going to do some tests tomorrow morning. Could you please tell me what happened at the dinner with Phyllis? I know Jeanne had a severe allergic reaction, undoubtedly to the MSG in the chicken dish. What I'd like to know is how long was she unable to breathe? How long was she deprived of oxygen?"

"I'm not sure, but it was several minutes. As soon as she passed out, I called 911, and the paramedics arrived within three or four minutes. They gave her an injection, and in just a few seconds, she began to breathe. They did put an oxygen mask on her."

"I know the brain can survive without oxygen for a short period of time, but I don't know exactly how long. What you told me will help."

"Was she having problems?" Judy asked.

"Not really. The only unusual thing was that she couldn't recall the year of her birth. She did know the date, however."

"Sometimes, that's a date I'd like to forget, too," she said with a bit of humor in her voice. "Is there anything I can do?"

"Not at the moment. Is there anything else you can tell me about the dinner?"

"I did find it strange that Phyllis seemed unconcerned about Jeanne. She just stood in place, staring at her, not moving to call for help when she fell to the floor. I made the call and put a pillow under her head. Phyllis didn't even open the door for the paramedics. I did. When Jeanne was breathing okay and the paramedics were preparing to leave, Phyllis pushed in to introduce herself to them. It was as if she had just awakened."

"That is very unusual behavior. Anything else you can tell me?"

"Only that as soon as the paramedics left, Phyllis said, 'Let's get back to our dinner before it gets cold," and she sat down and began eating.

"When Jeanne said she wanted to go home, I walked her to her car. That's when she said she thought Phyllis wanted to kill her. I returned to finish my dinner. However, at that point, I had lost my appetite and told her that perhaps I should leave—which I did."

"Thanks for telling me this. I'm sorry to have called so late, but I wanted to know what transpired this evening. It does sound very strange."

On his way back to his apartment, Jonathan pondered Phyllis's unusual behavior as described by Judy. *Could she have purposely put MSG in the Szechuan dish when she knew Jeanne was allergic to it? And then just stand by and watch her suffocate? It's a good thing Judy was there or Jeanne could have died.* When that thought struck him, he knew he would report this to Detective O'Neal.

CHAPTER 28

Jonathan rose early after a restless night so he could drive Jeanne to the hospital. After a quick cup of coffee, he refilled one to take with him.

"Good morning, Maurice. I'm just making a quick stop to pick up Jeanne," he said as he quickly disappeared into the building.

In a couple of minutes, they were on the street, and Jonathan asked Jeanne how she was. "Did you sleep well? Have you had anything to eat? Did you have coffee? If not, I'll share mine."

He didn't give her time to answer. He seemed more anxious than she. "Yes, I slept well. No, I have not eaten. It was too early for me. However, I'd like a sip of your coffee," she said as she reached for it. "Now, relax. I'm fine."

"We'll know that only after the tests."

Jonathan parked and scurried around to assist Jeanne from the car. "I hope you remember the name of the doctor we're to see."

"Of course I remember. It's a Swedish name." She hesitated, trying to recall it. "It's Doctor... something ... Just give me a minute." Then Jeanne said to the receptionist, "I'm supposed to see the Swedish doctor who treated me last night."

"That must be Doctor Larsen. He was on duty last night."

"Yes, that's the one. Where will I find him?" Jeanne asked.

"Let me check to be sure he's in. It's a bit early." She punched numbers on the phone. "Good morning, Nancy. Is the doctor in? He has a patient here. Thanks. I'll send her right up." Turning to Jeanne, she said, "You can take the elevator to the third floor. He's in room 305."

In the elevator they remained quiet, each lost in their own thoughts. Doctor Larsen greeted them, asking how Jeanne was.

"I'm okay. I slept well; so well, in fact, that I didn't wake up early enough to have breakfast."

"That's just as well. Some tests are best taken when fasting. When we're finished your friend can take you out for breakfast," he said giving a nod to Jonathan. "Another doctor, a neurologist, will be joining us. Jonathan, you may wait in the visitors' room while Jeanne and I go to the examining room."

"I can't go with her?" he inquired.

"We find testing is best done with no observers or distractions. We won't be long."

The doctor escorted Jeanne out and Jonathan sat down to wait. He hadn't brought anything to read or work on, so he casually glanced at the magazines all of which were on home decorating, cooking, sewing, the latest fashions—all stuff for women. Then he found a section on 'Cooking for One.' Some of the recipes seemed easy and economical to prepare. He made a note to order the book referenced at the end. He leaned back, stretched out his legs and closed his eyes, saying a brief prayer for Jeanne.

"Hey, sleepy head." He awoke with a start when Jeanne touched his shoulder. "I'm cleared to go to breakfast."

"Great. Then let's go."

Over breakfast Jonathan asked many questions, but Jeanne only told him there would be no answers for two or three days. "They have to analyze the results of the tests and see if there are any abnormalities. The doctors said that on the surface, everything looked good. Doctor Larsen will call me to come in and go over the results. Until then, don't worry."

"I know I tend to be a worrier," Jonathan said. "I probably inherited that from my mother. She worried about everything. I remember one day she said, 'I'm so worried' and when I asked why, she said, 'Because I can't think of anything to worry about.' That's the ultimate worrier."

"Well, I never worry. My mother was a worrier and I saw the futility of it. Her worry never changed anything, only made her anxious. So... my philosophy is, 'If you can do something about the situation, do it.

If you can't, say a prayer and let God take care of it.' That doesn't mean you don't have concern. But concern is different from worry. With concern you can take action. With worry nothing is accomplished. I have never worried."

"You are a very wise woman," Jonathan observed. "I'll try your method."

When Jeanne's second cup of coffee was poured, Jonathan said, "There's something I want to tell you."

"I hope it's good."

"I'm not sure, but you need to know what Judy told me. I called her last night after I took you home because you said she helped you to your car when you left Phyllis's. I wanted to know what she observed about you. You seemed okay and assured her that you could drive home safely. She told me how Phyllis didn't move to help you, almost like she was frozen in shock, and seemed so indifferent to your situation. It made me wonder if Phyllis had purposely added MSG to the Szechuan chicken when she knew you were allergic to it. Maybe she was trying to eliminate you."

"That went through my mind, too. You know she is jealous of me."

"Of you? Why?"

"Because you and I have become friends and she is in love with you. She thinks I'm keeping you from her."

Jonathan was quiet for a few moments before saying, "I'd never think of her in that way. I could never be more than an employer to her."

"As I have said before, I think she has mental problems. Do you think we should report what happened last night to Detective O'Neal?"

"Absolutely. Phyllis may have attempted to murder you, and she may attempt it again. You need to be very careful around her."

"I agree. No longer will I think of her as my friend."

They finished their coffee and reluctantly left the restaurant. As soon as Jonathan left Jeanne at her apartment, he called the police station and asked for Detective O'Neal.

"Sorry, he's not in on weekends. Can someone else help you?"

"No, but could you leave a message for him to call me first thing when he gets in? I'm Jonathan Crown and he has my number. Thanks." Now all he could do was wait.

Jonathan arrived at the appointed time to take her to the orchestra concert. It was filled with passion showing the many moods of Beethoven. It reflected the many emotional events Jeanne had recently experienced.

"Thank you, Jonathan. That's just what I needed. Now I can face tomorrow."

"You're welcome. It's what I needed, also. See you tomorrow." He left her at the door with a warm hug.

Sunday morning, Jeanne decided to attend church. The sermon was on trust. She must learn to trust God more and trust only those who were trustworthy. She thought about Phyllis and what she had done. She offered a prayer for her, that God would take care of her, but she would never trust her again.

At home, she decided a nap would feel good after the hectic couple of days she had. She never took naps, so why was she feeling tired and sleepy? Maybe her allergic episode took more out of her than she realized. She wanted to feel rested for her dinner with Jonathan so she stretched out on the sofa.

When Jonathan arrived, Jeanne met him at the door. "I'm ready for dinner."

"So am I," and they left in his Mustang to go to The Club.

"I'm so glad we are coming here again. I'm remembering the last time we were here," Jeanne said. "It was a special evening for us, as I recall."

"Yes, but any evening with you is special," Jonathan said smiling warmly at her.

They ordered their favorite wines, and began to relax as they savored their first sip. The candle on the table glowed with a rose tint, matching the roses in the vase. Soft music was playing in the background creating a most pleasant ambience.

"Jeanne, tell me more about your early life. Where did you grow up? What was your family like?"

"My family lived in the suburbs of a college town upstate. All of our neighbors were professional people. We lived in the same house my entire life. My father retired early from his job as the manager of a real estate company. My mother worked as a legal secretary until I was born, and then she became a stay-at-home mom. I was an only child, and no,

I don't think that made me self-centered. My parents saw to that. I'd say we were a typical American middle-class family.

"I attended local public schools but I did leave home to go to the university back East. I wanted to experience a new environment. That was where I first met Roger. I was infatuated with him. He was smart, ambitious, very good looking, and seemed like an ideal mate. When I graduated, I returned home and was immediately hired by a prestigious public relations firm. Within a year, Roger followed me and that led to marriage."

She paused and sighed. "The first several years were wonderful. We were in love. He didn't want me to work when I became pregnant with the twins, so I left my position and, like my mother, I became a stay-at-home mom. We were very comfortable financially. He was a good provider because of his position in business, which I never fully understood."

"Why was that?" Jonathan inquired.

"He wasn't exactly secretive about what he did, he just didn't talk about it much and I didn't ask questions." She remained quiet for a few minutes. "However, he must have done quite well because he left us very well off financially."

It was time to order dinner when the hostess approached their table with a menu. They started with a Caesar salad with a light dressing. He told the hostess they would consider the next course later. After refilling their wine glasses, she left to place their order, questioning the unorthodox way of ordering.

"Now it's your turn to tell me about your former life," Jeanne said.

"Actually, it seems I have a similar background. I, too, was an only child. However, my father died young, only in his 40s, and so my mother and I had an especially close relationship. My father had been an attorney. Perhaps that's why I became one. I always admired him. We lived in an upper-class neighborhood, just south of San Francisco. As did most of our neighbors, we had a gardener and a live-in maid, who was like a nanny to me. I attended the local public schools, as you did, and then attended Stanford University, where I obtained my law degree. Unlike you, I remained at home when attending the University mainly because I didn't want to leave Mother alone. She passed away the year after I graduated."

"I'm sorry. It must have been difficult because you were still quite young," Jeanne said sympathetically. She was quiet for a little while, thinking about all she had learned about Jonathan. Then she asked, "What did you do after you lost your mother?"

"It was painful to remain in my family home, so I sold it and moved to Southern California. I secured a position at my current law firm. It turned out to be a wise move. It wasn't long before I became a Junior Partner, and as you know, I am now a Senior Partner."

"Sometime along the way, you married Elizabeth. When was that?" Jeanne asked.

"Shortly after I became Junior Partner, and I felt financially secure."

"That would make sense. You are a very practical person," Jeanne said with a hint of teasing.

The hostess had taken away the salad plates when she asked, "Will there be anything else?"

Jonathan answered, "Absolutely. We are ready to order our main course."

"What will you have?" she asked Jeanne.

"I'd like the broiled lemon salmon with herb-seasoned rice and any vegetable the chef would choose to complement it."

"Very good. And you, sir?"

"I will have the same, and I like the idea of a surprise vegetable."

The hostess refilled their wine glasses, and left with their orders.

"It's interesting that we have some similarities in our backgrounds, such as being an only child and being raised by professional parents. One major difference is that I never had children of my own. I wish I had," Jonathan said wistfully.

"I'm glad I have the twins, especially now that Roger is gone."

"When Elizabeth died, I felt terribly alone. I even thought for a time that I might adopt a child. I soon realized I could never be a single parent. My work commitment would not have allowed room for a child. I probably worked so many hours just to fill the space in my life. However, it did allow me to become a Senior Partner."

"That's a good thing. You seem to really enjoy your work. I feel it's important to be happy in your profession. There are too many people who hate their job who complain every Monday morning about going to work. Personally, I look forward to Monday morning when I get to go to the office."

"That a wonderful attitude. It benefits the employers to have happy employees."

"Do you think Phyllis is happy with her job?"

"I hadn't thought about it. She's never complained, at least not to me. She is a good secretary, keeps everything well organized, and maintains my schedule efficiently."

"And she's well paid. That alone should keep her happy. Plus, she's working for a handsome and pleasant boss," Jeanne said, complimenting Jonathan.

"Well, that's true," he agreed in a self-deprecating tone.

The hostess arrived with their dinners and said, "Bon appétit" as she served them.

They continued sharing stories about their lives. By the time they had finished the main course, they knew a lot more about each other.

"I have never told anyone other than Elizabeth, as much about me as I have just told you," Jonathan said. "It felt good to share my life's story with someone who was interested."

"Thank you for sharing. As you may have guessed, I am interested in you. I find it easy to share personal information with you as well."

"Shall we have dessert?" Jonathan asked.

"Only if it's chocolate. Remember the one we shared before? Let's do it again."

When the hostess returned and removed their dinner plates, she asked, "Are you having dessert?"

Jonathan said, "Yes. The same decadent chocolate one we had before, which we'll share."

At the end of a three-hour dinner, they were completely sated, happy and relaxed. Jeanne had totally forgotten her ordeal two nights before.

"Sorry I kept you out so late on a school night," Jonathan said as he parked in front of her apartment building. "You may come in late tomorrow morning if you want to sleep in."

"Thanks for the offer, but I think I can make it at the usual time. Thank you for a lovely evening, and the enjoyable conversation. It was just what I needed."

Jonathan walked her to the elevator where he gave her an innocent, light kiss just as the doors opened. "Good night, Jeanne." He turned and left Jeanne smiling.

CHAPTER 29

Monday morning, Jeanne was humming as she dressed in one of the new suits she had purchased the day she went shopping with Phyllis. As she thought about that day and what a pleasant time she'd had, why did Phyllis try to kill her Friday night? It made no sense. Phyllis knew about the allergy because Jeanne had clearly told her about its effect when they had lunch.

When she arrived at her office, Phyllis was not at her desk. *Just as well*, Jeanne thought. *I'm not sure I want to see her today.* She went directly to her office and was glad to have enough work to keep her hidden in the research library all morning.

Jonathan called Detective O'Neal first thing when he arrived at his office. He told him about the near-tragic event with Jeanne Friday evening at Phyllis's house. They discussed what was the best way to proceed. Undoubtedly Jeanne should make a written report on what happened.

"Phyllis, has Jeanne come in this morning?"

"I think I saw her go by."

"Undoubtedly, she has gone to the library. I'll check." And he hurried to the stairs, descended quickly and went to find Jeanne. There she was buried behind books.

"Jeanne, good morning. I just talked with Detective O'Neal and told him about your event Friday night. He wants you to write a full, detailed report on everything you can remember about that evening.

Then he wants to talk with Judy. She wasn't in just now, but I'll leave a message for her." He finally stopped to take a breath.

"Well, good morning to you, too," Jeanne was finally able to say. "Yes, I will write down everything. Should I do it now?"

"Unless this is pressing work, yes."

She quickly put books away, gathered up her files and joined Jonathan at the elevator. As they exited, Jonathan saw Judy and asked her to come to his office as soon as convenient.

In her office, Jeanne immediately wrote in great detail the events of Friday evening. When she finished describing the medical testing procedures Saturday morning, she had written everything she could recall. She printed it out and e-mailed her report to the detective.

As requested, Judy went to see Jonathan.

"Why do you want to see him?" Phyllis asked. "Anyway, he's with a client right now."

"He asked me to stop in when I had a minute. Please tell him I'm free."

"I'm sure he won't be long. You can wait here if you wish."

"I'll be at my desk. Just give me a call and I'll be right over." Judy turned and left.

Phyllis was concerned why Jonathan would want to see another secretary, and why Judy?

Jonathan escorted his client out the door. "Please put these in this client's file," he said to Phyllis as he handed several papers to her.

As Phyllis reached for the file, she said, "Judy came by to see you, but she didn't say why. Do you want me to tell her you are free now?"

"Yes, please. This is a good time."

When Judy arrived, Phyllis took her into Jonathan's office.

"Thank you, Phyllis. That will be all," he said as he closed the door. "Please sit down. Judy, I need to ask you for a favor, or rather Detective O'Neal is asking it of you," he said very quietly. "He would like you to write a detailed report on everything that happened and was said at the dinner Friday evening at Phyllis's home. Could you do that?"

"Of course. Is there a problem?"

"There may be. We just need to clarify everything. There is some concern about why Phyllis would put Jeanne's life at risk. She knew about Jeanne's allergy. In fact, the detective may want you to come in to talk with him after he reads your report. Would you be willing to do that?"

"Yes, of course. Anything I can do to help?"

"Here is Detective O'Neal's e-mail address. Please send your report directly to him as soon as you can."

"Do you need a copy?"

"No… but on second thought, send it to me, also."

Phyllis asked Jonathan, "Is everything okay?" when Judy had gone.

"Yes. No problem. All's well."

Phyllis was not pleased with his answer. Usually, he shared everything with her; it was not like him to be secretive. Something was going on, and she planned to find out what.

Detective O'Neal eagerly read the report Jeanne sent him. It seemed very thorough, even though there was a time when she was unconscious and, of course, couldn't account for events then. When Judith's report came, it filled in the blanks. It certainly seemed that Phyllis did want to harm Jeanne. Since Judith was there, she probably saved Jeanne's life. After reading her report again, he had a more complete picture of what transpired that evening, but he knew he had to gather more information.

His next step was to talk with the paramedics who were called that night. Judith did remember the name of one of them, so he should be able to find them. He called the paramedic station that served the area of Phyllis's house and asked for Michael or his partner, both of whom would have been on duty Friday evening.

"Is there a problem, sir?" the supervisor asked.

"Oh, no. I just need to get some information from them regarding a call they answered last Friday evening. They are not in trouble; in fact, just the opposite."

"Michael and Jim come in around three in the afternoon. They are on evening duty. Can I have them call you then?"

"Would it be possible for you to contact them and ask at least one of them to call me at the station this morning? Here's the number. Ask for Detective O'Neal."

"Is it that important?"

"Yes, it is or I wouldn't ask this of them," the detective said firmly.

"Very well. I'll try to reach them now," he said, wondering why the police would need to speak with them.

It wasn't long before the phone rang at the detective's desk.

"This is Paramedic Michael. You wanted to talk to me?"

"Yes. Thanks for calling so quickly. You remember the call you responded to last Friday evening at the home of a young lady where one of her guests was having an allergic reaction?"

"Yes, of course. We arrived in time or she may not have recovered without some residual effect. Is she okay?" he asked with concern.

"Yes, she seems to be fine. However, I would like you and your partner to come to the station and give me a detailed report of what you saw, heard, observed or anything that might be helpful. Confidentially, I think it may have been done intentionally. We are still investigating that. Your observations may be most valuable."

"Certainly, we'll be glad to come in and tell you anything we can. Could we stop in around one o'clock this afternoon?"

"Perfect, and please don't mention this to anyone—not even your supervisor. If he asks, just say I had a couple of questions and all is well."

"Okay. We'll see you this afternoon." He immediately called Jim and told him they needed to go to police station regarding last Friday evening's event.

"Are we in trouble?" Jim asked.

"No. It's just a confidential meeting with Detective O'Neal. He wants us to give him a detailed report on our observations about the lady not breathing. Remember the three lovely ladies who were having dinner?"

"Of course. The one you liked; I think she said her name was Judy. Maybe he can help you find her," Jim said laughing.

"It wouldn't hurt to ask, and maybe I will."

"When do we have to see him?"

"At one o'clock this afternoon."

"Want to meet at Subway for a quick lunch first?"

"Sure, that way we can reinforce our memories of that evening before we see the detective. However, I doubt that we would forget anything, especially three beautiful women," he said smiling as he pictured the face of Judy.

At exactly one o'clock, Michael and Jim entered the police precinct and asked for Detective O'Neal. "We are the paramedics, Michael and Jim. He asked us to come in."

"Yes, he is expecting you." She buzzed the door open and said, "The last door on the left."

Michael knocked and Detective O'Neal called, "Come in, come in." He rose to greet them, shaking hands with each one in turn as they gave their names. "Thanks so much for coming in so quickly. I'm eager to hear what you have to say about your observations and what transpired Friday evening on your call to a house with three young women having dinner. Tell me everything in as much detail as possible. Oh, do you mind if I record our conversation?"

"No, I guess not," Michael said as he looked at Jim. "May we ask why?"

"Confidentially, your comments may be important regarding an intentional action endangering a life. In fact, at some point, you may be called upon for an in-person testimony."

"Okay. We're here to help, so let's get to it."

Detective O'Neal turned on the recording device and began with questions. "What were you told when you were dispatched on the call Friday evening?"

"That there was a female in distress who wasn't breathing."

"What was the exact time you arrived at the house?"

They continued answering all the detective's questions as thoroughly and succinctly as possible and in a very professional manner.

"The lady who was there told me about the behavior of the hostess; that she seemed so indifferent to the situation and may have been either in shock or just uncaring. Can you tell me if you observed her also?" the detective asked.

"Yes, the one called Phyllis did not move while we were there, just stared at the one we were treating. It was not until we were ready to leave and gave our names to Judy that she rushed over and gave us her name, almost in a flirting way. I was surprised by her behavior."

"Thank you. You have been very helpful."

"Speaking of Judy, do you know how we could get in touch with her? She was very helpful that evening and we just wanted to thank her. It's because of her our patient survived."

"I don't have her personal contact information, but she is a secretary at the attorney's firm Crown, Best and Carruthers. I'm sure you can find her there."

"Thanks. And let us know if or when you need us again." With that they headed for their work station. Michael left with a smile on his face.

"So what are you grinning about?" Jim asked.

"I really would like to see Judy again. Now I know where to find her."

"Well, it's time for us to go to work, so you'll have to wait until tomorrow."

"I know. I can wait one more day."

CHAPTER 30

Around noon, when Jeanne returned to her office, she opened her messages. The first one that popped up said *we need to talk.* She checked the address. It was the same as one of the previous messages. She hesitated about opening it, but she was curious if it had anything to do with what had transpired this past weekend. Should she or shouldn't she open it? She sat staring at the screen, fingers poised over the keyboard.

"Hey, Jeanne, are you ready to go to lunch?" Judy asked as she looked in the door.

Jeanne jumped, startled out of her thoughts. "Oh, you surprised me."

"I'm sorry. What were you reading that had you so engrossed?"

"I have an e-mail message I was pondering whether or not to open."

"Never open one when you don't know who sent it. That's my rule," Judy said with authority.

"I agree. This one, however, is from the same address as a previous one."

"Well, leave it for now, and let's go to lunch. It will be there when we get back, and you can decide then what to do."

"Okay." She closed the computer and joined Judy.

As they approached the elevator, Judy asked, "Shall we go to our cafeteria, or do you want to go out?"

"I've been cooped up in our library all morning, so I'd like to get out into the fresh air. Let's go to the deli. Another one of their sandwiches would appeal to me. How about you?"

"Sounds good to me," Judy agreed.

Just as they approached the deli, walking ahead of them were the two officers, Detective O'Neal and his partner. Jeanne wondered if she should tell the detective about her recent message. Officer Brandt saw Jeanne and Judy as he opened the door. "Well, look who's here again," he said.

Detective O'Neal turned and greeted them. "Would you like to join us for lunch?"

They looked at each other in question and nodded their heads. "We'd love to," Jeanne said. "But we go Dutch."

"If you insist," Office Brandt said as he held the door for them.

They placed their orders for their favorite sandwiches. Detective O'Neal was the first to speak. "Jeanne, are you doing okay now? Any problems after your medical event?"

"No. I'm doing fine. There seems to be no significant effects."

"That's great. By the way, Judy, I talked to one of the paramedics who treated Jeanne asking about you? Did you ever hear from him?"

"Yes, he called and I have a date with him this coming Friday evening. Thanks for telling him how to find me."

"You're welcome. He seems like a fine young man."

As their food was served, Jeanne said, "One never knows when or how you will meet someone special. I hope Michael turns out to be one of those." She turned to Judy. "That is his name, isn't it?"

"Yes. I'm surprised you remembered it. He told us just as he was leaving."

"I don't remember everything about that evening, but I remember how handsome those paramedics were. I was looking into the eyes of one when I regained conscientiousness. It was a great image to see," she said feeling a little embarrassed. "I understand that because of your timely call and the paramedics quick response, I recovered unscathed. Thank you again, Judy."

"I'd do it again in a millisecond, but I hope I never have to,"

"Changing the subject," Detective O'Neal said between bites, "I've been wondering, Jeanne, if you have received any additional mysterious communications?"

"Interesting that you should ask. I had another e-mail this morning from the same address as a previous one, but I didn't open it. I will be forwarding it to you."

"Yes, you should. We are still investigating the earlier ones, but have not identified the sender as yet. I'm sure we will. Our computer experts seem able to solve nearly everything in the electronic world. I have no idea how they do it, but..." He left it unfinished and took a bite of his sandwich.

"I'm eager to know who is sending the messages and what he or she knows that I should know. If the person ever elects to tell me, you will be the first to know," Jeanne said to the detective.

"I'd expect nothing less from you."

As soon as Jeanne entered her office, she pulled up the e-mail from the unknown sender and forwarded it to Detective O'Neal. She was sure it would not be long before the sender was identified.

Jonathan looked into her office. "Are you busy?"

"Not really. I just finished sending an e-mail to Detective O'Neal."

"Another unknown sender?"

"Yes. Did you want something?"

"Yes. I have a meeting out of the office with a client on Wednesday and I'd like you to attend it with me. I'll let you know what information you can assemble for it, but it should be no problem for you."

Jeanne was surprised, but quickly agreed to accompany him. "I'll be happy to help you, but why not take Phyllis since she is your secretary?"

"You are my assistant and that's what I need on Wednesday," he said firmly.

"Of course," Jeanne responded meekly. After all, he was the boss and she shouldn't question him.

"Oh, and we will be having lunch at his place. He suggested we bring our swimsuits. He has a beautiful, large pool. So dress casually. Until later," and he was gone.

Wow. That is different, she thought. She had never observed him at work, but this sounded less like work and more like a social visit. For now, she had work to finish in the library. Phyllis was at her desk, but

Jeanne kept right on walking. Their relationship remained cool ever since that infamous dinner at her house when she could have died.

Near the end of the day, Jeanne had finished her research. She returned some of the files to Judy for her boss and took the rest to Jonathan's office. His door was closed, and she placed the files on Phyllis's desk. "Please give these to your boss."

"He's not here. He already left for the day."

"Oh. Then perhaps I should keep them until tomorrow," Jeanne said as she quickly picked them up. She wasn't sure she could trust Phyllis with them because of the recent experience with a missing file.

CHAPTER 31

The phone rang as Jeanne opened the door to her apartment. She glanced at the screen, quickly wrote down the number shown and punched the talk button. As if she were the maid, she answered, "Blomgren residence," with a Swedish accent.

"Please leave a message for Ms. Blomgren," a man's voice demanded.

"Yeah, what is it?"

"Tell her to answer her e-mail with the subject line *information you need to know.*"

"Is that all?" but the line had been disconnected.

Somewhat concerned, Jeanne considered the request for a few minutes before calling Jonathan. However, before she could make the call the phone rang. It was Jonathan. "Hi. I was just going to call you. I had the weirdest phone call from some man."

"Do you know who it was? Did you get a number? What did he want?" Jonathan asked rapidly.

"Slow down and I'll tell you everything. No, I don't know who it was. Yes, I did write down the number he was calling from. I pretended I was the maid. All he wanted was to give me a message to open one of the e-mails I received."

"Which one was that?"

"The one that said *information you need to know.* Obviously, he is the one who sent it."

"You did forward it to Detective O'Neal, didn't you?"

"Yes, but they haven't identified the sender yet. Do you think I should open it?"

"No, not yet. Perhaps you should see what the detective says," Jonathan cautioned.

"All right. I'll wait for tomorrow," Jeanne said slowly. "By the way, you left the office early tonight. Is everything okay?"

"Yes, of course. I chose to skip out a little early. I needed to clear my head so I went for a short run when I got home. Now I feel much better."

"I'd like to do that, but I don't feel comfortable going out alone."

"And you shouldn't—not until we find out who is calling you and leaving e-mail messages. No, you stay in where you're safe. Go out only when you are with someone you trust."

"I should be able to take care of myself, but I do feel uneasy when I'm alone."

"That is normal. It may not be long before everything is resolved."

The next morning, she arrived early at the office and signed on to the computer. She stopped at a familiar address. It just said *we need to talk*. She called Detective O'Neal. He was not in so she left a message for him to call.

Phyllis stuck her head in the door and said, "Good morning. I hope all is well with you."

"Good morning. Yes, I'm fine, except for strange messages in my e-mail. I got another one just this morning. I don't know what to make of it."

"Is it the same address as a previous one?" Phyllis asked as the entered Jeanne's office. She looked over Jeanne's shoulder to see the wording on the screen. "It seems familiar, but I'm not sure who it is. I was wondering..." Phyllis said hesitatingly. "Would you like to have lunch today? We need to talk."

Jeanne paused for a minute while thinking about what had happened the last time they were together. At least going out to lunch would be safe, so she said, "Why not? We do need to clear the air between us. What did you have in mind?"

"Let's go to the French Corner Café."

"Sounds perfect. See you at noon." Jeanne was surprised about the invitation, but perhaps Phyllis was ready to apologize for what she had done.

A phone call startled Jeanne out of her thoughts. It was Detective O'Neal. "I'm returning your call. What's up?"

"I have another mysterious message in my e-mails this morning. It said *information you need to know.* That was all. So I'm wondering if you, or your computer nerds, have been able to identify who's sending these e-mails?"

"Yes, they have made some progress. Is the name Robert or Bob Baylord familiar to you?"

"No... No, I don't know who that is."

"We think he may be the one who is sending you e-mails. However, it's possible there is a different person as well."

Then Jeanne said, "A few days ago, I had a call from a man who asked to meet me one morning at the coffee shop at Sixth and Market, but I ignored his request. He may be the same one sending e-mails. Do you think I should respond to him?"

"Let's wait a bit and see what we find out about Robert Baylord," Detective O'Neal cautioned. "Give us another day or two." He paused. "I wish you had told me about the invitation to meet this person. We could have had someone there and perhaps found out who he is. If he tries to set up a meeting again, call me immediately. Okay?"

"All right. I'm just eager to get this resolved so I can feel safe again."

Jeanne met Phyllis at the front door on their way to lunch. "Thanks for suggesting lunch. It's been a while."

"Yes. I felt it was time to talk." Phyllis said nothing else as they walked toward the café. After placing their orders, Jeanne asked, "Did you want to talk to me about something in particular?"

"Well... yes, in a way. First, I want to apologize for what happened last Friday evening at my house. I had not remembered your allergy to MSG, and so I had used a small amount in the recipe as I usually do. I had never seen anyone have such an allergic reaction to anything, and so I think I was in shock seeing you in such a state. I hardly remember what happened. I'm glad Judy was able to take control of the situation."

"Thank you for the apology. Actually, I should have asked if you used MSG, but since I had told you about it a short time ago, I assumed you would remember. I'm just glad the paramedics were so prompt. Did you know one of them has asked Judy for a date?"

"No. That's great! So something good came out of the evening."

"It would seem so. They must have been impressed with Judy."

"So… are you okay now? I understand you went to the hospital."

"Yes. They did some tests, mainly to see if there was any damage mentally from me being without oxygen for several minutes. I haven't had the results yet, but I'm sure I'm okay. We can thank Judy for her actions, as well as the paramedics' quick response. I will be more careful in the future and always ask about the ingredients."

After a few minutes of silence while they attacked their crepes, Phyllis casually asked, "Do you know how often one has to have their car serviced? Like when to change the oil, check the tires, and such. I heard something on TV about how to keep your car running longer. I have never given it much thought."

"I've been told the oil should be changed every three thousand miles. However, with the new oil, you can go as long as five thousand miles. Your mechanic can advise you. Mine puts a little notice of the mileage in the corner of my windshield for when it's time to have it serviced.

"As to tires, someone said you should check the air pressure once a month. I never do. I'm sure your mechanic does whenever he services your car. But if you ever see them looking a little low, take them in for a check."

"Do you have any idea how long a battery lasts? The last one I bought was a five-year battery."

"They don't always last the full five years. Really hot weather is hard on them. Running the air conditioner drains them. However, driving the car regularly does help to keep them charged. You shouldn't have a problem with that since you drive to work every day."

Phyllis was quiet while she absorbed this information. Jeanne wondered why she was asking her these questions. She finally asked, "Are you concerned about your battery?"

"No, no. I was just curious. I've never given much thought to the upkeep of a car. My father always took care of the family car. I thought if I just bought one every two years or so, I'd never have a problem with maintenance."

"So that's why you were thinking of getting a new car, even though you like your convertible?"

"I guess."

They left the café and headed back to the office. Jeanne casually asked, "By the way, do you recognize the name Robert, or Bob Baylord?"

Phyllis abruptly stopped. She looked shocked, and responded, "How do you know him?"

"I don't know him. He may be the one sending me the mysterious e-mails. From your reaction, I sense you know who he is."

"I don't really know him, but I think I know who he is. But why would he be sending you messages?" Phyllis asked.

"That's what we are trying to find out. If you know who it is, please tell me. I want to know why he says *we need to talk* and that he has *information I need to know.*"

"I don't know how to contact him, and I've never talked to him."

"Since Detective O'Neal, and his computer nerds have been trying to discover the source of the e-mails, this is the one name that has surfaced. Would you be willing to talk to the detective about what you know?"

"I guess. It's only what I've told you."

"Any little bit of information may help. Let's call him when we get back to the office."

Jeanne put the call in to the detective's office and told him about her conversation with Phyllis. Then she put Phyllis on the line. "Yes, sir. I will be glad to come in. Will tomorrow morning be all right? See you then."

"What did he say?" Jeanne asked.

"He wants me to go to the station in the morning and go on line there. I don't know if I'll be much help, but when the police ask for help, you do what you can."

CHAPTER 32

Phyllis stopped at the police station on her way to the office. She was immediately ushered into Detective O'Neal's office. He introduced another person, Officer Martin. "Is that your first name or your last name?" she asked.

"It is my last name. My first name is Donald," he explained with a friendly smile.

Detective O'Neal was aware of the flirtatious way Phyllis looked at the officer. "Let's get to it," he said in a business-like manner. "Officer Martin has been researching the messages left on Jeanne's computer and he has found where some of them have originated. I'm told a name was familiar to you."

"Well, I don't really know who it is."

The officer pulled up the message on Detective O'Neal's computer. "Phyllis, look at this. Have you seen this before?"

She looked at it and froze. She stared at the screen without speaking.

"What is it? What are you seeing?" the officer asked.

It was a few seconds before she even blinked. "Have you opened the message?"

"Not yet. We've only tried to find the originating source, which led us to this name."

"Open it. It may give us a clue as to who he is and what he wants."

The officer clicked on read. The message said *I may know where the car is.* That was all.

"What car is he talking about?" the detective inquired. "I wonder if he's referring to Roger Ander's car. It has never been found since his death."

Phyllis sat down with a thunk and was so pale her freckles stood out.

Detective O'Neal asked, "Are you okay? You don't look well."

No response.

"Don, please get her some water. She seems shocked by this message."

As soon as officer Martin left the room, Detective O'Neal gently asked, "Phyllis, what do you know about this?"

She took a deep breath, exhaled it slowly, and then said, "I have no idea what he is talking about. I was just surprised to hear Roger's name. It's been several weeks, but I guess he is still..."

"I understand, but I think you know more than you are telling me."

Officer Martin handed the water to Phyllis. "Here, drink this."

Phyllis drank slowly, glad to have something to do. She would have liked to escape immediately, but the detective had more questions for her.

"Officer Martin, could you find and open one of the other messages from the same person?"

"Certainly, sir." With a few key strokes, the screen lit up with another single line: *information you should know.* He opened it. *"I saw someone move the car."*

Detective O'Neal was intrigued. "Since he sent these to Jeanne, she should respond to him. We need to find the person who sent these messages and have him come in for questioning."

Phyllis looked very uneasy. "Is that all you want from me? I need to get to the office."

"Yes, thanks for coming in. You have been very helpful. I'll call if we need you again."

Phyllis quickly left the detective's office, her heels clattering down the hall. As soon as she was outside, she took a deep breath. She was in the state of panic, not knowing what to do about the car. She wondered if this unknown person really knew where it was. *Had he seen me drive it from where it was parked? Why was he sending messages to Jeanne? Does he know me? Maybe if I remain quiet, I will not be identified.*

By the time she reached the office, she had calmed down a bit. She walked to her desk with her head held high as if everything was normal, but it wasn't.

"Phyllis, can you come in, please?" Jonathan called from his office.

She gathered up a pen and notebook and calmly walked into the room. "Yes, sir. What can I do for you?"

"I just had a call from Detective O'Neal inquiring if you were okay. He said you seemed very upset when you left the precinct. Are you all right? What happened?"

"Yesterday when I had lunch with Jeanne she asked me if I recognized a certain name. I said it was familiar, but I really didn't know who it was. Well, then Detective O'Neal asked me to come in to see the e-mails Jeanne has been receiving to see if I recognized them. When he opened them, the messages were succinct. They were about a car, but they don't know which one. When they mentioned that Roger's car was still missing and wondered if he might be referring to it, I guess just hearing Roger's name brought back memories."

"I see. So that's what upset you?"

"Yes, but I don't know why. It's been several weeks since we dated."

Jonathan was sure that wasn't the whole story, but he said, "I'm glad you are okay now. I have a couple of letters to write," and with that they went back to work.

Shortly after Phyllis left the police station, Detective O'Neal placed a call to Jeanne asking her to come in. "I have new information regarding the e-mails you have been receiving. It's time for you to respond to a couple of them, but I'd like you to do it here."

Jeanne knocked on Jonathan's door. "I had a call from Detective O'Neal asking me to come in. He has new information about my e-mails. Will it be okay for me to go now before I start my work in the library?"

"Of course. You need to get to the bottom of this mystery as soon as possible."

Upon arrival she stuck her head in the open door of the detective's office. "Good morning. I'm here."

"Thanks for coming in so soon. We'd like you to open your e-mails and send a response to the sender. First, I need to get our computer person here." He came immediately when called.

"Jeanne, this is Officer Martin who was able to identify the sender. Now we think it's time for you to take the next step."

Jeanne sat down at the computer. She clicked on read and saw the message *I may know where the car is.* "Well... this is interesting. What should I do?"

"We want to you answer him as you would to a person you might know."

Jeanne typed in *What car are you talking about? Where do you think it is?*

Surprisingly, there was an immediate response. *The car is a gray Mercedes-Benz. Is that yours?*

Yes, it may be. Do you know where it is?

I'm not sure, but I saw a lady drive it away from where it had been parked for a few days. When she returned she was with an Uber driver.

"*Thank you.* What else should I ask him?" she asked the detective.

"Ask if he'd be willing to come here and give us a full report."

She did, and the man, whom they assumed was Bob Baylord, hesitated, but finally responded affirmatively. He said he would come in later that afternoon.

When they retrieved the second message, Jeanne opened it to read *we need to talk.* To that one she replied that they would talk when he came to give his full statement to the police.

"Thank you, Jeanne, for coming in to deal with these. We may be coming to the end of the mystery. However, there are still some unanswered questions. I'm curious about the role Phyllis may be playing in these. Oh, not directly, but there seems to be a connection. We'll stay in touch."

It was nearly four o'clock when Jeanne had the call to meet with Detective O'Neal and the e-mail sender. When she walked into the detective's office, she was introduced to a handsome young man. "Jeanne, this is Bob Baylord. He has been trying to contact you, and now he has."

"I'm glad to finally meet you. I'm sorry I didn't respond to your message, but I never open an e-mail I don't recognize."

"I understand. Normally that's a good idea. I hope I didn't alarm you, but I wasn't even sure you were the right person. After reading about the missing car in the paper, I put it together with the information about the death, funeral and family and hoped you were the right person. It's easy to find almost anyone on the internet these days. That's what I did."

"Mr. Baylord has given me a full report about what he saw. He lives in the same neighborhood as Phyllis, but he doesn't know her. He observed the car sitting in the same place for several days. He said he saw a woman drive it away one morning. Go ahead and tell us what you were going to say."

"It was a Saturday morning and I was working in my yard so it was easy to observe the car. Within an hour she returned with an Uber driver. I've not seen the car since."

"Is that it?"

"Yes, except that I've been thinking about it—if there's a connection. My father lives alone out on the edge of town. He told me he just rented his garage to a lovely young lady. He sold his car because he is too old to drive and he could use the money. I agreed that it was a good idea."

"Could you give us his name and address? I'd like to check it out."

"Sure, but let me tell him. I don't what him to be surprised by police visitors."

"Of course. Tell him we will stop by sometime tomorrow morning. And thank you for coming in. You've provided some valuable information. An older woman who lives on that block gave us similar information about the car. It corroborates your story."

"It was nice to meet you, Jeanne, and I'm sorry if I alarmed you in any way," Bob said as he stood to leave.

"No problem. It has turned out to be an interesting, and hopefully a valuable contact. Oh, just one more question. Do you have a second e-mail address that you use?"

"Yes, I do. Why?"

"Because I received another e-mail from a different address that was confusing. Would you mind telling us what it is?"

"Of course." It was the one Jeanne had seen on her computer. Now they knew there was only one person sending her messages.

"That's a relief. I thought perhaps there was someone else being secretive. I'm glad to know it was only you."

CHAPTER 33

Wednesday morning, Jeanne looked forward to a day out of the office with Jonathan. She dressed casually in a skirt with a silk blouse and sandals, packed her favorite swim suit and left for the office.

When she walked in, Phyllis said, "My, you are more casual than usual.

"Yes, I was told to be casual today. We are going to a client's home.

Phyllis frowned, envious that she was not the one to go.

The drive out to the client's home took them through some of the most beautiful neighborhoods of Southern California. On the way Jeanne filled Jonathan in on the meetings with Detective O'Neal and the mysterious e-mail sender.

"Do you think Phyllis took the car?"

"It looks like it. We'll know after the police check with the owner of the garage."

They approached a large wrought iron gate at the end of the road. Jonathan reached for the call box to announce his arrival. The gate immediately swung open and quickly closed behind them. The long driveway led them up a circular drive surrounding a large fountain. Jeanne immediately thought of similar ones she had seen in Italy. Colorful flowers led them up a sculptured pathway to the front doors. Just as they stepped up to the entrance, the door swung open and they were greeted by the butler.

They were ushered into a large entry with a high ceiling in which was centered a beautiful stained glass sky light. It cast a rainbow of colors across the marble floor. They followed the butler to the reception room where they were announced to Mr. Marchant, the owner.

"It's good to see you again, sir," Jonathan said. "This is my assistant, Jeanne Blomgren."

"Welcome, Jeanne. I'm glad you could come. Come on out to the patio. It's a lovely day to be outside."

They walked through a couple of large rooms filled with elegant furniture and several original oil paintings, fresh flowers, and beautiful carpets. Jeanne was sure she had never been in such a magnificent home. Her eyes were wide open as she tried to take in everything. When they exited the house, the patio opened to an expanse of gardens around a large pool of crystal blue water. There was a small sculpture at one end from which clear water flowed.

A table with four chairs was waiting for them. "I've had the staff prepare a little refreshment. Help yourself to the lemonade. The pastries were baked this morning just for you," Mr. Marchant explained.

Jeanne sat where she could look out to the gardens. Jonathan sat across from her.

"Tell me, Jonathan, what have you been up to lately? Playing golf, tennis or just working?"

"Work has been rather busy so no golf recently. It is time to be out on the course again. Maybe we could schedule a game some Saturday."

"I'd like that. You just say when." Turning he asked, "Jeanne, how do you like working with Jonathan? Is he a severe task master?"

"Not at all. I'm really happy with the firm."

After a few more minutes of idle conversation, Mr. Marchant suggested they take a swim before lunch. "You did bring your suit?"

"Yes. Jonathan suggested that I should. Now that I see your beautiful pool, I'm glad I did."

"Even if you hadn't, I always have extra ones on hand." He led them to the rooms at the side of the pool where they could change. "There you go," he said as he opened the doors, one for each of them.

Even the pool's changing room was beautiful with bouquets of fresh flowers. *What elegance!* she thought. As soon as she donned her suit, she picked up a towel and exited to the pool. Jonathan was already in the water along with Mr. Marchant. She felt a little self-conscious, but she dropped her towel and dove into the water. She swam the length of the pool underwater and came up opposite the men. They looked at her with surprise.

"Where did you learn to swim like that?" Jonathan asked.

"I was on the girl's swim team in school. I wasn't particularly good at sports, but swimming was my thing."

"Well, I'm impressed."

She dove under the water again and swam back and forth with different strokes. The men just watched. "Well... aren't you going to swim?" she asked.

"Yes, of course," Mr. Marchant said as he swam off across the pool. Jonathan followed.

After several minutes of pool activity, Jeanne climbed out and retrieved her towel. She towel-dried her hair and finger-combed it. There was just enough natural curl to give her a carefree, casual look. By then the men made their last effort to swim the length of the pool, racing one another. They reached the end in a tie as near as Jeanne could tell.

"That felt wonderful," Jonathan declared. "Thanks for letting us come for a swim."

"I'm glad you enjoyed it. I did, too. Now, I'm ready for lunch. How about you?" He called, "Edward, we are ready for lunch." Then to his guests, "We'll dry off while we eat. Is that okay?" he asked looking at each one.

"Sure. I'm starving," Jonathan said as he donned his shirt, leaving it unbuttoned.

"Me, too," Jeanne agreed, putting on a light cover-up before she sat at the table.

A maid served vichyssoise to start, followed by a roast beef sandwich along with a small salad and a glass of a Rosé wine. When they had finished their lunch, Mr. Marchant said, "I understand you are partial to chocolate, Jeanne, and so we have a chocolate parfait for dessert." It arrived in a tall crystal glass showing layers of rich dark and light chocolate topped with whipped cream and chocolate sprinkles. With the first bite, Jeanne sighed and said, "Delicious."

Coffee was served in fine English bone cups. Since they both enjoyed black coffee they turned down the offer for cream or sugar, although Mr. Marchant enjoyed a dash of cream in his. When the second cup had been poured for each of them, Jonathan said, "This has been a delightful, relaxing time, but we do have a little business to attend to."

"Right," Mr. Marchant agreed. "Let me get my files. I have some information you need to see." He stood up and said, "Jeanne, you might like to get changed. I shan't be long."

Jeanne changed quickly. After a little repair of her makeup up she returned to the patio. "Would you mind if I walked in the garden while you tend to business?"

"But, Jeanne, you need to be with us. You'll be working on this with me. I've briefed Mr. Marchant and he knows we're a team," Jonathan explained. So Jeanne sat down ready to listen.

CHAPTER 34

On the drive home, Jeanne thanked Jonathan for including her in the meeting with Mr. Marchant. "It would be nice if we had more meetings like this one."

"Why is that?

"It was in such a beautiful setting. The swim and delicious lunch was more social than business. But I must admit, the business part was interesting, too. I had no idea you had such an important and wealthy client."

"Yes, he is an exceptional one. You can understand why we go to him, rather than he coming to our office. Tomorrow you can begin working on his case. I'm sure you understand it now and so can gather the required information. There's no rush, but I like to show efficiency. Mr. Marchant takes precedence over everyone else.

At her apartment, Jeanne checked for messages and retrieved one from Bob Baylord. It said *I told my father that you and Detective O'Neal would be stopping by to talk to him about the car in his garage. He said anytime would be fine.*

When she arrived at the office the next morning, she called Detective O'Neal gave him the message from Bob Baylord.

"Great. You need to go with me since you know the car. When can you get away?"

"I'm sure I can leave anytime. I'll just let Jonathan know. Will you pick me up?"

"Of course. Say, in about an hour?"

"Okay." She went to Jonathan. "Hi, I need a favor."

"Sure. What is it?"

"I had a message last night telling me we could check Mr. Baylord's garage anytime. Detective O'Neal will pick me up in an hour. Is that okay?"

"Naturally. We need to solve this mystery. Just check in with me when you return."

As she passed Phyllis's desk on her way to meet the detective, she said, "I should be back within two hours."

Detective O'Neal was waiting when she exited the building. As she greeted him, he said, "I am so excited to check out this garage. It may be what we've been looking for."

They stopped in front of the house and Jeanne observed, "The garage is out of sight from the street. A good place to hide a car."

When they ascended the steps, Detective O'Neal punched the doorbell. In a few seconds they heard shuffling behind the door and then it opened to an elderly man.

"Well, Officer, what can I do for you and this pretty young lady?"

"We came to talk to you about your garage."

"Oh, it's not for rent anymore."

"We aren't looking to rent it. I'm Detective O'Neal." He showed his badge. "We would like to know who rented it."

"Well, I can't tell you that. First, I don't remember the name of the young lady, and second, I told her it would remain locked. And besides I don't have a key for the lock."

"No problem," Detective O'Neal said. "Did she give you a check in payment?"

"No, she paid in cash for six months."

"I see..." He waited for a few seconds and then continued. "Would you mind looking at a picture—just to see if you recognize her?"

"Sure." He took the photo and held it up so he could peer through his glasses. "Yes, that's the lady who rented my garage. Red hair, and the prettiest green eyes. She's a beauty." He handed the photo back to the detective. "Is she in trouble?"

Ignoring the question, Detective O'Neal asked, "Did you see the car she put in the garage?"

"No. I never saw her bring a car in, but she could have done it when I wasn't looking."

"Would you be so kind as to show us your garage?"

"Well, I don't know what good that will do. You can't see in."

"That's okay. We'd like to see it."

"All right. I'll meet you out back. Just walk around there," he said as he pointed to the side of the house and closed the door.

Detective O'Neal and Jeanne were by the garage door looking at the lock when the owner opened the back door and toddled out leaning on a cane.

"Like I said, you can't see anything. Just an old garage."

The detective said to Jeanne, "It's just a standard lock. I may have a key that will open it. We'll need a court order, but that's not a problem." He turned to Mr. Baylord and said, "Thank you. You've been very helpful. We will be back to open the garage, but we'll call you first. May I have your phone number?"

"Of course." He gave him his number. "Shall I let the young lady know about your visit in case I hear from her?"

The detective quickly said, "No, please don't. Now that we know who she is we will contact her. Don't worry about it." They turned to leave.

When they got back to the car, Jeanne said, "At least we know Phyllis really did rent a garage. Do you think it was for a friend?"

"No, I don't, but we'll know for sure when we open the garage. As soon as I get a warrant, I'll let you know. You need to be with me to identify the car if it is Roger's."

Jeanne asked, "What do we do if it is his car? Well, technically it's mine. Do you arrest her?"

"Of course. She would be guilty of stealing a car, and that's a crime."

"I wonder how she thought she could get away with it?"

"Obviously, she didn't think it through. Now this makes me wonder if she may have killed Roger at the beach. Maybe we have uncovered a crime more serious than auto theft."

"You're right. How else could she have gotten the car?"

As soon as Detective O'Neal dropped Jeanne at her office, he went directly to the court house to request a search warrant.

Jeanne immediately went to Jonathan's office and knocked on his door. "I'm back."

"Come in and close the door. Now tell me. Did you find the car in the garage?"

Jeanne began the report. "She chose a good location. The garage is out of sight from the street and has no windows, so we couldn't see in. The owner, Mr. Baylord, is an older man, very nice and trusting. He recognized Phyllis from her picture and said she was the one who rented his garage. However, he never saw her bring a car in."

"So what's your next step?"

"Detective O'Neal is getting search warrant to open the garage. If my car is in there, she will be arrested for auto theft."

"And I will be without a secretary," he said with a frown.

The next morning the phone rang as soon as Jeanne entered her office. It was the detective.

" I've got the search warrant. Can you get away in about an hour?"

"Of course. I'll see you out front at ten fifteen."

Now she had to tell Jonathan she'd be going out with Detective O'Neal to verify the contents of the garage. She stuck her head in Jonathan's open door and said, "Just to remind you about my appointment this morning. I'll be leaving a little after ten."

"That's fine. Is everything going okay on the Marchant case?"

"Yes, but he referred to something from earlier dates and I don't have it in the current files. Are there some older ones?"

"Probably. I'll have Phyllis find them and give you everything for Mr. Marchant." He called to Phyllis and told her to give Jeanne all of the Marchant files.

"But... Why...," she stammered.

"Just do it," Jonathan said firmly.

"All right. It will take a few minutes. I'll bring them to you when I get them all together. Just don't get them mixed up."

"I'll be very careful. And thanks," Jeanne said with a smile. *Little does Phyllis know this might be her last day.*

In a few minutes, Phyllis appeared with a handful of files. "Here you are. This is all I could find," she said as she dropped them on Jeanne's desk. "Have fun."

Jeanne spent a few minutes looking at them and putting them in chronological order, then she left to meet the detective. "I should be back in about an hour or so," she told Phyllis.

Detective O'Neal was waiting at the front door. "Sometimes I hate this job," the detective said. "Well... not the entire job—just this part of arresting criminals, especially when they are as attractive as Phyllis. She seems like a decent person."

Jeanne quietly responded, "Don't forget this decent person tried to kill me."

"Yes. That has become part of her file. We may have to prove she did it intentionally."

As soon as they parked the car at Mr. Baylord's home, he opened the front door and directed them around back. "Did you get the warrant?" he asked.

"Sure did," Detective O'Neal replied. He handed it to him with flourish and waited while he looked at it.

When he decided it was correct, he said, "It's all yours."

The detective unlocked the padlock and removed it, lifted the latch and easily opened the door. There in front of them was the silver Mercedes-Benz. The detective said, "I need to check the registration for confirmation." In the glove compartment he found the registration slip made out to Roger Anders. He stepped out of the car and said, "Well, Jeanne, I think we've found your car."

To Mr. Baylord he said, "This car was stolen. It really belongs to this lady. It was her husband's car until he died several weeks ago. Now it belongs to her."

'Well, I'll be," Mr. Baylord said in surprise. "And she was such a nice young lady who I was happy to help. Does this put me in trouble?"

"Not as long as you were completely unaware of the lady's intentions. However, you may be asked to testify in court."

"Oh, dear," he said looking worried. "I've never done anything like that."

"That's okay," Detective O'Neal assured him, "we'll let you know when, or if it's necessary. Meanwhile, we'll leave the car where it is for now. At some point we will pick it up, but not today."

"Okay. I feel terrible about this, but how was I to know?"

"You couldn't have known. Don't worry about it. You did nothing wrong."

Detective O'Neal replaced the lock. "Please don't tell anyone about this—not even your son. We will provide him with all the information he needs to know."

"Okay. My lips are sealed. Should I return the money she paid me for the months not used?"

"No, you may keep it to cover your inconvenience."

"Thanks. I appreciate it," Mr. Baylord said gratefully.

"And thank you for your cooperation," Detective O'Neal said as he tipped his hat. "We will let you know when the car will be picked up."

As they drove away, Jeanne asked, "So what do you do now?"

"We'll need to search the car for evidence to connect her to the car, such as clothing, fingerprints, anything that would tie her to the car."

"So we can't assume Phyllis is the thief; we have to prove it?" she asked.

"Yes, that's right. No one saw her drive it into the garage. I will arrange to have the car picked up as soon as I have talked to Phyllis. I'd like to have the keys to it."

"Will you contact her at the office, or would you like to have her home address?"

"Yes, I would like her residence address. I'll go there this evening."

"As soon as I get to the office, I'll e-mail it to you."

Detective O'Neal headed back to his station. His first task was to request charges to be filed against Phyllis. He also made arrangements for the car to be picked up the next afternoon, after he talked with Phyllis. He assigned a couple of his deputies to accompany him that evening.

Jeanne stuck her head in Jonathan's office and asked, "Have you got a minute?"

"Of course. I always have time for you," he answered with a big grin. "Come in and give me a report on your findings."

Jeanne told him the car in the garage was indeed Roger's; now hers, of course. They chose to leave it there until tomorrow. Today would continue normally. "So until tomorrow nothing will be done. Phyllis is not suspicious."

CHAPTER 35

Detective O'Neal, along with two deputies, walked up to Phyllis's house. He punched the bell and waited. The door opened only a small crack, held by a chain, and one eye looked out. "Good evening, Phyllis. I'm Detective O'Neal. I wonder if we could have a minute of your time? I have a couple of questions for you."

"Oh, I guess so.."

"May we come in?"

She unlatched the door and opened it for them to enter. "What can I do for you?" she asked. "Is there a problem?"

"No, I don't think so. However, I think you may have information to help us. May we sit down?" he asked.

"Certainly." She moved the newspapers from the sofa. "May I get you something? Water or a soda?"

"No thanks, we shouldn't be long," the detective said getting down to business. "We need to talk to you about the garage you rented for your friend's car. Did you rent it from Mr. Baylord?"

"Yes. Why do you ask?" Her heart started to pound and she became slightly agitated.

"His son asked him about you because he was concerned about his father, who is older, and that he may not have considered the implications of renting to a stranger."

"I'm sure there was no reason to be concerned. I paid him in cash for six months."

"Yes, that's what he said. Does your friend live nearby? Mr. Baylord said no one has taken the car out, as far as he knows. He was concerned that if it wasn't driven, the battery would die."

"Oh, I'm not sure what my friend is doing. It's not my concern now."

"Perhaps you could give me your friend's name and I'll check on her—or him." After a few seconds' pause, he asked, "Do you happen to have another set of keys to the car? If so, we could check on it to be sure it's operating okay."

"That would be a big help," she said as she stood up. "I'll get them for you." She handed the keys to the detective and said, "Thanks for your concern. I appreciate it. You can let me know what you find." He took the keys and thanked her for her cooperation.

"Well, she certainly was nonchalant about it," he said as they got in their car. "If she's guilty of taking the car, she is covering it very well."

"The owner of the garage identified her as the one who rented it. If it was for a friend, who is the friend?"

"That's what we need to find out. First thing tomorrow morning, we will start investigating. Personally, I don't think we will find a friend."

Since it was still light, Detective O'Neal was eager to search the car for evidence. "What do you say we go to the garage right now and see what we can find?"

"I'm game—and curious. Let's do it."

They drove directly to Mr. Baylord's place and entered the garage. Since they still had the original search warrant they set to work, looking for anything that would tie Phyllis to the car. It was quite clean—no garbage, no papers, no personal items. However, Deputy Connors found a scarf in the glove compartment that definitely belonged to a lady. "If this was Roger's car, to whom does the scarf belong?"

Detective O'Neal took the scarf, bagged it and said, "This may be all we need." They closed and locked the garage and left.

The next morning, Deputy Connors began searching for the friend. He talked to Phyllis's neighbors, who never saw anyone with her. He talked to Judith at the office who said Phyllis had mentioned a friend, but she never said a name. In fact, no one he talked to thought Phyllis had any friends that she saw socially. The conclusion was that she made up the story about renting the garage for a friend. He did discover that she rented the garage the same week the car was moved from the street near her house. Was it a coincidence? He didn't think so. He gave his report to Detective O'Neal who agreed there was enough evidence for further investigation.

Having arranged to have the car removed from the garage, he met the tow truck at the house. He gave the keys to the driver. After the car was gone, he gave the lock and key to Mr. Baylord and said, "Thanks so much for your help. You may have these for your next tenant."

"Thanks, but I'm not sure I want to rent it again."

"I can understand that." After a brief pause he said, "I will be in touch with you again only if we go to court."

"I hope you don't have to, but I will be available if necessary." He slowly closed the door.

Back at the precinct, Detective O'Neal put a call in to Jonathan. "We have the car in police custody now. We did find a scarf in it that may belong to Phyllis. I would like to have her come in for questioning. Could she come in now?"

Jonathan transferred his call to Phyllis. He waited until she came to him and asked if he would take her to see Detective O'Neal. Since it was approaching the end of the day, he agreed.

"I have no idea what he wants," Phyllis said sounding worried. "I've told him everything I know."

"He's just trying to clarify some details. You know how they are—just being thorough."

As soon as they arrived at the police station, they were ushered to the Interrogation Room. Detective O'Neal entered and greeted them cordially. "Thanks for coming in so quickly," he said in a friendly voice. "First of all, I wanted to tell you we found the car in good condition. No problem in getting it started."

"That's good. But then it hasn't been there all that long."

"Phyllis, we have been trying to locate your friend without success. Surely you must have a contact phone number, at least a name."

With that, Phyllis became visibly uneasy. "Of course, I probably have it some place at home. Why do you need it?"

"We found an item in the car that we thought your friend might want."

"What? ...What is it?"

He reached down for his briefcase and took the bag out that held the scarf they had found in the glove compartment. He held it up. Phyllis turned pale and inhaled so quickly she choked.

"Where did you get that?" she asked angrily.

"It was in the glove compartment of the Mercedes-Benz. Is it yours?"

She glared at it as if it were a dangerous creature. "I don't know. No... it can't be. It must belong to my friend."

"The friend no one can find? Phyllis, I'll ask you again, is this your scarf?"

She looked away, not wanting to face anyone. "Jonathan, please take me home."

"I'm sorry," Detective O'Neal said, "but I will need you to be available for more questioning. I'll let you go now, but don't leave town." He stood up and nodded to Jonathan.

While driving Phyllis home, Jonathan asked her, "Is that scarf yours?"

"It might be. I had one similar to it," she said defensively. "What difference does it make?"

"It might make the difference of you being guilty or innocent. I think you had better tell the truth and answer the detective's questions honestly."

A little more meekly, she said, "Yeah, I guess so. I just hate being accused of something he can't prove I did."

"I don't think he was accusing you of anything." He dropped her off, saying, "See you tomorrow." Jonathan thought, you acted guilty of something. But what? Is there more to your story than just hiding the car?

CHAPTER 36

The next day, Detective O'Neal told Jonathan he thought they had enough evidence to arrest Phyllis for car theft, which was a felony. Her response to the scarf found in the car convinced him she was guilty. He discussed the best way to proceed. "I could just go to the office when Phyllis is at work and arrest her, but I think it would be better to do it a little more quietly. There will be a couple of officers with me when we make the arrest. We have no way of knowing how she will respond to being taken away by police officers."

Jonathan assured the detective he would help in any way he could.

Later in the day the phone rang, and since Phyllis was out, Jeanne picked it up, "Mr. Crown's office."

"Hello, may I please speak with Jonathan Crown?"

"Detective O'Neal, is that you? This is Jeanne."

"Oh, yes. Actually I'm glad you are there. I should speak with Mr. Crown first, however."

"I'll put him on." She handed the phone to Jonathan and closed the door.

"Yes, Detective, what is it?" He listened a few seconds and said, "I'll put us on speaker for Jeanne."

Detective O'Neal began to tell his plan. "In deference to you, and others in the office, could you ask Phyllis to remain for a few minutes after the others have left?"

"Certainly," Jonathan said. "Should Jeanne be here, too?"

"That might be a good idea. If you can have a reason for them both to stay late, that would cover our arrival, say about a quarter past five?" he asked.

"Sure. I can do that."

Just as he hung up, Phyllis returned to her desk. "Sorry to be out for a few minutes. Do you need anything?" she asked Jonathan as she watched Jeanne leave his office.

"Not right now, but I think I may need you a little later."

Jeanne began reading the old Marchant files. She had a couple of questions, but decided to hold them until the end of the day. She stopped by Phyllis's desk a little before five. "Phyllis, as you know, I'm working on Mr. Marchant's project. I have a couple of questions." She was sure Jonathan heard her. "Could you come to my office and see if you can help me?"

"Well, can't it wait until tomorrow? It's nearly five o'clock."

"It shouldn't take you long. I just need some information about his property. You probably know right where it is."

Jonathan poked his head out his door and said, "It's okay, Phyllis. It will make up for the few minutes you were out earlier."

Phyllis grudgingly rose from her desk and followed Jeanne. She sat by her desk with her back to the door as Jeanne slid the files over to her. Jeanne told her what she was looking for and that something seemed to be missing. As they had their heads together looking in the files, Detective O'Neal quietly approached the doorway. When he was standing in the center of the door, Jeanne could see two deputies directly behind him. She nodded to him and rose to her feet.

"Thanks, Phyllis. I think we should quit for the day," Jeanne said so that the officers would know it was Phyllis sitting there.

Before Phyllis could turn around, Officer O'Neal stepped into the office and said, "Phyllis, I'm placing you under arrest for being in possession of a stolen vehicle. Please put your hands behind you." He quickly tried to place handcuffs on her wrists.

Phyllis opened her eyes in surprise. "What are you doing?" she shouted. She lashed out at the detective with her one free hand. She kicked at him and screamed, "You can't do this. You don't know anything." Her eyes flashed green fire.

The two deputies entered the room and tried to subdue Phyllis, holding both of her arms so she could not strike the detective. "I'm innocent. I've done nothing wrong." She kept screaming and fighting to get free. They finally got the handcuffs on both wrists.

"We're taking you to the station where you will be booked for stealing a Mercedes-Benz from this lady," Detective O'Neal said as he looked at Jeanne. Jonathan came out of his office as they led her toward the elevator.

"You beast," she screamed at the policeman. "You're hurting me." She saw Jonathan and called, "Jonathan, help me. Tell them I'm innocent," she begged.

"Sorry. I can't do anything now," He turned and went to Jeanne. "Are you okay?" .

"Yes, but that was a bit upsetting. I've never seen her so angry. She scares me. That was a good idea to have them come after hours. I wouldn't have liked the other employees to see or hear that."

"I'm sorry to see her like that, but she broke the law. The only thing I can do is get her a criminal lawyer. I'll have someone stop in to see her tomorrow. We'll let her cool off tonight."

"I know you care about her," Jeanne said. "This must be difficult for you. She may want you to represent her. Can you?"

"No, I'm her boss, and besides, I'm not a criminal lawyer. She needs someone who knows how to defend her. Let's just go home. We'll deal with everything tomorrow."

"I'm for that," Jeanne said with a sigh. "It's been a rather tense day. I'm glad it's over. I am sorry for Phyllis, but she brought it on herself. I just don't understand why she took the car, and then hid it in a rented garage. What was she thinking?"

"Obviously, she wasn't thinking clearly. Perhaps we'll get some answers when she goes to trial," Jonathan responded. "Come on. I'll walk you out." They were the last ones to leave.

Jeanne was glad to get home to her quiet apartment and have a glass of her favorite wine. She tried not to think about Phyllis, but she kept replaying the scene in the office when Detective O'Neal made the arrest. Phyllis was clearly out of control with anger. She must have known

Jeanne was in on the plan. Fortunately, Jonathan stayed in his office and so he played no part in the arrest which went off rather smoothly.

The next morning dawned with a few clouds in the eastern sky which dispelled multiple colors across a blue-gray background. When Jeanne arrived at the office, Phyllis's desk was empty and Jonathan was not in yet. It seemed strange to have no one to greet her. She decided to see Judy.

"Good morning, Jeanne. What's up?" Judy asked.

"You missed the excitement yesterday. Detective O'Neal found my car in the garage Phyllis rented and so he and two officers arrested her right here."

"No! Sorry I missed it."

"She was very upset and more angry than I have ever seen her. It was not a pleasant sight. We arranged for Phyllis to stay a little late. It was very thoughtful of them to do it after everyone had gone."

"Now Jonathan is without a secretary. Will you fill in for a while?"

"Maybe, but I'm not really a secretary." She saw Jonathan come in. "We'll talk later."

"Good morning, Jonathan. What can I do to help you today?"

"Well, first thing I need to advise the partners about Phyllis. Could you call each one and ask them to come to my office immediately?"

"Sure, I'm on it," and she went to her office.

In a few minutes both partners arrived showing concern. Jonathan said he had some unfortunate news to share with them. He told them about the arrest made last night and that Phyllis was no longer employed by the firm. It took him a few minutes to explain what had been happening and assured them that everything was under control. "The only other employees who know about Phyllis are Jeanne and Judith. We've all agreed it is best to say that she is on an extended leave for personal reasons."

Jonathan's first task was to find a secretary. He called Marianne, who had been on leave, and asked her if she would consider coming back a little earlier than planned. He didn't give her any of the details, but said he really could use her help.

"How soon do you need me?" she asked.

"As soon as you can arrange it. Meanwhile, I have an assistant who can help me."

"I need to make some arrangements, but I think it may be possible. I'll get back to you tomorrow."

"That's fine. I'll appreciate it immensely. Until tomorrow…"

Then he called Judy and asked her not to mention anything about Phyllis to anyone other than to confirm that she is on an extended personal leave. The next call was to an attorney friend to see if he would consider taking Phyllis as a client. He agreed, and so Jonathan gave him all the details about her recent arrest. He said he was not to be involved in any way. He asked him to visit Phyllis soon at the jail and let her know he was her attorney. With than done, he released the whole incident from his mind.

Jeanne settled into the Marchant project. She felt relief now that Phyllis was incarcerated in the local jail. She had only one question on her mind—*When am I going to get my car?* The phone rang breaking into her thoughts. It was Detective O'Neal. "Good morning, Detective. How are you this morning?"

"I'm well, thank you. I wanted to update you on Phyllis. She has been placed in a cell by herself since she was highly agitated last evening. We were concerned about the safety of others, as well as herself. Her attorney has just arrived, and she has been giving him a bad time. She says she wants only Jonathan. She won't even talk to this one. By the way, his name is Gary Warner. Do you know him?"

"No, I don't, but if Jonathan sent him, I'm sure he is good. As you know, Jonathan is not a criminal attorney so he would not handle Phyllis's case. Doesn't she understand that?"

"No, I've explained that to her, but she won't accept it. She's not being rational. Maybe we'll just let her sit alone for a while until she is ready to talk to Mr. Warner."

CHAPTER 37

Jonathan took the call from the attorney. "What have you gotten me into?" he asked. "I've never had a client who is so angry."

"I'm sorry. I had no idea she would respond like that."

"She says she will talk only to you."

"But we both know I'm not a criminal attorney, and since I'm her boss, I can't represent her. She has to understand that."

"Perhaps if you join me and explain that when I meet with her next, she will accept me."

Jonathan hesitated and finally said, "Okay. When do you want me there?"

"Since this is Friday, and I'd like to have her post bail before the weekend, could we do it around noon today?"

He glanced at his schedule and agreed he'd be there at noon. He wasn't eager to face Phyllis. If she thought he was partially responsible for her arrest, she would undoubtedly take her wrath out on him. Jonathan told Jeanne he was meeting with Phyllis and her attorney at the jail at noon. "She is not willing for Mr. Warner to represent her as her attorney."

"But surely she can understand that you can't be her attorney," Jeanne said.

"You and I know that, but she is not accepting it."

Mr. Warner was waiting for him in the lobby of the police station. "Thanks for meeting me. I've never had a client who was as hostile as this young lady. She seems very devoted to you."

"She has been working for me for about a year. In all of that time, I've never done anything to encourage more than a professional working relationship."

"Office romances can be very difficult and usually result in disappointment for both parties. You were wise not to encourage her. However, in my brief encounter with her, I feel she believes there is more to your relationship. I just want to be sure there isn't."

Jonathan responded firmly, "I can assure you there isn't, and there never has been nor will there ever be."

"Good... so shall we go talk with the lioness?" Gary asked with a smile.

The sergeant escorted them to the interview room where Phyllis sat impatiently waiting. As soon as they entered the room, she stood up and rushed to Jonathan opening her arms for a hug. The sergeant quickly stepped in and said, "No physical contact is allowed. Step back and sit down."

She reluctantly did as she was told and said, "Thanks for coming, Jonathan. I don't know what I will do without you to help me."

"Phyllis, I cannot be your attorney. First of all, as your boss, I could not represent you. But more importantly, I am not a criminal attorney. You need someone to represent you who knows how to handle felony cases. I referred Gary Warner to you because I believe he is the best, but you must cooperate with him. Tell him the truth about everything." Jonathan paused and said, "If you wish I will sit in for a few minutes while you start talking with Mr. Warner."

"Yes, please do. I will feel more comfortable with you here," she said contritely.

"Is that okay with you, Gary?" he asked.

"Certainly. However, I cannot get into the facts of the case with you. I must retain the client-attorney privilege."

"I understand. Just tell me when to leave."

Phyllis interjected, "But I don't want him to leave. Please let him stay." Her voice took on a whining quality as she begged like a little child.

The men looked questioningly at each other with surprise at her change of demeanor. The angry, hostile woman had become a helpless, sniffling child-like person.

"All right, Jonathan can stay while you and I get acquainted," Mr. Warner said. He wanted her to know that he was in charge. Jonathan nodded his head as Gary began with simple questions.

"Would you like a glass of water before we get started? It's rather warm in here."

"Yes, please," she said with her eyes downcast.

The sergeant was asked to bring water for each of them. "Now, Phyllis, is there anything you need that Jonathan could bring you? Something to read, or...?"

"No. I won't be here long enough. You're going to get me out of here." Her angry demeanor returned as quickly as it had left.

"Yes, we will be working on that. Now, I would like to get to know you. How long have you been working for Mr. Crown? Where did you work before? Do you like your work assignments?" He continued with open ended questions about her personal life, friends, activities, hobbies, and such. She gave short, curt answers to all of his questions. It gave him a general idea of her personality and interests and showed what a limited life she led. He shared a little about himself, as well, trying to make her willing to be more open with him.

"Do you know why you are here?"

"Yes, I'm accused of stealing a car, but I didn't."

"Right now, I'd like you tell me about the car. What kind is it?"

She hesitated, and asked, "What do you mean? What kind? It's a car."

"Is it a sedan, a convertible, what make? A Chevrolet, a Cadillac, a Ford, or...?"

"I own a convertible. It's red." That was all she said.

Mr. Warner could see that this was not going to be easy. He looked at Jonathan who nodded, looked at his watch, and said, "I need to get back to the office for an appointment with a client." He stood up and said to Phyllis, "You're doing fine. Just work with Mr. Warner, please. He will keep in touch with me."

"Don't go," Phyllis cried. "I need you."

"No, you need an attorney who can help you," and with that he left the room.

Mr. Warner said nothing. He waited silently. It was quite a while before she even looked at her attorney. He was writing notes on his tablet, ignoring her completely.

"What are you writing?" she asked in an angry voice.

"Just notes on our conversation so far. Is there anything else you'd like to tell me?"

"I'll tell you nothing. I'll talk only to Jonathan." With that she turned away.

"That's okay." He closed his notebook and put his pen in his pocket. He stood up and said, "I'll leave you now to go back to your cell. I'll check in with you tomorrow when you might be ready to talk to me."

"No, don't leave me here. I want to go home," she whined.

"Sorry. It's too late today. I'll see you tomorrow," and he left her with the deputy. He really hated to leave her, but she had to be reasonable and accept him as her attorney. Perhaps after one more night in lockup she would be ready to cooperate.

When he returned to his office, he called Jonathan to report on what had transpired. He was assured that he had made the right choice. "Jonathan," he said, "I really think Phyllis is not rational. I think she needs to be seen by a psychiatrist. What do you think?"

"I agree, but do you think it is too soon? Perhaps after she knows you a little better she will begin to cooperate."

"That's possible. Let's wait and see how she is tomorrow. We'll discuss it after my next session with her."

"Okay. Call me then," Jonathan suggested. He was concerned about her mental state, but he had to leave everything up to Gary. He was a good attorney, and so he would trust him to do his best for her.

Jeanne worked on Mr. Marchant's account which was detailed and confusing. Once she sorted chronologically through the files, things began to make sense. By the end of the day, she felt she had made great progress and would soon design the next steps for him to take.

She leaned back in her chair and took a deep breath, letting it out slowly. She realized her body was tired from leaning over her desk for hours. What she needed was a good massage. Just then Jonathan poked his head in her door and asked if she was okay.

"Yes, but I am tired. I was just thinking about getting a massage when I leave."

"I know a good masseuse if you need one."

"Yes, I'd appreciate a referral."

In a minute he returned with a business card which he handed to Jeanne. "He is excellent, and if you wish, he can come to you. His motto is "Have table, will travel."

"What a great idea. I will give him a call. Thank you."

Jonathan hesitated in the doorway. "Jeanne, it's been a stressful week. How about if we go to our club for dinner tonight?"

Jeanne said with a smile, "How do you always know what I need? I'd love to go to dinner after I get a massage."

Fortunately, when she called, the masseuse was available and willing to meet her as soon as she got home. She left the office eager to have a relaxing treatment before going out with Jonathan. She had just time enough for a quick shower when the bell rang. Alexander announced a gentleman with some equipment had arrived.

"Please send him right up."

An hour later she was relaxed and ready for the evening. She dressed thoughtfully, wanting to please Jonathan. She chose a blue-green silk dress that reminded her of water in a lake when she moved. Silver sandals, a silver clutch and silver hoop earrings completed her ensemble. She did a quick turn in the full-length mirror and was satisfied with what she saw. She hoped Jonathan would be, also.

She opened the door to see Jonathan standing there with a single white rose. "Oh, it's beautiful," she exclaimed. She stepped aside and took the rose from his outstretched hand. She put it to her nose and inhaled deeply, enjoying the fragrance. "Would you like a glass of wine before we go?" she asked as she put the rose in a silver vase.

"Yes, that would be lovely. May I pour it for us?"

"There's a bottle open in the refrigerator. Will that one be all right?"

He took the bottle out and saw it was her favorite Pinot Grigio. "Of course. It's perfect."

Jeanne sat the rose on the table by the sofa and Jonathan carried the two glasses of wine to the living room. He handed one to her and said, "A toast to us."

"To us," and they took a sip. They sat side by side enjoying the evening view of the landscape. No need for conversation. It felt good to be quiet.

CHAPTER 38

Having dinner at The Club was becoming a regular event, which Jeanne enjoyed immensely. They spent a few minutes catching up, and Jeanne mentioned that Mark had called. "I told him about my mysterious e-mails."

"Yes, I'm glad some of the mystery has been solved with the identification of Bob Baylord's e-mails and the location of your car."

Jeanne was pensive as she asked, "How was Phyllis when you saw her at the jail?"

"Very defensive. She is not cooperating with her attorney at all. We were hoping to get her out on bail this weekend, but decided it was best not to. In fact, Gary saw her Saturday morning, and she wouldn't even talk to him."

"In a way I feel sorry for her. Have they made arrangements for her to see the psychiatrist?"

"I'm not sure, but I'm hoping she will meet with Dr. Meredith soon."

"I wonder if she will even talk to him?"

"It will be interesting to see what transpires," Jonathan stated. "Meanwhile, let's just enjoy our time tonight."

Monday morning dawned with a cloud-filled sky. *Just like I feel*, Jeanne thought as she looked out on the park. However, the day brightened when she answered a phone call from Mandy. "Hello, Sweetheart. It's good to hear your voice so early in the morning. Is everything all right?"

"Yes, of course. In fact, everything is wonderful. First of all, I'm getting all A's, and second, I've met a wonderful classmate and we're dating. I may bring him with me for Thanksgiving."

"Well, that sounds serious. Of course, I'd love to meet him. What's his name?"

"Jackson. Jackson Wellborn. Actually, Jackson Wellborn the Third. Isn't that romantic?"

"Yes, it does sound very sophisticated. Where is he from?"

"Mom, I have to get to class. I'll tell you all about him when I see you at Thanksgiving." With that she was gone, leaving Jeanne with numerous questions. She decided to call Mark and find out if he knew Jackson.

"Mark, I just had a call from Mandy. Do you know her friend, Jackson Wellborn?"

"I've met him. He seems like a good enough bloke. Why do you ask?"

"Well, Mandy says she plans to bring him with her for Thanksgiving. Do you think they are serious?" Jeanne asked with concern.

"They haven't been dating very long so it can't be very serious. I'll talk to him and see what he has to say. Will that help?"

"Yes, of course. I just want her to be happy, but careful."

"I understand. Gotta go. I can't be late for class."

Jeanne trusted Mark to look out for his sister. Thanksgiving was not far away, and she was eager to have them both home for a few days at the beach house.

She tackled the work on her desk, finished preparing her report and e-mailed it to Mr. Marchant. She printed a copy for Jonathan and went to his office to give it to him. She stopped abruptly when she saw a strange woman sitting at Phyllis's desk.

"Hi, I'm Jeanne. Who are you?"

"Hi, I'm Marianne, Mr. Crown's secretary."

Just then Jonathan appeared. "I see you two have met. Sorry I didn't get a chance to introduce you." To Jeanne he said, "Marianne was my secretary before Phyllis. I encouraged her to return." He turned to Marianne and said, "Jeanne is my new assistant. Well, not real new; she has been here for a few weeks."

"Jonathan, here is a copy of the report I sent to Mr. Marchant." Jeanne handed it to him, and with that she was gone leaving the secretary following her with her eyes.

"She's lovely. Where did you find her?" Marianne asked.

"It's a long story, which I may tell you some day," he said with a secretive smile.

"I look forward to hearing it." She spent the next several minutes reorganizing everything in the desk, removing all of Phyllis's personal items and putting them in a box. She was glad to be back in her own space and working with Jonathan again. The time off to recuperate was great, but she was anxious about getting back to work. Jonathan had told her only a little about why Phyllis had to leave, but she was sure to learn more as she got to know Jeanne.

Marianne called to her as she passed her desk and said, "You have a message from a Mr. Marchant." She handed the note to Jeanne.

"Thank you," and continued to her office. As soon as she sat down, she looked at the note which only read *call when convenient*. She couldn't tell if he was happy or upset with her work. She immediately dialed his number.

"Hello, Mr. Marchant. This is Jeanne. You called?"

"Yes. Thanks for getting back to me so quickly. I just wanted to tell you I read through all the material you sent and I'm very pleased with the thoroughness of your work. I'm looking forward to receiving the second installment."

"Thank you. I'm glad I could be of help. I should be finished with the next installment by the end of the day. Tomorrow at the latest."

Jeanne sat quietly enjoying the feeling of satisfaction of a job well done.

Phyllis had spent her third night locked up by herself in a small, sterile cell at the local jail. *Surely, she will be willing to talk today*, Detective O'Neal thought to himself. He greeted her in a very pleasant manner, asking how she was.

"What do you think?" she said angrily. "I've been in here without proper food, bored to death, not able to sleep on such an uncomfortable bed... Where is Jonathan? He's supposed to be taking care of me?"

"Jonathan is not your attorney. You need to talk with Gary Warner, who is your attorney." After waiting quietly for a little while, he said, "We have arranged for you to have a visitor. Dr. Meredith will be in this morning."

"Is Dr. Meredith a man or a woman?"

"Why do you ask? Does it make a difference?" the detective inquired.

"I suppose not. I do like men better than women—generally."

"Then you are in luck. Dr. Meredith is a man, so you should get along very well." With that he left her alone.

She sat on her bunk wondering why a man she didn't know would be coming to see her. But *anyone would be better than being all alone in here,* she thought. She stretched out on her bunk and stared at the ceiling. *I've got to get out of here. Maybe I can get my visitor to help.* She began to think of a plan to use Dr. Meredith to help her. She was just about to fall asleep when there was a knock on her cell door. She sat up with a start and waited as the key in the lock turned and the door opened.

"Hello," a very masculine voice said. "Would you like a visitor?"

Phyllis was surprised to see a very well dressed, good looking man appear. He was quite tall, dark hair and eyes as black as coal. However, they were not menacing. They had a sparkle with a hint of humor in them. She immediately stood up and responded with a flirtatious smile. "Well, well... Aren't you a welcomed sight? May I assume you are Dr. Meredith?" she asked.

"Yes, I'm your visitor today." He shook her hand and said, "So glad to meet you, Phyllis," as he observed her carefully. "May I sit down?"

She pointed to the one chair in the room, and she sat on the edge of the bed. "Make yourself comfortable. At least as comfortable as one can be in a cell," she said with dry humor. "So what are you a doctor of?"

"I'm a doctor of psychiatry. Does that surprise you?"

"I'm not sure. I've never met one before. I guess that means you study one's brain?"

"It's really more than that. We evaluate the entire person and help them develop and maintain a healthy mind. My first assignment is to determine if you need one."

"A psychiatrist, you mean?"

He nodded affirmatively.

"How do you do that?" she asked with sincere interest.

"We talk. We get acquainted and share information. That's the easy part. So... let's get acquainted. Tell me about yourself."

"You first. Tell me about yourself," she responded. "I would like to know you before I tell you everything."

"Fair enough," and he began telling her about why he became a psychiatrist, where he got his degree, where he had lived before coming to Southern California, what his favorite foods were. As they talked, Phyllis began sharing a little about her life. After an hour, he said he had to leave, but that he would like to come back again to visit.

"You can come anytime," Phyllis said. "I think I'm going to enjoy our visits." She gave him a warm smile as he took her hand to say goodbye.

He was let out and Phyllis sat down to reflect on their visit. She determined that talking with a psychiatrist was rather pleasant. She looked forward to his next visit.

CHAPTER 39

Upon returning to his office, Dr. Meredith transcribed his notes. He called Detective O'Neal and told him that he felt he had gained Phyllis's confidence and in future visits he would be able to delve into her mental state. Nothing was obvious at this point.

In the afternoon, Attorney Gary Warner approached Phyllis. She was in a much better mood and greeted him saying, "We need to talk."

He was surprised but enthusiastically agreed. "I understand you had a visitor this morning. How did that go?"

"Very well. I like Dr. Meredith... and he is very good looking," she added with a half-smile. "We had a good visit. He's coming back tomorrow."

"I'm glad to hear it. Now... if I'm going to help you, you need to tell me everything about why you are in here. You need to be honest, holding nothing back. I needn't tell you that everything you say in here is privileged information between me, your attorney, and you, the client. To get started I will ask you a few questions. Ready?"

"I guess so," she said as she clasped her hands in front of her.

For nearly an hour they talked about everything relating to the Mercedes-Benz. She insisted that Roger had given the car to her, but she didn't have the pink slip. "He must have died before he found it." The attorney had not planned to get into that topic since he had been retained to deal only with the theft of the car.

"It's getting late. Let's leave that discussion for another day. At this point, I will recommend you be allowed to post bail and go home until there is a court hearing."

"Oh, thank you! I want to get out of here." She stood up ready to make an exit.

"Not so fast. The paperwork has to be done and the money paid."

"Well, get going then. Hurry it up," she said impatiently.

After meeting with Detective O'Neal and arranging for bail, she was issued a release with the understanding that she was not to leave town. The detective was concerned because if she was found to be involved with Roger's death as well as the theft of the car, she would not be released. Murder was more serious. However, as of now they had no proof. She was issued her personal items and a deputy drove her home.

Detective O'Neal advised Jonathan of Phyllis's release from jail. He also updated him on the progress with her attorney after her meeting with the psychiatrist. Jonathan was relieved that finally she was talking with the attorney.

Marianne had removed everything belonging to Phyllis from her desk. When Jonathan came out of his office, he asked, "What is this?" as he pointed to the box sitting by her desk.

"That's what was in the desk that Phyllis might like to have returned to her. Would you like me to do that?"

"You might want to wait a day or two." He saw a photograph on top of the items and bent over to look at it more closely. He lifted it out of the box and studied it. He frowned and said, "I think I may keep this one." It was a picture of Phyllis at the beach with the scarf that was found in Roger's car, around her neck. She was holding a wide-brimmed straw hat. *This photo is going to Detective O'Neal,* he said to himself.

That evening, he called Jeanne to report his findings. She was not as surprised as he expected her to be. "It is the evidence we need," she said. "I just hope Detective O'Neal can put it all together."

"Also, Jeanne, you need to know that Phyllis posted bail today and she is home. She actually talked with her attorney and he arranged for her to be released. She had her second session with the psychiatrist. She seems to like him, maybe a little too much, if you know what I mean."

"I'm sure he will maintain a professional relationship, but at least he got her talking."

Monday morning, Jeanne turned on her computer and saw her messages. There was one from Phyllis. It read *Since I can't come to my office, could you gather up my personal items and bring them to me?* There was no please; just the curt request. She wrote back telling her that she would do that sometime today. However, she knew she should check with Jonathan and Detective O'Neal to be sure it was okay.

She had just delved into the Marchant project when her phone rang. Impatient about the interruption, she brusquely answered, "Yes, what is it?"

"Well, good morning to you, too," Detective O'Neal said. "Is everything okay?"

"Yes, I'm sorry. I shouldn't have been so abrupt," she said contritely. "What's up?"

"As you know, Phyllis was released from jail this week. She indicated there were personal items in her office that she would like returned to her."

"Yes, she sent me an e-mail asking me to bring everything to her. I'm not sure I should be the one to do it."

"That's why I'm calling you. Do not see her. She, and her psychiatrist, said something that makes me concerned about you. Let someone else return the items to her."

"Thanks, I will," she said pensively. "And thanks for the warning." She disconnected the line and tried to return to her work. Her mind kept thinking about what she had been told. *Was Phyllis really a danger to her?* She went to see Jonathan. "Marianne, is Jonathan free?"

"He has no one in his office. Just knock."

She knocked softly and slowly opened the door when he responded.

"Do you have a minute?" she asked politely.

"Sure. What is it? You look upset."

"I am a little, I guess." She told him about the e-mail from Phyllis and then the call from Detective O'Neal. "It makes me feel uneasy. What is she capable of?"

"Who knows at this point? We can't trust her. Don't go near her," he said adamantly. "We can have a courier take her things to her. I'll take care of it." He called to Marianne and asked her to arrange for a courier to pick up and deliver Phyllis's personal items to her at home. "You should have no contact with her, for two reasons: first, we can't trust her to do you no harm, and second, you may have to testify at her trial so it's imperative you have no personal contact with her. Understood?"

"Yes, sir," she said with a feeling of relief. She was glad to get back to the solitude of her office. She took a break only to join Judy for lunch in the cafeteria. She told her of the warning to stay away from Phyllis.

"I'm not surprised. Phyllis has been acting differently lately. Perhaps it's due to her feeling guilty. I'm glad you've been warned about her. Just be careful," she said.

"Thanks. I will." After a brief pause, Jeanne asked, "Have you seen the young paramedic lately?"

"As a matter of fact, I have. We went to the movies the other night, and he calls occasionally just to talk. I think we are becoming good friends. I really like him."

"That's great. I'm so glad for you."

By late afternoon, Jeanne had completed all she could for Mr. Marchant. She wrote it up, gave a copy to Jonathan and e-mailed it to Mr. Marchant. It was too late to start on anything new, so she used a few minutes to write to her children. She wanted to confirm their arrival for Thanksgiving, and if anyone would be coming with them. It was still a couple of weeks away, but she had to make plans. Jonathan would be invited, of course. If each of the twins brought a guest, that would make six of them. A perfect number for her dining room table.

On her way out she passed Jonathan's door and he called to her. "Do you have a minute?"

"Of course. I was just leaving since I was finished with all my work for today. I hope you don't mind that I leave a few minutes early."

"Not at all. You've earned it. I just wanted to tell you I'm impressed with the work you have done for Mr. Marchant. Well done!" Jonathan said with a smile. "See you tomorrow."

Jeanne went out with a big smile on her face. It was good to be appreciated. *Returning to the work world wasn't so bad after all,* she thought, *particularly with a boss like Jonathan.*

At home, she reflected on the work for Mr. Marchant and realized he was a man of varied interests and talents. She had been impressed with him, and his home when she met him, but after working on his project she was doubly impressed. He was someone she would enjoy knowing. She didn't know he felt the same way about her.

CHAPTER 40

When Jeanne arrived at the office the next morning, there was a message from Mr. Marchant on the computer. She immediately opened it with a feeling of trepidation. *Why am I uneasy about opening this?* She decided her unease was only because he was such an important client and she didn't want to do anything to displease him. As soon as she read his message, she relaxed. *I'm very pleased with your work, Jeanne. I have something more for you to do. Would you be willing to come to my place tomorrow morning?*

Jeanne was surprised by his request and knew she should ask Jonathan about it before answering. She asked Marianne. "Is he busy?"

"He's on the phone right now. We never know how long he will be. I'll call you when he is free."

When Marianne called to say Jonathan could see her now, she gently knocked on his door. "I have a question."

"Come on in. What is it?" Jonathan asked with concern.

"I have a message from Mr. Marchant. He wants me to come to his place tomorrow morning. He has something else he wants me to do. I haven't answered him yet. I thought I should check with you first. Should I go?"

"Probably it would be fine, but I'm surprised he didn't ask me first. Just so he knows you are not his personal assistant, but mine, I'll give him a call. In fact, I'll do that right now." He called to Marianne and asked her to get Mr. Marchant on the phone.

"Good morning, Mr. Marchant. Jeanne just told me you asked her to come to your place tomorrow morning. I just wondered how long you expect her to be there." After a brief pause, he continued, "That will be fine. I just need to know her schedule. She has other projects she's working on," Jeanne shook her head and Jonathan continued, "but yours gets top priority." He was silent for a few minutes. "He apologized for not checking with me first, so now he understands I'm your boss, not he. Thanks for checking with me."

"I'm glad I did. By the way, you may have to give me directions to his home. I didn't pay attention when you were driving."

"Here's his address. I'm sure you can find it using your G.P.S. Just in case you get lost, here's his phone number, too. He said you shouldn't be there very long, so I'll expect you back here before lunch. Are you okay, going on your own?"

"Of course." she said with a smile as she left his office.

The morning passed quickly. "Marianne, can you join me for lunch?"

"Yes. Just give me five minutes and I'll meet you at the elevator."

Jeanne walked over to Judy's desk while she waited for Marianne. "Judy, have you heard from Phyllis since her release?"

"No, and I hope I don't. I'm not sure what I would say to her. Have you heard anything?"

"No, but I don't expect to. I'm sure she is very upset with me because I was with her when she was arrested. She probably blames me for it. Here comes Marianne. We'll talk later."

Jeanne joined Marianne at the elevator and said, "Would you like to go out to the deli today rather than to our cafeteria?"

"Yes, that would be great. I haven't been there in ages; not since I went on leave. Do they still have those humongous sandwiches?"

"Of course. That's their mainstay."

They wound their way down the walkway to the deli chatting idly as they went. As soon as they entered the deli, Marianne said, "Oh, I'd forgotten how good this place smells. It makes one hungry just to walk in."

"Yes, it does, and I'm starving. I know exactly what I'm going to have."

Marianne perused the menu carefully. She eventually decided and they ordered their sandwiches. Then she asked," Can you tell me why Phyllis left so quickly?"

Jeanne hesitated not knowing how much to tell her. "Well, she had some rather serious personal problems which she had to deal with, but I don't know, or can't tell you all the details."

"That's okay. I was just curious. I'm glad I could come back to work for Jonathan. He sounded desperate."

"I'm sure he would be with only me to work with him. I'm definitely not a qualified secretary."

"So what do you do?"

"Mostly research, not only for Jonathan but sometimes for the other partners, too. I really enjoy it, except for being isolated in the library for hours at a time. I just started working for one of his clients on a special project, which is proving to be quite interesting."

"Which client is that?"

"Mr. Marchant. Do you know him?"

"Yes, I do remember him. He is what we call a *special client*. You're lucky that he likes you. He is very particular, as I recall."

Their sandwiches arrived and they hungrily took a bite. Marianne closed her eyes and sighed, "This is better than I remembered."

Jeanne continued, "I just hope Mr. Marchant will like the work I do for him. I don't want to disappoint him, or Jonathan."

"From what I hear about you, there is no danger of that."

While eating, Marianne asked Jeanne many questions getting to know her. Likewise, Jeanne asked Marianne about her life. "May I ask why you were on leave?"

"I developed some serious health issues and just needed a few months to resolve them."

"Oh, I'm sorry, but I'm glad you have recovered and can be back at work."

As they left the deli, they met Detective O'Neal and Officer Brandt coming in.

"Well, we meet again," the detective said. "This must be your favorite place for lunch, also. So who's your friend?" indicating Marianne.

"This is Marianne, Mr. Crown's secretary. She worked for him before Phyllis. These are two of my guardian angels, Detective O'Neal and Officer Brandt," she said.

"So pleased to meet you," the detective said as he tipped his cap to Marianne.

"Likewise," she responded.

When they arrived back at the office, Jeanne said, "Marianne, when Jonathan returns, please let him know I'm back in my office."

"Will do. And thanks again for having lunch with me." She followed her with her eyes, wondering if there was more to her relationship with Jonathan than only being his assistant. It was just a feeling she had.

Jeanne sat at her desk looking at the blank wall. *I must get some artwork for that wall,* she said to herself. The few green plants she had acquired had helped dispel the sterile atmosphere, but there was a need for color.

A phone call interrupted her thoughts. "Yes, Detective, what can I do for you?"

"I didn't want to mention it to you when I saw you at the deli because I don't know Marianne or what she knows of our ongoing saga, but I have some new information relating to Phyllis. I need to show you something. Could you pop in to the station for a few minutes at the end of the day?"

"Yes, I think that would be fine. Say, about four thirty or so?"

"Perfect. See you then," and he was gone.

Now she wondered what new information he had to show her but it must be important. Since she would be going directly to Mr. Marchant's in the morning, as she left the office she took what she needed for that meeting.

When she arrived at the detective's station she was ushered directly into his office. "You sounded a little mysterious. What do you have to show me?" she asked with curiosity.

Detective O'Neal opened a file on his desk and took a photograph out. "This was among things in Phyllis's desk," he said as he handed it to Jeanne. "Do you recognize the scarf she is wearing?"

"Yes, of course. It is the one you found in Roger's car."

"I agree. This proves she was in his car, and is the one who rented the garage to hide it. I think we now have enough evidence to take her to court for car theft. However, I still would like to know if she is also responsible for his death."

"Unless there is a witness, it's only conjecture on your part, but I feel that she must have been there when he died. Otherwise, why would she have taken his car? It may have been an accident and she panicked, or she pushed him down on the rocks purposely and left him there."

The detective was silent for a few seconds, then said, "I agree. Now I need to find a way to prove her guilt, or get her to confess, which I doubt she will do." After a long pause while stroking his mustache, he continued, "Thank you for coming in. Now I need to plan our next move."

CHAPTER 41

Jeanne awakened earlier than usual anticipating her meeting with Mr. Marchant. She wasn't really feeling anxious, but more like eager to see him again, and to begin a new project. She planned her attire to be more professional than it was on her first visit.

When she arrived at the large gates, she punched the call box. As soon as she identified herself, the gates swung open and she drove up the long driveway, around the fountain and stopped at the front entrance. Edward, the butler, met her at the door and ushered her into the library. "Mr. Marchant will be here shortly,"

Jeanne had barely sat down when Mr. Marchant entered and greeted her warmly. "Thanks for coming. Would you like a cup of coffee before we start?

"No, thank you. I've had my allotment for the morning."

He jumped right in saying, "I'm eager to have you help me with a project. Let's sit over here at the table. I have a few papers for you to peruse."

He pulled out some architectural drawings, not of a building, but what looked like gardens. "I understand you are very good at research, so... I would like you to research what should go into a very special garden. That includes not only plants appropriate for this climate, but other items such as benches, walkways, sculptures, fountains, and whatever you think would make a one-of-a-kind beautiful setting to enhance this property."

"Why ask me? Your gardener might be better qualified."

"I'm asking you because I feel you are very creative and innovative. If I had a gardener do it, it would end up like every other garden in the city. I want something different—something unique."

Jeanne took a deep breath and let it out slowly. "It would be an exciting project, but I'm not sure I'm the best person to take it on."

"Here. Take these preliminary rough drawings and think about it. You don't have to use any of these sketches. They were just some ideas I was toying with. You can do something entirely different. Your only limitation is the amount of space you have to work with, and I'm sure it's adequate." Mr. Marchant handed the papers to her. "I will provide a landscape architect to work with you, but it will be your plan. You can create whatever you want."

Jeanne slowly stood up and took the rolled up drafts. "I'm overwhelmed at the moment, but I will think about it. I've never done anything like this. It will be a challenge."

"I know you are up to it. I was impressed with your ideas when we first met." With that he walked her to her car. "I'll expect to hear from you within a week. And thank you." He turned and went back into the house leaving Jeanne wondering if she really could take on this request.

When she arrived at her office, she pondered how to tell Jonathan what was being asked of her. If she agreed to take on this project, would she still have time for Jonathan? She would just tell him everything and see what he thought she should do. She ambled out toward Jonathan's office and asked Marianne if he was free. He was on the phone.

"Just let me know when he is finished."

"Is everything all right? You seem a little upset."

"Oh... Yes, yes... I guess so." She slowly turned to wait for Jonathan. She sat at her desk considering her situation until Marianne called to say he was available. She took the sketches with her, still not knowing what she should do.

She nervously said, "Hi. I'm reporting in. I just returned from meeting with Mr. Marchant. You won't believe what he's asking me to do."

"What is it?" he asked with curiosity.

Jeanne told him Mr. Marchant was asking her to design a unique garden on his property. "My concern is... well, actually I have a couple of concerns. First, I feel unqualified to do such a project, but it would be fun to design a garden of my dreams. Second, if I agree to do this, it probably would take a lot of time and I am here for you first of all."

"Well... it is an unusual request," Jonathan agreed. "It's not in our firm's normal purview."

"That's what I thought. If I agree to accept this project, it would be out of the office—on my own time, but I don't know if I will have that kind of time."

Jonathan considered what she should do. It occurred to him that perhaps Jeanne would end up working for Mr. Marchant and not for him. *In fact, that might not be a bad idea.* As he thought about it, he realized it would make his pursuing a relationship with her much easier. He finally said, "I think you should consider doing the project. I know you would be good at it, and it might lead to your working for him full time."

"Oh, but I wouldn't want to leave you, and this firm."

"Think about it," he responded. "If you no longer worked here, it would be much easier for us to date and see where our relationship goes. Here we have to be careful. And remember, it was you who said 'there can be no in-office romances,' so what are we doing?"

"You're right. It would be more comfortable not having to hide our dating. But do you think I should try something new, and so different?"

"I respect Mr. Marchant's request. He wouldn't ask you if he had any doubt about you. I have none, either. As I've said, you can do anything you put your mind to."

"I appreciate your confidence. I just wish I felt the same."

They sat in silence, just looking at each other lost in their own thoughts. Finally Jeanne said, "I have a week to get back to him with an answer. That will give me time to do some preliminary designs to see if I can come up with something unique." She left Jonathan's office smiling.

Marianne noticed a difference in Jeanne from when she went into his office. "You look much more relaxed than when you went in— and happy now. Jonathan has a way of making that happen."

"Yes, he does." Since she had not been assigned any work, she had time to think about what it would be like working for Mr. Marchant. She liked him as a person, and felt he would become a good friend. He had always maintained a professional attitude with her, which was important. She started a list of questions for the next time they talked, assuming she was going to accept his invitation.

She was so engrossed in the project that she didn't realize lunch time had come and gone. Perhaps this was a sign that she would enjoy this new challenge. She looked at the preliminary sketches she had been given, and saw nothing intriguing. The only thing she could use was the perimeter of the space, in which she could make a unique and artistic statement. Her first task would be to research the kinds of plants—trees, shrubs, flowers and such, that would work in the local climate and changing seasons, which were nominal.

Her phone rang startling her out of her dreaming. It was her son. "Mark, how nice to hear from you. Is everything okay?"

"Yes, it is. I'm eager to get home for Thanksgiving, and I'm bringing a friend."

"That's wonderful. Who is your friend?"

"A fellow classmate. We've become good friends and when I told him where I was going for the holiday, he said his family was too far away and they couldn't afford the air fare. I told him to come with me. He knows Mandy, also."

"We'd love to have him join us. Mark, do you have a minute, or maybe longer? I have something I want to ask you."

"Sure, what is it?"

Jeanne told him about Mr. Marchant's request. "I need to answer him in a week. What do you think I should do?"

"Mom, I can't tell you. It's something you have to decide if you want to do it, and have the time. Since you are seriously considering the project, I would confirm that you are capable of doing it. Remember how much you enjoyed working in the garden at our old house?"

"Yes, I did," she said pensively. "But it might mean leaving my job with Jonathan."

"But you would still see him, just not at the office. In fact, that might be better."

"You're right. Thanks for listening and reinforcing my confidence in my abilities."

"You're welcome anytime. See you next week. We'll be flying down after classes Wednesday afternoon." The call was disconnected as they said goodbye.

She was unaware that Thanksgiving was next week. She realized she should go to the beach house this weekend to get it ready for the family and their guests. She called the housekeeper and asked her to do a good cleaning of the beach house before Thanksgiving. Also to make up the two guest rooms and baths. There would be five of them there for the holiday weekend, six for Thanksgiving. Then she called Mandy.

"Hi, sweetheart. How are you?"

"Hi, Mom. I'm fine. Are you still planning to have Thanksgiving at the beach house?"

"I certainly am. Are you bringing a friend? Mark is."

"Yes, I am bringing a friend from my science class. Her family is in Montana, and it's too far to go for just a couple of days."

"Well, I'm delighted to have her. What happened with Jackson Wellborn the Third?"

"Oh, we're still friends."

"Will you be flying down with Mark Wednesday afternoon?"

"Yes. We plan to rent a car so we'll have it for the weekend. You won't need to pick us up."

"That's great. I'll be at the beach house this weekend getting it ready for your visit."

"Thanks, Mom. You're the best. Gotta go. See you next week. Love you," and she was gone before she heard Jeanne's reply.

The time to leave for the day was announced by Jonathan looking in her office and saying, "Are you spending the night here? It's time to go home."

"Yes, of course. I was lost in thought about Mr. Marchant's offer and about Thanksgiving. You are still planning to spend it with us?"

"Of course. I wouldn't miss it. Are the children coming home?"

"Yes. I just talked to them, and they each are bringing a friend. There will be six of us for dinner. I must go this weekend and get the house ready for guests. Would you like to come along?"

"Sounds wonderful. I'll be happy to join you. Also, I need to check on my house. Now, it's time to leave."

Jeanne gathered up her things and joined Jonathan at the elevator. Everyone else had left. After they got in the elevator he leaned over and placed a light kiss on her cheek. "I hope the security camera was off," he said with a chuckle.

CHAPTER 42

At home, Jeanne settled down at the kitchen counter and unrolled Mr. Marchant's sketches. She studied them, taking note of the items that appeared important, such as a fountain and a stage area. He must be thinking of entertaining in the garden. A stage area would be good for small out-door concerts. If there was a band then there should be an area for dancing. She'd have to consider the types of entertaining he liked to host. This was going to be fun, but challenging. First, there was research to be done. That was easy for her, except a botanical category was different.

As she thought about all these things, she realized she was excited about doing the garden project. She didn't need a week to decide; she knew now that she would accept the request. Then if it took too much time from her current employment, she'd resign. Having made that decision, she was ready for some solid food.

There were times when she loved to cook. Thanksgiving was one of them. She created the menu for the dinner, but also made menus for the other meals while the twins and their friends were home. By the time she retired for the night, she felt organized for the holiday weekend and she had made an important decision about work.

She walked into the office, poked her head in Jonathan's office, and said a cheery, "Good morning. I've made a decision."

"I'm glad. What is it?"

"I'm going to accept Mr. Marchant's invitation to work on his project," she said with firmness. "And if I don't have time for it and you, I will submit my resignation to you."

"Good for you. I'll support you in whatever you do."

"Thank you. I appreciate that. Now do you have work for me today?"

"Yes. Let me get it together and I'll bring it to your office."

Jeanne greeted Marianne as she walked by her desk. "How about lunch today? I missed it completely yesterday."

"Okay. Let me know when you're ready."

Jeanne started looking up information about trees. There were hundreds of different kinds, so she narrowed her search to Southern California coastal areas. She was totally engrossed in reading about them when Jonathan entered.

"I hope I'm not disturbing you."

"Oh, no. I'm just reading about trees, which I will do later," she said contritely.

Jonathan briefed her on the work. "I will be out of the office for a few hours today, but I'll be back by late afternoon.'

"Thanks, I'm sure I'll be fine." Now it was back to the library.

Judy called to her as she walked by. "Jeanne, guess what?" Without waiting for an answer, she continued, "Remember the paramedic, Michael?" Jeanne nodded. "Well, he asked me out again. We're going to dinner on his day off—and maybe dancing."

"That's great! This may be a budding romance. Keep me posted," she said as she continued on her way. She was pleased for Judy. She remembered Michael was the one who had saved her life at the dinner with Phyllis.

At the appointed time, Jeanne met Marianne for lunch. "Have you been to the French Corner Café?" she asked.

"No, but I love French food. Is it close?"

"Yes, we go there occasionally. So let's do it today."

Off they went chatting as they drifted down the crowded walkway. When they arrived, they were seated immediately. They each ordered chicken mushroom crepes with a small salad and a bran muffin.

"This is delicious," declared Marianne. "I'm glad you suggested this place. I'll come here again, with or without you. You know, my husband and I spent some time in France. I learned to love their food... and their wines. They make delicious sauces, and their fresh-baked bread is to die for."

They continued talking about France, and other countries they had visited until it was time to get back to the office.

"Thank you for suggesting the French Café. I loved it," Marianne said.

"You're welcome. We'll do it again one day," and she went to continue her research, which she finished before it was time to go home.

Since she had a few minutes, she decided to call Mr. Marchant and tell him of her decision. She closed her office door and made the call. "Hello, sir. I've given a lot of thought to your proposal and am really excited about working on the project. So... my answer is yes. I accept your challenge and will do my best to create a unique and amazing garden on your property."

"I'm delighted to hear that. When can you start?" Mr. Marchant asked.

"How about right after Thanksgiving weekend? My children are coming home with a couple of their friends for the holiday and so I will be busy preparing for that."

"I understand. I'll expect to see you Monday after Thanksgiving and we'll get started."

"What time shall I arrive?"

"Let's not make it too early. I start slowly on Mondays. Will ten o'clock be okay?"

"That would be perfect. I'll be there," she replied. "Meanwhile, have a happy Thanksgiving."

Now she'd have to tell Jonathan, but he said he'd support her in whatever she chose to do. She was confident she had made the right decision.

On her way home, she thought about Phyllis's recent behavior. She did seem rather defensive since the dinner at her house. That dinner in itself was a criminal act, which had to be proved. She thought perhaps the psychiatrist would be the one to determine her guilt or innocence. She decided to check with the detective tomorrow and see if he's had a report on Phyllis's sessions with Dr. Meredith.

As she prepared her dinner, she thought about her new job. Designing a unique garden was going to occupy her thinking, and time, for quite a while. She would let it remain in the back of her mind while preparing for Thanksgiving with her family; it would percolate ideas to be used when she started to work on it.

The next morning when she arrived at the office, Jonathan called her into his office before she went to hers. "What's up?" she asked with surprise.

"I just got off the phone with Detective O'Neal. He feels the picture of Phyllis wearing the scarf we found in your car, coupled with her theft of the car is enough evidence to implicate her in the death of Roger. He wants to file murder charges against her, which would take precedence over the auto theft charge. He said that without a witness to the accidental death, or murder, it will be hard to prove, but he thinks they may be able to get her to confess."

"That would be amazing, and I hope he's right," Jeanne agreed.

"He feels the psychiatrist may be a key in getting her to admit her role in everything. She seems more open with him."

"Is he going to arrest her now on the suspicion of murder?" she wondered.

"I don't know. He didn't say. I just wanted to let you know the latest on what's happening."

For the rest of the day she contemplated her new project. As she was walking home, a red convertible made her feel uneasy as it drove slowly by her. *Is it following me?* The driver waved. Of course, she had forgotten Phyllis had a red convertible. She waved back, but hoped she would not stop, nor that she would follow her to the apartment.

Jeanne made quick decision to stop at the market and do some unnecessary shopping, allowing time for Phyllis to go on her way. After checking out, she stopped just inside the door. She looked both ways and did not see a red convertible so felt it safe to venture out. She hurried home without seeing Phyllis again. Why did it make her so uncomfortable? Actually, if she would admit it, she felt fear.

When she arrived at her apartment building, she told Alexander about the car that seemed to be following her. "Maybe I'm feeling paranoid, but do let me know if you ever see a red convertible here."

"Yes, Ms. Blomgren. I'll be aware of it, and I'll tell Maurice also."

"Thank you. I feel safe when you are here."

She entered her apartment and immediately called Detective O'Neal. Relieved that he was still in his office, she told him about seeing Phyllis and that she felt fear.

"Did she threaten you?"

"No, she just waved like a friend, but she had been driving by me very slowly. I don't know how long she may have been following me. I ducked into the market and when I came out I didn't see her anyplace."

"That was a good move on your part. Tomorrow I'll check with her to see how she's doing, and also talk to her psychiatrist. I was thinking I'd wait until after Thanksgiving to bring her in on suspicion of murder, but after this episode, it may be wise to get her off the street. Thanks for telling me about this."

"You're welcome. I don't trust her. What if she feels I'm responsible for her arrest?"

"Until we get her in custody again, I recommend that you not walk alone. Would you like a security guard with you?"

"No, I think I'll be okay. I'll be careful and drive to and from the office. I do feel safe here with Alexander on guard at my entrance."

After finishing that conversation, Jeanne poured a generous glass of Sauvignon blanc and turned on the classical music station. She was delighted to hear Chopin waltzes being played, which helped lighten her mood.

Jonathan called. "Just checking in to see how you are?"

"I'm glad you called. I had a rather unpleasant experience on the way home from the office. I reported it to Detective O'Neal."

"What happened?"

Jeanne told him about Phyllis following her and how she felt afraid. "I'm probably being paranoid about her, but I'm not going to walk alone anymore."

"Good decision. What is the detective going to do?"

"He'll talk to her tomorrow. It would be gratifying if he could get Phyllis to admit to her role in Roger's death."

"Yes, that would solve a lot of problems."

She concluded the call and retired hoping nightmares would not encroach on her sleep.

CHAPTER 43

While driving to their beach houses Saturday morning, Jonathan said, "I'm really looking forward to dinner with your family. It should be great fun."

"You have no idea," she said. "And since I don't know the friends they are bringing, we don't know what to expect. I'm sure they will spend a lot of the time on the beach. I just hope the weather will be as nice as it is today."

"That's only five days away so it should be. Today is perfect for being here."

"Let's meet for lunch around one," Jeanne said as Jonathan went to his house.

Jeanne immediately opened some windows and did a quick inspection of the house. The housekeeper had done a thorough job. Everything was perfect. She slid open the glass doors to her room and let the cool ocean breeze fill the space. She walked out on the balcony and looked at the ocean with its long sandy beach. A few people were out enjoying the sun. She wondered why she had never made an effort to know her neighbors. If they were going to spend more time at the beach, she would change that.

She wandered down to the kitchen and took an inventory of the refrigerator's contents, which were very meager, and then did the same for the cupboards. She completed the shopping list for everything necessary for the weekend with the twins and their friends. Then she realized she needed to get food for this weekend for her and Jonathan.

When Jonathan arrived, she suggested they have lunch at the local seafood restaurant just down the street, and then do their grocery shopping after.

Lunch was served on the restaurant's outdoor patio. Seagulls soared overhead and their calls were annoyingly loud. Some of them ventured down where they begged for food scraps.

"I think it's time to go to the market," Jeanne said, "even though I'd like to remain here."

With Jeanne's shopping list in hand, they selected the items needed for Thanksgiving dinner and for the three-day weekend. Of course, there would be left-over turkey for sandwiches.

"Jonathan, it just occurred to me that I really need to take Wednesday off to be here to prepare for dinner the next day. May I have the day off?"

"May I have it off as well?" he asked with a chuckle.

"I thought you were the boss."

"Yes, but sometimes the boss has to stay on the job. Of course, you may have Wednesday off, and if I can as well, I'll join you."

Jeanne ordered a turkey to be picked up Wednesday afternoon when she would purchase the perishable items. She was excited about the weekend. It was going to be especially enjoyable with Jonathan for their first holiday together—and with the children.

They finished their shopping and headed home. "Jonathan," Jeanne asked quietly, "what would you think of visiting a couple of our neighbors this afternoon?"

He was silent for a time, and finally said, "I think that's a good idea. We don't know any of them, but we should."

"That's what I was thinking. Perhaps we could take a bottle of wine from my collection and introduce ourselves."

As soon as they arrived home, they transferred the supplies into her kitchen. By the time they finished putting everything away, it was approaching wine time. Jeanne selected a bottle of wine from her stash and said, "Let's go meet a neighbor."

They went first to a neighbor on one side of Jeanne's house. No one answered the door.

"I saw a few people walking on the beach earlier today, so someone must be here."

Jonathan punched the doorbell of the next house and they waited for a response. He tried it again and a gentleman appeared behind the glass door.

"Yes, what is it?" he asked.

"I'm Jeanne. I live a couple of doors down from you and we wanted to introduce ourselves. This is Jonathan," she said as she indicated him with a sweep of her hand. "We brought a bottle of wine for you, assuming you enjoy a fine wine."

"It's very thoughtful of you. Would you like to come in?" he asked cordially.

"Yes, thank you. We'll only stay a few minutes," Jonathan said. "We don't want to interrupt if you are busy."

"We're never busy at the beach. We come here to relax. By the way, I'm Matthew," he said as he reached out his hand for Jonathan's. "Let me tell my wife we have visitors." He left briefly and returned with a regal-looking woman. They both appeared to be in their mid-fifties. "This is Mildred," he said looking adoringly at her. "These are a couple of our neighbors, Jonathan and Jeanne. They've brought a bottle of wine for us."

"How thoughtful of you," she said with a slight accent. "Shall I get some glasses for it?" Without waiting for an answer, she went to a cupboard and retrieved four crystal wine goblets with gold-trimmed rims. "These will do," she said as she sat them on the coffee table. "Matthew, dear, you may do the honors, unless Jonathan would like to?"

"I would be pleased," Jonathan said as he quickly rose to open the wine.

There was a moment of silence before anyone spoke. Jeanne was the first to ask a question to encourage getting acquainted. "How long have you lived here?"

Matthew answered, "This is our weekend home, which we've had for a few years. We live mostly in a townhouse in the city."

"Same here. Jonathan and I both work in the city and so we spend very little time here. Oh, by the way, we're not married; just good friends," she said. "His house is just a few houses down from me." She wondered why she felt she had to explain this to relative strangers.

"We realized we didn't know any of our neighbors, and thought it would be a good idea to know who lived near us," Jonathan explained. "We became aware of the need to know people on our beach after an accident here a several weeks ago."

"What was that?" Mildred asked.

Jeanne explained how she had come upon a dead body down by the rocks and when she went for help that was when she met Jonathan. "Until then, I had known no one here. Now I know you two," she added with a smile.

Matthew frowned as he said, "I do remember something about that event. That was you? We didn't venture out to see what was going on. We tend to keep to ourselves."

"As does everyone else living on this beach," Jonathan said. "But that's part of the attraction to living here."

"I agree," Matthew said. "However, I can see why it might be wise to at least know who lives here if for any reason you need someone, as was your case. Was that ever resolved?"

"Yes. It's behind us now," Jeanne said. She didn't want to get into that so she changed the subject. "My family will be here for Thanksgiving weekend, and so we were here getting the house ready for my twins and their friends."

Jonathan stood up, "I think it's time to go. It was great to meet you."

"Same here. And thanks for the wine. Feel free to stop in anytime when you are here."

"I'd love to do that," Jeanne said. "Goodbye for now."

They left feeling good about having made one, actually two friends on their beach. "That was rather pleasant," Jeanne said. "I think they will be very good neighbors. They are a little older than we, but young in spirit."

"Great observation. I agree."

When they arrived back at Jeanne's house, she said, "Jonathan, you seemed to abruptly take leave from our visit. Was there a problem with them?"

"No. I just felt we had been there long enough, and I didn't want the conversation going into more personal information. We don't know them yet, and so we have to be careful."

"I understand. I do tend to be more trusting of people than perhaps I should."

"I think that was demonstrated in your so-called friendship with Phyllis."

"I agree, but I hope I have learned my lesson. Thank you for keeping us on track when meeting new people."

Since it was approaching the dinner hour, Jeanne suggested they prepare their meal at her house, to which Jonathan agreed. Jeanne put their place settings on the counter for informal dining. After eating a few bites Jeanne said, "This has been an enjoyable day,"

Jonathan agreed. "But the day is not over yet."

"So what do you have in mind?"

"I'm not sure. Perhaps after dinner we could sit on your balcony and watch the sunset."

"That's a lovely idea. How about taking our dessert there also?"

They cleared away the makings of dinner, served the raspberry cheesecake onto small plates, and trudged up the stairs to the balcony outside Jeanne's room. The sun was low in the sky and scattered clouds hung low on the horizon.

"This is a perfect way to end a day," Jonathan said as he sat down facing the ocean. He took the plate Jeanne offered. "This is beautiful," he said admiring the colorful dessert.

"Fresh raspberries are one of my favorite foods. The other one, as you know, is chocolate." She continued, "I'm glad we decided to do this. It's been ages since I have enjoyed such good food and good company in this beautiful place." She settled into her chair with a relaxing sigh and took a bite of the rich dessert.

They enjoyed the quiet time while they nibbled at the cheesecake. They watched the sun slowly dip into the ocean. The clouds put on a colorful show reflected in the water. The waves carried the colors onto the beach. The glow in the sky spread over them like a canopy. Little by little the colors faded, gradually entering the field of darkness. All they could see was the rim of white foam as the waves broke on the sandy shore.

Jonathan reached for Jeanne's hand without a word and just looked deeply into her eyes. She responded with a smile. Without speaking, they arose and with their arms around each other they walked to the railing of the balcony. Jonathan turned to Jeanne, lifted her chin and placed a serious kiss on her open lips. He pulled back and said, "I've been wanting to do that all day."

"I'm glad you finally did," Jeanne said with a slight smile. And with that she returned his kiss, putting her arms around his neck and pulling him closer. It felt wonderful to be held like that. She didn't want to let him go.

Jonathan breathed deeply and easily picked her up and carried her into the bedroom. They kissed passionately when he placed her on the bed and laid down beside her. There was no rush and they took their time getting to know each other in a new, but intimate way. Jonathan caressed her face and kissed her gently. "You are the first woman I've kissed since Elizabeth died'."

"And you are the first man I've kissed since Roger died," she replied. "It felt kinda good," she added with smile.

With that he kissed her again, lingering a bit longer this time. When he released his arms from around her, he reluctantly said, "I think it's time for me to go back to my place." He sat up, looked down at Jeanne with a happy smile, and said, "Perhaps we can continue this another time."

She had mixed feelings about his leaving, but agreed it was time. She accompanied him to the door. They shared one last kiss as they said good night and he left with a glance over his shoulder to see her close the door.

CHAPTER 44

Jeanne awakened with a smile on her face. She couldn't remember a day she enjoyed as much as yesterday. Jonathan certainly had become a very special friend; in fact, he may become more than a friend. As she considered that possibility, she realized she might be open to love again. She would just wait and see if he felt the same. The signs he gave yesterday indicated he might.

She dressed casually and descended to the kitchen to make coffee. She turned on the radio to the classical music station. Bach was pealing from an organ. She turned it up so that the music filled the entire house. It replaced being in church—a perfect way to start a Sunday morning. She realized it took very little to make her happy. Jonathan made her happy.

As soon as she had that thought, he appeared at her door. "I smell coffee. Is there enough for two?"

"Of course. Come in and I'll fix something to go with it." She turned the music down just a bit. "I hope you like organ music on a Sunday morning."

"Absolutely." He poured himself a cup and sat at the counter watching Jeanne as she prepared a few slices of French toast.

"I'm glad you arrived in time for breakfast."

"Well, I must confess. I had to or I would go hungry. I didn't purchase any food for myself. We concentrated on the weekend with the children and I gave no thought to what I needed. So... I guess you are stuck with me."

"I can't think of anyone I'd rather be stuck with," she said smiling warmly at him. He said nothing, but he gave her a sticky kiss on the cheek.

"Jonathan, would you do me a favor this morning?" she asked hesitantly.

"Of course. What do you need?"

"It's not what I need, but more what I need to do."

"And what's that?"

"Would you go with me to the rock pile at the end of the beach? I need to be there to let go of the past with Roger."

"I understand. Whenever you're ready, we'll go."

"Thank you. You really are a good friend. I owe you more than just breakfast."

By mid-morning, Jeanne was ready to leave the house for a walk along the shore. She talked as she walked, remembering the day, and the reason she met Jonathan. "It was mid-afternoon when I finished reading a very good book. I don't remember now which one it was. I decided to walk to my favorite place for a last look at the ocean before going back to the city to start a new job. The day was beautiful and I felt so free. I remember a light breeze was blowing my hair across my face...."

They were approaching the rock pile. Jeanne hesitated before ascending the rocks. "I need to do this," she said as she started up the rocks as she always had. Jonathan followed close behind. When they reached the top, she stood quietly lifting her arms to the sky. "I remember saying, 'I'm free, free to be me' to wind and the ocean. Then I turned to climb down. That's when I saw him." She covered her eyes as if she didn't want to see that place again. Jonathan put his arms around her and held her close. A few tears seeped out of her eyes and soon she was sobbing. It was the first time she had cried, really cried, since Roger had left. Jonathan just stayed quiet and held her. After a few minutes, she was all out of tears.

They descended carefully without looking in the crevice where Roger had fallen. A smile came back to her face and she said, "Then I found you... and my life changed."

They walked hand in hand back down the beach at the water's edge. They took their shoes off and walked barefoot letting the cool water cover their feet. Seagulls floated overhead on the ocean's breeze, as free as Jeanne felt. Then she said, "Thank you, Jonathan, for doing this for me. I feel a full release from my past now. I'm ready for my future life."

Jonathan didn't know what to say so he remained silent. He just hoped he would be a part of her future life.

As they approached his house, he noticed the young girl in the house next door. He said, "Let's go say hello to Margaret."

"Who's Margaret?"

"She is the daughter of the people who own the house next door to me. I met her one day when I came out here to inquire if anyone had been seen in the area the day you found Roger. I haven't seen her since. Perhaps her parents might be here for the holiday and we could meet them."

They walked up to her house, knocked on the door and called, "Hello, Margaret. It's Jonathan. I wanted you to meet Jeanne who lives a couple of doors over."

Margaret came out on the patio to greet them. "Hi. I'm glad to see you and to meet Jeanne. Since I am on break from school I decided to spend it here. My parents will be out for Thanksgiving. Perhaps you could meet them then."

"That would be lovely," Jeanne said. "My children and their friends will be here, too. You might like to meet them."

"I'd like that. Where do they go to school?"

"They attend Stanford University in Palo Alto. Where do you go?"

"I'm at USC, in my second year."

"You should have a lot in common, so I'm sure you would enjoy meeting each other," Jeanne assured her.

Jonathan said. "We'll plan on meeting your parents next weekend, and introducing you to Jeanne's family."

"I'll look forward to it. Goodbye for now." She turned to go back inside and suddenly stopped. "By the way, did you find the book you were looking for that day?" she asked.

Jonathan looked puzzled for a moment, and then remembered the reason he had talked to her. "Oh, the book. No, I think it's gone forever. I hope whoever found it has enjoyed reading it."

As they walked back to Jeanne's house, she asked, "What was that about the book?"

He told her how he used that as an excuse to ask if they had seen anyone in this area the day Roger died.

"That was very clever of you."

"Yes, it was," he said with a smug smile. "In fact, it was she who told me she had seen a woman with a wide-brimmed hat going up the embankment at the end of the beach that afternoon."

"You didn't tell me that. She may be a witness if Phyllis ever goes to trial."

"I thought about that."

They returned to Jeanne's place feeling pleased to have seen Margaret and open the door for a friendship.

"I suppose we should close up our houses and get ready to drive back to the city," Jonathan said regretfully. "We can leave whenever you're ready."

"Okay. Give me an hour or so." She walked over to him and gave him a quick kiss on the cheek. She turned and went straight to the kitchen, smiling at him as he went out the door.

When Jonathan called from downstairs, she answered, "I'm ready. I'll be right down."

A wide smile creased his face when he saw her coming down the staircase. "Hi. My red chariot is waiting to deliver you back to your castle."

"How romantic you make it sound. But aren't chariots supposed to be gold?"

"That's only in story books. I hope you are not disappointed."

"Not at all, especially since the driver is so handsome."

She locked the door and they reluctantly headed back to the city.

"Jonathan, I've been thinking about my job with you and my new one with Mr. Marchant. How would you feel if I went to work for him full time."

"As I told you, I would support you in whatever you decided to do. I mean it."

"I appreciate that very much. As I've thought about working in a relatively new field, and the size of the project, I'm sure it will be a full-time job." She hesitated for a time, and then continued, "And given what happened between us this weekend, it might be more comfortable not working together when we have to see each other every day."

"I agree in one aspect. It will be hard to see you in such close proximity and keep my hands off of you. Besides, you have said we must keep personal relationships out of the office. I think that will be impossible to do now. Therefore," he said with authority, "I think it would be best if you resigned this week."

"You won't mind if I don't give a two-week notice?"

"Let's say you did, making it effective the day before Thanksgiving."

"Thanks, I appreciate that. I'll prepare a letter of resignation as soon as I get in the office."

They were quiet as they approached her apartment. As Jeanne reached for his hand, she said, "This weekend has been a major turning point in my life—for a number of reasons. Thank you for your part in it."

"You're welcome. Anytime I can be of service," he said as he leaned over and kissed her. "See you tomorrow."

It felt good to be back in her own apartment after such a life-changing weekend. Her friendship with Jonathan definitely had gone to the next level. Now she could focus on the future—right after Thanksgiving.

As she thought about her new job, she hoped she had made the right decision to work full time for Mr. Marchant. She had a good job with Jonathan, but since their relationship had changed, she knew it was best for her to resign. Now they could enjoy their relationship out of the office. She knew the job with Mr. Marchant would be challenging, but when did she ever back down from a challenge? Looking forward to tomorrow, she fell into a restful sleep.

CHAPTER 45

"Good morning, Marianne," Jeanne said pleasantly. "By the way, Jonathan said I can have Wednesday off. My twins will be home for Thanksgiving, and we're spending it at the beach house. I really need to have the day to prepare a dinner for six, and for the three days the twins and their friends will be with us. What are your plans for Thanksgiving?"

"Nothing special. We are going to my husband's family home for dinner. I'm taking dessert, which is much easier than preparing a complete festive meal."

"It's good to be with family. Now, off to work," and she went to her office.

She immediately turned on her computer and wrote her letter of resignation. It was a very formal letter addressed to Jonathan and dated exactly two weeks prior to this Wednesday. She printed it out to give him later. She placed a call to Detective O'Neal. He answered immediately. "Good morning, Jeanne. Anything new with you?"

"No, but I was wondering if you had a chance to talk with Phyllis and find out why she was following me the other day."

"No, I have not talked to her. I have a call in to the psychiatrist to see if he will meet with her today. I think he is the only one she will open up to. I have given him a list of questions for which I would like to have answers. I'll see if he will be successful in getting them."

"Thanks. Please keep me posted."

"Of course, I will."

When his phone rang, it was Dr. Meredith. The detective told him of Phyllis following Jeanne on the street and asked if he would visit her soon. He was hoping the psychiatrist could get something from her that would make it easier for him to indict her for murder. He had kept copious notes on every conversation with anyone who had contact with her over the past several weeks. Her file was getting quite thick.

Dr. Meredith met with Phyllis and as he perused the list of questions from Detective O'Neal, he became aware of the importance his sessions held. He also knew he was sworn to maintain client-patient privilege. He had to find a way to convince Phyllis to acknowledge her actions under oath at a court hearing. At this point, she seemed to be in denial. However, the more they talked the more he became aware of slight discrepancies in her stories. His one concern was her abnormal attitude about the death of Roger. *I think I need to talk with Jeanne.*

After he concluded his session with Phyllis, having made very little progress, he put in a call to Jeanne.

"Would you have some time later today to meet with me? I need to ask you about your relationship with Phyllis."

"Certainly. What time would you like me to see you?"

"Would right after lunch, say... one-thirty work for you?"

"Yes, I'm sure that would be okay. Where shall I meet you?"

"Could you come to my office?" He gave her the address.

Jeanne wondered what he would want, but realized it was important or he would not have asked to see her. "Jonathan, I need to be out of the office for a little while right after lunch. Dr. Meredith has asked me to come see him. Is it okay?"

"Of course. It will be interesting to hear what he says."

She met Judy at lunch who talked about Michael and how they were becoming good friends. "I owe it all to you," she said. "Well, not exactly, but because I called 911 the night we were at Phyllis's, I met Michael. I'm sorry for the reason, but I'm glad it was he who was on duty then."

"I'm glad, too. I knew you'd meet someone special someday, and that was the day."

As soon as they entered the deli, they were met by Detective O'Neal and Officer Brandt just leaving. "This seems to be our favorite place," the detective said as he held the door for them. "By the way, Jeanne, have you heard from Dr. Meredith?"

"Yes, in fact I'm meeting with him right after lunch."

"Wonderful. I'll be eager to get a report," and he was gone.

"Is there anything you want to tell me?" Judy asked as they were seated.

"Dr. Meredith is the psychiatrist working with Phyllis. He probably wants to hear my side of the stories she is telling."

"I'll bet they are different," she responded with a smile.

When Jeanne returned to the office, she retrieved her car and drove directly to the office of Dr. Meredith. As she entered the reception area she was greeted with soft music. The comfortably cool room was decorated in warm earth tones.

Dr. Meredith immediately appeared. "It's good of you to come on such short notice. Come on in and let's get acquainted," he said as he led her into his office. He sat on one end of a leather couch and motioned for her to join him on the other. "We'll keep this conversation informal. I just needed to know a little more about you and your relationship with Phyllis. What is your background? How long have you worked at the legal firm? Just tell me anything that would help me know you."

"All right. Here goes. I am a mother of teenage twins, a boy and a girl. I recently became a widow when my husband was killed, or died. It happened near my home at the beach, and that was where I met Jonathan. I have been an assistant to him for only three months or so." She continued telling him everything that had transpired during the past three months. He asked a question now and then but let her tell her story. He was particularly interested in what she said about a so-called friendship with Phyllis and their interactions, including the near disaster with the dinner at her home. He made a mental note of her observations which differed from Phyllis's.

"Well, you certainly have given me a lot to think about," Dr. Meredith said. "If I have other questions, may I call you?"

"Yes, any time if I can be of help. I am concerned about Phyllis, but also I'm afraid of her."

"That's understandable given her behavior. I suggest you to have no contact with her."

"I don't plan to," she said firmly.

Dr. Meredith stood up, indicating the visit was over. "Thanks again for coming in. It has been very enlightening."

On her way back to the office, she realized she had talked nonstop for nearly an hour. Dr. Meredith really was easy to talk to. She could see why he made a good psychiatrist. She smiled to herself, and wondered what he thought of her. *Maybe he was analyzing me.* She nearly laughed out loud at the thought. She hoped he'd found her normal; at least well balanced. *Maybe someday I'll ask him."*

She looked in Jonathan's office when she returned. "Hi, I'm back," she said quietly.

He looked up. "Oh, yes... come in, come in. Have a seat and tell me how it went with Dr. Meredith."

"Overall, I think he was pleased. He asked a few questions but mostly I just told him everything, every little thing I could remember. I couldn't help but wonder what he thought of me. Was he analyzing me?"

Jonathan laughed. "I often wonder why we are so suspicious of psychiatrists. I doubt he would have any concerns about you. You are about as normal as anyone I know. But then, I'm not a psychiatrist."

With that, she handed him her resignation, and asked, "Do you have more work for me?"

She spent the next two days working on tasks for Jonathan. Before leaving, she cleaned out all her personal items from her desk. She stopped by Judy's desk to tell her that she had resigned and would be working for Mr. Marchant. "I will miss seeing you, but I'd like to keep in touch. I want to know how things go with Michael so call me whenever you want to talk. I'll do the same."

"Of course, I will miss seeing you here, too, but we'll stay in touch."

Jeanne took the elevator down to the garage level for the last time. Although she had been at Crown, Best and Carruthers only a few months, it seemed a lot longer as she thought about all that had transpired while there.

When she arrived at her apartment, she realized that for a few days she was going to be an unemployed widow and single mother. The phone rang. It was Jonathan. "I just wanted to tell you I let the others partners know you had resigned to accept another position. They were sorry to see you leave, as am I, but I'm sure you have made the right decision."

"Thank you. I do feel good about it."

"I already miss seeing you in your office, but now I can see you out of the office," he said with a smile in his voice. "I'm looking forward to Thanksgiving with you and your family."

"Me, too. I'll be going to the beach house tomorrow. Will you be going there after work, or are you still planning to take the day off?"

"I plan to, unless something comes up to keep me from it."

"Whenever you get there, please come by for a glass of wine."

"Will do. See you soon," and he signed off.

CHAPTER 46

Early Wednesday morning, Jeanne packed for the holiday weekend. Before she left the apartment, she called Detective O'Neal to see if there were any new developments and to let him know where she would be. She told Alexander she would be away until Sunday evening.

When she arrived at the beach house, she realized she had neglected to get fresh flowers. She dashed to the local flower market and selected what she needed for all the rooms. While she was arranging flowers in various containers, there was a knock on her door.

"Hello, Margaret," she said surprised to see her neighbor standing outside the door. "Is everything all right?"

"Yes. I saw you arriving and wanted to let you know my parents are here and they would love to meet you. Could you and Jonathan come over this evening around six for a glass of wine?"

"How nice of you. We'd love to. Jonathan is driving out today so I'm sure he will be here by then." She hesitated for a few seconds, and then continued, "My children, the twins and their friends, are arriving sometime today. Perhaps you would like to meet them. You could come here and leave us older people at your house. What do you think?"

"I think that's a great idea," she agreed. "See you later."

Now I'll prepare snacks for the young people. We'll just have a generous selection of hors d'oeuvres for all of us; no dinner, she decided.

She heard happy, excited voices and then the door burst open with the arrival of the twins. "Hi, Mom." It was Mark and Mandy, each with a friend in tow. "This is my mom," Mark explained. "This is my friend, Brad, and this is Mandy's friend, Gwen. I guess you can call my mom Jeanne."

Jeanne greeted them saying, "We're so glad you could come."

Brad was the same height as Mark and had an athletic build. Unlike Mark, he had dark brown, nearly black hair with a slight wave. An unruly lock fell casually over his forehead.

"Mark will show you to your rooms so you can get settled and prepare for a fun-filled weekend."

It was amazing how much energy exuded from young people. As soon as they had changed into swim wear, the boys headed out the door to the water. Mandy and Gwen lingered a little longer. Gwen was smaller than Mandy, in fact would be considered petite. Her brown eyes sparkled when she smiled. Her sandy-blonde hair was long and straight, pulled back into a pony tail, which made her look younger than she may have been. They soon left to join the boys. Jeanne knew as soon as the sun set and the air cooled, they would be in.

It was late afternoon when Jonathan arrived. He went to his house first and noticed the young people in the ocean. They were the only ones brave enough to swim in the cold water. As soon as he unpacked, he started out the door on his way to Jeanne's when Margaret appeared.

"Hello, there," he said. "Are you here with your parents for the weekend?"

"Yes, and I wanted to tell you they would like to meet you, and so you and Jeanne are invited to come for a glass of wine at six o'clock. Jeanne said that would be fine."

"Well, it's fine with me, too. See you then."

He hurried over to Jeanne's and went in without even knocking. Seeing her on the sofa, he leaned over to give her a kiss on the cheek.

"Oh, I'm glad you're here. The children came in, said hello, and immediately went swimming. Now that you are here, do you want to help me in the kitchen?"

"Absolutely. Just tell me what to do."

They started working in tandem very efficiently preparing healthy snacks for the evening, and small sandwiches for the young swimmers. As they completed the food preparation, the children emerged from the beach.

"Wipe as much sand off as you can and head for the showers. Snacks are ready for you."

The four young people appeared ready to devour whatever they found. Fortunately, she had prepared enough to keep them happy.

Jeanne said, "A young neighbor, Margaret, is going to be joining you later. She is a student at USC spending the weekend at her parent's house just down the beach. They have invited Jonathan and me to join them for wine at six and so we invited Margaret to come meet you. I hope that is okay."

"Of course. I'm sure she would have more fun with us than with you old people." Mark said with a grin.

"We're not so old," Jonathan stated.

"Sorry. It's just that..."

"Don't worry about it. We understand. We were young once."

A light banter continued between them as their guests grew more comfortable with the adults. It was going to be a great weekend, Jeanne concluded.

When six o'clock arrived, Jeanne and Jonathan cautioned their children to make Margaret feel welcome and just enjoy themselves. They walked to the neighbors, and were greeted by Margaret. "Please come in. These are my parents, Tom and Amy," and to them she said, "This is Jeanne and Jonathan. Now you all have fun getting acquainted while I go meet the twins. See you later," and she bounded out the door.

Jonathan handed a bottle of Jeanne's favorite wine to Tom and said, "It's good to meet you. We've been neighbors here for quite a while and yet had never met. Thanks to Margaret, now we have."

"How did you happen to meet Margaret?" Amy asked.

"One day I was looking for a book my friend lost. Margaret was here and I asked her if she had seen it when she was walking on the beach. That was it."

Tom said, "We don't know any of our neighbors. We tend to keep to ourselves. It might be different if we lived here full-time."

Amy offered hors d'oeuvres as Tom poured wine for each of them. "Margaret tells me that you live right next door."

"Yes, that's right. I'm surprised we hadn't met before, but then, I've not been here very often. Then when I am, I tend to bury myself in my work."

"What kind of work is that?" Tom asked.

"I'm an attorney." He left it at that.

"Which house is yours?" Amy asked Jeanne.

"I'm two doors down from you."

"How long have you had the beach house?" she asked.

"Several years. We bought it before the children were in high school. We thought it would be a good place to spend weekends and holidays. And it has been."

"We like it here. It is so peaceful. A great place to get away and relax," Tom added.

"What do you do, Tom?" Jonathan asked.

"I'm a professor at USC. I teach economics and business classes. I must say, it does help with covering the tuition for Margaret, since we get a reduction as faculty. USC is an expensive school."

"Yes, and so is Stanford, where my twins attend," Jeanne said.

"What are they majoring in?" Tom asked.

"Mark is studying architecture and Mandy is interested in the medical sciences. How about Margaret, what is her area of interest?"

"She is an artistic soul," Amy said. "She is a musician as well as an artist. She hasn't really decided on one focus yet. I think she'd like to work in a museum someday. But we'll have to see what direction she'll take."

The evening proceeded with lively conversation as the neighbors got acquainted. When Jonathan felt they had completed the wine hour, he stood and said, "It's time to let you get to your dinner, and we to ours. I'm so glad we have finally met one of our neighbors."

"I agree with that," Jeanne said as she followed Jonathan to the door. "We wish you a Happy Thanksgiving."

As Jonathan and Jeanne walked back to her house he said, "A lovely couple. I'm glad to know them. Too bad we didn't meet them before."

"Yes, but I guess we weren't ready yet."

Jonathan wasn't quite sure what she meant, so he remained quiet.

They arrived at Jeanne's, to find that the twins and their friends had gone to their rooms early. She did hear them talking quietly.

She and Jonathan went upstairs to the outside deck and sat to look out at the darkening ocean. The sky still glowed with remnants of the sunset.

"What time shall I come tomorrow?" he asked.

Jeanne thought for a moment and then decided mid-morning would be good. "I don't want you too early. You distract me. I'm planning on dinner around four o'clock."

She gave Jonathan a quick good night kiss and retired to her room. As she slipped into her bed, she smiled and thought how fortunate she was. This was going to be a very special holiday. Sleep came easily and so did dreams.

CHAPTER 47

Thanksgiving morning dawned with a clear sky and only a few scattered clouds on the Western horizon. Jeanne entered the sun-filled kitchen, made coffee and before she had her first sip, Mark and Brad entered.

"I smell coffee," Mark said.

"Help yourself."

Brad poured himself a cup and said, "It's so quiet here. I slept more soundly than I ever remember."

"I'm glad," Jeanne said. "That will give you energy for the day's activities. I suspect more swimming will be included."

"Of course it will," Mark agreed. "That's the best part of living at the beach."

Then the girls joined them. "What's for breakfast?" Mandy asked.

"I'll let you make whatever you want. Now I have to get to work. Mark, would you lift the turkey out of the refrigerator for me, please? I need to prepare the stuffing for it."

"Here, I'll do it," Brad offered as he quickly reached for it. He easily lifted the big bird and placed it on the counter.

"Where does your family live?" Jeanne asked

"Our home is in a small town in northern Wisconsin. It originally belonged to my grandparents. It's where my father, and then I, grew up."

"And where is your family home?" Jeanne asked Gwen.

"It's just my mother and I. We live in Butte, Montana. We were on a family farm, actually it was a ranch, until my father died. Now we live in town."

The conversations between the young people continued as they shared information with each other about their families and their homes, which pleased Jeanne. Everyone was busy when Jonathan appeared.

"Good morning," he declared. "I hope you left some coffee for me."

"If not, we can make more," Jeanne said as she gave him a welcoming smile. "In fact, I'm ready for a second cup so it's definitely time to make another pot."

"So what are your plans for the day?" he asked the young people.

"What else but to go swimming?" Mark responded.

"I just heard on the news that a storm may be brewing in the West. If so, you'd better plan to swim earlier today."

They looked out to the ocean and saw only a few clouds on the distant horizon. "Well, it looks like it's a long way off so I don't think we'll need to worry about it," Brad said.

"Sometimes a storm at sea affects the tides on the shore," Jonathan explained. "So just pay attention to the waves when you're out there."

"Will do," he said as he settled down to eat the breakfast the girls had prepared.

"What may I do to help?" Jonathan asked Jeanne.

"Just stay out of my way. I'll let you know if I need help." She worked best without distractions, and Jonathan definitely was a distraction.

Once the young people had finished their breakfast, they headed out for the day. Jonathan stopped them at the door and said, "Remember what I said about being aware of any change in the waves or the tide. Storms can erupt rather quickly over the ocean. This is a private beach so we don't have a life guard on duty. Just be careful and watch out for each other."

"We always do," Mark said. "All of us are good, strong swimmers. In fact, Brad is on the swim team at the university."

"Good to know. Have fun and enjoy the water." With that he let them go, even though he felt a bit uneasy.

That left him and Jeanne alone. When the turkey was ready to go into the roasting pan Jonathan lifted it. "How much does this thing weigh?"

"Around sixteen pounds. Of course, the stuffing adds to it. I'm sure it will be enough for dinner with a lot left over for sandwiches tomorrow. Sometimes I like it better the next day."

"I agree. There's nothing better than a cold turkey sandwich with cranberry sauce."

Jeanne opened the oven door for Jonathan to insert the turkey. "It will take a few hours, which gives us time to walk on the beach and talk."

"I'm for that," he said as he escorted her out the door. They walked down to the water's edge and saw the young people frolicking in the waves. A slight breeze stirred the air and sea gulls soared overhead. After several minutes, they returned to the house just in time to see Margaret walking through the sand to join the others in the water. "I'm glad she has made friends with our kids," Jonathan said.

Jeanne stopped abruptly and said, "Do you realize what you just said?"

"What did I say?"

"You said 'our kids' as if they were yours and mine."

"I said that without thinking," he stated with surprise. "And this weekend I do feel partially responsible for them."

"I appreciate your concern for them. It's nice to have you help keep an eye on the four of them."

When it was time to work on other aspects of dinner, Jeanne turned on the classical music station and set about puttering in the kitchen. Jonathan sat down in a chair where he could see the kids in the water. He noticed the clouds were growing in the distance. Soon the breeze was stirring the leaves and blowing the sand.

"The storm seems to be approaching faster than expected," Jonathan said with concern. "I think the kids should come out of the water pretty soon. Perhaps I'll go down and tell them." He left Jeanne looking out the window at the gathering clouds.

When he was near the water's edge he saw Brad quite a ways out and he called to him, "Brad, you need to come in." He didn't hear him, so he said to Mark, "Will you signal for Brad to come in? He's too far out. With the storm approaching it's not wise to be out there."

Mark waved his arms hoping Brad would see him. He did wave back. Mark could tell he was swimming but he was not making any progress toward shore. He and Jonathan immediately knew something was wrong.

"Mark, I think he's caught in a rip current. We need to help him. If you swim out to him, you can guide him along the shore until you get out of the pull of the current. He may not realize what is happening and does not know how to get out of it."

"Okay, I can do that," he said with an edge of fear in his voice. Mark dove into the rising tide and swam out to Brad.

"What are they doing?" Gwen asked. "They should not be out that far."

"I think Brad got caught in a rip current," Mandy said. "He is a strong swimmer but not as strong as the pull of the tide. Mark is going out to help him."

"But won't Mark be in the same situation?"

"No. You see, he knows how to get out of a rip current. Mark has been around the ocean for years, and Brad hasn't. He may not even know what a rip current is."

"What is a rip current? How does it work?" Gwen asked.

"Often when there is a storm at sea it changes the ebb and flow of the tides causing a strong one to pull everything back into the ocean. So even though that storm seems far away, it has affected the tide here."

"That sounds very dangerous," Gwen said with concern.

"It can be if you don't know what to do."

"Will Mark be able to help Brad back to shore?" she asked as they watched the two figures swimming toward the outcropping of rocks down the beach.

They anxiously walked along the shore in the direction the boys were going watching their progress. Mandy's heart rate increased as she silently said a prayer, "God, give them strength. Bring them in safely." They held their breath praying that the boys were going make it before they were exhausted. Brad had been struggling for quite a while before anyone recognized he was in trouble. He was nearly exhausted by the time Mark reached him.

"Mark, help me. I can't seem to get to shore. What's happening?"

"Brad, relax. Just follow me," and he began swimming.

"But I want to get to the shore!" Brad shouted.

"Just follow me and we'll get there." Fortunately, Mark knew just how to swim with the tide. It was several minutes before he felt less pull. He began swimming slightly toward the shore. He looked over his shoulder to see how Brad was doing. He didn't see him. "Brad, where are you?" he shouted. He turned back and dove into the waves. He didn't see Brad. He surfaced and called to him. He took a deep breath and dove down again. Finally, he saw Brad struggling under the water. He swam to him and pushed him up to the surface. Brad took a breath, coughed and relaxed all of his weight onto Mark. Mark held him up while trying to swim toward the shore and cried, "Brad, help me."

Brad responded with, "I can't. I'm too tired."

"I know, but we are almost there. Stay with me for a little while longer."

Mark let them relax and float on the water for a few seconds. The waves were increasing in size and so he knew they had to get to shore. "Come on, let's go," he shouted as he began pulling Brad along with him. "You can make it just a little way further." The beach was slowly getting closer. Mark was getting very tired, also. Finally, his feet touched the sand and he pulled Brad up with him. Using what little strength they had left, they waddled up the beach and fell into the dry sand. "We made it," Mark said. "You're safe now."

"Thanks," was all Brad could say.

Jonathan had been following their progress along with the girls. They all ran around the rock outcropping, splashing through the waves not caring if they got wet. With relief, they saw the boys stretched out on the sand.

Mandy ran over to Mark and fell down beside him. "Mark, are you okay?" He just groaned and looked over at Brad.

Jonathan stood by and looked at the exhausted pair. Finally he said, "Well done, Mark. Now let's go back to the house." He helped the boys, pulling them up one at a time.

They all traipsed slowly along the damp sand not saying a word. Margaret went to her house and the others entered theirs to be greeted by Jeanne with a hug for each one. She was relieved to see them all home safe. "Now you go get changed and prepare for our Thanksgiving feast."

Everyone was quieter than normal, even Jonathan was subdued. They all had experienced a traumatic incident, but fortunately it had a happy ending. They would discuss it whenever Brad was ready. Now, they had dinner to think about.

"Mandy, would you and Gwen set the table, please?"

They immediately set to work putting China plates, silver ware, holiday napkins and crystal goblets on the table.

"Mom, may we all have wine with dinner?"

"Yes, I think that would be all right. Gwen, are you and Brad eighteen?"

"Yes, we are."

"Then, you may add the wine glasses to the setting. It is time for a celebration."

Jonathan removed the turkey from the oven and set it on the counter to rest. It looked picture perfect. He added ice to the glasses, poured the water and Mandy lit the candles. Soon everything was on the table. Jeanne selected the wine which Mark uncorked. She indicated where each one was to sit. As she looked around the table, she smiled and said, "I'm so thankful to have all of you here. Now tell me what each of you is thankful for."

They took turns sharing their thanks and when the last one spoke, which was Jonathan, he said, "Now we thank God for all of this good food, great friends, His protection and our love for each other. Amen." They all said, "Amen."

Jonathan was assigned to carve the turkey, which he did expertly. They all hungrily consumed great quantities of food. When they had their fill and cleared the table, Jeanne brought out the pumpkin chiffon pie. She served coffee to those who wanted it and they sighed with pleasure at their first bite of the pie.

Brad, who had been very quiet during the meal, said, "This is the best pumpkin pie I have ever had. It's different."

"That's because it's chiffon. We prefer it to the standard kind."

"I agree. You must give me the recipe so I can have my mother make it."

"I'd be happy to give it to you," Jeanne said pleased that it was such a success.

When everyone had finished eating, Mandy said, "Mom, you go sit down now. We'll do the cleanup."

"No, you're the guests."

Mandy firmly said, "You did all the cooking. This is the least we can do. So go now." She gently pushed her mother out of the kitchen.

Jeanne reluctantly left with Jonathan leading her to the enclosed patio where they could watch the sunset. Sitting beside one another, Jeanne said, "This was a nearly perfect day."

"Why do you say 'nearly perfect'?" Jonathan asked.

"It was except for the possible tragic event with Brad. I'm so glad Mark knew what to do and is a good swimmer."

"Yes, you must be very proud of him. I know I am."

"Yes, I am proud of both of my children. They have grown into wonderfully responsible young adults."

Soon all the young people came out to join them and observe the dramatic sunset. Jeanne said, "This is a perfect way to end a special holiday. Thanks to all of you for making it so."

Jonathan reluctantly left Jeanne saying, "I'll see you at breakfast, assuming I'm invited."

"Of course, you are expected to be here, but perhaps you should arrive a little late."

"And why is that?" he asked.

"We do need to appear proper to the young people," she said with a slight blush. "We don't want them to jump to an erroneous conclusion."

"I'll be discreet," and he was gone.

CHAPTER 48

The clouds that had descended on the beach lingered into the morning. The sun was totally blocked out by the gray cloud cover. Jeanne was thankful that yesterday was a beautiful day for the children to spend in the water. Today she didn't expect them to go swimming.

As soon as Mark appeared, Jeanne suggested he build a fire in the fireplace. "It will not only warm up the room, but will make it a bit more cheery."

The boys brought in wood for the fire. "There is nothing like a fire on a dismal morning. This weather is so different from yesterday. Does it always change so drastically at the beach?" Brad asked.

"Yes, it can change quickly. However, usually by noon the clouds will have cleared and we'll have sun again," Mark explained.

"What's for breakfast?" Mandy asked as she as Gwen emerged from their room.

"I'm making blueberry pancakes."

"Wonderful. Can we help?" Gwen asked.

"You girls can empty the dishwasher and set the table. Jonathan will probably be here soon, so set a place for him, too."

With a big yawn, Brad said, "I need coffee. Is it ready yet?"

"Yes. Grab a cup and help yourself," Jeanne said. "Milk is in the refrigerator if you need it. We drink it black."

"I'll take it black today, too," Brad said.

"Good morning, everybody," Jonathan said as he burst through the door. "I smelled coffee and followed the scent." He grabbed a cup and eagerly took a sip. "So what's on the schedule for today?" he asked with enthusiasm.

"We haven't decided yet," Mark said. "I'd like to go on a hike. Would you, Brad?"

"Yeah, that sounds great. Do you have good hiking trails around here?"

"Yes. It just depends on how long a hike you want. Mandy, do you and Gwen want to come, too?"

They looked at each other and then slowly shook their heads. "No, I think we want to go see some of the shops and just poke around town."

They all sat in their usual places and devoured breakfast. Having made their plans for the day, they dressed appropriately for their chosen activities and set out on their adventures. The boys took a supply of turkey sandwiches to have for lunch while out in the hills, bottles of water, and a handful of chocolate chip cookies which Jeanne had made for the weekend snacks.

Mandy and Gwen waited until midmorning to leave for their day in town. They planned to be back for lunch when they would have their turkey sandwiches. That left Jeanne and Jonathan on their own.

"Have you made plans for today?" Jonathan asked.

"No. I was so preoccupied with the children that I gave no thought to us."

"That's good, because I have an idea. Let's drive up the coast a ways and go wine tasting. There are some small family-owned wineries in the area that produce some excellent wines."

"How do you know that?" Jeanne asked with surprise.

"I have been doing some research. Until I met you, I had no reason to investigate them. Now we need to visit them and increase our wine collection."

"That's a wonderful idea. I'll leave a note for the kids to let them know we'll be back in time for dinner. They can take care of themselves until then."

The rest of the day, actually the rest of the weekend, passed with everyone doing what they enjoyed. The Thanksgiving weekend had been all Jeanne had hoped it would be. The time she spent with Jonathan only strengthened their friendship. In fact, they were definitely becoming more than just friends.

As she thought about getting back to her apartment in the city, she realized that Monday she was beginning a new job. Another chapter in her life would begin with Mr. Marchant. Her new assignment would not be in an office, but in a beautiful house surrounded by magnificent gardens. They would become her new focus. The thought left her feeling insecure, but excited. She reminded herself that she liked a challenge. This certainly would be one.

Sunday the children left to return to school promising to be home for Christmas. Jonathan left for the city after they enjoyed the last of the turkey sandwiches. Jeanne was the last one to leave the beach house after checking that everything was secure. It had been a wonderful weekend with the family and their friends—one that Jeanne would remember for a long time.

At home, she called the housekeeper and asked her to wash all the linen, and generally tidy up the beach house in case they were there for Christmas. She was rather tired from the busy weekend, and after a light snack, she retired. She had just closed her eyes when the phone rang. Without thinking she answered it. It was Jonathan.

"Hi. I just called to say goodnight and to tell you again that I really enjoyed the weekend."

"Thank you. It was a good weekend, wasn't it?"

"Yes. Now I wish you a good night's rest and an enjoyable first day at your new job." Jeanne fell asleep knowing Jonathan really cared for her.

CHAPTER 49

The night produced the soundest sleep she'd had in a long while. Jeanne awakened to the music of Scarlatti and greeted the day with enthusiasm. She carefully chose clothes for her first day with Mr. Marchant—casual, yet elegant. Not knowing exactly what she would be doing, she selected comfortable shoes in case she chose to ambulate through the gardens. While drinking her second cup of coffee, she looked at the sketches she had drawn of her ideal, but imaginary garden. She added a list of plants—shrubs, trees and flowers—to consider including in the design. However, she needed to do more research on plants that would thrive in the Marchant location. She had been assembling a pallet of colors and it occurred to her that she didn't know his favorite color. She would discuss that with him this morning.

At exactly ten o'clock, Jeanne punched the call button on the gate. She announced her arrival and the gate swung open immediately. The butler greeted her at the door, and suggested she park behind the house, near the back entrance. She realized she was no longer a guest, but was now part of the staff. As she turned the corner she saw the chauffeur pointing to a parking space under a carport. There was her name indicating her own parking space. She was official.

"Thank you," she said to the chauffeur. "I guess you know who I am."

"Yes, ma'am. I am William. Let me know if there is anything I can do for you."

"I appreciate that. Right now, just point me to the entrance from here."

"Right this way." He escorted her to the patio entrance where Mr. Marchant was waiting.

"Good morning, Jeanne. I see you have met William."

"Yes, and thanks for my very own parking space. It's the first time I've had my name on a space for my car. It makes me feel special."

"You're welcome, and you are special," he said with a warm smile. "Are you ready to get to work?"

"Absolutely. Where do we start?"

"First, let me show you to your office. Right this way." He led her into a small hallway along side the patio. He opened a door, ushered her in, and said, "This is your personal space. I think it has everything you will need: a walnut desk and an ergonomic chair, computer and printer, telephone, fax and a copy machine, filing cabinet and a drafting table. Just let me know if there is anything missing and I'll get it for you."

She scanned the room. "It has everything, except a coffee maker."

"I'll have one sent in immediately," he responded seriously.

"Oh, no. I was kidding," she said feeling embarrassed. "However, on second thought that might be nice. I do drink a lot of coffee. No cream or sugar."

"Just out the door to your left is the bathroom, and then beyond that is the kitchen. Please feel free to make yourself at home." He left her standing there in awe of the beautiful space she had for her own private office.

She sat down in the comfortable leather chair and put the file with her sketches on the desk. After removing the pencils and pens from her purse, she was ready to get to work. She turned on the computer and sent a brief message to Jonathan giving him her new office phone number. She also advised Detective O'Neal of her new work location and how to contact her. At this point, no one else knew where she was. Of course, her e-mail address remained the same so she could hear from everyone anytime.

She began reviewing plants, making a list of appropriate ones including sizes and colors. Once she had a selection to begin considering, it was time to walk the space with them in mind. She set out with a notebook in hand. She first considered the view from the house and patio, as well as the area around the swimming pool. The entire morning was spent in the garden as she made sketches of changes she would consider. By the time she finished her first analysis, it was noon. She went back to her office where she eagerly sat down at her desk. She barely had taken a relaxing breath when there was a light knock on her office door.

"Come in?" she said as a question.

It was the cook. "I have prepared a light lunch for you. Would you like it served on the patio?"

"Yes, that would be lovely. I'll wash up and be right out."

As soon as she sat down, a beautiful salad was placed in front of her along with a French roll and a glass of iced tea. She was asked, "Is there anything else you would like?"

"No. This is lovely. Thank you." Jeanne decided this was going to be the best job in the world. She just hoped she could make Mr. Marchant happy.

"Hi, there," Mr. Marchant said as he approached Jeanne when she finished her last bite of salad. "How did it go this morning?"

"Very well. I spent the time walking through the area trying to get a feel for the space. It will be a challenge, but I am certain I will come up with a plan, not only to please you, but to enhance your property."

"And that's what I'm expecting." Then he asked, "May I join you for dessert?"

"I'd like that. I want to share some of my preliminary ideas with you. I can use your feedback before I go too far astray," she said with a self-conscious laugh.

As soon as the chocolate sundae was placed in front of them, she began to share her thoughts about the garden. He kept nodding his head in approval and she kept describing everything to him. She got the feeling she was on the right track with her ideas. "As soon as I am a little more sure of how everything will look, I'll give you a drawing of my plans. Before any actual work is begun, I want to be sure you approve it."

"I appreciate that. I'll look forward to seeing what you may develop."

"Mr. Marchant, what is your favorite color?"

"Why, it's yellow. I like it because it is such a happy color. Why do you ask?"

"I'll keep it in mind as I design the garden."

"Thank you. Now, I'll let you get back to work, and I'll get to mine. By the way, just tell the cook what you would like for lunch. She will prepare something for you every day." With that he was gone.

Jeanne was totally lost for words. She sat quietly for a moment rethinking everything that had just transpired. She picked up her iced tea and took it to her office. She thought about how best to develop the plans for creating a unique garden. First, she would divide it into sections, making each one special and unique. That way she could tackle the huge project in smaller parcels. With that decision made, she was ready to start putting the plans on paper.

CHAPTER 50

Jeanne was tired when she got home from her first day at the Marchant Estate. A glass of Chardonnay was most welcome, along with music of Debussy. She kicked off her shoes and stretched out on the sofa, letting the music wash over her. She was startled by the ringing of the phone. It was Jonathan. "How was your first day working for Mr. Marchant?"

"Exhausting, but I enjoyed it. The project is a challenge. However, it's going to be a lot of fun, too."

"That's great." There was a long pause then he said, "Jeanne, I had a call from Detective O'Neal today. He said they arrested Phyllis for murder, as well as car theft."

"Oh, I'm not surprised. Did he tell you if they had substantial information now?"

"No. He only told me they probably would be asking me, as well as you, to be available to testify at some point. He said he would contact you."

"I haven't heard from him yet. I did let him know where I am during the day. Perhaps tomorrow I'll hear from him."

"You'll have to tell Mr. Marchant about Phyllis at some point if you are called into court."

"I'm sure it will be okay. He's letting me set my own schedule. Of course, I'll let him know when I have to be away. Until then, we'll let the detective deal with Phyllis."

She was awakened by a loud ringing. She glanced at the clock to discover it was already eight o'clock. She answered the call from Detective O'Neal. "My, you are calling early, but I'm glad you woke me."

"I'm so sorry to have awakened you," the Detective said apologetically. "I wanted to talk to you before you went to work."

"That's okay. My schedule is more flexible in my new job. So what do you need?" she asked as she stifled a yawn.

"I wanted to let you know we arrested Phyllis for murder yesterday, or rather Sunday. Of course, you'll need to be available to testify when she goes to court. I'll let you know when that is."

"I appreciate that. I feel better knowing she is no longer on the streets. How did she respond to her arrest?"

"As you might guess, she caused quite a scene. There was lots of screaming and lashing out at the arresting officer. We went to her home Sunday afternoon with the warrant. As Phyllis was escorted to the police car, she created quite a disturbance. She did not go quietly."

"I can imagine what it was like after having been a witness to her arrest in the office."

"One of the officers experienced some of her nail scratching to his arms and face. Nothing serious, but enough to draw blood."

"That's terrible," Jeanne said sympathetically. "Do you think Phyllis has a mental problem?"

"She has been under the care of Dr. Meredith, the psychiatrist. I'll let him answer that. We are considering the dinner she prepared for you and Judith, and her seeming to follow you in her car one day. Was there any thing else that you recall?"

"Only when she hid a file at the office hoping to get me in trouble. She was always jealous of me because she thinks she is in love with Jonathan and I was coming between them. You know Jonathan's deceased wife was Phyllis's sister? I think she never accepted that he chose Elizabeth and not her."

"I did not know that," the detective said with surprise. "That may explain part of her behavior. I'm sure the psychiatrist has discovered that, but I may ask him."

Jeanne was eager to get back to her garden project. As before, when she arrived at the large gates she was admitted immediately. The butler greeted her, "Good morning, Ms. Blomgren. Mr. Marchant asked me to give you the gate code so you may come and go as you please. Just enter it on the key pad when you drive up," he said as he handed her the note.

"Good morning, and thank you, Edward. I appreciate it." She went to her office feeling comfortable with having the gate code; that meant she was trusted. She went directly to work on the garden section closest to the house. Since that was the area Mr. Marchant and his guests would see first, it needed to be special. She already knew he liked roses, as did she, and he had mentioned his favorite color, which she kept in mind as she selected plants to include. The morning progressed quickly and it was lunchtime before she realized it.

The cook quietly knocked on her door and said, "Since it is quite cool today, I've prepared your lunch in the small dining room. When would you like to have it served?"

"If it's ready, now would be fine. I am hungry."

As soon as Jeanne was seated, she inhaled the tantalizing aroma of the soup when she dipped her spoon in for a taste. "Umm... Delicious. By the way, I don't remember your name. You seem to know mine is Jeanne Blomgren. What's yours?"

"It's Mrs. Anna Jensen. You may call me Anna."

"Thank you, Anna. Are you Norwegian or Swedish?"

"I'm Swedish," she said proudly.

"So am I," Jeanne responded. "Now I know why I like your cooking."

Anna blushed a little and muttered, "Thank you," as she left.

Jeanne was returning to her office after finishing lunch when she was stopped by Mr. Marchant. "Hello, Jeanne. Do you have a minute?"

"Of course, Mr. Marchant. My time is your time," she said with a little humor. "What can I do for you?"

"Let's go to your office."

Jeanne led the way. "What's on your mind?" she asked as they sat down. She folded her hands on top of the desk hoping to look relaxed, even though he made her feel uneasy.

"I just wanted you to know I will be out of town for a couple of days this week. You will have access to the house and your office. There is always some staff here so you won't be totally alone. However, I have engaged a landscape architect to work with you. He will be here tomorrow morning to meet you. His name is Armando. I want to be sure you and he are compatible and that you will be comfortable working with him. I trust you will let me know."

"Absolutely. I doubt there will be a problem. I can get along with almost everyone." She had said almost everyone thinking of Phyllis. "Now, I have a question for you?"

"Fire away," he said as he sat up straight.

"Would you like to see my preliminary sketch for the first section of your garden? As you know, I've divided your property into sections making it easier to develop the design."

"Yes, that was a good idea, and I would love to see what you are developing."

Jeanne spread out her initial drawings on the large drafting table. As she explained what she was thinking, why she chose certain plants and colors, she tried to clarify the aesthetics of the plan. All the while, Mr. Marchant was nodding his head as if he understood and agreed. He did ask a couple of questions and made an occasional suggestion. At the conclusion of her presentation, he said, "I like what you are doing. Continue on."

She couldn't help but break into a huge smile. "Thank you. I will."

The next morning, Armando appeared shortly after Jeanne arrived at her office. "I'm Jeanne Blomgren," she said as she reached out her hand. "And you must be Armando."

"Yes, I'm pleased to meet you. Mr. Marchant has told me a little about you and what you want to do to his property."

"That's one way to put it," she said smiling. "I do have plans to make it very special. Let me tell you what I have in mind."

She proceeded to tell him about working in small sections, but making it all cohesive in design and color. She also told him what she thought about the use of the space. There needed to be a place for small gatherings, perhaps a stage for concerts, but nothing obtrusive. She admitted that she didn't know a lot about plants, but had done research for those suitable in this climate.

"May I see your preliminary sketches, or is it too soon?"

"I'd be happy to show them to you and get your input. I've worked on just the first section." She retrieved her sketches and spread them out on the table. Armando silently viewed them.

"You've done an excellent job... so far. I may share a few suggestions with you, if you're open to them. Mr. Marchant made it clear that the garden is to be your design. I'll respect that."

"Thank you. I will need your help and knowledge. I know what I want it to look like, but I may not know how to implement that look. That's where you come in," she said looking questioningly at him. "Are you interested in working with me?"

He was delighted with what he heard and immediately knew he would enjoy working with her. "Yes, Ma'am. I would very much like to work on this project with you."

"Then, let's get started. Come to my office. It has a space where you can work."

She showed him the drafting table which pleased him. "I'm not good at creating an accurate drawing. That's your expertise as a landscape architect. Come tomorrow morning around ten o'clock with your pencils sharpened and we'll get to work. I'll go over the entire plan with you and then we'll focus on just one section at a time. Will that work for you?"

"Sounds fine. See you tomorrow."

She was pleased to have someone so knowledgeable and professional working with her. She finished the day with a smile on her face.

As soon as Jeanne arrived home, she called Jonathan. She was so eager to tell him about Armando that she could hardly wait for him to answer his phone. When he finally did, she jumped right in with telling him how excited she was working for Mr. Marchant and on the project, and now with Armando, the landscape architect.

"Slow down, Jeanne. I can tell you are excited and happy. I think you have found your new passion."

"I think you're right," she said after a moment's pause. "This job is not work; it's fun. I come home energized."

"You are fortunate to have found something so enjoyable and rewarding. I'm happy for you." Jonathan meant that sincerely. "Now... will you have time for me this weekend?"

"Of course. I'm eager to see you. What do you have in mind?"

"Would you like to see a matinee performance of a new play Saturday and then dinner at The Club?"

"That sounds lovely. I haven't been to a theater production for some time. I read that this new play is a good one."

"Yes, that's the word. So it's a date. I'll pick you up at one o'clock. Until then, I'll keep you in my thoughts."

Before Jeanne could respond, he was gone. Yes, she would keep him in her thoughts, also. He was in her dreams that night as well.

CHAPTER 51

Armando proved to be a talented and enthusiastic asset to the garden project. His drawings clearly identified the garden's layout and Jeanne's drawings indicated the color patterns. When Mr. Marchant returned they were ready for his approval for the first section, which he gave immediately. Of course, he wanted to see the rest of the garden's plans before any work would begin.

On the first Tuesday of December, Jeanne had a call from Detective O'Neal advising her the trial for Phyllis would begin the next week. "You need to be available when called to appear in court. Can you get away from your job?"

"Yes, I can arrange to be there when asked," she told him. "Do you have any idea how soon it might be?"

"No, but I would expect you to be called early because you found the body. That's what started the whole thing."

"Of course. I wish I could attend the entire trial, but I do have a job."

It was time to tell Mr. Marchant. He looked up when Jeanne knocked and asked, "Is everything all right?"

"Yes. The project is going well. However, something has come up that I must tell you about. It has nothing to do with my work here. Do you have a few minutes? This may take a little while."

"Yes, what is it?" he asked with curiosity.

Jeanne began by saying, "I may have to appear in court soon regarding a murder trial."

Mr. Marchant looked shocked and said, "If you must, you are free go when needed."

"I feel I should tell you about it so you will understand." She began at the beginning and told him everything relating to Phyllis and Roger. "And that's how I met Jonathan."

When she had finished, Mr. Marchant took a deep breath and let it out in a low whistle.

"Thanks for sharing that with me. I had no idea of what you have gone through. If I can be of any help just let me know."

"By allowing me to have time to appear at the trial is a start."

"If you want to spend more time there, do. We have no set deadline."

"Thank you for understanding. If I can attend some of the trial I would like to." She stood, indicating she was finished.

By Friday, they had nearly finished the design for the second section. There was one problem unique to this section, but it turned out to be the best part of the design. The natural spring just above his property fed a small creek that ran along side and into his property. Jeanne and Armando were able to incorporate it into the garden, which enhanced the over-all design. They wanted to create a quiet and romantic place for contemplation.

"We have done a good job," Jeanne told Armando. "I think we can submit our design for Section Two on Monday. Now, let's call it a day and go home a little early. I'm sure your family will be happy to see you."

"Thank you, Ms. Blomgren. I'll see you Monday."

"Armando, you may call me Jeanne."

"Yes, Ms. Jeanne," he responded with a shy smile.

Jeanne's phone rang just as she prepared to leave. She hesitated, not wanting to answer it. "This is Ms. Blomgren," she said in her professional voice.

It was Mr. Marchant. "I was just calling to see if everything is okay and to let you know I will be in Monday morning. I'm eager to see what you have for me."

"We have finished the plan and drawings for Section Two. They will be ready for your approval—or not. However, I think you will like it."

"Great! Since it is nearly the end of Friday, I suggest you go home and have a pleasant weekend. See you Monday." Before she could thank him, the call was terminated.

On the weekend, she and Jonathan attended the theater. They had mixed feelings about the play—Jeanne liked it but Jonathan was not sure. It gave them a lot to discuss over dinner at The Club. It was one of the few times they had differing opinions. It was finally agreed that when it comes to the arts—whether it's music, art, dance or theater—it is "in the eye, or ear, of the beholder" as to how one responds. No one is wrong, just different.

"Now that we have that settled," Jonathan said, "we can discuss other things. Tell me all about the garden project."

Jeanne told him what they had done and how she enjoyed working with Armando. "I'm so happy you introduced me to Mr. Marchant. His project is exactly what I needed to keep me busy and productive."

"You're welcome. I miss you at the office," he said as he reached for her hand, "but I'm glad you are happy with your new job."

They reluctantly left The Club. When they arrived at her apartment, Jeanne invited Jonathan to come in. Jeanne turned on their favorite music, sat on one end of the sofa, kicked her shoes off and curled her feet up under her. Jonathan sat down next to her. Jeanne drew in a deep breath, let it out slowly and asked, "Do you have plans for Christmas?"

That took Jonathan by surprise. "No. Since Elizabeth died I've ignored Christmas. It will never be the same."

"I understand. Perhaps you could spend this Christmas with me and the twins. Would you?"

He remained quiet but finally said, "Maybe. I'll think about it."

"Okay. No pressure, but I want you to know we'd be happy to have you."

"Will you be at the beach house again?"

"I'm not sure. It will depend on the weather. Right now, I think I'd like to stay here. I'll check with the twins and see what they'd prefer for their two weeks off." She inhaled and asked, "Do you have plans for tomorrow?"

"Nothing special. Why? Did you have something mind?"

"I wondered if you'd like to go to church with me?"

"Sure. I'd like that."

"Let's attend the ten o'clock service, then we can come here for brunch."

Jeanne walked him to the door. He turned and took her in his arms with a warm embrace. He lowered his head and placed his mouth on hers in a deep and passionate kiss. She opened her mouth to his as she melded into his arms. Jonathan slowly pulled away and said, "Good night. See you in the morning."

She quietly closed the door and stood against it reveling in that kiss.

Sunday morning dawned with bright sunlight sneaking through the crack in the draperies. Jeanne crawled out from her cocoon and enjoyed a leisurely shower. Since brunch was on the schedule she had just a small glass of juice and apiece of toast. At exactly nine thirty, Jonathan knocked.

"My, don't you look handsome," Jeanne said when she opened the door.

"You look very nice, too. That is a beautiful suit—and so are you."

Jeanne blushed slightly at the compliment. "Thank you, sir," she responded as she quickly walked to the elevator. Once inside, Jonathan leaned over and gave her a gentle kiss on the cheek.

"What was that for?" she asked.

"Nothing special. Just because..."

The organ music that greeted them at the entrance to the church was by a contemporary composer she didn't recognize. It was majestic and solemn—perfect for establishing a worshipful stance. The service proceeded with the singing of hymns and, of course, a sermon. This one was on The Power of Love. The pastor talked about the various kinds of love: family, country, friends, sweethearts, and the greatest of all—God. It was an inspiring message. The organist must have known Jeanne was there because he played a Bach postlude which made her church experience complete.

As they exited, Jonathan announced, "Now, I'm ready for brunch. You did promise it, you know. What are we having?"

"We have a choice. Which would you prefer: a mushroom omelette or Belgian waffles with fresh blueberries, or strawberries?"

"That's a difficult choice. I like both." After a few seconds, he finally said, "Let's have Belgian waffles. Can we do a mixture of strawberries and blueberries?"

"Of course. We can do whatever we like."

They enjoyed working and eating together. When the last of the champagne had been ingested, they sat down with a cup of coffee in front of the large windows to appreciate the view of the park. Their conversation covered myriad topics, and finally Jonathan asked, "Are you ready to testify in Phyllis's trial?"

"As ready as one can be. I have no idea what questions her lawyer will ask."

"As I always say, just tell the truth as only you know it, and you'll be okay. I think the trial is to start this week. Have you told Mr. Marchant you may have to be there?"

"Yes. I told him the whole story and he said I should do whatever I have to."

Jonathan yawned. "Jeanne, I think I need to go home and take a nap. That generous brunch and champagne has made me drowsy."

"I, too, am ready for a nap. You don't need to leave. You can nap here... if you wish."

He hesitated a moment and said, "That's a great idea. Let's do it."

They went up to her bedroom and laid down side by side on top of the comforter and closed their eyes. They spoke no words, only turned and smiled at each other. Jeanne knew Jonathan had dozed off when she heard the soft rumble coming from his throat. She drifted into nothingness.

The next thing she was aware of was a hand on her cheek. She slowly opened her eyes and saw two beautiful brown eyes staring at her.

"You look so peaceful sleeping. I'm glad you are awake because..." and he leaned over and kissed her lightly at first, and then more passionately. She responded in kind. They lay quietly for a time with arms wrapped around each other, just enjoying the closeness.

"This is nice," Jeanne said. "I like having you here."

"And I like being here. We must do this more often," and he kissed her again. He raised up and said, "I really must be going. The day is nearly over and I have to prepare for a case starting in the morning."

Jeanne slowly got up, stretched and said, "If you must go I won't detain you, but I'd love to have you stay longer...as long as you like."

"I'll be back another day, I promise."

Jeanne followed him to the door and accepted another brief kiss as he left.

CHAPTER 52

The ringing of the phone as she entered her office Monday morning jump-started Jeanne's day. When she answered, she was surprised to hear the voice of Gary Warner, Phyllis's attorney.

"Good morning, Mr. Warner."

"Good morning. As you may know, Phyllis McNeil is being arraigned this week on two counts: murder and car theft. I'm not sure yet if they will be handled separately or together at the trial. The judge may decide. When she does go to trial we will want you to be available the first couple of days since you were the one who discovered the body."

"I understand. That will not be a problem. Just let me know the exact times as soon as you can. I do have to let my current employer know when I'll be away."

"Of course. I'll be in touch," and with that he was gone.

Jeanne was glad things were progressing toward a trial. Meanwhile, she wanted to get the second phase of the garden plan completed.

Armando walked into the office with a cheerful, "Good morning, Ms. Jeanne. Let's finish Section Two today. I already have some ideas for the third section."

"Great. So do I," Jeanne added enthusiastically. "Let's get to work and compare ideas."

Together they reviewed the work on Section Two, made a few minor changes and by noon declared Armando's drawing complete. They took their sketches to Mr. Marchant's office. He looked very serious as he perused them. He asked a few questions, made a few positive comments and in general was very pleased with their work.

"Jeanne, you have incorporated some very innovative ideas. You are extremely creative and as they say, you 'think out of the box.' I like it, particularly the way you blend the sections with a meandering natural pathway. I am eager to see the rest of your plan. Will the next section deal with the performing space?"

"Yes, and I'm having great fun thinking about what kinds of performances or events that could be held there. Is there anything special you would like?"

"I'm sure that whatever you design will meet my expectations. You have complete freedom to do whatever you want. However, I will hold the option for final approval."

"Of course, and thank you."

For the next few days, Jeanne and Armando sketched ideas, talked about events, the space, the acoustics and overall visual appearance. By the end of the week, they were ready to present Section Three plans to Mr. Marchant. When he saw the area designed for performances he immediately said, "We need to plan a special concert for the opening of the gardens. A chamber orchestra or a band for dancing, or...," he said with excitement.

Jeanne looked at Armando and said, "I'm sure the remainder of the garden designs will be finished by Christmastime. However, it will depend on how long it will take to implement them before we make plans for an opening event."

Armando said, "Once everything is approved, work can start almost immediately. I can have constructions crews lined up, ready to go whenever you say the word."

"I think we could plan on a late spring opening," Jeanne commented. "That's a perfect time for the garden; flowers will be in bloom and the lawns will be green. It may be a rush, but I think it can be done."

"That would be perfect. See if you can make it work," Mr. Marchant said.

Jeanne and Armando looked at each other, smiled and vowed to meet the schedule. Together they sketched out plans for Section Four, which included the swimming pool area. Naturally, they chose not to change the pool and surrounding deck, nor the dressing rooms, but they did change the landscape. By the end of the week, they were ready to get Mr. Marchant's approval of Section Four. They had designed each section to blend into the next so it appeared to be one continuous plan. Trees of various foliage and height framed the spaces and provided a backdrop to the garden. Armando's architectural drawings were so precise Mr. Marchant had no problem envisioning the entire project. When he saw the completed plan, he immediately gave his approval to go ahead.

"Since Christmas is approaching, why don't you plan on starting the physical work right after the holiday? You both have worked hard, so you deserve a little time off to enjoy Christmas with friends and family. Armando, you can get the crews scheduled to start the work. Jeanne, you can get the necessary new plants ordered. Other than that, I'll see you after Christmas. Have a merry one."

"Thank you. Merry Christmas to you, too," Jeanne and Armando said simultaneously. They put their work away and left to enjoy the Christmas holiday.

Jeanne realized she had been so busy with the garden project, she had neglected to make plans for Christmas. It was just a few days away and she had done no shopping for gifts. The twins would be home, and Jonathan would be joining them Christmas day. She was glad Mr. Marchant gave her some extra time off since she really needed it.

As soon as she arrived home, she started making lists of tasks: gifts for the twins, a gift for Jonathan, something for Alexander and Maurice, and the menus for Christmas Eve and the Christmas dinner. She also had to prepare for the twins being home for a couple of weeks. She expected them arrive this weekend, which meant she had better get to work. Based on projected weather reports, she decided they would stay in town for Christmas. The twins might go to the beach house sometime during their holiday if the weather permitted.

Early the next morning, the small screen on the phone showed the name of Gary Warner, Phyllis's attorney. She hesitated before answering, and finally said, "Yes?"

"Good morning, Jeanne. Sorry to call so early. I'm planning to meet with Phyllis this morning and I wanted to let you know she will be going into court Monday."

"Thanks for the heads up, Do I need to be there?"

"No. I'm not calling you to testify yet. However, the prosecutor might."

"So I guess I might hear from him soon? It's too bad this is happening Christmas week when we all are busy with holiday activities."

"Yes, it is unfortunate, but Phyllis wants to get this over with as soon as possible, and she is guaranteed a speedy trial."

"I understand. I'll be available whenever I'm needed."

Fully awake, Jeanne climbed out of the warm hollow of her bed and launched into the day's busy schedule. Gathering her lists in hand, she ventured into the market place. Now that the twins were older, it was much more difficult selecting the appropriate gifts for them. And then there was Jonathan... She didn't want to get anything too personal, and yet it had to be meaningful. She also wanted to get a gift for Judy, who had become a good friend.

By noon, she was not only tired, but hungry and so she decided to drop into the French Corner Café. As soon as she entered she heard someone call her. "Come over and join us," Judy invited. She was with Michael and so Jeanne hesitated interrupting their private lunch time.

"Are you sure? I don't want to intrude."

"Not at all. Please sit down. Michael, you remember Jeanne?"

"Of course. It's good to see you again," he said smiling warmly at her. "I will always remember you as the one who brought Judy and me together."

"I'm glad something good came out of that unfortunate evening," Jeanne said as she slid into her seat. "Have you ordered?"

"No, we just arrived and are still reading the menu. Here, you can look at this one," Michael said as he handed it to her.

"Thanks, but I really don't need to see a menu; I already know what I want. We used to come here so often that I may have memorized their food selections."

They placed their orders and Jeanne said, "Phyllis's trial starts soon. At some point, I think each of us may be called in to testify."

"I would expect that," Judy said. "We haven't heard from anyone yet. Have you?"

"I had a call this morning from Gary Warner, Phyllis's attorney, telling me the trial was starting next week. I appreciate his advance notice."

"It's unfortunate that it starts just before Christmas," Michael observed.

"They probably will have only a couple of days in court and then take a break until after the holiday. At least I hope that is what will happen," Jeanne said. "The twins will be coming home and I want to have time with them."

By late afternoon, Jeanne had completed her shopping. She just hoped the receivers would be as pleased with her gift purchases as she. She put on a CD of music by Schubert. It contained her favorite: the *Trout Quintet.* She kicked her shoes off, sat in front of the picture window and let out a long relaxing sigh as she sipped on her favorite wine. It had been a productive, but tiring day, and having lunch with Judy and Michael had been a pleasant interlude.

Since the twins were coming home this weekend, she decided to let them get the tree and decorate it. That would give them something to do for a couple of days.

CHAPTER 53

The twins arrived at the apartment late in the day in a rented car so they could have their independence while on vacation for a couple of weeks. Their conversations went late into the night covering myriad topics from school programs and their latest dates to Jeanne's new job and her impending court appearance. Jeanne brought them up to date on Phyllis, her arrest for murder in addition to car theft.

Mark asked, "So...do you have Dad's car now?"

"No. It is still in police custody until after the trial. At that point, I think I will sell it and divide the proceeds between the two of you. Now it's time to retire." She said good night and turned out the lights.

The next few days were busy getting ready for Christmas. The twins went shopping for a tree, which they dutifully decorated. Jeanne wrapped the gifts she had purchased and placed them under the tree. As soon as she placed the wreathe on the door, she declared that it was beginning to look like Christmas. A call from the attorney disrupted the holiday spirit when she was asked to appear in court the following morning.

"Of course, I will be there," she answered. "Do you know how long it will take?"

"Not long. We just need to swear you in and get your testimony on when and how you found the deceased. You will be called back another day, which may not be until after Christmas."

"I am surprised you are starting the trial before the holiday."

"Yes, but we do have a couple of days to get started. There will be a lot to cover." He signed off saying, "I'll see you in the morning at nine."

Jeanne told the twins she would be in court the next morning. They asked if they could go, too. Since a trial is open to the public she said, "Yes, if you really want to."

"I think it would be educational for us," Mark said. "We've never been to a court trial, so it will give us a chance to see the legal system at work."

"Yes," Mandy chimed in. "We need to be there for you."

Jeanne agreed she'd like them there. She was surprised that she did not feel apprehensive about testifying. She just wished Jonathan could be there. When he called her that evening she told him about going to court in the morning.

"I would like to be there, too. If I can get out of the office I will drop in."

"No problem," Jeanne assured him. "If you're not there I'll give you a full report."

"I'll count on it." After a brief pause, he continued, "I'm surprised I have not been called since I was with you that day. Perhaps they'll get to me later."

"I'm sure they will. Until tomorrow, good night."

Jeanne rose early so she would be fully alert for her court appearance. She and the twins arrived at the court house a little before nine. They found the correct room where they were greeted by Gary Warner, the attorney who had called her in.

"We're first up on the court document this morning. Just be seated until you are called."

"Thank you," was all Jeanne had time to say. She and the twins took their seats and the side door opened. Phyllis was led in dressed in her own clothes rather than the orange jumpsuit Jeanne was expecting to see. She looked tired, but that may have been because of the lack of makeup. They did not make eye contact. Phyllis kept her eyes downcast.

The judge entered and called the court to order. Jeanne noticed there were few people in the courtroom. Undoubtedly some were people who made a habit of visiting courtrooms and a couple from the press who were assigned to cover that room and judge.

The judge announced the first case, which was Phyllis's, and the prosecutor addressed the court. He stated the defendant was being accused of murder as well as car theft. He requested that the two accusations be tried separately. He waited quietly while the judge read from the file in front of him. Finally he said, "It appears that the two are related. I think it would be prudent to consider them together."

"Thank you, your honor."

"Then you may proceed," and with that the trial officially began.

The prosecuting attorney read his formal statement saying they would prove Phyllis guilty of murder, and ultimately stealing the victim's expensive car. He set the stage of where, why and how the crime was committed by her. As far as Jeanne could tell, he had stated his facts accurately. She was called to the stand as a witness.

After she was sworn in, the attorney asked, "Were you the person who first found the victim on August...?" He looked at his notes and couldn't immediately find the date, so he continued, "the end of August of this year?"

"Yes," Jeanne answered confidently.

He asked her questions about that day at summer's end and she told her story again in great detail, just as she had done for Detective O'Neal. When she had concluded, the attorney told the court he wanted to reserve the right to question her again at some future time.

Then it was time for Mr. Warner to cross-examine her. When he addressed her, it was the first time Phyllis looked at her. Jeanne kept her eyes on the attorney as she answered all of his questions, which related to the day she found Roger dead among the rocks. She remained very consistent in all of her comments. He said, "That will be all for now. Thank you for coming in." She was excused. As she walked back to her seat, she registered surprise at seeing Jonathan enter through the back doors.

The prosecuting attorney called Jonathan to the stand. He asked him some of the same questions Jeanne had answered. Even though Jonathan had not heard Jeanne's comments, his answers were exactly the same as hers. The same was true when Gary Warner questioned him. The two of them set a solid foundation for the remainder of the trial.

The judge adjourned the session and said it would be continued after the holiday. Phyllis was escorted back to her cell after looking at

Jonathan with a very sad expression. Both Jeanne and Jonathan showed no reaction to her. They left the courtroom quietly.

"I was surprised to see you this morning," Jeanne said to Jonathan.

"I was surprised with an early morning call asking me to come, but to wait outside the room until I was called in. I guess they didn't want me to hear what you said."

"Well, you said exactly the same things I did. You were asked the same questions they asked me. Now they know the truth."

One reporter came over and asked if he could interview them. They declined. They agreed to not discuss any part of the trial with anyone outside of their family. Now all they wanted was to enjoy the Christmas holiday together, and so they concurred to dismiss everything about Phyllis and the trial from their minds.

CHAPTER 54

Everyone gathered at Jeanne's apartment. They savored assorted snacks while they discussed plans for Christmas Eve. Jonathan declined to be included for Christmas Eve. He said, "That time should be for family only. I'll be happy to join you Christmas Day." They could not dissuade him.

After he left, Jeanne and the twins talked about how this Christmas would be different from previous ones. For one thing, Roger was no longer with them. The family had always been together for special holidays, and they were celebrated in the family home of many years. This year, they were in Jeanne's new apartment. If the weather permitted, the twins said they might go to the beach house for a day or two, otherwise they would remain in the city with Jeanne.

Jeanne turned the Christmas tree lights on as the sun was setting. "Mark, would you start a fire in the fireplace, please? It will brighten the room for Christmas Eve."

While Mark built the fire, Jeanne prepared her usual Christmas Eve meal for the three of them. They enjoyed a quiet meal of traditional Swedish foods, along with mulled wine.

"Are we going to continue our tradition of opening one gift tonight, Christmas Eve?" Mark inquired.

"So you think you are getting more than one gift?" Jeanne asked with a smile. "But yes, we should continue that tradition."

They retreated to the living room and by the fire Jeanne gave each of them one gift, which they eagerly opened, and they gave one gift to Jeanne.

"I like this custom," Mandy remarked, "but now that we are older, will Santa Claus come tonight with more gifts for us?"

"I'm sure he will, assuming you have been good this year," Jeanne said with love.

Christmas Day arrived with a bright morning sun, the first in a couple of days. Jeanne was in the kitchen making coffee when Mandy bounded in. "So when can we open presents?" she asked with excitement.

"Not until your brother is up and Jonathan arrives. Meanwhile, what would you like for breakfast?"

"May we have cinnamon French toast with bacon?"

"I think that is a great suggestion. Will you help?" They set about preparing a Christmas breakfast.

Mark wandered in yawning and asked, "When's breakfast?"

"Soon," Jeanne answered. "Jonathan will be over any minute." Just as she placed the egg-soaked bread in the buttered pan there was a knock on the door. "Mandy, will you get the door? It's probably Jonathan."

His jovial voice shouted, "Merry Christmas! It's a beautiful day." His arms were overflowing with colorfully wrapped packages, which he immediately placed under the tree.

"Indeed it is," Jeanne replied. "Merry Christmas to you, too. The first piece of French toast is cooking so you are right on time."

As everyone sat down for breakfast, conversation was spontaneous and enthusiastic. Jeanne relished watching her family's interaction with Jonathan.

As soon as they had finished eating, Mark said, "It's time to open presents. I will play Santa Claus." They gathered in the living room and he picked a package from under the tree. He handed it to his mother. "This one's for you. It's from Mandy and me."

Jeanne took her time opening the package. "You know I need nothing." Finally, the wrapping fell away and revealed a gold picture frame which held a recent photo of the twins. "Oh! It's beautiful," she exclaimed. "And I did need this." She hugged each twin as she thanked them.

Thanks were extended to Jonathan for his gifts, which they said really weren't necessary. It took several minutes to remove all the paper and ribbons scattered around the room.

It was Mandy who said, "This has been a very happy Christmas. I was concerned that the first one without Dad might not be."

"I agree," Mark added. "We have survived a difficult year. Thanks, Mom, for making it possible."

"It took all of us working together. I couldn't have done it alone." She glanced at Jonathan and added, "We owe a lot to Jonathan, our attorney and friend."

Jonathan stood up and walked over to Jeanne, smiling as he said, "And thanks to all of you for including me in your family today." His arms encircled Jeanne in a long and warm embrace. Mark and Mandy just looked at each other and smiled.

Late in the afternoon, Jeanne and Jonathan were sitting in front of the living room window enjoying after-dinner coffee when Jonathan suddenly said, "Let's go for a walk." He grabbed Jeanne's hand and pulled her out of the chair. Jeanne lifted a jacket from the hall closet, Jonathan donned his jacket and they left the apartment telling the twins they'd be back soon. They walked to the park across the street and strolled down the winding pathway to the fountain in the center of the lawn. The shadows were lengthening in the setting sun.

"Let's sit for a minute," Jonathan said as he pointed to the sculpted bench. "There is something I want to talk to you about."

"Okay. What is it?" Jeanne asked with curiosity and some concern.

"Do you realize we met about four months ago?"

"Yes, but it seems longer. So much has happened in that time."

"True. We have come to know each other quite well, don't you think?" he asked as he reached for her hand.

"Yes, we have, and I've enjoyed every minute of it."

"Jeanne, I didn't think I would ever love any woman again after Elizabeth, but I think I'm falling in love with you."

Jeanne was quiet as she looked into Jonathan's brown eyes. She couldn't respond with words, but she leaned in and kissed him. Only then could she say, "I think it might be mutual."

Jonathan smiled with happiness and proceeded to respond to Jeanne with a more passionate kiss. "Jeanne..." He hesitated. "Jeanne, would you consider marrying me?"

"I might consider it," she said with a playful smile.

"How long do you need to consider?"

"Oh... not long." She looked at Jonathan and continued, "Maybe a minute or so."

Jonathan grinned from ear to ear as he said, "In that case, will you marry me?"

"Yes. Yes, I will marry you," Jeanne said enthusiastically with a smile matching his.

They sealed the agreement with a kiss, and another...

After pausing for a brief moment, Jeanne said *"Jag alskar dig."*

Jonathan looked at her perplexed.

"Oh, it's I love you in Swedish."

"As far as I'm concerned, you can say it in any language, and as often as you wish."

"In that case, *Je t'aime* and *Te amo*. Will that do for the time being?"

"That's a good start," he answered with amusement. "Now, I have one more gift for you," Jonathan said as he reached into his pocket and pulled out a small package. He placed it in Jeanne's hand. "Open it."

She slowly removed the wrapping to reveal a small black box with her name on top lettered in gold. She lifted the lid to expose the most beautiful diamond and blue star sapphire ring she had ever seen. "Oh, it's beautiful," she said breathlessly. "May I wear it?" she asked expectantly.

"Of course. That's why I got it for you." He picked up her hand. "Here, let me put it on for you." He easily slid it onto her fourth finger.

Jeanne knew at that moment she belonged to Jonathan, and he to her.

"Jonathan, you had this ring in your pocket all day? How did you know I would say yes?"

"I hoped you would. Now, the next question is, when do we tell the twins? I'm sure they will think it's too soon after losing their father."

Jeanne was quiet for a time as she pondered the answer. "Yes, it may seem too soon, but being older, in our mid-forties, why would we wait? The twins know you, and I'm sure they want us to be happy. You make me happy." She hesitated and then thoughtfully said, "Perhaps we can compromise. Let's have a long engagement."

"How long are you thinking?"

"Maybe we could plan on a summer wedding, which will be nearly a year after Roger's death, and besides the new Marchant gardens will be finished. I'd like to be married there. What do you think?"

Jonathan readily agreed. "That's an excellent idea. Even though I'd love to be married sooner, I think your plan is perfect. We will wait to announce our engagement to anyone other than your children. Of course, we need to get Mr. Marchant's agreement to hold our wedding in his new garden."

"I don't think that will be a problem. After all, I did design it for such events. We may be the first wedding to take place in the beautiful new space. That will give us nearly six months to develop plans for our special day." She paused and then said, "First, let's go home and tell the twins." Jonathan agreed and they walked back to the apartment, hand in hand, smiling all the way.

When they approached the apartment building, Maurice greeted them at the door. "You must have had a merry Christmas; you both look very happy."

"That we did," Jeanne said. She was bursting to tell him why, but it would have to wait. They hurried to the elevator, eager to share their good news with the twins. "Mandy, Mark, where are you?" Jeanne called as soon as they entered the room. "Come in here, please."

They slowly came out of their rooms with questioning expressions. Mandy asked, "What is it? Is something wrong?"

"No, not at all. We have some news we want to share with you."

"It must be good news," Mark observed. "You both look happy."

"Yes, we are. We are very happy," Jeanne said as she looked up at Jonathan. "Jonathan asked me to marry him, and I accepted."

"Oh, Mom, that's wonderful!" Mandy exclaimed as she gave her mother a big hug.

Mark agreed and said, "Great! I'm very happy for you... for you both." Then he said, "Welcome to the family. Will I call you Dad, or...?" he asked Jonathan.

"Just call me Jonathan," and he smiled as they shook hands.

Jeanne explained that it was going to be a secret for a while. They were the only ones to know. Then they discussed the reason for waiting, and said they would have an early summer wedding. The twins agreed with the plan and they would comply with their wishes.

Then Jeanne showed them the ring with a delicate spray of diamonds diagonally placed around the oval-shaped blue stone. "It's perfect for me."

"I agree, Mom," Mandy said. "He couldn't have given you a better one. It's absolutely beautiful. Isn't it, Mark?"

"Yeah. I've never seen one like it. Did you have it made special?"

"As a matter of fact, I did. I wanted something unique for a unique person," he said smiling at Jeanne, who gave him a quick kiss on the cheek.

"Well, you are one of a kind, too," she told Jonathan. "I believe this calls for a celebration with champagne."

Mark handled the task of uncorking the bottle while Mandy retrieved the crystal flutes. They toasted the happy couple and then settled down for a lengthy conversation about their future. Jeanne observed her happy family, which now would include Jonathan.

CHAPTER 55

Jeanne went back to the Marchant Estate on Monday and met with Armando before presenting their completed plans to their boss.

Midmorning, Mr. Marchant appeared at Jeanne's office and said, "I'm ready to see your plans. Do you want to bring them to my office?"

"Yes, we will be right there." They hurried to his office.

"Now let's see what you have," Mr. Marchant said eagerly.

Armando confidently unrolled the plans on the large table and placed weights on the corners to keep the pages flat. There were four separate plans, one for each section, but they had combined them into one large page so he could see how they all fit together. Mr. Marchant took his time studying them. He asked a few questions, and Jeanne had an immediate answer. Only once did she defer to Armando.

"I am particularly surprised, and pleased, at how you included the natural stream in the plan. That stream is like a bonus to my property."

"I agree. I wanted to make it a special place—one where you would want to spend some quiet time."

"I really like the general layout. It's perfect."

"May we begin the work now?" Jeanne asked.

"Of course. Just be careful, but do whatever is necessary."

They left his office ready to start construction. Armando had alerted crews about starting work this week, so when he made the call to give the go-ahead, they responded enthusiastically. Jeanne had no idea how long it would take the landscape crews to implement the new design before the new plants could be embedded. Armando said he would tell her when it was time to have them delivered. For now, she had to wait.

The murder trial for Phyllis was back in session. Jeanne was not called in immediately, but was asked to be available when needed. She did tell Mr. Marchant that she may have to be away occasionally. Also, she told Armando that she would be involved in some court proceeding and may be in and out. "No problem," he assured her. "It will be a while before you are needed. I'll let you know." With that she felt free to attend some of the court hearings.

The topic of Roger's car came up, and Jeanne was called up to identify it, and the scarf found in it. Even though the trial was about suspected murder, the car played a role in it. She confirmed the detective's story about its discovery in the rented garage. It all seemed so cold and calculated now. Jeanne answered dozens of questions with "yes" or "no" until the attorney seemed satisfied that they had all the information they needed.

Phyllis appeared to be very uncomfortable. *She must be feeling guilty*, Jeanne said to herself. *I wonder if she will admit to killing Roger, even if it may have been accidentally?*

At the end of the third day, the judge said, "We are approaching another holiday weekend. I'd like to conclude this hearing before then. If the attorney's have no further evidence, I would like to submit this case to the jury. Before I do, however, I'd like to ask the defendant one question. Did you kill Roger Anders?"

Phyllis sat up straight, her green eyes flashing anger, "No... Yes... Maybe." She raised her voice and shouted, "It was an accident!"

The judge responded with surprise, and quietly said, "Why don't you tell us all about it—everything?"

After a long pause, Phyllis looked directly at the judge and said, "I know you are trying to make me guilty. I won't accept that. I won't stand for it!"

"Then tell us what happened that day at the beach."

Instead of answering the judge, she set off on a tirade about Jonathan, Jeanne, the detective, and anyone else she could think of, including Judy. When she seemed exhausted, she became silent and glared at the judge. She clearly was not accepting responsibility for her own actions.

The judge sent her back to her cell pending a psychiatrist's evaluation. He allowed the jury to adjourn until after the holiday.

Jeanne was sorry to have seen what transpired in the court room. When Jonathan called that evening, she related the court scene to him. "I've never seen anyone rant like she did."

"Do you think it's possible she is acting so she can get off the murder charge by pleading insanity?"

"It's possible. Do you think she is that clever?" Jeanne was quiet while she considered other examples of her unorthodox behavior. "There was the dinner episode when she tried to kill me with MSG. And the time when she hid the files at the office to get me in trouble with you. She is not showing signs of a rational person. What do you think?"

"I think we will have to depend on the psychiatrist to make that determination," he said with sadness in his voice. "Meanwhile, New Year's Eve is coming up and I wanted to invite you to be my date at a party given by my law firm. "Will you? I know I should have asked you sooner, but I hope you don't already have a date," he said teasingly.

"Of course, I don't. I'd love to go with you. It will be good to see members of the firm. I've missed them."

"Wonderful! It will be at the top of the Majestic Marvel Hotel downtown."

"Oh, I've always wanted to see it. I hear they have the best restaurant in town."

"So I hear, too, and the best view in the city with glass-lined walls of the circulating room. However, they will be hard pressed to have better food than The Club."

The twins attended a New Year's Eve party with some of their school friends. Jeanne was with Jonathan at his firm's party until the early morning hours. They were still up when the twins arrived home.

"Did you two have a good time," Jeanne asked them.

"Yes. It was great seeing our friends from school. So how was your date?"

"We had a great time. That room at the top of the hotel is spectacular. They had a good band for dancing, great food, and endless champagne."

"My firm knows how to throw a party." Jonathan said.

"Did you know the room at the top of the hotel makes a complete turn every hour?" Jeanne asked. "You can see all over the city while dancing or dining."

Jonathan interrupted and said, "Now I am exhausted, so I'll say good night to everyone and wish you all a Happy New Year."

Jeanne walked him to the door and stepped out to enjoy a lingering good night kiss. "Will I see you tomorrow?" she asked.

"Of course. I plan on watching the New Year's game with you. I never miss it."

"Neither do I. It's the only time I watch football. This year is special because USC will be playing against Stanford. We can't miss this one!"

"Right. I'll see you then," and he left stifling a yawn.

Mark was waiting when Jeanne came back into the room. "Mom, I wanted to tell you that Mandy and I were given tickets to the game tomorrow. Our friends knew we would want to be there. You don't mind if we go, do you?"

"Of course not. You need to be there. After all, it's your school that's playing. Besides I'll be here watching it with Jonathan."

"Thanks. Good night. See you in the morning... sometime."

Jeanne retired thinking about what next year would hold for them. She experienced a sense of excitement when the garden wedding crept into her thoughts.

CHAPTER 56

Jeanne awakened early enough to see the start of the Rose Parade on TV. While sipping her coffee, she marveled at the beauty and creative designs of the various floats. A couple of them gave her some new ideas for the Marchant gardens. She quickly wrote them down with sketches so she could recall them when back at the office.

The twins ambled out midmorning ready for coffee but not much else. Mandy poured herself and Mark some cereal. They watched the end of the parade while crunching on the cereal and then dressed for attending the football game.

"Mom, we're meeting our friends in Pasadena, and going with them to the Rose Bowl," Mark explained. "Parking is impossible, so we'll leave our car at their house and go in the limousine they've rented for the day."

"That sounds very luxurious. Have a great time. We'll be rooting for your team," Jeanne said as she bid them goodbye.

Jonathan arrived in time for a quick lunch before watching the exciting game with Jeanne. It was well played by both teams. The score was tied in the fourth quarter. Jonathan jumped to his feet when the quarterback threw a long pass to the tight end, who caught it on the run and kept going into the end zone. It was the winning touchdown for Stanford. Even Jeanne was shouting. Their team had won!

The twins were very excited when they returned late to the apartment. Of course, they talked nonstop about the game. They knew the return to school tomorrow was going to be one of celebration on campus.

Jonathan said goodbye to the twins, "Will we see you on Spring break?"

"Probably," Mandy said. "If we do come home, will we work on the plans for your wedding?"

Jeanne responded, "Of course. We want you to be involved."

As Jonathan left he said, "Goodnight, Jeanne. When will I see you next?"

"One evening this week I'm sure. Or maybe more than one," she said hopefully. She walked to the door with him and they lingered with an amorous kiss. This holiday season had been one of the happiest Jeanne could remember.

She arrived at the Marchant Estate to be greeted by several large pieces of equipment removing sections of the current garden making way for the new one. Armando was standing guard at the edge of the first section giving directions as needed to the work crew. Jeanne joined him. "Good morning, Armando. I see the work is underway."

"Good morning, Jeanne. Yes, it has begun. It's exciting to see your design take shape. Moving dirt is easy with this equipment so we should complete this first phase in about a week."

Jeanne had ordered plants to arrive next week. For now, she wanted to incorporate some of the ideas she got from the rose floats and adapt them into Section Two.

During this work schedule, Jeanne was called in again to testify in the court case. This time she was asked about the dinner at Phyllis's. She retold everything she could remember, as well as the resulting examination at the hospital.

Then Judith was called to the stand and she was asked to tell her experience at the dinner. Her testimony supported Jeanne's and filled in the time when Jeanne was unconscious. After her testimony, the paramedic, Michael, was called to the stand. By the time all three of them had told their experiences, the jury had a very complete picture of that event.

The next time Jeanne was called to testify, it was regarding Roger's car. Bob Baylord was also in court to testify the same day. Even Detective O'Neal appeared in court to tell how they determined the car had been in Phyllis's possession. The scarf, the picture, the observations of her neighbors all had corroborated that Phyllis had been in possession of the Mercedes-Benz. Because of the timing and the way she had obtained the car, the attorney then opened the door to the possibility that she was guilty of murder—the murder of Roger Anders. At that point, the judge called for a recess until the next morning.

Jeanne was concerned about the timing of the trial and the installation of the Marchant gardens. She hoped she would not have to be in court very long. As soon as she returned to the Marchant Estate, she asked Armando if she could talk with him before they left for the day. As soon as the workmen left, Armando went to Jeanne's office and knocked. "You wanted to see me?" he asked

"Yes, come in and have a seat. There is something I need to tell you." She hesitated, not knowing exactly how to tell him why she would be away occasionally. "Armando, you may have noticed I leave for a couple of hours sometimes. I may need to be away again, perhaps for a little longer and so I wanted to tell you why."

"You don't need to explain it to me."

"I know, but I think I should." She began telling him about having to appear in court for a murder trial, as well as car theft. "The murder was of my husband, who's car was stolen by the alleged perpetrator. So as you can imagine, I need to be on call for the trial."

"Wow! I would never have guessed that reason," he said with surprise and sympathy. "Can I do anything to help?"

"Not really. Just cover for me with our project if I'm not here. Mr. Marchant is aware of my circumstances. I don't want to slow the work down. I know you are fully capable of handling everything. In fact, you're probably better at it than I. Of course, I will check in whenever I can. Meanwhile, I will be here tomorrow, unless I get an early call." She stood up ending the conversation.

"Thanks for telling me. I will do my best."

Jeanne felt relieved having shared everything with Armando. She knew he'd do well on his own. All the plans were drawn and approved so the workers just needed to follow them. She trusted Armando to keep apprised of the progress, hourly if needed.

Jonathan had called every evening to see how Jeanne was and to get updated on the trial. He did ask her, "May I see you this weekend? I think it's time for a quiet dinner at The Club."

"I agree. Let's plan on Saturday afternoon to do something fun and then have dinner."

"What did you have in mind?"

"I haven't been to a movie in ages. If there is a good one, could we do that?"

"I'd like that. A Saturday matinee is always fun. It reminds me of when we were kids and would go to the movies on a Saturday afternoon."

"I really need to do something to get my mind off everything that's going on. A movie and dinner with you should do it."

"Then it's a date."

Since it would be a couple of days, or more, before Jeanne could commence her work in the garden, she chose to attend the trial as the murder phase continued. The more she listened, the more she was convinced that Phyllis was mentally unstable, and it seemed that her attorney did, too. Undoubtedly, he was going to try to get her declared innocent by means of mental incapacity. She didn't think Phyllis should be found innocent, but perhaps delay sentencing until her mental state could be proved. During the next two days, she heard testimony by Detective O'Neal, Jonathan, Bob Baylord, Judy, by the partners Mr. Best and Mr. Carruthers, the psychiatrist, and then she was called back. It was when Phyllis asked to testify on her own behalf, that it became obvious that she was not mentally stable.

When the prosecuting attorney asked her the first question, she didn't give a direct answer, but went into a soliloquy that didn't make sense. She talked about Judy being her friend, and then turning on her, about being in love with Jonathan and their plans for a future together, about Jeanne who came between them and how much she hated her, and then concluded by talking about Roger as if he were still alive and had come into her life at just the right time. She even showed the jeweled hair comb she was wearing as a symbol of his love. The tirade ended by her saying, "I have nothing more to say. I just want to go home and be left alone."

At that point, the judge said, "I can only declare this person mentally unstable and not competent to stand trial for murder at this point. As to the auto theft, she is hereby ordered to release the Mercedes-Benz to its rightful owner, Jeanne Blomgren. I sentence Phyllis McNeil to a mental institution until such time she is declared capable of standing trial. Court is adjourned."

Everyone breathed a sigh of relief. Jeanne acknowledged that the judge had made the correct decision. Jonathan said, "Thank goodness that's over," and gave Jeanne a hug. Bob Baylord shook her hand, and so did Detective O'Neal.

"Detective," Jeanne said, "Thank you so much for your consistent work until everything was resolved."

"Just doing my job," he replied.

Jonathan walked Jeanne out of the courthouse and asked her, "Are we still on for Saturday at the movies?"

"Absolutely. Now that the trial is over, we need to celebrate. Oh, perhaps that's not the correct thing to say. I'm sorry for Phyllis, but I'm glad she will get help."

"Let's put that chapter behind us. We can celebrate our new chapter," he said smiling as he thought about their impending marriage.

Jonathan called to Judy, Michael and Detective O'Neal and asked them, "Would you like to join us for some wine at the bar down the street from our office? We deserve a little time to relax."

They responded affirmatively. And so while they sipped wine, they reminisced about the adventure of the past few weeks.

CHAPTER 57

Jeanne arrived at her office early and went directly to Mr. Marchant's office. He was staring at his computer and so Jeanne knocked softly. "Oh, Jeanne. Come in. Is everything okay?"

"It is now. I wanted to tell you the trial is over so I won't need to be away anymore."

"Was she convicted of murder?"

"Not really. She was declared mentally incompetent so she was sentenced to a mental facility for treatment. I will get the car she stole, which I will sell. I'm just so relieved to have this behind me."

"Yes, I'm sure you are. Thanks for letting me know."

Jeanne smiled and said, "Now it's back to work. The project is going well. Armando has been doing a great job keeping everything on track. Feel free to check it anytime. After all, it is your garden." With that she went to inspect the work herself. Excavation of Section Two had begun. At the rate the work was being accomplished, she felt the entire garden could be completed within a month or a little more.

"Well, what do you think?" Armando asked as he walked up beside her.

"I'm impressed with how much has been accomplished. I guess it's time for me to schedule the delivery of the plants."

"By the way, have the benches been made?"

"Good point. I'll check on them. How about the fountain in Section Three? It should be installed along with the irrigation system."

"Yes, there is a lot to consider. Between us I'm sure everything will remain on schedule," Armando assured her. Jeanne felt very comfortable with Armando supervising the project.

In the following days, no major problems occurred. It was difficult getting the area with the natural stream installed to her satisfaction, but Armando did it. The large trees arrived and were placed in the strategic places to provide needed shade and to frame the garden, yet keeping the views in all the right places. They had retained many of the original trees.

A parade of trucks brought cement for the fountain, the performance platform and pads for the benches, which had been designed and crafted by a local artist. They were placed strategically throughout the garden. Jeanne helped plant the flowers and shrubs to provide color and design to please the eye from any angle. The sketches she had drawn made it easy for the army of gardeners to embed hundreds of plants.

By the end of the month, Jeanne was placing the final few flowers around the patio. The project was complete. Of course, in two or three months' time all of the flowers would be blooming and the color pallet would be very appealing to the eye.

Jeanne went to get Mr. Marchant to give him a tour of the garden. "Do you have time for a little walk?" she asked.

"Yes, of course. Is it time for the final view?"

"It is. I would love to give you my personal tour."

"Let's go," he said enthusiastically. "I've been eagerly anticipating this day."

They entered the garden off the patio on a pathway that was wide enough for two to walk side by side. Armando followed behind. "I'm glad this is not just a cement walk," Mr. Marchant said. "You have created a lovely garden pathway." A few comments were made which indicated Mr. Marchant was pleased with what he saw. When they arrived at the stream, he chose to sit on the bench placed beside it. Jeanne and Armando stood nearby, saying nothing.

Finally Mr. Marchant spoke, "This is my contemplation bench. It's so peaceful here."

They wandered on and came to the performance area with a small stage as a backdrop to an open area for social events. "This is beautiful," he said. "I can visualize music performances, cocktail parties, dances..."

He was interrupted by Jeanne saying, "And I visualize it for something special."

"What's that?"

"A wedding." She hesitated and then said, "I would love to be married here. Jonathan and I are engaged. Would you consider a late Spring wedding here?"

Mr. Marchant was doubly surprised by her question; he didn't know she and Jonathan were to be married, and he had never considered hosting a wedding. After opening and closing his mouth a couple of times, he said, "I think that's a marvelous idea. You will be the first wedding in this beautiful garden you have created."

"Oh, thank you, Mr. Marchant. It will be the perfect place for us to be married." She hesitated and then continued, "If you'd like to give the space a test before then, you could host a cocktail event or a small concert. I'd be pleased to help you with it."

"That might be a good idea. I'll think about it."

They continued the tour ending back at the pool area and the patio.

"Thank you for the tour. You have done an excellent job. Your design is better than I anticipated. I love how you incorporated the natural stream and the romantic gazebo at the edge of the forest. Because it is of natural wood, it blends in so much better than the standard white one would. What is that delicate flower you planted around the gazebo? It smells so sweet, but not overpowering. I've never seen it anyplace."

"It's Daphne. It likes the shade and cool weather so it should do very well there."

"The wooden benches scattered throughout give places, not only to rest, but to enjoy the view. You have created a romantic garden. I can see why you want to be married here."

Jeanne's work with Mr. Marchant was finished. He invited both her and Armando to join him for a glass of wine on the patio. Edward poured a fine California white wine into crystal glasses and they toasted each other for a job well done. Mr. Marchant handed them each an envelope and said, "Thanks for making a lovely place even more beautiful. I am very pleased. However, I would like you to check in regularly for a while to be sure it is all working properly. Jeanne, perhaps it would be wise for you to brief my gardening staff on the care of all the new plants.

Armando, I'm sure you will leave the blueprints of the irrigation system so when, or if it needs repair, staff will know what to do."

They both agreed to his requests and thanked him for allowing them to work on such an interesting project. They left after gathering up their personal belongings. Jeanne hugged Armando telling him how much she enjoyed working with him. "Of course, I want you to come to our wedding. I will see you then, if not before."

"Thank you. I will be there."

Jeanne reluctantly returned to her apartment. She would miss working with Armando. Now she was unemployed again, except for occasionally checking the garden for Mr. Marchant. Now I have time to plan our wedding, she said to herself.

When Jonathan called that evening, Jeanne said wistfully, "Let's go to The Club tonight."

"Okay. Any special reason?" Jonathan asked.

"Maybe. I do have something to tell you."

"What is it?"

"You'll have to wait until tonight," she said firmly.

When he arrived at the apartment, Jeanne greeted him with a welcoming kiss and they immediately went on their way. As soon as they were seated at their usual table, Jonathan asked, "What is it you have to tell me?"

"We finished the garden. Mr. Marchant is very pleased with it, as am I. It looks better than it did on paper, better than I imagined. I want you to come see it. Of course, all of the plants are still quite new, but in a couple of months they will have matured."

"I'd love to see it. When can I?"

"Any time you can get away. He wants to have a small event in a couple of months, such as a cocktail party, or a concert, to christen it. I promised to help him with it."

They continued sharing all that had transpired in their lives. It seemed they would never run out of conversation. Finally, Jeanne asked, "Jonathan, would it be all right if we announced our engagement soon? It's hard to keep the secret."

"Yes. That would be fine with me. I've been wanting to tell my partners."

"Great! What do you think about having our wedding around the end of May or the first week of June?"

"I'd like that," he said grinning. "Even sooner, if you want."

"No, I don't think so. I don't want to feel rushed. We'll need at least three months to get everything done."

"Okay. What do we do first?"

"Let's host a small party with our closest friends to make the announcement. We could have it here at The Club... or at one of our apartments. What do you think?"

"Would you mind having it at your place? I think your space is so beautiful, and it's large enough to handle the number of people we would invite?"

"I'd like that," Jeanne responded with a smile. "But I'll have a caterer to help. I want to be free to enjoy the party, too."

"Then it's settled."

They left The Club feeling good about the next step in their future.

CHAPTER 58

Jeanne walked through the garden and found the new plants thriving. Now she could focus on her wedding. Her first task was to plan the announcement party. It would be informal—no printed invitations, just a phone call or personal invitation. In order for the twins to attend she would schedule it for the upcoming school's holiday weekend.

She called the twins. Mark said, "That sounds great. I'll be there."

Mandy said, "I had made plans, but yes, I'll be there."

With that settled, she called Jonathan to tell him her plans. He readily agreed. "So..." she said, "Do you want to invite the partners, your secretary and their spouses, and any clients and friends you choose?"

"Will do. I'll let you know who and how many. Yes, I'll keep the surprise."

Jeanne called Judy and asked if she and Michael could come to their party. She didn't tell her more than that; she wanted to keep the surprise. She also invited Detective O'Neal and Officer Brandt with their spouses, her doormen, and of course, Armando and his wife. She included their new friends from the beach community. It was an eclectic group of people, but that would make an interesting party. As soon as she heard from Jonathan to confirm how many would be coming, she called the caterer and arranged for food and drinks.

The day for the announcement arrived. The twins came home the evening before. Jonathan came over in the morning, not so much to help but to be with Jeanne and control his excitement. The caterer and a server arrived on time and prepared everything efficiently. When the first guests, Judy and Michael, arrived, Jeanne and Jonathan were relaxed in the living room ready to receive them. The twins greeted the guests at the door, introducing themselves and showing them in. One by one, or two by two, everyone arrived and soon the room was filled with lively conversation.

When Jonathan was sure everyone had champagne, it was time to make the announcement. He took Jeanne's hand and stepped in front of the large windows overlooking the park. Sporting a big smile, he tapped his crystal glass and said, "Perhaps you are wondering why we have called you all together today. You may not know each other, but we know all of you. And each of you is special to us in some way. Therefore, we wanted you to be first to know that Jeanne and I are to be married this Spring. Here's to us," he said as he lifted his glass to Jeanne with a touch of hers. They drank, as did all the others.

There was a cacophony of sound as everyone wished them well and asked numerous questions. Jeanne showed her beautiful diamond and star sapphire ring to everyone. It was a time of celebration, not only of the engagement, but of the ending of the criminal event that had consumed so much of their time.

The sun had set and city lights had come on by the time the party ended. The mid-afternoon cocktail party had been a success. Mr. Marchant was the last to leave. At the door he said to Jonathan, "I would like to have your wedding as the first one in my new garden designed by Jeanne. I hope you will agree to it."

"Thank you. I think we'd like that," he said while smiling at Jeanne. She nodded in agreement.

As soon as the door was closed, Jeanne sank down on the sofa with a sigh. "I'm engaged to be married," she said as she looked at her blue sapphire ring.

Jonathan sat beside her and said, "You are going to be my wife."

They kissed and said nothing more. They were totally unaware of the caterer and the twins putting everything away. It was only when Mandy said, "Mom, they are finished and ready to leave," that Jeanne joined the present. She thanked the caterer as she paid her and said she might want them to cater the wedding reception in about three months, to which she had a favorable response.

Jonathan took his leave suggesting he come by the next afternoon. Jeanne eagerly agreed. "I want some time just for us," she said.

The twins went back to school the next morning, Jeanne slept late, and then waited for Jonathan to arrive. They settled on the sofa with Chopin's music playing softly in the background and they began to discuss their plans for the wedding. Jeanne showed him her list.

"You certainly are well organized," he observed. "Maybe I should prepare my list of tasks. Or you can just tell me what to do," he said grinning at her.

"I'm sure we both want a small wedding. So, in that vein, I want my daughter, Mandy to be my maid-of-honor. I think I'll ask Judy to be a bridesmaid, and that's it. Who do you want to be your best man? Mark could be a groomsman, if you'd like?" she asked hesitantly.

"Yes. Absolutely. As to a best man..." he said thoughtfully. "I think I'd like to ask one of our partners, Mr. Carruthers. I've known him the longest, and he has been my mentor."

"That's a great idea. He would be perfect."

Just as the sun was setting, Jonathan said, "Jeanne, I have a question to ask you."

"Yes? What is it?" she asked with concern.

"About our honeymoon... Do you want me tell you what I have in mind, or would you like me to surprise you?"

She was quiet for a little while pondering his question. "Well... I feel I can trust you to plan something I would appreciate. So... Surprise me," she said firmly.

"Thank you," was all he said. He did have a plan in mind.

In a couple of days, Jeanne went to check on the gardens. She ambled through each section and found everything doing well. Now that her work was finished, she could appreciate the design. There was a special focal point in each section that invited one to pause and enjoy the space and the view. She agreed with Mr. Marchant about his favorite place at the contemplation bench near the stream. As she approached it, he was sitting there. She walked up quietly, not wanting to disturb him, however, when he saw her he motioned her to join him.

"Come, sit a while," he invited as he made room for her beside him on the specially designed bench. They sat quietly for a moment listening to the trickling of the natural stream. "I come here nearly every day to have a quiet moment and clear my mind."

"I'm glad. We all need a quiet place." She sat still for a few minutes and finally said, "May I ask you something?"

"Of course. What is it?"

"I've been thinking about our wedding here in a few months. Since I have no parents living, would you be willing to walk me down the aisle?"

Mr. Marchant looked surprised, but smiled and said, "I'd be honored."

"Thank you," was all that needed to be said.

They stood up together and walked back toward the house, stopping briefly at the site for the wedding ceremony. It was perfect.

CHAPTER 59

Jeanne was enjoying her second cup of coffee, when Mr. Marchant interrupted her quiet time. Delighted to hear from him, she greeted him with a light-hearted, "Good morning. How nice to hear from you."

"Good morning. I have some good news for you."

"Oh? What is it?" she asked.

"I was at a social event the other evening and mentioned we had just completed my newly designed garden. It so happened that one of the guests covers landscape projects for a major magazine. He asked me several questions and then asked if he could come see what we have done. How could I refuse him?"

"You couldn't, nor should you," Jeanne agreed.

"He was here a couple of days ago and was duly impressed. I told him about you, and he may be contacting you for an interview. I hope you don't mind."

"I guess not," she said hesitantly.

"Good, because you need to be recognized for your design. Now, to another subject. I do want to hold a small event here to christen the garden. Will you help me?"

"Of course, I said I would. What do you have in mind?"

"I was thinking a music concert would be appropriate. And I am eager to check out the acoustics of the performance area. What do you think?"

"I like that idea. Would you like a chamber music concert?"

"Yes, I would prefer that to a band for our first event. Could you arrange that?"

"I think so… it depends on… well, do you have a budget?"

"Of course, just put together whatever you think would work best in the space and I'll take care of it."

"When do you want to have the event?"

"It needs to be when the weather is a little warmer, since we will be sitting outdoors. How about sometime in late March or April?"

"That sounds good. It will take a little while to secure the musicians. That may determine the date."

"Great. You go ahead and set that up. Just let me know the date as soon as possible."

"Will do. And thanks for asking me."

Jeanne was excited to begin working on another project. What to do first? How does one secure professional musicians for a private concert? Jeanne spent the morning brainstorming when it occurred to her the best place to find musicians was from the local symphony orchestra. She called the symphony's office and told the secretary what she needed. Her request was immediately sent to the principal first violinist, who in turn contacted fellow musicians and procured an appropriate ensemble for a garden concert. When he told Jeanne who he had assembled, she was delighted.

"Now all we need is a convenient date for everyone. I'm thinking sometime in April when the weather is warm."

The violinist responded, "The orchestra has a series of concerts in March, so your suggested time should work. Could we do it around the middle of April?"

"Yes, that should be all right for a Sunday afternoon concert. I think I told you it will be in the gardens of the Marchant Estate. I just need to get his approval. I'll get back to you soon."

Mr. Marchant was delighted and granted his approval. When everything and everyone was in place for the concert, she was free to continue working on their wedding plans. Just as she settled down with them, she had a phone call from the editor of the magazine Mr. Marchant had told her about. He was wanting to interview her and have a tour of the gardens.

"I'll be happy to meet with you anytime at your convenience," she said.

"Could we meet at the Marchant Estate day after tomorrow at ten in the morning?"

"Yes, I will be there." And she was.

They toured the entire acre, stopping the longest at the contemplation area with the water feature. Their cameraman took a multitude of pictures, the editor asked numerous questions, and Jeanne enjoyed sharing her experience and thoughts about the garden.

"Thank you for the tour. We plan on featuring this garden in an upcoming issue of our national magazine. Is it all right to quote you in the article?"

"Of course." Jeanne had a quick thought. "Would you like to attend the small concert here in April? That way you can appreciate the performance area and hear the acoustics. I'm sure Mr. Marchant would like that, too."

"Thank you. That is an excellent idea. Just send me the details." With that he left after commenting that this was one of the most beautiful and unusual gardens he had ever seen.

Jeanne was pleased and thought perhaps this was another career to consider, if she ever needed one.

The next several days were devoted to wedding plans. Each day she checked off another item on her list of tasks. Jonathan said he was accomplishing everything according to the plan. "When you come over this weekend we need to design our wedding invitations. I'll have some sketches we can consider, but you need to be thinking about what you want them to say."

"I'm on it," he told her. "Since we're having a garden wedding it will be a little less formal, I suppose."

"Of course. No tuxedos, just white dinner jackets for the men, and short cocktail-style dresses for the ladies. I'm not sure what I will wear, but it will not be long and white."

"Whatever you wear, you will be beautiful," he said with meaning.

When Jeanne settled down at the table that evening, Jonathan presented his few scraps of paper bearing suggestions for wedding invitations. She placed hers beside his and they spent time reading, discarding, and then finally writing the one they wanted using ideas from each of them. The final version was informal and suited them perfectly.

"Are we going to write our own vows?" Jeanne asked.

"Of course. I already have written mine, although I may do some editing."

"You're ahead of me. I'll get right on it," she said smiling at him. "Are you going to tell me about your plans for our honeymoon?"

"No. All I'll tell you is plan for a month-long trip. Remember you said you wanted me to surprise you."

"That's true. I can wait." Jeanne knew she could trust him to make plans for something she would enjoy. But a month-long honeymoon? She never would have thought of that.

CHAPTER 60

The day of the concert was fast approaching. Invitations had gone out to a select group of Mr. Marchant's friends and business associates. Of course, Jeanne and Jonathan were included, along with Armando and his wife. Nearly one hundred guests were expected, including the Mayor and the editor of the magazine who was preparing the article on the Marchant gardens.

By the first week of April most of the flowers were in bloom and the garden was splashed in color. Humming birds had arrived to feast on the nectar provided for them. Dozens of song birds were building nests in the trees and bathing in the fountain. When walking through the garden one was surrounded by nature. A lively grey squirrel ran across the pathway. It was exactly what Jeanne had dreamed of creating.

The morning of the concert, Jeanne and Jonathan were there to assist Mr. Marchant's staff. Chairs for the audience were carefully placed, large plants provided a backdrop for the stage, and climbing roses nearly covered the trellis above.

Just after noon the musicians began arriving. They were directed to the stage area and one of them said it was the most beautiful setting in which he had ever performed. They were eager to hear the acoustics. After tuning their instruments, they began with a Strauss waltz.

Jeanne and Jonathan were delighted with the sound, as was Mr. Marchant. After playing the first few measures of music, they stopped and the first violinist said, "This is amazing. The sound is truly beautiful, a perfect blend. You have created an acoustic wonder out of doors."

They continued playing their music getting used to the sounds. Then it was time for guests to arrive.

Edward, the butler, directed guests down the path to the performance area where Mr. Marchant greeted each one. As soon as everyone was seated, Mr. Marchant said, "Thank you for coming to this inaugural event. I want you to meet Jeanne Blomgren, the designer of the gardens, and Armando, the landscape architect." They both acknowledged the recognition. "Please wander through the gardens following the concert of light classical music and enjoy their designs."

Following the exceptional concert, the reception on the patio included champagne and a bountiful selection of hors d'oeuvres. Jeanne and Armando were asked questions about the garden. The editor of the national magazine was particularly complimentary about the appearance and design of the grounds and the quality of sound in the stage area. Mr. Marchant was enjoying his first event there, too.

Jeanne was visualizing their wedding which would take place there in a few weeks. She asked Jonathan, "Can you imagine how this will look for our wedding?"

"I'm not good at visualizing things, but if it will be anything like this, I'll be happy."

"It will be even better when more flowers are in bloom. I love the way the roses, my favorite flower, surround the stage."

Guests were beginning to leave after having walked through the garden. They stopped to tell Mr. Marchant how impressed they were with the design and the music. Several of them complimented Jeanne and Armando on the unique garden. All in all, the afternoon event was a great success.

"Thank you, Jeanne, for creating such a wonderful space for me. It truly is unique. It is everything, and more than I imagined. I had a great time this afternoon. I think you have a new career in the making," he said with a teasing smile. "Now we will look forward to your big event—the wedding."

"Yes, we are eager to be married here. Thanks again for allowing us to have our wedding in this special place."

When they arrived back at Jeanne's apartment, Jonathan said, "Jeanne, I'm impressed with how you created such a splendid event. You are an amazing woman."

"Why, thank you. It was fun, but a lot of work. Our wedding will be easier now that we've had a trial run in the space."

"Well, I'm eagerly anticipating our next event."

She just smiled in response and said, "I am, too."

The twins returned home on Spring break eager to help Jeanne with the wedding. When they visited the Marchant gardens, they were amazed.

"Mom, did you really design this?" Mark asked as they walked through the entire acre.

"Yes, I did. I'm surprised myself. I had no idea I could do this when I first took it on. Of course, I had help from Armando, but the concept was mine."

Mandy said, "It really is impressive. This will be the most beautiful wedding ever. The rose covered stage is a perfect setting for exchanging vows."

When they returned to the patio, Mr. Marchant was waiting. "What do you think of your mother's work?" he asked the twins.

"It's amazing. She's amazing," Mark said.

"You have the most unusual and beautiful garden of anyone," Mandy said. "My favorite place is at the contemplation bench by the small stream."

"It's mine, too," Mr. Marchant agreed. "Now would you like to join me for lunch?"

"Oh, we didn't expect that," Jeanne said, "but that would be lovely."

Anna served grilled chicken Caesar salads and freshly baked rolls to the four of them. They lingered over cinnamon Swedish cookies and coffee. The twins enjoyed conversing with Mr. Marchant about plans for the wedding as well as for the reception, which would be held on his patio.

On the way home, the twins talked nonstop about the beautiful setting for the wedding and about Mr. Marchant and his property. The date had been established as Saturday afternoon, the first weekend in June. Everything was in place. The numerous tasks were completed over the next several days.

The twins returned to school too soon as far as Jeanne was concerned. They did have time to select their dresses. The next time she saw them would be for the wedding.

Jeanne invited Judy to join her for lunch. "It's time to discuss my wedding in June for which you will by my bridesmaid. Can you meet me at the French Corner Café next Saturday at noon?"

"Yes, I will be there."

"I've missed seeing you. I want to hear the latest on Michael. Is he still in the picture?"

"Yes. Very much so," she responded with a smile in her voice. "We see each other quite regularly."

"I'm so glad. Perhaps you two could meet Jonathan and me for dinner one evening?"

"I'd love that. Just say when."

"I'll check with Jonathan and let you know."

CHAPTER 61

That evening Jeanne suggested, "Since Judy will be my bridesmaid it would be nice to treat her and Michael to dinner and talk about the wedding. What do you think?"

"I think it's a great idea. I'd like to know Michael better. It looks like he and Judy might be getting serious."

"I agree. How would you feel about having them join us at The Club? It would be something special for them."

"Let's do it on a Saturday. I always think of that as a date night."

Jeanne arranged the dinner with Judy and Michael for the next weekend. They met at her apartment before going to The Club. When Jonathan arrived, he greeted Jeanne with an affectionate kiss on the cheek.

Shaking Michael's hand he said, "It's good to see you. I remember you are the one who saved Jeanne's life."

"I was just doing my job," he responded slightly embarrassed.

"And it was a good job. I'm glad you did it so efficiently," he said as he gave Jeanne a little hug. "The final medical report indicated she suffered no ill effects."

They continued chatting until Jeanne said it was time to go to dinner. They took Jeanne's car with Jonathan driving, since his car was too small for the four of them.

"Yes, Phyllis told me you drive a small sports car—a red Mustang," Judy said. "Oh, sorry. I shouldn't have mentioned her."

"It's okay," Jonathan responded. "She has been a large part of our lives and so we can't forget her completely." That was the last mention of Phyllis.

Judy and Michael were duly impressed with The Club; with the service and the elegance of the evening. Their conversations flowed easily. "Thank you so much for inviting us to have dinner with you here," Judy said as they finished their chocolate dessert. "It was an evening to remember. I hope we will continue being friends after the wedding."

"I agree," Michael added. "This was special."

"You're both welcome," Jonathan said as they left for home.

The next morning Jeanne picked up their wedding invitations. After getting them all addressed, she relaxed when she dropped them in the mail. Now she was committed to getting married, not that she had second thoughts about it. She knew she was in love with Jonathan and he with her. That was the only criteria.

It was the end of May when the twins returned home for the summer. They immediately jumped in to help with wedding activities. Jeanne, Mandy and Judy went for their dress fittings.

"Mom, I really like the dress you chose. I think the ice blue color is just right for you."

"Thank you. I feel good in it, so it must be the right choice."

After buying comfortable but elegant shoes, they brought their purchases home and settled down to discuss the wedding–and their future.

"What kind of cake are you having?" Mandy asked.

"A French vanilla white cake with a Belgian chocolate center layer."

"Of course. You must have chocolate. You can't go a day without it," Mandy said teasing her. "But I feel the same."

"When is the rehearsal?" Judy asked.

"We'll go to the Marchant Estate early Friday evening, when Mr. Marchant is hosting a rehearsal dinner in his home. There will be eight of us including the minister."

"Who is presiding over the ceremony?" Mandy asked.

"Reverend Holmquist from the Presbyterian church."

"Good. I always liked him. He has a great sense of humor, so his services were never boring. I wonder what he will do at your wedding."

"Why do you ask that?" Judy wondered

"He can be a prankster. But don't worry about it, Mom. I'm sure he will be just fine. He undoubtedly will have a joke or two to share, though."

Mark walked in and asked, "So what have you been doing all day?"

"We've been shopping," Mandy said. "We picked up our dresses for the wedding and bought shoes. We are ready for the big day. What about you? Did you get your clothes?"

"Yeah. Jonathan, Mr. Carruthers and I got our outfits."

Jeanne reminded him of the dinner Friday evening and that it will be dress-up affair at the Marchant residence following the rehearsal.

"Yes, I remember," he assured her when he left the room.

As Judy was leaving, Jeanne invited her to come to her apartment Friday and go with them to the Marchant Estate. "Jonathan and Mr. Carruthers will meet us there," Jeanne said giving Judy a hug. "I feel like this is really happening."

"So am I," Mandy said. "Once we got our dresses it hit me—my mother is getting married!"

During the simple meal that evening, the twins assured their mother that they were really happy for her, that they liked Jonathan and fully approved of and accepted him as their stepfather.

"So where will you live after you're married," Mark asked.

"Jonathan plans to move in here. This apartment is larger than his. However, we think we'd like to get a new house. We might even have one built if we find a perfect place for it. It would be fun doing that together. We're in no rush."

Mandy was delighted with the idea of a new house for them. "I think that's the best idea you've had. Just be sure you include space for us to visit," she said as she looked at Mark.

"Of course. You will always be welcome at home, wherever it is," Jeanne assured her.

The rest of the week was filled taking care of details with the caterer, the photographer, the musicians, the baker and the florist. Jeanne was happy that Mr. Marchant and his staff were handling the reception. It was his gift to them. With nearly a hundred guests, that was a substantial gift. Anna was preparing the rehearsal dinner from Jeanne's menu.

On Friday, everyone arrived at Mr. Marchant's home at the same time. Andrew, the butler opened the large doors and greeted them. He escorted them to the living room where they each were offered a drink. As soon as their orders were given, the minister arrived and joined them. The maid and the butler served their drinks and hors d'oeuvres. Soon they all were chatting as old friends.

Mr. Marchant led the way to the garden for the rehearsal. He hesitated at the edge of the patio, turned to Jeanne and said, "Thank you for planting yellow daffodils by these steps. You remembered my favorite color. They are the first flowers I see when I look out here."

"After they are finished blooming, they will be replaced by yellow daisies or tulips," Jeanne explained. "You will always see your favorite color someplace in the garden."

They continued to the stage area and as soon as they were in their places, Reverend Holmquist gave instructions for the event. The wedding participants would be in the changing rooms by the pool and enter from there. He talked them through the ceremony, each one playing his or her role. At the conclusion with the kiss, they would all proceed to the patio for the reception.

Jeanne surveyed the garden from the wedding site and was very pleased. The roses covering the trellis overhead were in bloom giving off their subtle scent. She smiled in self-satisfaction at what looked like the perfect place for a fairy-tale wedding. As she turned to Jonathan, he kissed her gently and said, "I love you, and I love the garden you created for our wedding. Thank you." Jeanne just smiled.

The photographer took several pictures of the wedding party. He said these would be some of the most beautiful pictures he had ever taken because of the surrounding garden. Jeanne was pleased to hear so many compliments on the garden.

The dinner served in the formal dining room was impressive. Two servants placed and removed plates unobtrusively. The menu consisted of crisp spring greens with fresh raspberries and candied pecans to start. This was followed by wild mushroom soup served in soup cups with miniature crisp toast circles. The main course was veal medallions seared in butter and herbed crumbs, along with parsley buttered potato cubes and nutmeg seasoned petite green peas in a light cream sauce. Of course, fine wine was served with each course. Champagne was poured when the chocolate dessert was served. It was a smaller version of the chocolate parfait which Jeanne had the first time she had lunch with Mr. Marchant. A perfect ending to a dinner to remember. Everything was delicious and done to perfection. Jeanne thanked Anna profusely when the meal was finished.

After-dinner coffee was served in the living room along with Swedish chocolate mints. Conversations were lively and continued long into the evening. The wedding participants had become good friends and both Jeanne and Jonathan were pleased with their compatibility. They reluctantly left, knowing they would return the next afternoon.

CHAPTER 62

It was the day of the wedding. Judy came to Jeanne's apartment, and Mark went to Jonathan's. Judy drove the women to the Marchant Estate, and the men followed a little later, with Mr. Carruthers as the designated driver. Mr. Marchant greeted them as they arrived. The best man, Mr. Carruthers, and Mandy, as the maid of honor, made sure everyone and everything was ready to start the ceremony.

The musicians arrived and set up on the small stage. Edward directed the guests to the wedding site. When the first ones appeared on the patio, the string quartet began to play music of the Romantic composers. At the appointed time, they changed to Pachelbel and played his famous Canon in D to which the wedding party walked. The Reverend Holmquist was the first to take his place. He was followed by Mr. Carruthers and Mark, and then Jonathan. They looked splendid in their off-white coats, navy pants, and ice blue ties. Then Judy entered carrying a bouquet of yellow and blue flowers with white orchids. She was followed by Mandy in the same sky blue dress with her flowers held in front as she walked onto the stage and took her place opposite Mr. Carruthers.

When the Canon reached its climax, Jeanne appeared in her ice blue dress carrying a small bouquet of yellow roses and white orchids. Jonathan smiled at the first glimpse of her, and his eyes followed her as she approached the stage on the arm of Mr. Marchant. They locked eyes as she took her place at his side. The minister began, "We are gathered here today in this beautiful setting to..." and so he continued with the standard marriage ceremony. Jeanne and Jonathan stated their personal vows and exchanged rings. "And now I pronounce you husband and wife. You may kiss the bride," which Jonathan did with passion. The string quartet played Mendelssohn's Wedding March. Everyone applauded as the couple left the stage and walked to the patio where they greeted each guest. "It was a unique and beautiful wedding," one guest said. "I'm glad I was here."

"I'm glad I was, too," Jeanne said as she looked at Jonathan, her husband.

The food was served buffet style and guests could sit at tables covered in ice blue cloths scattered around the patio. The fare consisted of beef, chicken and shrimp k-bobs with vegetables cooked over an open grill. Hot cheddar biscuits were plentiful as well as a selection of fine wines. The string quartet had moved to the patio and continued to provide appropriate music during the reception.

When all the guests were seated, Jeanne and Jonathan took their place at a table in the center of the patio. Judy and Mandy took food to them and Mr. Marchant poured their wine. He then instructed the servants to take care of them as he joined the guests.

It was time to cut the cake. Mr. Carruthers stood up and asked for everyone's attention. He gave a meaningful toast to the couple wishing them well as they build their lives together. The twins welcomed Jonathan into their family and said how happy they were that their mother found someone special to be in their lives. Tears of happiness formed in Jeanne's eyes and she blinked them away.

The bride and groom cut the cake together and shared a piece. "I might have known there would be chocolate," Jonathan said with a smile when he saw the first slice. Then he invited everyone to enjoy it with them. The servants cut the cake and served each guest. Coffee was poured and they all lingered for a time.

Jeanne and Jonathan changed into their traveling clothes. When they exited, they walked hand in hand through the tables of guests and were showered with rose petals. A limousine was waiting with their luggage to take them to a hotel before going on their honeymoon. Jonathan had told the twins when they expected to return home, but no one else knew. He told no one where they were going.

"Alone at last," Jonathan said as the limousine slithered down the driveway and out the gates.

Jeanne laid her head on his shoulder with a sigh. "Alone, but together," she said.

They arrived at the Majestic Marvel hotel and were escorted to the Presidential Suite. Champagne on ice was waiting along with a bowl of fresh strawberries.

"This is lovely," Jeanne exclaimed as she perused the room. "The view from the balcony is spectacular. I'm glad you chose this hotel again."

"I thought you might like it," Jonathan said as he encircled her with his arms. "We can have dinner sent up to our suite whenever you'd like. Meanwhile, let's relax and have a glass of champagne." He popped open the bottle and poured the sparkling liquid into the crystal flutes. "Here's to my wife. May she always be as happy as she is today."

"And to your happiness, too. May our love be entwined around our hearts forever."

They enjoined their arms as they took their first sip.

Their first night together was everything Jeanne had dreamed of. It was romantic and surpassed all her expectations. Jonathan was an artful lover and Jeanne responded in kind.

In the morning after a light breakfast in their room, they left for an extended trip around the world. When they entered the limousine to go to the airport, Jeanne said, "We met at the end of summer, and now we start our new life together at the beginning of summer."

ABOUT THE AUTHOR

As a music composer and author of children's books and this novel, Kathryn B. Hull is a member of ASCAP and SCBWI. She is a State and Nationally Certified teacher of music with an active piano studio in La Quinta, California, having taught music in both elementary school and college. She is a member of MTNA and CAPMT, having served on their boards for a number of years. She promotes the arts and music education through her work with numerous community organizations. She has a Bachelor of Arts degree with a major in music and minor in English. She is listed in Who's Who of American Women among several others. She is the recipient of two Life Time Achievement Awards.